A RAK

"Married? You and I? After knowing and loving my Reggie you think I'd have come willingly to your arms?" Joanna reached for the reins that Pierce still held and tugged at them. "This conversation is absurd, Your Grace. I find it boring in the extreme."

Much to her surprise, Pierce laughed. Her surprise intensified when he lifted her onto Lad's back and handed her the reins. In his eyes was a reflection of soft humor instead of the expected hard but steady gleam. "You little spitfire," he said softly, his hand laid on her boot. "I think I'll love you more now that you're a bit seasoned than I did when I lost you." He backed off and raised his hat, staring up into her bemused features. "I look forward to seeing you soon, *Mrs*. Wooten—when you return to the London scene, if not before." An eyebrow quirked and he smiled. "I think it'll be before, don't you?"

ELEGANT LOVE STILL FLOURISHES –
Wrap yourself in a Zebra Regency Romance.

A MATCHMAKER'S MATCH   (3783, $3.50/$4.50)
by Nina Porter
To save herself from a loveless marriage, Lady Psyche Veringham pretends to be a bluestocking. Resigned to spinsterhood at twenty-three, Psyche sets her keen mind to snaring a husband for her young charge, Amanda. She sets her cap for long-time bachelor, Justin St. James. This man of the world has had his fill of frothy-headed debutantes and turns the tables on Psyche. Can a bluestocking and a man about town find true love?

FIRES IN THE SNOW   (3809, $3.99/$4.99)
by Janis Laden
Because of an unhappy occurrence, Diana Ruskin knew that a secure marriage was not in her future. She was content to assist her physician father and follow in his footsteps . . . until now. After meeting Adam, Duke of Marchmaine, Diana's precise world is shattered. She would simply have to avoid the temptation of his gentle touch and stunning physique – and by doing so break her own heart!

FIRST SEASON   (3810, $3.50/$4.50)
by Anne Baldwin
When country heiress Laetitia Biddle arrives in London for the Season, she harbors dreams of triumph and applause. Instead, she becomes the laughingstock of drawing rooms and ballrooms, alike. This headstrong miss blames the rakish Lord Wakeford for her miserable debut, and she vows to rise above her many faux pas. Vowing to become an Original, Letty proves that she's more than a match for this eligible, seasoned Lord.

AN UNCOMMON INTRIGUE   (3701, $3.99/$4.99)
by Georgina Devon
Miss Mary Elizabeth Sinclair was rather startled when the British Home Office employed her as a spy. Posing as "Tasha," an exotic fortune-teller, she expected to encounter unforeseen dangers. However, nothing could have prepared her for Lord Eric Stewart, her dashing and infuriating partner. Giving her heart to this haughty rogue would be the most reckless hazard of all.

A MADDENING MINX   (3702, $3.50/$4.50)
by Mary Kingsley
After a curricle accident, Miss Sarah Chadwick is literally thrust into the arms of Philip Thornton. While other women shy away from Thornton's eyepatch and aloof exterior, Sarah finds herself drawn to discover why this man is physically and emotionally scarred.

The Widow
and the Rake

Jeanne Savery

ZEBRA BOOKS
KENSINGTON PUBLISHING CORP.

ZEBRA BOOKS are published by

Kensington Publishing Corp.
475 Park Avenue South
New York, NY 10016

First Printing: November, 1993

Printed in the United States of America

With love to my husband, Tom.
May he continue to say
he's known one worse housekeeper!

One

Wrinkling her aristocratic nose, Lady Joanna Wooten, nee Lady Joanna Ransome, fastened the last button of her dull brown riding habit. It had done yeoman service in the Peninsula where Lt. Reginald Wooten had taken her immediately after their marriage. She had neglected to replace it during those busy weeks in England while Napoleon was incarcerated on Elba, so it had had to serve during their stay in Brussels. Then Reggie had died at Waterloo . . . but she wouldn't think of that. It had been well over a year since Waterloo.

She hated it, the habit. She could hardly bear to put it on. But being a woman prudent with her more than adequate fortune, Joanna was determined to suffer with it patiently until she could order one in deepest blue, in the starkest of Hussar styles, one she knew would become her more than any other. She could see it in her mind, the lines softened by crisp white lace above the high collar, longer lace at the wrists, and lots and lots of lace on the petticoats which would flirt from beneath the long skirt. She took a last look in the mirror and shook her head. For now, she thought, picking up her gloves and crop, it would do. In a very few months she would end her extended official mourning, and the only thing which pleased Joanna about that fact was that she would again wear colors.

Joanna peered out into the hall and, despite her nearly twenty-four years, felt much as she had as a young girl escaping from her governess. Seeing no one, she hurried to where a steep stairway was hidden behind a panel. The closest route to the stables, it had been familiar to her from childhood. Moving quickly, aware that at any moment she might be caught by one of her brother's retainers, who, in his absence, depended on her, she passed through the low door. A moment later she left the house, still wary of ambush. Ever alert, she strode off at a pace which would have caused palpitations in all those who had had a hand in training her as a lady. It wasn't far and she was soon peering in the open doors to the stables.

She brightened. "Good day to you, Sam."

Joanna felt only a brief sense of relief before again worrying she might not escape the responsibilities that weighed so heavily upon her. Sometimes she wondered how she'd drifted into becoming her brother's de facto factotum at Midbourgh Court.

"Is Lad looking forward to a run as much as I am?" she asked.

Peering up from under grizzled brows at the tall woman he'd known from the cradle, her brother's head groom grunted expressively. His disapproval of Her Ladyship's choice of mount was an old grievance. Lady Jo, as the old servants called her, was a bruising rider. It was his own teaching that had made her so, but that didn't change the old man's mind about Lad. It simply was not proper for the daughter of the sixth Earl of Midbourgh to ride a long-legged, rawboned, spirited gelding. Not that the old earl would have objected if he were still alive. *He'd* have laughed and thought it a great joke. The new earl was a man of a different cut, thank the Lord, aware what was due him and proper for his sister.

Sam agreed with the new earl; far better Lady Jo be satisfied with the well-mannered gray the seventh earl, her brother, had bought her. Lord Midbourgh said his gift would make a pleasant and biddable mount for his sister. The seventh earl was one to make his wishes known and, in his self-complacent way, assume that sufficient, never giving the matter another thought.

Sam snorted softly. He could guess the newest Lord Midbourgh's response if he were made aware Lady Jo would have nothing to do with his gift. He'd grumble and moan and shake his head, then wonder why he had to have such a hoyden for a sister. Doing a bit of grumbling himself, Sam went to saddle the mettlesome roan. "A nice ride for my niece, said she." Sam shook his head. "Lad," he told the gelding, "you be no horse for a lady. You never were and you never will be and I'll be blamed if she comes to ruin." The animal, as if agreeing, bucked gently. "Whoa there."

With one eye on the house, Joanna couldn't hide her impatience when she called, "Sam, don't take forever." She wished immediately that she hadn't spoken so harshly but she *needed* her hour with Lad before she again took up her daily responsibilities. Then there was Elizabeth, her niece. No. She wouldn't think of that problem. She'd reached a decision concerning Elizabeth. Assuming her ridiculously easygoing and self-centered brother would co-operate!

Joanna patted Lad's arching neck and held up the sugar she had handy. The gelding's soft muzzle tickled her and she patted him again. Sam gave her a hand up into the sidesaddle and, carelessly arranging her skirts, she set off. She was barely out of the stableyard when a halloo from the old man had her pulling up the prancing roan. Joanna twisted around to look back at him. "Yes, Sam?"

"A couple of those out-of-work soldiers came through the village this morning. Vicar fed them before sending them on, but maybe it's best if you ride on Midbourgh property today." He looked anxious. "They can be pretty desperate rogues, m'lady."

Joanna felt an impotent rage at the thought of Wellington's brave men, his "infamous army," released from service with no way to earn a living. Over a year had passed and many were still out of work and, in the current economic climate, had little chance of finding any. Her heart went out to their plight but, beyond giving money to the vicar to aid his charitable efforts, there was little she could do. She sighed. "Thank you, Sam." Obediently she turned Lad's head in the prescribed direction and Sam, having long ago given up on making her take a groom with her, let her go.

On her return to Midbourgh Court he'd understood her grief and the need for long solitary rides as had no one else. By now they'd become a habit. Even so, he thought, perhaps today he should insist . . . but she was off toward the north boundary and surely the vagrants had taken the east road toward Canterbury where they might find work in the Kentish fields now the harvest was upon them . . .

10

* * *

The home woods opened out and Joanna urged Lad into a longer stride, taking the low stone fence into the stubble of the first field with ease. She didn't glance toward the towering chimneys of the neighboring estate barely visible through a gap in the gently rolling hills. When she'd first returned home, she'd avoided this direction. Her concern, however, that she might accidentally encounter the Duke of Stornway had abated as she'd learned more about that erratic peer's present way of life. It seemed he rarely returned to the estates he'd inherited while still in leading strings.

Joanna had long ceased sighing over memories of her childhood when she'd trailed behind her brother and Pierce Reston, youths a dozen years her senior. Later Pierce had become a wild young man, but still he'd been carelessly kind to a girl left too much alone. She was thankful he no longer seemed to have an interest in his country dwellings. Particularly White Stones.

She was equally thankful the Dowager Duchess of Stornway, his mother, had retired to Bath and that she was not required to meet the reproachful eyes of the woman who had aspired to be her mother-in-law. His Grace, Pierce Reston, had been a desultory but nevertheless favored suitor until Lt. Reginald Wooten appeared in London.

The handsome officer had been introduced to her at a ball. He was a dashing young man in regimentals, still a trifle pale, though recovering nicely from a shoulder wound. He'd taken one look at Joanna and declared he would win her and take her with him when he returned to the Peninsula. Joanna had taken a similar look into his laughing eyes and agreed.

Immediately Pierce became a dog in the manger. To the surprise of all who knew him, he lost his town bronze and made a cake of himself. When he'd had the effrontery to kidnap her and carry her off, he'd nearly destroyed her affection for him.

A timely rescue by Reggie had changed her brother Henry's implacable determination that his sister not throw herself away on a mere soldier, his will previously set against her equally strong determination to marry her Reggie. Joanna smiled at the memory. Pierce, did he but know it, had done her a favor. After the rescue she'd threatened to tell the *ton* how she'd been carried off and *not* tell them her dearest Reggie had arrived in time to save her from Pierce's machinations. That and her insistence she'd not marry Pierce even if Henry prevented her marriage to Lieutenant Wooten had done much to change her brother's mind!

A long meadow appeared, and once over a barred gate, Joanna let Lad out. She'd not bothered with a hat, believing the years in the Peninsula had ruined her complexion for life, and now she relished the wind against her face. She loved feeling the power of the animal carrying her with long strides across the grass, the wind tugging at her tightly bound hair. A clutch of sheep scurried out of their way and she laughed.

She didn't notice the two figures watching her from the end of the field. Nor did she notice the lone rider on a black stallion partially hidden in the deep shade of the woods just across the estate boundary.

* * *

12

His Grace, the fifth Duke of Stornway, grinned widely as he watched Lady Jo ride. He admired the sight of her slim figure as she leaned forward in the saddle, urging the big gelding on. A lock of hair whipped out of its bonds, another found freedom, and soon a pale banner of flowing sun-gilded hair trailed in the wind of her passage. Should he join her? The duke decided it wouldn't be prudent.

Realizing he'd lost Joanna through taking her for granted had been the hardest lesson he'd ever had to learn. Now he watched avidly, wondering how long he must wait before she went to London to chaperon her niece through the chit's first season. Surely it would be soon. He'd seen Henry's daughter, a spoiled little miss if ever there was one, in the village with a group of young people. The girl was ripe for trouble. Jo would have to bring her to London no later than next spring. The duke groaned at the thought of so many months of waiting, but until then he could not put his plan into action. This time he'd court her assiduously as she should have been courted years earlier.

It had seemed a good plan when he'd made it, but he hadn't expected her to mourn so long. With this glimpse of her, his impatience grew nearly out of bounds. Patience had never been his strongest virtue and now it seemed no virtue at all. Maybe he *would* join her. Maybe . . . His hands tightened on the reins and Apollo, his stallion, tensed. He reminded himself of his plan. With a sigh, Pierce relaxed and his mount settled.

It was a good plan. Even though the wait was far longer than he wanted, he mustn't spoil it. Given a second chance, Pierce was determined to court Joanna properly. Surely not all the affection she'd once felt for him had disappeared in that insane moment when he'd determined to have her for himself and damn the young officer who'd appeared from nowhere to win her heart and hand.

Joanna laughed again, the sound drifting to him. He ached with the desire to get reacquainted with the woman who had somehow spoiled all others for him. Would she be the same wildly courageous girl with whom he'd fallen in love? Or had her experiences in the Peninsula changed her?

Pierce had heard tales he could scarcely credit of the hardships she had endured following her husband on his campaigns, and had admired her more than ever. Wooten's death at Waterloo would have affected her, too. Would he even like her once he got to know her again?

Pierce watched the gelding jump the stream at the end of the field, watched her control the rangy beast's playful reluctance to settle down. Her mount was obviously full of energy. He danced, tossing his head and pulling on the reins, but she soon mastered him. Pierce's eyes never left her as she dismounted and dropped the reins over the horse's head so he could graze while she strolled near the stream. A gentle rise was mottled by a large patch of brambles and a copse of alder threw shade over the stream. It made a beautiful setting for a lovely woman. . . .

Joanna thought of the past, a smile teasing her mouth. Reggie would joke her unmercifully for her strict adherence to mourning, laugh at her, and tell her she was a little prude and not to be so silly. *Little*. A deep chuckle trickled up her throat to be followed by a suppressed sob. She extended one boot-clad foot and looked down her length. Only someone as tall and strong and wonderful as her dearest hey-go-mad Reggie could ever call her little! She came to the flat boulder on which she often rested while thinking about the past. The sun bore down on her and she searched her pockets for a handkerchief. Pulling off a glove, she dipped the square of linen in the stream. . . .

Other eyes noted the rawboned but magnificent gelding, the well-kept tack that indicated wealth. They were a little confused by the rider's drab garment but there had been a flicker of gold on the hand she bared before wetting a handkerchief to cool her face. The two ex-soldiers were aware she'd be carrying none of the ready. Why would she want money when riding on private land? But that ring would bring enough for a meal or two and who knew what other baubles she might wear about her person? They conferred, plotted a bold plan, and, slipping bush to bush, approached her.

The first Joanna knew of her danger was when a man slipped from behind the nearest bush and raced to grab her. One hand passed around her waist, his other slipping around her cheek to cover her mouth tightly. Joanna struggled helplessly as the second man grabbed her left wrist, pulling at the broad wedding band.

"Easy now, lass. We won't be a hurtin' you but we be needin' this more than you."

It was a gruff voice and Joanna immediately stilled. The voice went on to apologize in a soft country tone, and the second man, fooled by her seeming acquiescence, relaxed a trifle, Joanna bit him.

"For heaven's sake, Turner," she declared. "What are you about?"

"Mrs. Wooten?" An expletive and immediate apology were followed by a rude demand that his partner release their captive.

Hands on hips, Joanna glared at the two men. "Is this any way for Wellington's best to behave?"

"Now Mrs. Wooten," coaxed the speaker, "you know we'd never have bothered you if'n we knew it was you." The man she'd called Turner cuffed his friend. "Don't ye know enough to take off your hat for a lady?"

Joanna laughed, happy to see her late husband's batman, a man who had helped more than any other in her adaptation to life in Spain. A thunder of hooves turned her head and the laugh broke off sharply, her heart pounding wildly.

"Oh, Lord, Turner, we're in the basket now," she said. "You two keep your mummers dubbed, you hear?"

The unknown soldier looked shocked at Joanna's use of cant, but Turner growled at him to heed his betters and be quiet. Joanna turned fully to await the arrival of the newcomer. Pierce Reston, the one man she most dreaded ever again seeing, was invading her life at the most inopportune moment possible. He arrived in a swirl of dust, dismounting quickly, and moved toward the waiting trio. Joanna noted concern in his features, in his eyes, but couldn't know that in his mind he felt an even stronger sense of surprise the men weren't escaping and a deeply hidden elation that he'd been forced to come to her side.

"Good day, Your Grace."

The duke's gaze flickered toward her, then back to the men he watched warily, wondering at their docility.

"You're trespassing," she went on with hastily assumed poise, "or have you avoided White Stones so long you've forgotten the boundaries?"

Had he really been that tall and broad when she'd left England with Reggie? Joanna spoke coldly, hiding the unexpected flutter in her breast and hurrying into speech before he could answer. "To what do I owe the unexpected and unwanted honor of your presence? I thought I made my thoughts on that subject quite clear the last time we met."

When the men showed nothing more than nervousness—the one who'd held Joanna more than the other—Pierce looked fully at Joanna. He'd last been this close to her in a dimly lit private parlor in a small inn not far south of London. One expressive eyebrow rose. "I assumed, under the circumstances, you might not object, Mrs. Wooten."

The soft drawl she remembered all too well, hardened on the "Mrs." His deliberate mistake, the misuse of her title, caused Joanna's palms to sweat. She resisted the need to wipe them along her habit. It was much too important she get rid of the duke and see what she could do for Turner and his friend than that she wonder at the distress she felt.

"Circumstances? Good heavens, Your Grace, do you mean my old friends from the army?" She was proud of her ability to dissemble and assume an air of surprise.

He dropped all pretense of formality. "Cut the 'Your Grace' business, Jo. I'm certain you are not safe with these two." He turned quickly as one man made a restless movement and frowned as his partner

17

muttered quick warning not to be a fool, that all was well. "Mount up like a good girl, Jo, and I'll see you away from here before taking these vagrants off to Matthews. He'll know what to do with them."

"Oh yes." Loathing filled Joanna's voice. "Our perceptive justice. Certainly he will. He'll clap them in prison and throw away the key. No thank you. I'll see to them myself."

"And how might you do that?"

"Sarcasm is just what I'd expect of you, Pierce. You haven't changed one whit."

"You haven't answered my question," he said coldly, ignoring the insult. Inside he felt as chilled as his tone implied. This was *not* how their first meeting was supposed to go.

"I will put them to work, of course. Turner is an honest man. I know him well. I'm very sorry to see what has become of him and will do what I can to put it right. He was a good friend when I badly needed one."

"And your friend's friend?"

Joanna, suddenly unsure, cast a look at her husband's old batman. Turner nodded. "I can trust him as well. And I'd prefer your room to your company, if you don't mind."

"I do mind. If you insist on taking these men to Midbourgh Court, I'll accompany you until I know there are others to see to your safety."

"In that case, I suggest we go. The sooner I'm returned to the Court, the sooner you can return to whatever dire emergency forced you to come to White Stones. And the sooner you do, the sooner you can settle the problem and return to Town."

"London?" His eyebrows rose. "At this time of year?" Since she was still speaking to him, Pierce

18

forced himself to relax and his habitual bored manner returned. "No one is in London now. Perhaps I'll go to Brighton while Prinny continues in residence there."

Pierce turned to catch the two horses, only to find the man called Turner holding the reins and waiting respectfully to help Joanna mount. He gritted his teeth as she thanked the rough-looking man.

"I will see you both presently at the Court," she said, "where we will decide what is best to be done with you. Turner, I depend on you."

"If you be offering us positions, Mrs. Wooten, we'll be there like a flash. Honest work isn't easy to come by these days."

She gave directions and moved off, not checking whether the duke was ready. He was, of course. She heard the splashing as his stallion followed Lad through the stream. Joanna gathered her courage, derided the fluttery feeling she couldn't seem to control, and trotted on, knowing she faced a difficult interview once they were out of earshot of the two ex-soldiers.

A rueful smile crossed her face and just a tinge of regret. How Pierce must hate her. He'd avoided her so carefully up to now. Only the fact that he was a gentleman must have made him come to what he'd thought was her rescue. Too bad for him, she thought, that he'd felt required to do so.

She'd done the unforgivable when she'd rejected his suit in favor of Reggie's. A lowly officer against a highborn lord of the realm! Reggie, a mere lieutenant in an admittedly famous regiment with an income one might, with generosity, call a competence, was no suitable match for Lady Joanna Ransome, especially when compared to the Duke of Stornway. Pierce had never looked kindly on insults.

Joanna sighed deeply. She remembered how surprised she'd been at his rage when she informed him she was marrying the lieutenant. She'd then laughed incredulously at his threats to force her into marriage—until he'd had the audacity to actually carry her off. He'd had the reputation of a rake, been far too careless of appearances, but until that night had, in all their long association, been heedlessly kind to her. She couldn't quite rid herself of nostalgic memories of the young man who'd allowed her to trail behind him as he'd toured his estate. And years earlier, when she'd been just a child of six or seven, he'd often cajoled her brother, Henry, into allowing her along on their milder adventures, teaching her to fish and whatnot.

Still, the idea he was hopelessly in love with her had been the biggest bouncer he'd ever uttered and she'd just been telling him so when Reggie, dear Reggie, appeared and took her home. Joanna grinned an unladylike grin. It hadn't been *quite* that simple. First she'd had to dissuade her betrothed from a duel with Pierce by informing Reggie she wouldn't be married with Pierce's blood on her conscience. The duke had laughed, telling Reggie he'd meet him where and when he liked and they'd see who married Joanna, but she'd outfaced the two angry men and all had ended peacefully.

When the two riders reached a wide place in the path through the home wood, Pierce touched Apollo's sides and rode forward until he could catch up Joanna's reins. She glared at him. The drawl was absent when he ordered, "Just one moment of your precious time, my lady disdain."

20

Pierce held her gaze until Joanna, unable to withstand the steady look, turned her head. Dismounting, he came to her side. Strong hands reached for her slender waist and lifted her down. Joanna immediately turned her back on him, an action for which he silently thanked her. He wasn't sure, if she were facing him, if he could restrain his desire to kiss her. The moon-pale hair streaming loose in wild tangles down her back was, however, very nearly an equal temptation. Pierce restrained his impulses sternly. This lady was no longer an innocent fresh from the schoolroom, protected by that innocence. He wondered if she'd known that night in the wayside inn, she was in no real danger from him, despite his threats. Times had, however, changed. She was now a desirable widow who had participated in the pleasures of the marriage bed. Once he had her in his arms Pierce wasn't certain he could control himself.

"Well, Your Grace?"

"It isn't well, Joanna. I had no opportunity to apologize for that, hmm, contretemps just before your marriage." He paused, then went on softly, "Joanna? I wish to do so now."

Joanna, her large eyes wide with disbelief and challenge, turned. "Contretemps? Is *that* what you call kidnapping and threats and placing me in an intolerable position?" She was angry to discover her eyes burning with unwanted tears, and the words ran on in an attempt to cover her sudden descent into missishness. "Do you know that until after we wed, my Reggie doubted my word that nothing had occurred between us? That for that last interminable week before our nuptials, I suffered his patient worried looks." *And more*, she thought, *so much more*. "I had

21

to put up with the knowledge he feared the worst of me!"

Pierce frowned. "He can't have known you if he doubted you. You're the straightest woman I've ever met." Pierce was intensely aware of having his love once again within arm's reach, though he carefully avoided moving closer. "Doltish behavior on his part, Joanna," he added.

There was a rustling in the nearby bushes but neither Joanna nor Pierce noticed. Joanna, surprised by his response, rediscovered the pain she'd felt before her virtue was proved. It had been the one stain on her love for Reggie, that he doubted her right up to their wedding night. She'd never told anyone how his behavior had changed, how, during that week, he'd once made demands on her which she'd avoided only by the opportune arrival of her flighty and invalidish sister-in-law. Nor had she ever spoken of how roughly he'd taken her that first time, sure in his own mind she'd either succumbed willingly or been forced by the handsome and socially powerful man now facing her.

Joanna had forgiven her young husband, of course, understanding that his suspicion and anger were based in feelings of inferiority and insecurity when he compared himself to the nonpareil. And, of course, he'd taught her to love their loving, but somehow the purity of her feelings for him had been tarnished. Not that she'd thought of that for years. The fact that Pierce upheld her honor smoothed balm over a wound she was surprised to find still festered. It was good to know Pierce would have believed her. The knowledge almost softened her feelings toward him.

"I thought him a dolt from the beginning," he

22

said, his soft drawl impinging on her thoughts, "but you could never see it."

That was going too far and any softer feelings disappeared. "Reggie was not a dolt. He was the best of all the scouts." Joanna had been in constant fear for her husband's life but she'd hidden it from him, showing him a smiling face whenever they could be together. "Old Hooky said so more times than I can count," she went on, goaded by Pierce's scornful expression.

"What Wellington said was that your Reggie took more chances than any other and lived and breathed for every opportunity to risk his skin." Pierce's sarcasm bit into Joanna's heart. He was putting into words suspicions she'd loyally thrust away whenever Reggie had volunteered for some new and dangerous mission. "I'm surprised your precious husband lived as long as he did." Pierce's uncertain temper sent him on a course sure to put him in the basket. "In fact, I expected you home within the year. I'd rather counted on it," he finished more quietly, his indigo eyes holding her indignant sherry-colored ones.

"And what possible good would it have done you if I had been—home—so soon?" Her voice wobbled slightly on the euphemism for being an even younger widow.

"We'd have been married and our nursery boasting two or three lusty brats."

Joanna gritted her teeth, but her temper faded at his soft voice and the warmth in his eyes.

"*Years,* my lovely Joanna. Do you have any idea what torture those years were to me? Knowing you were bedded by that rash young fool, thrust into one dangerous situation after another, forced to live a life you were never bred to, making do with the humblest

23

of housing and, for all I knew, going hungry at times?"

Again neither noticed a branch move unnaturally as if someone wished a better view. Instead Joanna's suspicion warred with unwelcome feelings of excitement and anticipation. Too, his knowledge surprised her. How *could* he know what her life had been like? Drat the man.

She ignored the rest and went back to his insouciant claim they'd have been married. That she knew was a lie. If he still wished to marry her, he'd have appeared immediately after her required year of mourning and begun courting her all over again. She mustn't let him think it mattered. Joanna drew a deep breath and attacked.

"Married? You and I? After knowing and loving my Reggie, you think I'd have come willingly to your arms?" She reached for the reins he still held and tugged at them. "This conversation is absurd, Your Grace. I find it boring in the extreme."

Much to her surprise, Pierce laughed. Her surprise intensified when he lifted her onto Lad's back and handed her the reins. In his eyes was a reflection of soft humor instead of the expected hard but steady gleam. "You little spitfire," he said softly, his hand laid on her boot, "I think I'll love you more now you're a bit seasoned than I did when I lost you." He backed off and raised his hat, staring up into her bemused features. "I look forward to seeing you soon, *Mrs.* Wooten—when you return to the London scene if not before." An eyebrow quirked and he smiled. "I think it'll be before, don't you?"

Again she had to still those fluttery feelings. It wouldn't do to trust Pierce's words no matter how she might wish they could forget the hurt she'd given his pride. Much to her surprise, she found she longed to renew the comfortable friendship they'd once had. Not love. Never love. Pierce didn't understand that tender emotion. And Pierce was a dangerous man when he felt his honor wounded. She must remember that.

Joanna tossed her head, unaware that his eyes gleamed in appreciation. "'Tis my one regret that when I return to society I must force myself to be polite to you, Duke. 'Twill quite ruin the season for me." His chuckles followed her as, rosy-cheeked, she trotted away toward the stables where busy lads could be seen working industriously under Sam's watchful eye.

Pierce watched until she reached the head groom who handed her down from the tall gelding. Then he turned to Apollo, mounted, and after one last wistful look toward his love, moved back down the path toward White Stones.

His Grace, the Duke of Stornway wasn't quite out of sight when Lady Elizabeth Ransome, niece to Lady Joanna, pushed aside a branch and stepped onto the path. Sleek black curls peeked from under a girlish straw hat. The demure effect of bonnet and dimity gown was contradicted by what her Aunt Joanna would privately label Elizabeth's conniving look. And if her aunt had been present to observe it, she would immediately have been on guard against her niece's latest machinations.

Two

After settling the question of Turner and his friend, Joanna sought the privacy of her room. The smile—something approaching an unladylike grin— which she'd felt obliged to check while with others, broke forth now she was alone. She allowed the bubbling, feeling freedom, then hugged herself and twirled like a green girl. Lud, it'd been exciting to spar with Pierce. Gratifying as well. Could he really have hinted he still wished her for his wife? Long in the tooth as she was? At almost twenty-four she was young to be a widow, but she'd long ago lost the dewy bloom of a chit in her first season.

Joanna approached the pier glass near the windows. Doubtfully she studied her complexion which had been ruined by the hot Spanish sun. The pale golden tan had never quite faded, nor the dusting of freckles across her nose and cheeks. Add to that fault her windblown hair, the pins having been lost early in her ride, and another fault, the badly worn habit with the sleeve seam showing a new rip . . . she looked the complete hoyden. No, Pierce couldn't possibly find her attractive.

Could he? Her gaze drifted down. Her figure, she thought, was adequate. Joanna unbuttoned her habit and shrugged out of it. The soft white bodice beneath it faithfully followed the thrust of her breasts. Reggie had loved her breasts. Would Pierce? Joanna blushed rosily at the thought and chided herself as she turned to her wardrobe. If she were thinking of the obnoxious duke as a lover, it was past time she got herself back in circulation and looked around for a respectable match—however appalling the notion of anyone other than Reggie as husband.

That the thought of remarrying crossed her mind at all shocked her and she instantly banished the notion. She'd settled her plans for the future. She would buy a house in London, find someone older, some respectable lady to live with her. Joanna counted over her relatives searching out a suitable companion-cum-chaperon and sighed as she realized there wasn't one with whom she thought she could abide sharing a home. Well, a solution to that problem could wait.

A knock preceded the bustling entry of Belton, Joanna's abigail. The woman had been not much more than a girl herself when promoted from nursery maid to abigail—well before Jo had been old enough to really need one. The two had said tearful goodbyes after Joanna's wedding because the bride could not take a maid to Spain. Having Belton with her again was one happy result of returning to Midbourgh Court after Waterloo. The much-loved maid was scolding even before she was fully in the room.

"Now then, milady. Let's get you out of that monstrous habit and into a proper gown."

Joanna let the soft country voice flow over her and thought again of Pierce. What a coup it would be if Pierce were to propose again rather than give the sort

27

of hints he'd given! The suspicions of his motives that she'd banished from her mind slipped into her thoughts, giving her pause. Propose? And what then? Leave her waiting at the church most likely, if she were silly enough to agree! He'd have revenged himself very well indeed.

"Hold still, do, Lady Jo. How am I ever to get these tangles out of your hair if you persist . . . ?"

Joanna snorted in a most unladylike way. Belton, thinking the sound a reprimand, stuttered into silence. Joanna didn't notice, telling herself she must get her imagination under control. Pierce was a gentleman and would never jilt a lady.

Besides, even if Pierce proposed she wouldn't, *couldn't* accept him. Not the man who had once tried to dishonor her. She sighed. It was as well she didn't believe his flirting words, didn't trust him. She pulled away from Belton, who was silently persisting in brushing her hair, and wandered to the windows.

"Now, Lady Jo. Please pay attention to what you're about."

But to see him again in London? To bandy words with him? Yes. She'd enjoy a light flirtation. The honesty to which he'd referred struck again, and she knew she'd enjoy much more than a flirtation.

Good heavens! What was she thinking? Indulging in an affair, which Pierce would undoubtedly make as public as possible in some "accidental" manner, was quite out of the question. Besides, even if she could trust him, her principles would never allow her to become a man's mistress! But those disturbing flutters—utterly intriguing, completely delightful, but definitely disturbing—were back with the thought, and no matter how she tried, Joanna's struggles to suppress them were only partially successful. She sighed, a sound Belton heard and about which the maid wondered.

For one moment a feeling of disloyalty filled Joanna, but Reggie's laughing eyes insinuated themselves into her mind along with his jesting voice telling her not to be a ninny. Life was too short, he'd say. One must fill every day and every moment with all it offered.

Not that he'd approve of His Grace as a partner in such games. He'd never quite lost his jealousy of the Duke of Stornway. Not in the more than three years they'd been wed. But life *was* short. Could be very short. Joanna's mouth drooped. Reggie's life had been short indeed. He'd passed his twenty-eighth birthday no more than a month before that fateful day near Waterloo.

Joanna straightened her shoulders, checked that she was neat and tidy, her pale hair brushed and firmly controlled in the tight bands she'd adopted with her widow weeds and, satisfied, left her room to fulfill still another necessary duty: a long overdue letter to her brother which would, she hoped, cut short his procrastinating ways and set in motion her plans for her niece.

Some four miles away at White Stones, Pierce joined his friend, Robert Merton, the Earl of Halford, in the library. He laughed as Rob closed his eyes, raising a handkerchief to his nose. "I know. I should have changed. But humor me, old friend. A bit of horsey odor won't kill you."

"A bit!" Rob waved a languid hand. "You've brought the whole demmed stables in with you."

"Cut line, Robert. You know I know your fribblish ways are a pose."

The handkerchief disappeared as quickly as it had come to hand, and Rob settled more firmly into his chair. "Habit, old man. Habit. One must never go out of character, not for a moment, you know."

"All that's over. Isn't it?"

Rob sighed. "I suppose so. Such a shame."

"You don't mean that."

The lounging man looked up at Pierce's sharp tone. "No. Of course I don't mean it. But I miss the excitement of those years when I pitted my poor wits against Nappy's agents. Life will become a dead bore if I don't find a way of stalling it off."

"I think *my* boredom is at an end," said Pierce.

He poured brandy for the two of them and sipped. His eyebrows rose at the quality which, despite the end of the war, was hard to come by, and lifting the decanter, he gave it a suspicious look. The brandy was, he suspected, smuggled—not that he'd raise such an embarrassing question with his steward. Putting it from his mind, he settled into a chair across from his friend, crossed his boots at the ankle, and studied his toes.

"How so?"

"How so what?"

Robert scowled. "How," he asked with overdone patience, "have you ended your state of boredom? There might be a lesson in it for me."

"I doubt it. Unless one in how *not* to behave!" Pierce hesitated then looked his friend in the eye. "This must go no further, Rob."

"When have I ever been a gabble-monger?" Intelligent interest glowed in the earl's eyes despite the

30

pretended belligerency of his words. He glowered at Pierce until the two of them chuckled.

"You've never been one to let your mouth flap. And that's why I wish to talk to you. Besides, it is old gossip and so out-of-date I don't suppose I should be concerned that someone might have overheard."

"Never known you, m'boy, to be so indiscreet as to let any cats out of any bags."

"Indiscreet? I sincerely hope I wasn't. However, at the time, I didn't think about anyone being nearby. Thing is, I have this vague feeling, now it's too late, we weren't as isolated as I'd thought. Or, rather, as I didn't think." Pierce scowled. "I wasn't in a state to think of anyone but the two of us."

"Oh? You met someone while you were out?"

"Remember Joanna Ransome?" Pierce tried hard for a casual note, but his friend knew him well. Besides, Rob had a long memory.

"Midbourgh's sister?"

The *ton* would have been much surprised at how alert Robert Merton appeared. He'd carefully fabricated the reputation of a care-for-nobody dandy, worrying about the set of his coat, the creases in his cravat, with never a serious thought in his head. The pose had been useful in the days he'd worked as a counterspy. Now the pose was habit and he rarely let his true self be seen—if it still were his self, that is.

"Seem to remember you had an interest there." He frowned. "Married some flashy redcoat and went off to the wars, didn't she?"

"Yes." Pierce gritted his teeth. "Went off to the wars and suffered no one knows how much hardship. I heard one tale of a hairsbreadth escape from French troops and another of a bivouac in a village where no house was fully roofed—and that in the winter."

The barely suppressed passion in Pierce's voice alerted Robert. "Would I be right in thinking you still have an interest there?"

"You would." Pierce glared. "That better not become the latest *on dit*, my friend."

"You wrong me."

"I know," sighed Pierce, "but I'm all on end. Today was the first time I've seen her in four and a half years." He tipped his jaw. "Let her know I'd seen her, anyway."

Rob nodded his understanding. With effort he controlled a chuckle. A vision of the Duke of Stornway hiding behind trees and spying on his love was one he found exquisitely funny. Then a distinctly unfunny thought intruded: "Did you also see her soldier?"

"You've not kept track. Her soldier died a hero's death at Waterloo."

"Did he now? Well, that's all right then." Rob sipped his drink, his eyes never leaving Pierce's. "Well over a year since Waterloo. You're slipping, old friend."

"I don't have the least idea what you think you're talking about," said Pierce, very much on his dignity.

"If you wanted to court the lady, you're a little dilatory about it, aren't you?"

"I'm not dilatory and I'm not slipping. . . . Just cautious." The slightest hint of desperation could be detected in Pierce's tone when he added, "This time nothing must go wrong."

"Ahhh."

Pierce glanced toward Rob and burst out laughing at the knowing look which went with the drawn-out sound of understanding. "You're right. It went very wrong before. I see you haven't forgotten the ass I made of myself at the time."

"Thwarted love's black brow. You were a dead bore for weeks. Yes, you definitely made a cake of yourself."

"You don't know the half of it. I bought a special license and kidnapped her." He aborted a movement toward a pocket hidden inside his coat.

"You what?"

"Right under the eyes of her betrothed and her brother. Not that Henry made the least push to stop me."

"No, Midbourgh wouldn't. But the cub did?"

"Of course. Worse, he caught up with us and succeeded in taking her away. From Joanna's reaction when he appeared, I knew I'd lost. I didn't return to Town until they were wed and off."

"Midbourgh would have upheld your suit," said Robert thoughtfully, his fingers playing with the rim of his glass.

"I did not want a woman forced into marrying me."

"Must be love."

"I told you . . ."

"You idiot. You've handled women since you were breeched. How could you have so mishandled the one you wished to make your wife? Is it still love?"

"The problem, dear boy, was quite simple," said Pierce, assuming a heedlessness which would have fooled no one. "I didn't know it was love until Wooten appeared on the scene. I'd been taking her for granted." Rob's brows rose. "Well, she'd been making puppy eyes at me for years and I assumed when the time was right . . ." Pierce stood and took

33

a turn around the room before straightening his shoulders and facing his friend. "I made," he said with dignity, "a gross strategic error."

"Which you decided not to repeat."

A rueful look crossed the duke's face. "Which I decided not to repeat. I had such plans, such dreams, about how we'd meet again." He sighed. "She's cross as a bear, Robbie."

"I assume from what you said earlier you must have referred to your, er, faux pas of five years ago."

"I tried to apologize."

"That was certainly an error. Should have ignored it, old boy."

"So it seems."

"Made an ass of yourself, my friend."

"I seem to do it with regularity when it comes to my dealings with Joanna. It doesn't seem fair: just when it is so important to retain every bit of savoir-faire I have, I invariably develop foot-in-mouth disease."

Pierce glowered at Robert who tried to suppress chuckles but ignobly failed. He felt quite out of charity with his old friend who couldn't control his abominable sense of humor. Finally, miffed, he took himself off and turned himself over to his valet. The smell of the stables had begun to bother him—at least it made as good an excuse as any for leaving Robert victor of the field.

The excited yipping of a half-grown terrier pup penetrated the preoccupied frown of the young widow writing industriously at the ormolu-decorated escritoire. Joanna raised her head to glance out the window beside her. The hand not holding the pen pushed aside the deep red drape, a fall of white lace dripping back from slim fingers to lay against the dark gray of her sleeve. A smile lifted the corners of her generous mouth at the sight of the gatekeeper's younger grandson.

The sturdy lad racing after his pet disappeared around the hedge hiding the stables. The smile faded, a sad look darkening her eyes. If only she and Reggie had been so blessed, she thought. She shook off the downcast mood and firmly turned back to the letter she was composing with much care. Her brother Henry simply must be made to attend!

Some minutes later the parlor door creaked open. Half-consciously Joanna made a mental note to have candle wax rubbed into the hinges, but she made no move to turn and greet the intruder invading her carefully contrived peace. Rustling skirts and the sound of soft sandals pattering in erratic movements around the room interfered with her concentration, but Joanna ignored the incontrovertible fact that she was no longer alone. A sigh, and then another more penetrating, reached her ears. Still Joanna wrote on. Finished, she reached for the silver sand with one hand as she quickly read through what she'd written.

"Aunt Jo?"

"In a moment, Elizabeth."

Joanna sprinkled her letter to her absent brother liberally, shook off the sand, and folded the heavily embossed paper he deemed proper to his station. She wrote the direction of his Brighton residence across the front in a firm rather unfeminine hand. A candle stood on the desk, and making deft use of the tinderbox, she lit it, centering a blob of gold sealing wax carefully over the fold. She pressed a seal into

35

it and set it aside, admitting she'd procrastinated as long as she could.

Her niece emphasized the necessity of facing her. *"Please*, Aunt Jo. 'Tis *important."*

The impatient tone irritated her, and Joanna wished, not for the first time, that she'd had the raising of her niece from a much earlier age. But the notion was, once again, rejected. If she'd returned to her brother's home at the death of her sister-in-law as Henry had wished, she'd have had that much less time with her beloved Reggie. . . . Joanna put such thoughts firmly out of her mind.

She was appalled when the depressing memory was instantly replaced by an insistent mental picture of Pierce, something that had happened far too often since their meeting that afternoon, thoughts of him insinuating themselves into her mind at the oddest moments.

Joanna turned in her chair. Her *duty*, she reminded herself, was to the spoiled beauty who was absentmindedly destroying a bouquet Joanna had, just that morning, arranged. The nostalgia roused by meeting Pierce must not interfere with her duty. She studied her niece's nervous manner and pouting face.

"'Twould seem it weren't so important after all," Joanna ventured when Elizabeth remained silent.

Her niece continued plucking petals from a particularly lovely rose while turning occasional speculative glances toward the calm figure of her aunt. Finally the girl came to some conclusion and affected a nonchalance that didn't fool Joanna for a moment.

"Oh, but it is, dearest Aunt Jo. It is terribly important."

36

Joanne repressed a sigh. "What has occurred to put you in such a pucker, my dear?"

Joanna knew her niece had spent part of the morning with her bosom bow, Lady Alicia Staunton, and Alicia had a way of putting Elizabeth's nose out of joint. The two girls had been best friends and rivals since they'd been in leading strings. And ever since Alicia had gone to London for last spring's season and returned quite the young lady, the situation had worsened. She assumed wrongly the current conversation was based in something said during the girls' latest visit. Joanna forced an interested look and gazed expectantly at her niece.

"Lady Bradford."

The utmost disgust in Elizabeth's voice made Joanna chuckle, despite the instant thought: *not this again.* The girl cast her aunt a glance pregnant with wounded feelings and flounced to the couch, seating herself in a flurry of ruffles.

"It is *not* a laughing matter, Auntie."

"It?" asked Joanna innocently.

"We have received no invitation to the Bradford Hunt Ball."

Just as she'd feared. Would they never settle the question? Joanna sighed.

"We must go, Aunt Jo. The thought that we might not attend is not to be borne."

The tragedy expressed by Elizabeth's drooping figure contrasted sharply with the furtive glance she tossed toward her aunt, measuring whether her chaperon was suitably impressed by the potential for disaster.

"Of course we've received no invitation." Joanna kept her voice even with effort. "If there's been one, it will, quite properly, have been sent to your father."

"But it is *we* who need one. Sending it to him who will not care for the humbug hunting here and will never think of us buried in the country is disastrous. No man," said the selfish young beauty, her high voice filled with loathing, "could possibly be more thoughtless than my father."

Joanna rose to her feet, her mouth firmed into a line her niece had learned to dread. "That is quite enough, Elizabeth. You will retract those words and you will go to your room where you will write in your best hand twenty-five times: "A froward tongue . . ."

"You treat me like a schoolroom miss!"

Joanna's eyelids drooped dangerously. She held the defiant girl's eyes for a long moment. Elizabeth batted her lashes, sparkling tears beading their length. Joanna ignored this ploy, too, knowing her niece capable of producing those tears at the slightest thwarting of her will. When sure her niece was thoroughly cowed, Joanna spoke.

"You, my dear, whatever you prefer to think, *are* in the schoolroom. And there you'll be until the season begins next spring. *As you very well know.* Even if Lady Bradford were so lost to propriety as to send us an invitation, I would be required to word a polite refusal."

The tears became real, the lovely face as plain as any youngster in a fit of temper. Joanna had discovered it best to ignore her niece's tantrums and did so now.

The stern little speech that induced Elizabeth's outburst offered no clue to Joanna's true thoughts on the subject. Her recent decisions concerning her niece's future had been the main focus of the letter to her absent brother who, although not so selfish as his daughter had implied, was absentmindedly complacent and undoubtedly held the comfortable view that it would be years yet before he must worry about finding his daughter a husband.

That was not, however, a subject to be discussed with Elizabeth. It would be soon enough when and if Joanna received a positive reply to her careful composition to her brother. It had become obvious to Joanna her niece was, in an evocative phrase she'd once heard used by a sea captain who'd been at Trafalgar, a loose cannon on deck. And so she'd told Henry, concluding they should bring Elizabeth out during the little season this fall and declining to be responsible if he refused to heed her advice and his harum-scarum daughter caused a scandal.

"It is more than the fact you are not yet out," Joanna went on in a kinder tone as the sobs ceased.

Memories of the excitement and the unbearable wait before her own first season flitted through her mind, and empathy for Elizabeth's impatience interfered with Joanna's usual good sense as she tried to explain to the girl why they couldn't go.

"It is also that I am still in mourning for your uncle. It would be quite irresponsible of me to allow you to attend a formal ball and unseemly for me to appear there."

"It's been well over a year, Aunt Jo."

"It doesn't seem it."

For a moment it appeared as if the sadness underlying the simple statement effected a softening in Elizabeth, and Joanna read sympathy in the chit's expressive eyes. The momentary compassion faded, however, and her young voice was again strident. "It isn't fair. Matilda Storling's going and she's never been presented. And Alicia and—"

"And, I doubt not," Joanna interrupted tartly, "a great many other people. That is quite enough on the subject. You become a dead bore, my dear Lizzy," a deliberate use of the childish nickname, "and don't think I've forgotten your words concerning your father. You will hand me the required lines in the drawing room before dinner. Since there is not a great deal of time, I suggest you begin. Twenty-five lines, Elizabeth," she reiterated in as stern a manner as she could contrive.

Ignoring the sputtering indignation from her thwarted niece, Joanna turned toward the door. Going into the hall, she heard the creak of the hinge. Again she reminded herself to have a servant wax the irritating thing, ruefully acknowledging the fact that she would undoubtedly forget. Again.

That night Joanna yawned widely as she lay in her big four-poster bed. What an exciting day it had been. A trifle too exciting perhaps when Turner's friend had his grubby hands on her, but on the whole she'd felt life coursing through her as she hadn't since before Waterloo.

The arrival of Turner and Martin had been fortuitous actually. A few months training under Dawson, Henry's butler, and Sam, his head groom, would have the two ready for similar positions in the home she intended establishing for herself as soon as her flighty niece was off her hands. Lord Midbourgh was unaware of his sister's plans. He'd try to throw a rub her way, thinking it totally improper and, worse, insulting to his dignity. *His* sister had no need to live anywhere other than under his roof. Joanna had spent a number of hours planning ways around his expected attempts to thwart her. Turner and Martin would be servants Henry couldn't bribe. She'd have their loyalty, not her brother. It was a step toward her future.

Reluctantly Joanna once again considered her meeting with Pierce. Meeting the duke had, in a way, been a blessing. It pointed out just how bored she'd become with the peaceful life at the Court. Perchance there'd been more than a little self-interest prompting her decision that Elizabeth must have her season? Perhaps deep down inside she'd wished to get back into society?

Pierce. Had he changed or had she merely forgotten? Joanna cast her mind back to those last meetings during her one and only season—and that curtailed by her marriage. Tall. Dressed in the restrained but elegant style Brummell had brought to fashion . . .

Restrained. Yes, that had undoubtedly been a problem. The sober blacks and subdued grays, no matter how well-tailored, could not compare in young eyes to the flashing gold braid on the crimson regimentals Lieutenant Wooten wore. Nor did Pierce's drawling voice and deceptively languid manner compare well to Reggie's quick stride and exuberant nature.

How young she'd been, thought Joanna . . . and sat up, appalled. Now why had she thought that? Surely she wasn't, now that she was older and wiser, comparing Pierce favorably with Reggie? Her beloved Reggie? Pierce the rake? The wild one? No. Definitely not.

Besides, just before she'd met her Reggie, there'd been that fortunate visit from Lady Cressida Clayton, then Merton, the Earl of Halford's sister. Lady Cressy, then in her fourth season, had warned Joanna about the sort of life Pierce planned for her. Joanna found herself once again infuriated by the very idea. Make her a docile wife, would he? Expect her to bear his brats and keep the homefires burning while he continued to live the life of a rake in London! How dare he!

The old anger faded as common sense returned and Joanna laid her head back on her pillow. She hadn't married Pierce. She'd met and married Reggie. The turmoil in her mind about her meeting with Pierce was a result of her current quiet life. It was simply that she'd seen no men in so many months. No presentable, interesting men, that is. There were, of course, the very young men of the local families and their stodgy fathers with whom she occasionally exchanged civil greetings. There was the vicar who, though an intelligent and well-educated man, was no longer young.

There were no others. The ennui she'd been telling herself would pass had led to her overestimating the delight she'd experienced in the first instant she'd seen Pierce; delight that had immediately been buried under her concern for Turner and returning memories of her last meeting with the duke.

Having settled to her satisfaction the reasons for her elation when Pierce galloped back into her life, she finally allowed herself to think about their conversation in the woods. No. He hadn't been serious when he'd implied he still wished to marry her. If he was, then that would mean . . . but no. He had never loved her and never would. He didn't understand the meaning of the word!

Besides, if he loved her he wouldn't have waited a day beyond the traditional year of mourning before contriving to see her. If that long! Pierce had never held propriety in high regard. And he'd not a patient bone in his body. On top of that, she'd heard enough about his current style of living to be certain he wasn't a man nursing a hopeless passion.

Pierce? Joanna laughed lightly at the thought of the Duke of Stornway nursing a passion, hopeless or otherwise. He was too proud to allow anyone to know his private thoughts. Joanna sighed. If she were to see him in London—and how could she avoid that possibility?—she must remember his reputation and not let her heart soften toward him.

Flirt with him? Oh yes. That would be quite enjoyable. A doubt occurred as she remembered how she'd felt in his presence. A discreet affair would never do. Flirt yes. But carefully. Take him seriously? Never. She mustn't forget Pierce had always gone to great lengths to right a wrong done him.

Joanna chuckled as she remembered the youthful Pierce. He'd, once or twice, concocted exceedingly ingenious ways to achieve revenge for some slight, although occasionally they'd gone wrong—the time he'd put glue on the pew where Squire usually sat, for instance. He'd been angry with the man for calling him gallow's bait, merely because the old man had caught Henry and himself poaching in Squire's trout stream. Oh yes, that plan had gone wrong, indeed. Squire's mother-in-law had been visiting and Henry, Joanna, and Pierce had watched, round-eyed, as the stiff-necked old lady had been ceremoniously seated right smack in the exact spot where Pierce had liberally applied the glue brush! None of them had stayed one instant beyond the end of the service that day! There'd been other occasions, too, when he and her brother Henry had ignored Joanna, the child, as they'd gone about their plotting.

Memories of his often humorous choice of revenge

43

faded as she reminded herself of the existing situation. She must not forget she'd given him the worst hurt a man could have: she'd rejected his suit for someone far below him socially and in possession of far less of the world's goods. Joanna wished she might believe the wounds were to his heart instead of his pride but she didn't. Pierce wouldn't allow such an insult. No matter how long it took to get back at her, he'd discover a way. There was the main reason why she mustn't believe a word if he persisted in trying to turn her up sweet.

So. She'd flirt with him all he wanted. At the same time she'd be careful she didn't get into a position where Pierce could achieve what must be his purpose. But why, having settled that quite satisfactorily, did she feel so depressed and unhappy? When she could discover no reason—at least, no acceptable reason—Joanna put it out of her mind and went to sleep.

Three

"Wait, Aunt Jo. Please wait."

Joanna turned in her saddle and bit her lip. What a picture Elizabeth made as, rosy cheeked, her dusky curls bouncing against the deep rose of her best habit, she ran toward the stables. It should have gladdened the heart of a loving relative. Still unsettled by her meeting with Pierce the day before, Joanna could feel nothing more than irritation. "I am riding to the village to visit one of your father's dependents, Elizabeth. I can't feel it a duty in which you'd enjoy participating."

For a moment the lovely face pouted, but, too soon for Joanna's escape, she brightened. "I'm sure the day is fine enough that I'll like the ride,", she said firmly.

At a snail's pace, thought Joanna, who had been anticipating a gallop. No acceptable objection occurred to her, however, and she sighed. "In that case," she said, "Sam will have your mare saddled and will, I'm sure, ask Jem to saddle a horse for himself."

"Surely we don't need Jem, Aunt." The beauty's eyes widened as they did when she wished to appear

45

particularly innocent. "You never take a groom when you ride."

"I am not a young miss not yet out. We'll take Jem."

Indeed, the well-trained staff had already supplied the required mare, the much-maligned gift Joanna had passed on to her niece. Jem was waiting to help Elizabeth into the saddle. She smiled at him and he reddened.

Jem idolized the girl. Every male Elizabeth knew idolized her—except for the vicar, prosy old man. For reasons Elizabeth could not comprehend the vicar seemed to disapprove of her—but it was a thought she rarely allowed herself to dwell on because no one else seemed to think her less than perfect. The duke, too, would find her irresistible, assuming her luck held and they met up with him. She knew he would. Then Alicia would see!

An hour later Joanna and Elizabeth were exiting a small cottage at the tail end of the village when two riders appeared around the curve in the road. Joanna bit her lip, but, behind her, Elizabeth brightened and surreptitiously straightened her pert little riding hat. Her luck *was* in!

"Hold, Robert," said Pierce, catching sight of them. "Good day, Lady Joanna."

His Grace and Lord Halford dismounted, and after Joanna introduced them to Elizabeth, the men helped the two ladies to their saddles. Pierce did a mental review of the preceding few minutes to discover how Lady Elizabeth had somehow maneuvered it so he was aiding her. He found himself disgusted that in his preoccupation with Joanna he'd allowed it.

"You've been visiting Granny Black?"

He spoke to Elizabeth but Joanna answered, and immediately Pierce turned toward her, resting his hand on Lad's neck.

"She isn't at all well, Pierce. I'm worried about her although she insists she has all she needs and it is merely old age."

Momentarily thwarted, Elizabeth fumed.

"Granny Black, ill? How sad that is. I'll be sure to visit her. Remember the tales she used to tell us?" He chuckled softly at the color in Joanna's cheeks.

"You know her stories left me with nightmares." Joanna blushed more rosily and turned from the eyes which, holding hers with an admiring gaze, unsettled her. "I was forbidden to listen to her."

"Not that that saved you. I, or your brother, managed to pass on most of them." Hiding his action from the others, he touched her hand.

Elizabeth giggled loudly enough to call attention to herself. "I like best the one about the girl who watched the smugglers."

"Smugglers? And a girl?" asked Robert. Lord Halford, recognizing the green girl's bid for Pierce's attention drew his mount alongside the young miss who had managed the impossible and out-jockeyed Pierce—even if it was only for a moment. "Tell it to me, Lady Elizabeth. I enjoy a good story," said Rob, wishing to help his friend.

Elizabeth's laugh trilled and she tossed her curls. "I'm sure His Grace can make a better tale of it." She flirted at her quarry from under her lashes and frowned when she discovered he was ignoring her in favor of her aunt. "Aunt, surely we aren't waiting here all day?" she added waspishly.

"Have you," asked Pierce softly, deliberately turning his back on the girl, "considered beating that pert miss?"

Joanna gave him a repressive look and said, "It is time Elizabeth and I were returning home. It was very nice meeting you, Lord Halford. Perhaps we shall run into you in London once we join the social whirl."

"Ah," drawled Robert, "you and Lady Elizabeth will come up for the little season?"

"Nothing is definite, m'lord. That decision is up to her father."

"But surely he wouldn't be so selfish as to leave such a lovely young lady languishing in the country and deprive us of such beauty?"

"My brother has definite notions on how to raise his daughter, Lord Halford," said Joanna mendaciously and unblushingly. "He'll decide when she is to make her come-out."

Robert smiled at Elizabeth and went on softly, "Brunettes are much in fashion, you know."

Elizabeth, who had barely glanced at Pierce's friend, gave Lord Halford a longer look. Had she been a little hasty when deciding to set her cap at Pierce? Here was a well-favored man who didn't look at her as if she were a field mouse in the pantry. His coat and buckskins, stylishly skintight, were far more fashionable, his slim build attractive. Best of all, he had a pretty way with words.

"I will be brought out no later than the spring. Perhaps during the little season this fall," Elizabeth asserted mulishly. "I have written my father and informed him it must be."

"'Tis a new fashion, Robert," drawled Pierce. "A girl still in the schoolroom now tells her esteemed parent how to go on."

48

"Don't encourage her, Pierce." Joanna's voice was too low for the others to hear. "She is very young, you know," she apologized to Lord Halford.

Velvet brown eyes twinkled into hers. "I have several sisters, Lady Joanna. I understand perfectly."

Elizabeth, ignored by all, knew she'd behaved badly. Not at all like the poised young lady she wished to appear. Nor could she see how to retrieve the situation. Angrily she again suggested it was time to go. "It is so dreadfully hot and dusty in the street, Aunt Jo. I'm sure it isn't good for your health."

Pierce tried to control himself. Really he did. He managed very well until he'd mounted Apollo. But then a roar of laughter had him bending over his stallion's neck. "The heat, Joanna? After the Peninsula?"

Robert's lips twitched but he suppressed outright chuckles, and Joanna just looked at her niece with an expression that boded no good to that young lady once they were home. With a sob of real emotion, Elizabeth turned her mare and kicked the much-surprised animal in the side. When the gray took off at a dead run, Jem, his mount not half so young and spry as the mare, struggled to turn it and started after her.

"Lud. Now we're in the basket," said Joanna, also off after the galloping mare. She barely noticed Lord Halford's startled reaction to her language and didn't care that Pierce was once again laughing—but this time at her.

A grim realization of impending disaster filled Joanna. Elizabeth's gray was a well-behaved little animal but accustomed to a very tight rein. Given encouragement for something other than their usual dawdling pace, the mare had the bit in her teeth.

49

Joanna closed in on the runaway but was unable to catch her. Pierce and Robert were late in comprehending the girl's danger.

The mare raced toward a low wall surrounding a horsey paradise: a meadow where running would be a delight. Despite her rider's screams, the mare took it easily. Elizabeth, however, did not. With one last terror-filled shriek, she tumbled to the ground. Joanna took the wall wide, not certain where her niece had landed. Right behind her Pierce and Robert sailed over as well, fearful their teasing had goaded the girl too much.

"Rob, old friend, there is a farm just round the next curve," said Pierce with calm authority as he dismounted. "Borrow a carriage of some sort for bearing that imp of Satan home." Lord Halford, after one look at the still figure, obeyed. "How is she?" Pierce asked over Joanna's shoulder. "Can you tell?"

"I don't know yet. Jem," she ordered, "ride home. Have Her Ladyship's bed prepared and go for the doctor." Jem, glad of something to do, his freckled face red with guilt that he'd not, somehow, saved his young mistress from a fall, raced off as fast as his elderly horse would take him. Joanna checked Elizabeth's limbs. "I don't think anything is broken but she must have hit her head." She rubbed at Elizabeth's wrists while Pierce watched the girl's face.

"She got off more lightly than she deserved then."

"Pierce, how can you be so unfeeling? How could I have allowed this to happen?" A touch of panic colored Joanna's voice. "How will I tell my brother?"

"Worried about your skin, Joanna? Can't think Midbourgh would have the energy to beat you."

"This is no time for levity," she scolded. "She

50

should have come around by now. Oh, what am I to do?"

"Stop blithering, Jo. She came around some time ago, but knowing she well deserves a scold, she's shamming it."

For a moment big blue eyes glared at him but closed almost immediately. Not, however, before Joanna noticed.

"Let her be," Pierce continued. "If nothing's broken, she'll have aches and pains which she deserves. She behaved abominably."

"Yes." Joanna, her fear allayed, feigned despair. "I think she proved she's not ready for a season. She'd never get vouchers for Almack's with such a wayward tongue. The only thing to do is to write my brother the sad news."

Elizabeth sat up with a jerk. "You wouldn't!"

"I wouldn't? And why not, miss?"

"Oh, Aunt Jo, please. You wouldn't, would you?"

"But you *have* behaved abominably."

"I didn't mean to. Truly I didn't." Elizabeth moved her arm and groaned at the pain. "Oh! I hurt."

"Good."

Pierce's terse comment fired the girl's temper. She glared at her tormentor.

"You, my girl, deserve every ache and pain. You are a spoiled little miss with no manners and less conduct."

"That's not true. Besides, who are *you* to scold *me* when you've behaved far, far worse?"

Pierce's eyebrow rose. "You should have no knowledge of my behavior—or if you do you should pretend you don't!"

"I know how you treated my aunt! Abducting her

against her will . . ." Elizabeth trailed off at her aunt's gasp.

Joanna's skin paled to a waxy white. "Pierce . . ."

"Since I doubt you told her that story I must assume she overheard our tête-à-tête yesterday." His mouth tightened. "No properly brought up young lady would deliberately eavesdrop on a private conversation. Your father," he told Elizabeth, "should have beaten you. Jo, er, *Lady* Joanna obviously has too soft a heart to put you in the way of proper behavior. Or perhaps by the time she came to you it was too late. You are forward and pert and not very honest." He studied her, his eyes skimming the heart-shaped face, the dusky curls, the slim figure, then turned back to Joanna. "However, the chit has some looks . . ."

It was Elizabeth's turn to lose color. Not at the scold but at Pierce's last comment. If he, a connoisseur, thought her only passable, perhaps . . .

"If," he went on, "you can train her to conceal the negative side of her character, she may contrive to make a decent match. Just don't let her try to attach any of my particular friends. I'll reveal the truth instantly."

"Then I'll tell what you did to my aunt!" stormed Elizabeth, hurt and bewilderment leading her to retaliate.

Joanna gasped. "That does it." She confronted her niece and, hands on hips, glared down at her. "You are an intolerable brat. I wash my hands of you."

Joanna turned and gave a short whistle. There was only Pierce to know and she didn't care if he thought her unladylike. Besides, he'd taught her to whistle in the first place and she was too impatient to catch Lad when she knew her mount would come at the sound. She was fighting her skirts in an attempt to mount without help when Pierce caught her elbow.

"Let me go," she stormed.

"Are you abandoning the chit? Leaving her behind?" When she struggled for freedom, he went on, his tone suggestive, "Alone. Here with me."

Laying her head against the leathers, Joanna breathed deeply. "You are right, of course. But my charming brother is going to have to bestir himself. I will not continue to chaperon a chit with no more conscience than a . . . a . . ."

"Peep-o'-day boy? A here-and-therian? One of the fashionably impure, perhaps?"

Joanna nodded firmly. "Any or all."

Again Pierce had to control ready laughter, something Joanna had been capable of drawing from him even when a child. It was so *good* to banter with her again! Wouldn't Joanna be chagrined when she realized she'd admitted knowing flash words that should never have sullied her delightfully formed ears?

Elizabeth felt chilled. Would her aunt really carry out her threat to leave the Court? And if so, how would it affect her? All the old tabbies would talk if her closest female relative refused to bring her out. She'd be ruined indeed. She'd never have a season. No. Aunt Joanna must not go. No, no, and no.

"Aunt Joanna?" she called in a weak voice. "I feel so awful."

"Good." Joanna's tone was tart.

Elizabeth opened her eyes wide. Had that been her gentle aunt saying that? "I hurt."

"Excellent."

"Please, Auntie . . ."

"Be quiet. You have done your aunt enough damage for one day."

Elizabeth opened her mouth, but another sharp look from Pierce's anger-darkened visage frightened her and she closed it. Tears dripped down her rosy cheeks. How could everyone be so unkind to her? It wasn't fair. What had *she* done after all? It was Joanna who had caused this fiasco, but her aunt was getting no blame. It *wasn't* fair. How could His Grace suggest she had hurt her aunt? She'd done nothing. Nothing.

The farm trap arrived and the two men lifted the girl into it, Pierce with rough efficiency and Robert with the gentle care that characterized his behavior toward the weaker sex. Elizabeth thanked Lord Halford with a faint smile and closed her eyes.

"Joanna?" Pierce held out his hand. She ignored it. "Come, love . . ." He smiled at her flustered look. "Up you go."

"Must I?"

His eyebrow quirked. "Your niece will undoubtedly need your support on the ride home."

At his dryly spoken words, Joanna glanced at her pouting niece and obeyed. The girl had made enough nuisance of herself today without pretending to swoon and tricking that nice Lord Halford into cuddling her under the mistaken impression the girl needed support! Joanna wondered if there was something she should have done in the year she'd had charge of Elizabeth. Or had the girl's character been ruined before her arrival? And why had she never noticed the tiresome chit was more than just a nuisance?

Elizabeth knew when she was defeated. She rode home in silence, squeezed into the corner of the trap with her aunt supporting her shoulders. Had there ever been such an awful day? Much to her consternation, she found the succeeding days no better.

54

Elizabeth tried every wile she knew to get back into her aunt's good graces but nothing worked. At every attempt she received reproachful looks, sometimes even a sense her aunt didn't *like* her. Elizabeth couldn't understand it.

Still more important, Aunt Joanna had written her father. What had been reported in that letter she didn't know but feared it wasn't to her advantage. The duke had brought out the very worst in her and had caused her loving aunt to turn from her. It was all his fault. Elizabeth concluded His Grace was no gentleman. A gentleman surely wouldn't have lectured her that way. No gentleman would have been so cruel. Besides, he'd thought her looks nothing out of the ordinary—and surely that couldn't be true. So on top of being a rake and a kidnapper, he was a liar.

Lord Halford, however, had a different cut. Elizabeth sensed his underlying gentleness and desperately wanted to meet him again. He was better looking than the duke, and he'd been kind, and best of all, he'd shown a proper interest in her. Besides, his dress was much more elegant than the slight disarray His Grace affected. It would be a great thing if she could attach such a man about town, *perhaps become engaged,* before she ever made her bow to society. Assuming she'd be allowed to make that bow! *That* would astonish Alicia Staunton no end. Alicia with her tales of how wary the London gentlemen were, how difficult it was to bring an acceptable *parti* up to scratch.

Alicia. Who had already had a season. Jealousy of her slightly older friend burned in Elizabeth's breast. If she could only attract Lord Halford's interest before going up to London, she'd have brought off a coup that would astonish Alicia and, by the way, make her season much more interesting from the start. Which brought her back to the problem at hand. How to meet Lord Halford again? Surely the two men would not long remain at White Stones? The duke never stayed long in the country and he'd already been there near to a fortnight according to servant gossip relayed by her abigail Betty. Something must be contrived. But to contrive anything at all meant regaining Aunt Jo's esteem.

Twice it had occurred to Elizabeth to apologize. Twice she'd rejected such a lowering thought. Admit she'd been in the wrong? Anger boiled through her at the very idea. Besides, hadn't Alicia told her it was a maxim of Brummell, that arbiter of the *ton*, that one should never apologize? On the other hand, how else was she to turn Joanna up sweet?

Elizabeth was musing on these matters one day as she was out walking. Her meandering, purposeless path took her toward the stables where she found that new man of her aunt's working on a wood carving. What was his name? Joanna's husband's batman was Turner. This one was . . . Martin? Was that right? "What are you doing?" she demanded.

The old soldier glanced up, surprised at the half-arrogant, half-curious tone. Slowly he rose to his feet, reaching for the soft hat covering his dull brown hair.

Good food and lack of worry about the future had done much to improve Martin's health and allay his bitterness but here was a young lady who had everything soft and, from what he'd been told, didn't appreciate a bit of it. Still, the girl was Mrs. Wooten's—or as he discovered she was properly called—Lady Jo's niece. He'd best try for respect.

"Just a bit of carving, miss."

"I see that. What are you carving? And why? Aren't you supposed to be working?"

Martin compressed his lips. When he'd served in the Army, he'd run into flashy young officers with just this attitude and hadn't liked them. But, he reminded himself, Lieutenant Wooten hadn't been that sort. Nor had his wife. "I do what I'm told, miss. And I've been told to take it easy for a week or so." With effort he kept his voice even. "As to the carving, 'tis a small hobby. See you?" He held up the half-finished statuette and Elizabeth's eyes widened. Still rough and unfinished, even so it had the look of Lad, Joanna's favorite mount. "This be a gift for Lady Jo. My friend Turner let slip Her Ladyship's birthday comes soon and I thought to show my thanks to her for her giving me work and hope for the future." The last came out with a tremble and his features hardened into a mask to hide the revealing emotion.

"Birthday? *Her birthday*. Of course!"

Without another word the beauty whirled away and, forgetting the dignity of her advanced years, Elizabeth raced toward the house.

"Now what do you think that was all about?" Martin asked the bit of wood in his hand. He got no answer, but relieved of the chit's presence, he settled back into the sun and returned to his delicate work. Soon he'd begin training in the management of a lady's stables. And someday, he'd been told, assuming he learned well, he'd have charge of Mrs. Wooten's horses. *Lady Jo's*, he reminded himself and wondered that she hadn't used her title while married which, as the daughter of an earl, was her right according to old Sam. Warmth filled him. Lady Jo trusted him. She intended giving him a position the likes of which he'd never hoped to have. And Martin, half believing her an angel sent from heaven just for his salvation, intended serving her to the very best of his ability.

Joanna looked up from her book reluctantly. It had been almost a fortnight since that last disastrous meeting with Pierce when her niece had shown just how unworthy she was of the name Ransome. How much longer, she wondered, could she keep up the cold disapproving front she'd adopted from the moment she'd realized the depth of Elizabeth's selfishness and lack of sensitivity to others? The girl must be made to understand she couldn't ride roughshod over anyone standing in the way of her wishes. Worst of all, whatever discipline was imposed on the chit was up to her. The short note she'd received in reply to her last two letters to her easygoing brother had been just what she'd expected: exactly no help at all.

"Well?"

"Please? Can't we be friends?"

"Really, Elizabeth, how can you even ask? You have shown yourself entirely untrustworthy, utterly selfish, and completely uncontrollable. You are scarcely the sort one would want for a friend."

Elizabeth felt something curl deep inside, a painful something she didn't recognize. She remembered the duke's analysis of her character when he'd scolded her. He, too, had seemed to dislike her. And the vicar . . . Was she really so bad? Was she so far beyond the pale that even her closest relative couldn't like her? The coldness sending creeping fingers throughout her body frightened her.

"Aunt Jo?" She juggled the box in her hands into a less awkward position.

Joanna didn't look up from the book in her lap. She didn't want her charge to see the pity in her eyes. "Yes?"

"I don't want to be . . . that way. I don't know what to do."

Joanna set aside the second volume of the new novel she'd been reading. For a moment she studied her niece. "How seriously do you mean that?"

"I don't know." The honest answer startled a blush into the beauty's cheeks and a chuckle from her aunt. The laugh was a hint that maybe she'd finally found the right approach and, dropping the box, Elizabeth slipped to her knees at Joanna's feet. "Am I truly so bad?"

"You are spoiled and thoughtless and selfish. I don't know if you are totally lost to good behavior or not."

"What do you mean by good behavior?"

"Thinking of others before yourself might be a first step."

Elizabeth frowned. "I don't understand."

Joanna sighed. No, the girl very likely didn't understand. She had never been required to think of anything but her own desires. "What did you feel that day while we were visiting Granny Black?" Her niece's frown deepened. "Be honest, if you can, Elizabeth."

The blush returned and the girl ducked her head. Her voice was muffled when she spoke. "Bored. Disgusted with . . . with her *smell*. She used to be so different."

"You liked her stories, didn't you? When you were younger and allowed to visit her?" Elizabeth nodded hesitantly and Joanna went on. "But now she is old. She's ill. And, yes, her illness causes an odor which is unpleasant. So she's useless to you since she is no longer able to entertain you?"

"But . . ." Elizabeth raised puzzled eyes. "You mean I should remember her the way she was, feel sorry for her now?"

Joanna sighed. "That's a start I suppose."

"There's more?"

"Don't you feel any affection for her at all?"

"Affection? For Granny Black?!" Elizabeth's eyes widened. "You mean you *like* her?"

"I love her."

"But she's just an old servant." Elizabeth's true bewilderment was obvious.

"She's an old woman, a human being. Someone who had a part in my youth and gave me affection. I'm not to return that love simply because she holds a different station in life?"

Intrigued by ideas which had never entered her head, Elizabeth settled back onto the rug. "Who else do you love?"

"Any number of people." Joanna named her old nanny, her governess, several other servants who had been at the Court since her childhood.

"But they are *servants*. One doesn't love one's servants." Elizabeth looked shocked, then uncertain. "Does one?"

"They are people with feelings, just as you are. Except they are kinder than you and understand loyalty and love. They are, actually, far more interesting than you are."

"What?!"

"My dear Elizabeth, they are all many years older than you. They have lived long and active lives. Of course they are more interesting than a chit who is not yet out of the schoolroom. A schoolroom, more-

60

over, of which you've taken no advantage, so far as I can tell, so that you've emerged from it ignorant and boring."

"I'm beautiful," said Elizabeth indignantly.

"So is a rose. Which fades after a few days."

Elizabeth's cheeks whitened. That *thing* in her chest tightened still more, painful and cold and frightening. "You mean that when I get old and I'm no longer beautiful I'll be nothing at all?" New thoughts, Elizabeth found, were very uncomfortable things.

"Nothing but a bitter old woman. Given the self-centered tendencies you show, there's a strong possibility you'll be a vicious old woman. Like Lady Keaton." Hope for the future of her charge beginning to emerge, Joanna kept her face from stretching into a grin at the horrified look on Elizabeth's face.

"But what can I *do*?"

"Try thinking of somebody other than yourself?"

Elizabeth looked around and reached for the box. "I have. Here." She thrust it into Jo's hands.

"What's this?"

Elizabeth's cheeks reddened a bit. "Well, it's your birthday . . ."

"So it is." Joanna felt a moment's surprise she hadn't remembered that fact herself.

"And I thought . . ."

"You thought?"

The red deepened and Elizabeth hung her head. "Well, at the time I hoped the gift would sweeten your temper and maybe you wouldn't think so badly of me. But now . . ." Bravely she met her aunt's eyes, "Well, I just want you to have it." Her gaze dropped to her fingers.

"Good girl."

Elizabeth's head bobbed up and her eyes widened. It was the first real approval she'd seen on her aunt's face since that horrid day she'd been thrown.

"I'm not saying that because you've given me a gift, Elizabeth."

"You're not?"

The girl's expression denoted such confusion Joanna had to control outright laughter. She forced herself to respond in a serious fashion.

"No, I'm not." She had to swallow a chuckle as Elizabeth blinked. "I'm approving the fact you were honest with me."

Elizabeth stared. "But when I was honest about Alicia Staunton's new bonnet, you were angry."

"Ah. The difficult line between the social lie and emotional truth. You are very young, Elizabeth, but you are not stupid. I'm sure, if you think about it, you'll understand the difference."

"You mean," Elizabeth said a few moments later, "one should be tactful when talking to one's friends?"

"Yes. Also honest with yourself. Did you really think the hat a fright or were you jealous?"

Elizabeth's laughter bubbled up. "Oh, the hat was definitely a fright. I'm sure you agree. I coveted the costume," she continued wistfully. "I've never owned anything half so modish."

Joanna swallowed another gurgle of laughter. Maybe encouraging Elizabeth to be honest was going to be a problem all in itself! "I see. So, jealous of the dress, you had to denigrate the hat."

"I don't know about denigrate," said Elizabeth naively, not knowing the meaning of the word, "but I probably wouldn't have been so cutting if I hadn't wished for the dress." Elizabeth smiled tentatively at her aunt. "Are you going to open your present?"

Joanna, deciding she'd accomplished more than she'd ever expected toward setting her charge's feet on the right path, opened the box. She lifted out an evening dress in the newest style, the color a smoky rose she'd never thought to wear. She held it next to the deep gray of her afternoon gown and suddenly the drab colors of mourning made her ill. Holding the new dress before her she walked toward the oval looking glass hanging beside the door and studied her reflection. It was perfect, just the sort of dress she'd been thinking of buying. She turned slightly.

"Where did you get this? How *could* you have gotten it?"

A flush darkened Elizabeth's complexion to an ugly puce. "You won't like it."

"I won't?"

"No." Elizabeth gulped, but bravely she confessed, "I sent a note to the duke and *all* my pin money and asked him please to order it for me. I was sure he'd know exactly how to go about it."

Joanna's look of disbelief, her stunned expression, told Elizabeth she'd been too honest. The girl looked down to where her satin-shod toe prodded the carpet.

"Tell me I didn't hear you say what I thought you said."

"I'm sorry."

"Sorry! Elizabeth, have you the least notion how much a gown such as this must cost?"

"I had *eight guineas*, Aunt Jo. Surely it couldn't have cost more than *that*."

Joanna just stared at her.

Weakly Elizabeth asked, "It would?"

"More likely ten times that, you little fool, or *more.*

63

You must return this at once to His Grace. At once. And tell him . . . oh, tell him you didn't have the nerve to give it to me after all and he can bestow it on his latest—no! No, for heaven's sake don't say that . . . Oh, I'm totally distracted!''

Elizabeth escaped the room while her aunt stalked from one end to the other. When, at last, Joanna looked around for her niece, the girl was gone. Only the dress, the lovely dress, remained in a heap where she'd dropped it. Joanna glared at it. Hot coals would be an infinitely more welcome burden than a dress Pierce had ordered for her.

How *dare* he? No man, no *gentleman,* she corrected herself, would give a woman not closely related to him something so personal. Not if he had the least respect for her. Pierce had used the opportunity dropped in his lap by her equally devious niece to show her exactly how he hoped to use her. Buying her a dress as if she were one of his doxies! All thought of her niece's conduct was lost in contemplation of Pierce's far more despicable behavior, the unforgivable insult. Joanna gritted her teeth, anger swelling to proportions that frightened her. *Why* she was so angry never crossed her mind.

Four

"Don't be a fool, Jo."

Pierce watched her stiffen in her saddle. He sighed, touched heels to the sides of his stallion, and closed the space between them. Catching her reins he pulled them both to a stop.

"I'd rather see your eyes than your profile, love."

"I will not be treated like one of your . . . your . . ."

"Lightskirts? *Cher amie?* A prime article?"

"Any or all."

Pierce laughed softly. "One result of following the drum, Jo, was to increase your vocabulary and *not* for the better."

"Fiddle." She hated the flush heating her cheeks but went on determinedly. "Most of the cant I know I picked up from you and Henry before I was out of the schoolroom."

"That blush becomes you." The blush deepened. "May I continue," he added after a moment of observing her, "or are we to brangle all day?"

"I am not a fool."

"You're a fool if you think I sent you that dress."

"But Elizabeth . . ."

65

"Sent me a note and a pitiful amount of money which I immediately forwarded to your brother along with the suggestion he try . . ." He held up his hand. "No, Jo, don't call me out for knowing the names of the best mantua-makers in Town—or in Brighton, for that matter. How can I help but know when such topics make up the greater part of a fashionable lady's conversation?"

"You wouldn't know the establishment personally, of course."

Pierce laughed, but there was something cool hidden beneath the coaxing drawl of his soft voice when he answered. "Why shouldn't I? I haven't a wife, Jo. My lady married someone else. Was I to wear the willow forever? Not my style."

"Damn you, Pierce!"

He ignored her interjection, going on as if she had not spoken. "You're home now. You'll be coming to London." The drawl warmed. "Do you think to ignore me? Will you turn a cold shoulder to my courtship?" His eyes teased her, invited her to laugh, and Joanna bit her lip. "I don't give up easily, you know. I'll follow at your heels like a lap dog. You'll need a heart of stone to turn me off forever."

Joanna struggled with her feelings, the desire to join his teasing fought with chagrin that she'd ever believed him capable of flaunting the social code to the point he'd have bought a dress for her. "I don't understand you."

"What don't you understand? That I loved you? That you married my rival? That I still love you?"

Love? Oh no, Pierce. "You don't know the meaning of the term."

"I know my love for you wouldn't be so selfish as

66

to ask you to endure all you endured with the Army!"

A bitter note was apparent in Pierce's tone and Joanna couldn't help sounding just a wee bit defensive. "We did very well, Pierce, and Reggie'd have had a promotion after Waterloo."

"And would have then dragged you off to the war across the Atlantic. Or perhaps to India next."

Jo stared rather blankly and Pierce watched a dreamy expression grow in her expressive eyes. Dreamy? Could she have *liked* the dangers and new experiences?

"Tell you what, Jo. Now there's no danger Boney will return, we'll take a long honeymoon on the Continent. Maybe go so far as Greece. Would you like that?"

The dreamy look in her eyes changed slowly; new dreams seemed to replace the old. Suddenly her vision cleared and she focused on him.

"Well?" he asked.

"Honeymoon? I'll tell you again, Pierce, and for the last time: I will not marry you."

"Joanna," he said in pretended wide-eyed horror. "Are you saying you'll go as my mistress?!"

Joanna suppressed a gurgle of laughter but just barely. "No, you fool. You know I wouldn't. I've planned my future and it has nothing to do with you." All animation faded from her features with the words.

Pierce didn't like this new expression half so well; her eyes lost the glow of excitement. It held too much resignation, too much quiet desperation. He loosened his hold on her reins and the two horses walked on side by side.

"Tell me your plans, Jo."

His low-voiced demand was so unobtrusive she barely noted it, only registering the fact someone would listen.

"I'll make my brother understand Elizabeth's much too hot to handle and must have her come-out. Surely it won't be difficult to get her settled. Despite her— her lack of character," she said with difficulty, embarrassed by her niece's recent behavior. "She is very lovely and she will have a more than adequate dowry. Yes, she should go off easily her first season. Then I'll be free."

"Free for what, Jo?"

"I'll find a small house in London. Somewhere not quite out of the way. And a companion. And . . ." Her voice trailed off as if she didn't quite know what would happen next.

"And find yourself *quite out of the way* of everything. No, Jo. It will not do. Much better to marry me."

"And," she went on firmly, her eyes flashing, "not have someone constantly telling me what will or will not do!"

She touched Lad's side and he obediently stretched his gait into a run. Pierce followed suit, and as they raced neck and neck, Jo's mood lightened. After jumping the stream and settling Lad's usual playful rebellion to stopping, she allowed Pierce to help her down. Her mood changed again as his hands lingered at her waist, her eyes caught by his.

"No, Pierce."

"Oh yes, my Lady Jo."

His fingers tightened and his head lowered, his features blurring as his mouth approached hers with an enticing slowness.

Oh God, the thoughts raced through her mind. A

68

year. More than a year since she'd been held and kissed and . . . But this was Pierce.

His mouth touched her temple.

Pierce who had kidnapped her and lied to her and seemed bent on continuing the farce. Pierce, the man who hated being bested and was now out to win . . . Win what? Not marriage. She didn't dare believe he meant marriage whatever his words.

Warm lips traced a line across her cheek, pausing near the spot where an occasional dimple lurked.

She didn't believe for an instant he really wanted to marry her. But he would want to prove to her she'd made a mistake marrying Reggie. So what *did* he want? To get her to admit she loved him and then, sneeringly, tell her to go to the devil? Or, more likely, beguile his way into an affair with the new widow?

Joanna jerked away just as his mouth brushed hers.

"No. No, no, no." She held his face away from hers. "I will not lower myself this way. Go away, Pierce."

"I'm a duke, Jo. Marrying me would not be lowering yourself."

She glared up at him, her fingers tugging uselessly to release herself. "You'd better watch out, Duke. One of these days I might take you seriously and then where would you be?"

"Take me seriously, Jo. Do," he coaxed. "I'll find myself just where I wanted to be five years ago. I love you."

"Oh, you *lie*. Why do you lie to me?"

Pierce's hands tightened at her waist. "Why won't you believe me? I tell you the secrets of my heart as I have never done to another woman and you accuse me of lying!"

"Maybe if you hadn't been involved with so many

69

really beautiful women I'd be more prone to believe you."

"Sarcasm? I'm a man, Jo. Of course there have been women. But only one I've wanted to marry."

"Oh yes. Of course only one. Nice, adoring, naive little Joanna Ransome who wouldn't for the life of her interfere in her husband's pleasures, who would blindly settle for home and hearth and maybe a little diversion once in a while in Town at the height of the season and—"

"Jo, you'd better stop. Right there. I'm becoming quite angry with you."

Indeed, she thought, he looked furious.

"You wouldn't have thought up that packet of drivel on your own. Who filled your head with such utter nonsense?" he demanded.

Jo stared into his eyes. Yes, he was angry. Very angry. And he sounded serious when he denied such intentions. Had Lady Cressida been spouting clankers? Had the older girl an ulterior motive (what a remarkable idea!) for "explaining" just what Pierce would want in a wife?

"Someone told you taradiddles. Someone drove you from me five years ago with lies and . . ." The darkening in his expression frightened her. "I want to know who it was, Jo."

She shook her head. As vicious as he looked, there was no knowing what he might do.

"It wasn't your brother. He wanted our marriage."

She blinked, relaxing a bit.

"And it wouldn't have been my mother. She, too, wanted it, hoping I'd settle down. Which I'd have done, blast you."

Joanna, freed from his hold, turned toward Lad, whistling softly.

"Don't think you're going to run from this, Jo. Either you tell me or I'll find out some other way. Someone will know."

"I think it's time I returned to the Court, Pierce. And time you calmed down. Nearly five years have passed, for heaven's sake."

"Five years you would have been mine if someone hadn't poisoned your mind against me. Poison which led to your marriage to that blasted officer."

She shrugged. "Believe what you will. I loved Reggie with all my heart."

"So *you* believed. Because you're that sort." His voice softened on the last words and Jo turned back. "Having made up your mind, you did it with courage and honor and loyalty. But you didn't love him, Jo. You were infatuated. *Me*, you loved."

There was just enough truth in his statement to tighten Joanna's throat. She had to get away from him. Now. Before he pried from her the name he wanted. Cressy Clayton was his best friend's sister. And poor Pierce would be torn between loyalty to Lord Halford and his desire for revenge. No, it was much better to forget the past. Forget the past and make sure the same thing didn't happen in the future.

But there was one thing she'd not forget. Their conversation convinced her Lady Cressida had lied and had deliberately turned her against Pierce. During her short season Joanna had found the older girl beautiful and sophisticated and with a sort of *knowing* that she, straight from the schoolroom, could not hope to possess.

Cressy Clayton had been Lady Cressy Merton then, Lord Halford's sister, and starting her fourth season. That, in itself, should have told Joanna something.

71

Cressy might have been considered by the highest sticklers to be on the shelf. As beautiful as she'd been, there must have been a reason for her spinster status and that reason might have been an obsession with Pierce, mightn't it?

On the other hand, within months of her own marriage to Reggie, Cressy had married the rich Mr. Clayton, a man old enough to be her grandfather. And she'd been widowed longer than Joanna. Not that Cressy had seen fit to go into deep mourning. She'd been back in the social whirl long before the first year was out, or so Joanna had heard. More recent gossip had it that Cressy was deeply in debt. So why didn't she take a second husband, one who could afford to keep her in the style she preferred? Perhaps Cressy still hoped to lure Pierce into parson's mousetrap?

Had Cressy had that in mind when she'd filled Joanna's idealistic soul with lies about what Pierce wanted in a wife? Frightening her with visions of being shunted aside and ignored once she'd supplied Pierce with an heir? Joanna's temper roiled at the thought and she almost gritted her teeth, wishing she could confront the hussy with her questions.

"Joanna, I'm waiting for an answer."

"Then you'll just have to wait, won't you?"

"I begin to remember a negative aspect of your generally admirable character."

Joanna looked over her shoulder questioningly.

"You are abominably stubborn, my girl."

Lights danced in her eyes and she turned, leaning against Lad's side, her arm raised and her hand on his mane. A gurgle of laughter fought for freedom and finally achieved it. "Oh, Pierce, do you remember that summer I insisted you teach me to swim? What was I? Eleven?"

"I refused." His mouth spread in a grin, his gaze softening with amusement.

"And I told you if you wouldn't teach me, I'd have to teach myself?"

"And I had to drag you out of the ornamental pond when you jumped off the middle of the bridge. I ruined a brand new pair of boots, you pernicious brat. Were you aware of that?" His laughter faded rapidly. "If you ever again scare me as you did that day, I'll tan your hide—as I should have done then."

"That is the most ungentlemanly thing you've ever said to me, Pierce."

"I'd've smacked you then—only you were half-drowned and already miserable. But you were still stubbornly determined you'd learn to swim."

"I achieved my end, didn't I? You agreed to teach me, didn't you? I did learn."

"And you say *I'm* selfish and only want my own way!"

"It's as well I did, Pierce."

Her sober expression brought an alert look to his eye. "The Peninsula? You might have drowned?"

"We were under forced march orders. A river had to be forded. One of the, er, women dropped her baby. If I'd been unable to swim, I might not have had the nerve to go after it."

"So you went after the little bastard. Weren't there any men there who could have rescued it?"

"That *little bastard* was a much-loved infant. Just because the woman was no better than she should be doesn't mean she was incapable of maternal feelings! And no, the men couldn't have helped. They had their hands full, once again doing the impossible just

73

as old Hooky always demanded—Oh, forget I mentioned it."

His hands settled on her stiff shoulders. "Heroines are all very well, my dear, when they aren't the woman I love. I don't like the idea you were in danger."

"I wasn't in any danger. The current wasn't *that* fast. If the stupid horse I was on that day hadn't had a ridiculous aversion to water, I'd have barely gotten wet. As it was, we caught up with the march quite easily."

"You mean they went on and *left* you?"

"It was an army, Pierce. They were under orders."

"My God, woman, it is a damn good thing that husband of yours is already dead. I swear I'd beat him to within an inch of his life and then draw and quarter him for—"

Her hand muffled his words and he glared at her. "I would appreciate it if you'd loosen your grip on my shoulders, Your Grace. I'd like to wear my brother's birthday present to dinner this evening without a fine set of bruises for additional adornment."

Pierce let her go as if he were burned. He hadn't been aware just how firmly he'd been gripping her. His fists opened and closed on air. Would she have bruises where he'd held her? "You'd drive a saint to perdition, Jo."

"Then isn't it a good thing I turned down your delightful proposal? I'd certainly dislike being responsible for sending your saintly character into a decline." His bark of sardonic laughter delighted Joanna, but she wasn't about to let him know it. "And now I really must return to the Court, Pierce."

He lifted her into the saddle and straightened her

74

skirts. "Where did you get this dowdy old habit, Jo? When I have the dressing of you, you'll never wear anything but the best available."

"Pierce, you will desist from making statements which make me sound like your latest ladybird!"

"I will?"

She glared at his patently faked innocence. "You'd better."

"You take snuff so beautifully, my love, I can't resist teasing you. As you well know, I merely meant that when we're wed I will delight in spending a fortune making you the best-dressed woman in London. I'll take you to Paris twice a year and . . ." Joanna glowered and he chuckled. "Even that . . . that *thing* you're wearing doesn't detract from your loveliness. Think what you'd do for the latest Parisian fashions and most exquisite fabrics."

"I am not poverty-stricken, Pierce. I have a quite adequate fortune and will, once I'm out of mourning, supply my own wardrobe."

"Ah. I might have known your brother wouldn't take my advice. He sent a drab gray or did he become adventuresome and provide you with something in muddy violet?"

"You will never know, will you?"

Surprise made his voice sharp. "Of course I will."

"I must go." She lifted her reins and trotted toward the stream.

"I look forward to seeing Henry's choice this evening."

She pulled Lad around abruptly. "What do you mean? Where will you see me?"

Pierce strolled toward her. "You did say you'd be wearing the new gown this evening, didn't you? I'll see it then, of course."

He frowned as she continued to look perplexed. At her questioning expression Pierce's eyes narrowed.

"Jo, you've invited us to dinner, haven't you?"

"*Invited* you? You and Lord Halford?" He nodded. Jo goggled. "*This evening?* Invite a pair of bachelors for dinner when Elizabeth and I have no host! Where did you get such a skitterwitted notion?"

"Jo, you *must* know . . ."

A horrendous suspicion touched her mind, formed, grew. "Elizabeth!" she said with horror. "Surely she knows better . . ."

"You *weren't* aware."

Her expression confirmed his statement.

"It isn't so bad as you just suggested, Jo. Not just the two of us, I mean. I, personally, know three families who will arrive on your doorstep just before eight this evening." He chuckled. "There has been some grumbling that you don't keep country hours, my dear."

"Do you suppose," asked Joanna with wry humor, "my charming niece thought to inform our housekeeper she's invited half the county to dinner?"

He laughed. "Surely she wouldn't do something so chuckleheaded—but," he added after a thoughtful pause, "perhaps you'd better go home and make sure of that point."

"It was supposed to be a surprise," wailed Elizabeth.

"It would certainly be a nice surprise if we'd found it necessary to stretch a meal for two to feed . . . Just how many have you invited to this dinner party, Elizabeth?"

Her voice dropping away to almost nothing, Elizabeth told her.

Cook had hysterics and had to be calmed. Their old butler, Dawson, went into a quiet panic at the state of the silver and commandeered a couple of gardener lads to help polish it. Elizabeth, understanding the importance of her error, offered to do extra bouquets and proceeded to throw the head gardener into a temper by picking all the blooms in his favorite display. Jo's maid followed her from place to place demanding her charge come have her hair washed and that she rest before she took her first step back into society in over a year. By seven o'clock that evening Jo was not only exhausted, she was ready to murder her whole household starting with Elizabeth.

Nevertheless, by a quarter to eight, order had returned to the Court and Jo took a moment to check her niece. For once the girl had used good sense. She had not cajoled her maid into lowering the neckline of her gown. She had not chosen family jewels far too old for her but was wearing a pretty string of beads and only one bangle on her wrist. She had not experimented with her hair but allowed it to be dressed in a simple style suitable to her age and status. Nor did she balk when informed she'd have to play her latest piece on the small piano in the salon for the entertainment of their guests later that evening.

Joanna nodded approval and heard Elizabeth's relieved sigh. It occurred to Jo that her niece had been treating her with a wary reserve quite unlike the girl's normal insouciance. Had Joanna become so unpredictable as all that? Yes, perhaps she had. It wasn't just Elizabeth who worried about bringing another peal down over a somewhat less-than-innocent head. Others had begun to treat her with that extra care that indicated they didn't quite know what to expect of her.

Poor Elizabeth. If she wanted someone to blame for her aunt's erratic behavior, she could blame Pierce. Joanna sacrificed him to Elizabeth's temper without a qualm. It was, after all, his fault!

Guests began arriving and Joanna felt a sense of approval as she watched Elizabeth make painfully polite conversation with the vicar. Joanna spoke with Susan Templeton, his middle-aged niece and housekeeper, before moving on to welcome Mrs. Storling and her daughter Matilda. Others followed rapidly.

The Duke of Stornway and Lord Halford arrived when the salon was nearly full. Pierce made his way to their hostess's side. "I see your fears were unfounded, Jo," drawled Elizabeth's bête noire as they waited for the last of the guests.

Jo's eyes met his in a speaking look. "That, Your Grace, just shows what an unknowing one you really are. You should have been here an hour ago!" Joanna felt pride in her brother's people that they had managed so well.

He looked around the drawing room, noted the bouquets, the sparkling chandelier, the polished furniture. "Got all this out of holland covers in the nick of time, did you?"

"Pierce!" She pretended outrage at his teasing. "You can't think we live under covers? Henry's heart would fail him. You know such an idea would be appalling to anyone with his notions of consequence."

Pierce smiled that special smile that started in his eyes and ended with the crooked curve of his lips which, years ago, raised a flutter in her breast. She wasn't pleased to discover it still did and frowned slightly.

"Take a damper, Jo. I'm teasing you. That gown, by the way, is a distinct improvement over that ghastly habit."

"I should think it would be. I've bought nothing new since I purchased mourning. And that didn't include a habit."

Pierce stepped back and raised his quizzing glass, studying her closely. "The rose is an excellent color for you. We'll remember that when ordering your trousseau." He grinned. "Don't think to stop me with that missish look, my dear. Not only will it not work, but such a prudish expression is out of character and not to be believed."

Dinner was announced and Pierce offered Joanna his arm as was correct. He was, after all, the premier peer in attendance and Joanna was hostess.

Across the room Elizabeth accepted the awkward escort of a neighbor's smitten younger son. She scowled at the glowing way Joanna looked up at the rake, glowered at the way her aunt laughed at something he said. It was quite obvious that Aunt Joanna was succumbing to moon-madness. Something would have to be done to save Joanna from terrible embarrassment at the least, or, at worst, a broken heart and scandal—assuming the Dreadful Duke really was pursuing her aunt. Elizabeth, like her aunt, assumed the worst of Pierce Reston.

Just as Pierce and Joanna left the drawing room, the front door was opened by the harassed butler who had veered from his way to the dining room at the sound of the knocker. Two more guests entered the hall.

"My Lord," stuttered Dawson. "Were we expecting you?"

"I should hope," said Henry Ransome, Lord Midbourgh, in a casually pompous tone, "you'd always be expecting me. Well, don't just stand there, man. Let us by." He shoved his hat and cane at a hovering footman and helped his guest from her traveling cape.

"Father!" Elizabeth dropped her escort's arm and ran toward the newcomers.

"There, there. Mustn't muss m' cravat, kitten."

Elizabeth stepped back and noticed the lady standing just beyond her father. Why was the lady glaring at her?

"Cressy, you haven't met me daughter, have you?"

"You talked about her as if she were still in leading strings, Henry. If you didn't acknowledge the chit as your daughter, I'd be certain you were hiding one of your—"

Lord Halford's soft but determined voice cut her short. "That's quite enough, Cressy."

"You!" Cressida's well-shaped brows rose in an arc. "Well, brother dear, I'd never have thought to find you at a country do such as this appears to be. It is a party, is it not?"

"Aunt Joanna's birthday dinner." Elizabeth quailed at the look the *tonnishly* dressed lady pitched her way.

Cressy turned slowly to face Joanna. Rage and hate filled her. Her eyes sent daggers toward Joanna Ransome Wooten who had sent Pierce to the right about and practically into a decline—which was *not* the result Cressy had expected five years earlier when she'd fed the chit a careful set of lies. "Ah yes.

80

Joanna . . . Wormton?" she said, deliberately getting Joanna's married name wrong.

"Cressy . . . Clayman? Is it really you?"

Joanna heard Pierce's muffled laugh and spots of red appeared in her cheeks. How could she have allowed herself to come to pulling caps with the malicious woman? She turned to the butler standing rigid at his post.

"The company will return to the drawing room, Dawson. Do what you must and inform us as soon as you are again ready to serve." She turned to find her brother's housekeeper standing respectfully nearby. "Mrs. Landy, please show Lady Cressida to a room where she may freshen up." Finally she turned to her brother. "Henry?"

"I'm fine. Just fine. Didn't expect to find a crowd, my dear. But happy you decided to celebrate your birthday. Brought you a little something . . ."

He'd shed his many-caped coat and handed it and his gloves to another footman. Now he dug into his watch pocket and handed Joanna a tissue-wrapped packet. "Nothin' much, my dear, but when Elizabeth reminded me it was your birthday, just thought it might be nice to toddle over from Brighton and wish you happy. When Cressy heard I was coming, she begged to come along." His voice dropped to a confiding tone. "Not sure if she wanted a repairing lease away from her creditors or if she knew Pierce was in residence at White Stones. Ah, well. We've room to put her up, now, haven't we?"

"How, hmmm, *thoughtful* of you to bring her, Henry." *Thoughtful, my foot. You were too lazy to find a tactful way of saying no, you complacent idiot!* Joanna kissed his proffered cheek, told her brother she'd open his present later, and pushed the packet into her reticule, all the while controlling an urge to hit him with the Sèvres vase sitting on a nearby table. "Do go into the drawing room now so Dawson may take care of the table."

Joanna wondered just how long she'd be required to play hostess to the woman who had schemed and lied and ruined her relationship with Pierce. Oh, it was too much! Joanna wished she could turn into smoke and waft away up the nearest chimney. After spending hours that day soothing her household, she did not feel up to dealing with her brother. Or the problem of adding two additional places to her perfectly arranged table. Even less did she feel like fending off Cressy's barbs, and from the looks of the scowl she'd worn as she climbed the stairs behind Mrs. Landy, the barbs would fly thick and fast.

"Should I deal with her tonight, Jo?"

Jo dropped her hand from her forehead. "Oh. Pierce. I didn't see you there. I thought I was alone. Do go on into the drawing room . . ."

Her eyes raised to meet his when, his fingers gently touching her cheek, he interrupted her. "Don't put on society manners with me, my love. I can easily turn Cressy up sweet if you want me to."

"Flirt with her, you mean?"

" 'Twill be an onerous duty, love, but if it will lighten your burden, I'll force myself."

"When you have to force yourself to flirt with the greatest beauty in a room," said Joanna tartly, "you'll have one foot in the grave. No. I take that back. You'll be flirting with someone on your deathbed. You'd have to be buried with no pretty ladies in sight."

Pierce smiled. "That's better. I feared you'd lost your fighting spirit." He put a hand on her waist and led her toward the drawing room but stopped just short of the doors. "I do not, by the way, consider Cressy Clayton the most beautiful woman here tonight. You hold that honor."

"Another clanker! If not Cressy, then Elizabeth is the loveliest. Pierce, will you see she doesn't cause a scene?"

"If you wish. But only for your sake."

"I do wish. I simply can't handle another crisis today. You wouldn't believe what has gone on here since I saw you earlier."

"Elizabeth thought she'd done all that was necessary simply sending out the invitations?" asked Pierce. Joanna nodded her tired head. "In this case," he soothed, "I suspect it was simple lack of forethought on her part. But satisfy my curiosity: why did she send them?"

"Although it might have been to force my hand concerning our social life, I believe she truly did it to please me. I agree the muddle she caused was through thoughtlessness but she's learned a lesson from it." An impish smile lit Joanna's face. "I made her follow me around as I soothed first one servant and then another and made her apologize to the head gardener for ruining his best display for the bouquets tonight."

"I'm surprised she isn't laid upon her bed," was Pierce's mocking comment.

Joanna threw him a speaking look that said that was exactly where *she* wished she could be, and Pierce, thwarting the footman, opened the drawing-room door for her.

"Back into the fray, my dear. Death before defeat and all that tosh and bother."

She smiled at his nonsense as he'd desired her to do.

Robert touched his shoulder. "We've got to do something about Cressy."

Pierce turned to his friend. "Robert, you've hit the nail on the head in your usual brilliant fashion. I've promised Lady Jo I'll turn her up sweet." He smiled at Jo but turned back to Robert when his friend said it wouldn't do. "Why not?"

"Pierce, you've spent years convincing Cressy she hasn't a chance with you. Flirting with her will have her hoping again and then what?"

"Any better suggestion?" he asked, wondering why Joanna stiffened slightly at Robert's words.

"Yes."

Robert, adopting a stern look, let himself out into the hall. Pierce put his shoulder against the door and prevented it from completely closing. Joanna was pleased by his maneuver. She was curious as to how Lord Halford planned to handle the vicious woman.

Joanna stepped closer, and she and Pierce pretended to be deep in their own conversation while eavesdropping on the one going on in the hall. Joanna didn't feel a twinge of guilt at their despicable behavior and wondered at herself.

"Cressy," came Rob's voice through the crack, "a word with you."

"There isn't time. Dinner's about to be served."

"One word."

"Oh, all right. But make it fast, Robert."

The tapping of a feminine toe against the polished wood of the hall floor was quite clear to the listeners.

"I don't think you're attending, Cressy." The toe was silenced. "Bills, Cressy. That great wad of bills you recently sent my secretary."

"What about them?" There was a shrill note in Cressy's usually well-modulated voice.

84

"Do you want them paid?"

"What a stupid question. Of course I want them paid." The tapping toe could again be heard but the tempo now had an agitated note. "Why else would I have sent them?"

"Then, my dear, you'll behave yourself."

There was a long silence, then a deeply indrawn breath. "I haven't a notion what you mean, Brother dear."

"You do know. Your rudeness to Lady Joanna was inexcusable and I won't have it. You've thrown yourself at Pierce for years. I'd think by now you'd have realized he loathes you, but no, you notice how he looks at Lady Joanna and you can't bear it. Then, too, you've discovered another beauty is to challenge your place in the *ton*. Lord Midbourgh's daughter's looks beat yours to flinders, and the knowledge is making you sick, isn't it? Cressy, I know the evil of which you're capable when your jealousy's aroused and I warn you, you will *not* spoil this evening or I'll return those bills to you without a second thought."

"You wouldn't want to see your sister in debtor's prison."

"Wouldn't I?" Robert's voice took on a thoughtful note. "I wonder. Our father spoiled you rotten, Cressy. I've very nearly given up on you. I think the *ton* would actually give me a medal if I allowed you to reap the consequences of your actions."

"How dare you!"

"How dare you think you can go your length again and again and never pay the piper?"

"Robert . . ."

"I am not asking you to behave, Cressy. I am telling you. Not one groat will you see from me ever again

85

if you do one thing to cause any of Henry's family pain."

Pierce quietly closed the door and watched Joanna mingle with her guests. She'd moved away abruptly when Robert mentioned Cressy's jealousy. Was it *Cressy* who had lied to her? He sauntered across the drawing room to where Henry was talking to Lord Bradford, certain in his own mind that Cressy's fangs were pulled . . . at least until her bills were paid.

Five

Joanna lay against her frilly pillows and stared into the cloud-dotted sky visible through the windows Belton had uncovered minutes earlier. She sipped overly sweet chocolate, grimaced, and set her cup aside. Why could she never remember to tell Mrs. Landy she preferred coffee in the morning?

Her maid bustled in from the dressing room, two morning gowns in her hands. "Which will it be, Lady Jo?"

Joanna wrinkled her nose. Neither was her wish. Last night, for the first time since Reggie's death, she'd worn a flattering color. The drab gray on the left made her as ill as the rusty black on the right.

"Have I nothing else, Belton?"

"Thought that would be the way of it," said the woman complacently. "Thought once you saw yourself in that new gown you'd not want to creep back into raven dark again."

There was satisfaction in Belton's tone. The servants had high hopes that this time the duke would manage to make their mistress his wife. If Joanna had been aware of their views, she'd have ordered them to perdition.

"You've something up your sleeve, Belton."

"Well, just a thought, Lady Jo."

"Do tell," she coaxed, absently sipping the chocolate. "Don't keep me in suspense."

"Thought to have a look in your old trunk."

Belton was obviously trying to be nonchalant, thought Joanna, but wasn't quite achieving it. She put on an expectant look.

"Didn't have anything much to do last night once I had you looking respectable and off downstairs to your pleasures, you know."

Joanna smiled. "So you went to the attics and dug out my trunk."

"Yes, Lady Jo. I did."

"And what did you find in that trunk, my dear Belton?" Joanna dropped the teasing tone and sighed. "What *could* you find that wasn't so out of the way I might still wear it?"

"Well, nothing quite in current style, to be sure. But Mrs. Landy and I, we took a peek at what the ladies were awearin' and . . ."

"And?"

Splotches of color lit the maid's cheeks. "Well, we thought . . ." Again she paused.

"I'm not much interested in what you *thought*, Belton. What did you do?" At the mischievous tone Belton relaxed. "Belton?"

"'Tisn't much," she mumbled and disappeared into the dressing room.

When she returned, Joanna felt tears pushing at the back of her eyes. "Oh, Belton. You must have worked all night!"

"Do you think it will do, Lady Jo?"

88

"Do? It's perfect." Joanna slid out of the high bed and crossed to where her maid displayed a gown in her favorite deep blue and sprigged with tiny pink flowers. She took the sides in her hands and lifted it, spreading it so she could appreciate the details of a high waist trimmed with a narrow lace and a modest but not prudishly high neckline, again trimmed with lace. The sleeves, elbow length and with a further touch of the lace, were much in fashion, too. "You've done wonders. I remember this. Long, tight sleeves and it had wide blond lace at the shoulders, didn't it? But I'm sure it's fuller now."

"Yes. The neckline was quite out. And the sleeves weren't right." Belton blushed. "As to the skirt, there was a spencer lined in the same material which we unpicked and well . . ." She finished the sentence with a shrug.

"However you did it, dear Belton, it's right up to the mark." She smiled a watery smile and flung her arms around Belton, dress and all.

"Here now, m'lady, give over, do," her maid scolded fondly. "You'll crush it and I'll have to press it again."

Joanna released her and twirled across the room. Suddenly she felt young again. She'd gone into mourning for Reggie. She'd done her duty. Perhaps, to compensate for the resentment she'd felt at his death, *overdone* it. The new and very flattering rose gown, last night's simple dinner party for only forty-four people—even such mild dissipation had shown her how bored she'd become.

It was time to live again. A vision of Pierce's face as it had neared hers, the heat of his palms through her habit as he'd bent to kiss her, the anticipation she'd tried to deny all returned to haunt her. Sensations she thought she'd never feel again swept in an uncontrollable storm right through her body. Live? Love? *Pierce?*

Joanna stood before the washstand and scrubbed her face, taking the towel Belton handed her without noticing what she was doing. She must remember Pierce's nature. Must remember to what lengths she'd known him to go, getting even for some infinitesimal slight he'd endured. Now he wanted revenge for the slight her refusal to marry him had been. That *must* be what he wanted. Not that he'd be averse to indulging in any dalliance she'd allow along the way . . .

The gown slipped over her head and Joanna stood quietly as Belton hooked it up. Pierce would tease and taunt and flirt and have her right back to where she'd been before she'd met Reggie: ready to throw herself at his feet and let him walk all over her! But she was older now. More mature. And she wouldn't allow that to happen. Not that she'd have let him walk on her even then. She'd had far too much spunk to put up with just anything. But now she'd tease him back. And she'd give him taunt for taunt. And if he flirted? Oh yes. She'd flirt with him. . . . Kiss him? a tiny voice in her mind asked. Oh yes . . . Joanna fidgeted. *No.* No, she wouldn't. Of course she wouldn't. She mustn't. It wouldn't be the least bit proper to kiss him.

"Hold still, Lady Jo," fussed her maid as she shivered. "I'll never get this hooked if you won't hold still."

Obligingly Joanna held still. For all of ten seconds. Then she remembered her brother had arrived the preceding evening. Worse, he'd had Cressy in tow. Worse yet, they were staying, he'd said, for the Bradford hunt and ball before returning to Brighton. Oh, it was too much!

"Botheration."

"Don't you like it?" Belton sounded hurt.

Joanna looked in the pier glass and noted her reflection. "The gown is absolutely beautiful, Belton. I don't know how to thank you."

"Then what . . . ?"

Joanna frowned at the question, then remembered and blushed. "I was thinking of something else."

Belton nodded wisely. "That witch who arrived with your brother, I'll be thinking."

"How did you guess?"

"Me and Mrs. Landy, we had a little talk last night while we worked on this. Mrs. Landy, she says if Lord Midbourgh marries that woman, she for one will look for another position. And she didn't think she'd be the only one."

"My brother would go into apoplexy if Mrs. Landy left."

"Yessum. But she won't work under a mistress like that one would be. You should see Mrs. Clayton's maid. Poor little rabbit jumps at her own shadow. Mrs. Landy says one can always judge a mistress by her maid." Belton nodded in agreement.

"Ah. And how does she judge me, Belton?"

"Away with you and your teasing, Lady Jo. You know you're a right one and that's a fact."

"Such flattery will go to my head. Belton, I don't think you need worry about Lord Midbourgh remarrying. I've heard no rumors he's setting up to become a Benedick. Nor do I think he'd get leg-shackled with someone like Mrs. Clayton if he were in a mind to wed again."

Belton nodded, smiling at the information. "I'll see

the others hear that, Lady Jo. Now will you sit still? Just for a few minutes?"

This time she managed to do so but was relieved when Belton laid down the brush and set the last pin.

"Are you finished?" Joanna looked in her dressing-table mirror and decided she liked the softer arrangement Belton had given her hair that morning.

Along with the drab colors, it was time to give up the skinned-back look she'd adopted at Reggie's death.

"That will do nicely, I think," she said as Belton placed a lacy cap over her creation. "Thank you, Belton."

"You'll be wanting to do some shopping now, I'm thinkin'."

Joanna laughed. "You can't put one over on me, Belton. You're tired of the country yourself and hope to get into town. Well, suddenly I find I wish that, too. Perhaps I'll ask my brother to take us back to Brighton with him when he returns. There must be one or two decent modistes in Prinny's favorite summer resort."

"How long does His Lordship think to be home?"

"He mentioned the Hunt Ball, Belton."

"He had no business bringing that nasty woman with him. Not with his daughter and you here, too."

Even for Joanna's usually easy ways, the implication behind her maid's comment was a bit free. "Belton, I understand you, of course, but Lady Cressida is not Lord Midbourgh's mistress. She came because she wished to see her brother," Joanna said in sternly repressive tones, although she knew it was more likely Pierce after whom Cressy was chasing, "Since she can't stay in a bachelor establishment such as that at

92

White Stones, Henry invited her here where I'm available to play propriety."

Undaunted by Joanna's reprimand, Belton sniffed. "Pity you'll have to put up with Her Majesty."

"Belton, I'm relying on you, on all of you, to help me keep the peace."

"I'll pass on that word, too, Lady Jo. We're aware of who will have to patch things up if they go wrong."

On that dark thought Joanna took herself off to the breakfast room where she found her brother refilling his plate from the heavily laden sideboard. "Find everything you need, Henry?"

"I'd think you'd lost your touch, m'dear, if I didn't. Cook's done us very well. Try some of the deviled kidney. Cook has just the right touch with it. Can't get the same anywhere else."

"I'll ask her for her recipe and send it to your cook in Brighton."

"Already tried that but 'tweren't the same. Think it must be that one can't get decent kidneys in town." He added another spoonful to the pile on his plate. "Wonder why I stay there."

Joanna laughed. "Because of all the things one *can* find in town I suspect."

Her brother agreed amiably and reseated himself. "Much surprised to get that note from Pierce, Jo."

Joanna stiffened at the reference. "It was my fault, I'm sure. I should have known Elizabeth well enough to have stopped her, but I had nary a hint she'd do something so outrageous as to write him and ask him to do such a thing."

"Oh. The dress. No, 'twasn't that. Glad to help. It was what he said about Elizabeth." Henry cogitated as he chewed. "Think he has an interest there?"

Joanna choked on a mouthful of toast. When she stopped coughing, she looked to see if her brother were serious. He was.

"Just what did Pierce say in this note of his?"

"Something about her being a rare handful and I should see to my responsibilities. Might it be he wants me around so he could ask me for her hand?"

"You've windmills in your head."

"Ah. You've an interest there yourself, have you?" Henry frowned. "But if that's the case, why'd you whistle him down the wind the first time?" He studied his blushing sister. "Well, you're more up to his weight than my little Elizabeth. Think I'd prefer to see her wed to someone more her own age. Not that he'd not be a good match, mind." He poked at a kipper, speared it. "Pretty little thing, Elizabeth. Surprised."

"She's a diamond but Pierce isn't interested in her."

"Turning *you* up sweet, my dear?"

"No, he isn't. Oh, I admit he's trying. But I'm convinced he's merely out for a little sport at my expense. As you said, I turned him down once. His pride was hurt. Now he thinks to wind me around his finger and leave *me* at a stand. You know Pierce, Henry."

Henry mulled that over in his slow way, shook his head. "Won't wash, Jo. Wasn't seen in London till after you went off with that nobody of yours. And when he did show his face, it was black as thunder forever and a day. Seemed to be doing his best to ride with the devil, too. Bets were, he'd lose his fortune before the year was out." Henry chuckled around a bite of roll. "Only problem was, he seemed to win more than he lost."

"Pierce was gambling to excess?"

Henry nodded. "The man had the most unnerving luck. But didn't care a whit if he lost or won. Seemed all the same to him."

"I didn't hear anything about that."

"Don't suppose you got much gossip where you were, m'dear." He looked at his plate and sighed as he scooped up the last of his kidneys. "These really are very good, Jo. You should have some."

Jo shuddered and assured him toast and coffee were quite sufficient.

"In any case, Pierce came to his senses before any real damage was done." Henry glanced at the door. "Well, Cressy. Don't just stand there. Come in. Come on in." He raised his voice. "Dawson?" The butler appeared as if by magic. "Serve Lady Cressida whatever she wants. Kidneys are very good, Cressy."

Cressy shuddered quite as dramatically as Joanna had done. It almost made Joanna wish she'd taken the kidneys. Even in so slight a manner she hated agreeing with the sly Cressy.

"Did I hear you telling Lady Joanna something about Pierce?" asked their guest.

"Old history, Cressy. Old, old history."

Old history, thought Joanna, which finally explained why Cressy had married an old goat like Clayton. Pierce must have made it bluntly clear he wasn't in the market for a wife.

"I thought my dear brother had gone north to his estates," said Cressy, turning her malicious gaze on Joanna. "How long has he been at White Stones?"

Joanna hoped Dawson wouldn't discuss this conversation in the servant's hall. Her story for Belton, that Cressy wished to consult her brother, would be proven the lie Belton assumed it to be. "I really

95

couldn't say, Cressy. I ran into Pierce a couple of weeks ago. Then Elizabeth and I met both him and Lord Halford the next day. *That* was a disaster."

"Yes. You wrote me about it." Henry chuckled. "Silly puss."

"Joanna wrote you about meeting up with my brother and His Grace? Why?"

"Seems my little daughter made a fool of herself. Wasn't hurt too badly was she?"

"A few aches and pains she richly deserved. That's all."

"Her mare ran away with her," explained Henry to the bewildered Cressy. "Threw her," he went on when their guest continued to look confused.

"But why should you write Henry about *that*?"

Joanna kicked Henry under the table to prevent him telling Cressy just how much a fool Elizabeth had been and said, "Henry is her father, Cressy. I have the responsibility of informing him of her health and condition. Of course I wrote him about the accident."

"Quite right. Quite right," muttered her brother, sensible at last of the impropriety of revealing too much. He might not be the greatest wit in the world but he wasn't blind to Cressy's all-too-noticeable faults. "Well, since I'm here I suppose I'd better see my agent. No problems, are there?" he asked, his expression both wary and hopeful.

"None of which I'm aware," said his sister repressively.

"Cut line, Jo. Of course you'd know. He'd have come to you first, m'dear, knowing you'd sort things out if you could." He beamed at the two women and strolled out of the breakfast room.

"Well!"

"I assume all is well."

"I refer to the fact Henry thinks *you* could manage his estates."

Since for more than a year Joanna had been doing essentially that for her lazy brother, she was forced to grit her teeth to repress the hot words burning her tongue. "I'm sure you know best, Cressy."

Cressy, unsure if she'd been complimented or insulted, decided to try another tack. "Have you been ill, Joanna?" she asked overly sweetly.

"Why no." Joanna's eyebrows rose and her eyes widened. "Why do you ask?"

"Your complexion, my dear. Such, hmm, high color surely could only be the result of an illness—perhaps something you picked up abroad?"

Joanna's temper was on the verge of boiling over until Cressy's words cooled it, touching off a wave of laughter instead—much to the lady's obvious chagrin.

"Yes, Cressy, definitely something I picked up abroad. It's called sunburn. There is nothing to be done and I've learned to live with this odd golden color." *You're her hostess, Joanna reminded herself. So act like one.* "Now, do tell me, what would you like to do today?"

"You mean there *is* something to do in the country?"

Joanna drew in a deep shaky breath before responding. "True, things are very quiet, Cressy, but I seem to remember you ride?" She also recalled just how cowhandedly Cressy rode and made a mental note to send orders to the stables as to the sort of mount she should be provided. "There are some lovely walks . . . Or you might like to recoup your looks by resting?" *Oh, bother,* thought Joanna. *I didn't mean to be catty. Really I didn't.*

It was Cressy's turn to grit her teeth. "I think I'll ride. A groom will show me the way to White Stones?"

"An excellent notion." Let Pierce and her brother deal with her. "I'll send a message to the stables at once. Now if you'll excuse me, I'll have a few words with Mrs. Landy." Cressy blinked. "Our housekeeper. She's been at the Court since she went into service and is a wonderful woman. My brother has often said the Court would fall to ruin without her."

Having given Cressy a clue as to Mrs. Landy's place in the scheme of things—just in case she was wrong and her stupid brother actually ended up marrying the jade—Joanna smiled thinly and left the room. She felt almost complacent for having brushed through breakfast with nary a squabble. Or scarcely a squabble, she rephrased her last thought. Joanna was, after all, incurably honest. At least with herself. At least most of the time.

Cressy scowled after her hostess, venting her spleen on Dawson because she'd lost her favorite quarry to the duties of her day. But Cressy's attempt to put the poor man to the blush was unsuccessful since he took her outrageous demands and criticisms in stride. His calm manner merely exacerbated her always uncertain temper.

Of course, if Dawson *had* shown his irritation or allowed himself a step out of place, she'd have been equally irritable. Not completely without self-awareness, Cressy smiled at the thought.

She pushed such frivolities aside. Recently it had been brought to her attention that she'd better remarry before her reputation was completely lost. There'd been that strong hint from Princess Esterhazy that she'd find herself without vouchers to Almack's if she didn't reform her ways, and anything was better than that. Besides, there were her debts and Rob was more and more snippy about paying them. So she'd make one more play for Pierce before, again, finding a rich old man to save her groats.

Cressy was still stinging at Joanna's cattish hint that her looks were off when Elizabeth entered. Elizabeth, with all the glow of youth as well as a perfect heart-shaped face echoed by her heart-shaped mouth and topped by a magnificent head of dusky dark hair. Cressy, at twenty-eight, knew and hated the fact that her beauty was fading. Here was a naive tool for revenge and Cressy wasted no time charming the tiresomely beautiful daughter of the house. She put herself out to describe all the delights of a first season while subtly putting the fear of social ostracism into the chit if she so much as looked to be the least bit fast or interesting.

Which *should*, thought a happy Cressy, leaving the cowed schoolgirl to her thoughts, keep the young lady in line. Elizabeth would be too petrified to reveal the least sign of the delightfully teasing personality with which she'd gathered the young bloods around her the night before.

Cressy's good mood wouldn't have lasted five minutes if she'd been aware of just how up to snuff Henry's daughter was. The girl had taken the lady's measure with the first hint that Elizabeth's beauty wasn't all she thought it, that having a more than adequate dowry wouldn't compensate for the least show of gauche or fast behavior, and finally, that only the most boring and proper behavior could save such a nonpareil as she knew herself to be from returning in ignominy to her family estates without one offer to her name. Elizabeth had had too many young men whispering in her ear to be so easily convinced.

Elizabeth was thoughtful, not cowed, when Lady Cressida Clayton left the breakfast room. She'd discovered in her immature breast a great dislike for Cressy Clayton and *not* because the creature had denigrated her looks. Elizabeth wasn't lacking in intelligence despite the fact that, so far, she'd made little practical use of it. And she had more than her share of imagination. She looked back on her own behavior of the past few months and cringed. Was she to become just such a malicious creature as Lady Cressida, never happy unless she made someone else unhappy?

Joanna would have been very glad to know her niece had not forgotten her little lecture about the fate of spoiled and petted beauties who persisted in their self-centered and thoughtless ways. Here, thought Elizabeth, in one of her few attempts at self-analysis, was just such an Awful Example as Aunt Jo had had in mind. And it wasn't, thought Elizabeth, a very pretty picture. She determined to mend her ways.

Elizabeth had a magnificent plan in her head. Lady Cressida was just the sort of female a well-known rake like the Duke of Stornway should favor. She would be a perfect foil to lead His Grace's attention away from Elizabeth's beloved aunt. Once he developed an interest in Cressy, he would be thoroughly occupied and wouldn't be breaking Aunt Joanna's heart. Or worse.

Curious, Elizabeth spent a few moments in contemplation of what that "worse" might involve. That it had to do with seduction, an activity in which rakes indulged, was common knowledge. But beyond that she was lacking in detailed information. Her governess had hinted it was quite awful and to be avoided at all costs if one were to retain a shred of reputation. Therefore, Elizabeth concluded, to save her aunt, it was obviously her duty to see that the Disreputable Duke had every opportunity to make up to the Awful Example.

"And what, then, am I to ride?" Cressy asked Sam after being denied Elizabeth's gray and then Lad—an animal she'd picked at random. "The cart-horse?"

Sam, primed by Lady Joanna's orders, wasn't the least intimidated by the crop the lady wielded in front of his nose. "There's nary a slug in His Lordship's stables, milady. How about that bay?"

The gelding was being tacked up when Elizabeth arrived on the scene. "Are you riding? May I go with you?"

The pretty manners didn't help Elizabeth's cause, but the thought that Cressy could leave behind the groom did. "I'm riding over to White Stones to see my brother. You may show me the way." Cressy slapped her crop against the side of her boot as she waited impatiently for Elizabeth's mare to be saddled.

Elizabeth, forcing a smile, suggested that because the day was so fine they go the longer route by road. She'd have suggested the same thing if the day hadn't been fine, but Cressy wasn't to know that. Cressy was pleased she needn't worry about mud—or worse—splashing her skirts or about the necessity of jumping any really high gate or hedge. She liked riding no better than Elizabeth did, although her seat was somewhat better.

Three-quarters of an hour later Pierce's butler, his

nose in the air, informed them His Grace and Lord Halford had ridden out.

With *her* nose in the air, Cressy informed the butler, "We will await them in the salon."

Elizabeth ventured a caveat. "Do you suppose your brother has the intention of visiting *you* at the Court?"

"The devil you say." Cressy laughed. Her one saving grace was the ability to laugh—on admittedly rare occasions—at herself. "I believe you have the right of it. They most likely went cross-country. Well, girl, what do you suggest?"

Elizabeth suggested they return at once. She clinched her argument when she suggested, "With my father in residence, Aunt Joanna will be forced to ask them to stay for nuncheon."

Cressy silently agreed Joanna would ask the men to lunch—but attributed her own motives to the woman she hated so much. Joanna, she believed, was, this time, a rival worthy of her. There had been a look in Pierce's eye last night when his gaze rested on Jo which had been unmistakable and intolerable. There was also the fact he was lingering at an estate he'd avoided for years and was—mistakenly—believed to abhor.

The only reason Cressy could find for such behavior was the notion Pierce intended laying siege to Joanna. It was a courtship she'd thwarted once and would, if she could, again. She'd desired Pierce since laying eyes on him when her brother had brought his new friend home from Balliol one university vacation years ago. If she couldn't have him, and she'd nearly admitted he'd never bite on her lures, Pierce would not be allowed to have what *he* wanted either. Somehow she'd thrust a spoke in his wheel. Again.

Cressy turned the bay and hit him sharply with her crop.

Elizabeth followed, her heart in her throat, but she was determined to keep up however uncomfortable the ride and however difficult it was to stay in her saddle. Although unaware of Cressy's plans, she was equally determined to thrust that spoke in His Grace's wheel.

"Come now, Joanna. You've procrastinated in every way possible."

"I've told you I cannot go riding, Pierce." Joanna turned her shoulder, straightening a flower in a vase. "I am, as you very well know, my brother's hostess and it would be grossly impolite to go off . . ."

"Cut line. I'll wager you don't care a groat about playing hostess to Robert's sister. Besides, Henry brought her, so she's his guest, not yours. Let *him* entertain her. All that is red herring. What you *are* doing is attempting to avoid any sort of tête-à-tête with *me*."

"If you want the word with no bark on it, then yes I am. Now will you please go join Henry and Lord Halford in the library?"

"Did you say please?"

"If you please or if you don't, just *go*."

Pierce tugged at a strand of her hair, loosening it. "That's more the Jo I remember. Don't let Cressy get under your skin, love. She'll try, you know."

Joanna found herself contrarily chagrined Pierce did as he'd been bid, striding off toward the library. She watched him go with a troubled frown before turning on her heel and heading for the garden. Pierce was right, of course. She longed to put on her

103

habit and ride out her temper on Lad's back. She longed for the peace and quiet she'd enjoyed before Pierce reappeared in her life. She longed for Reggie to . . . No, she didn't!

Joanna stopped short, staring unseeingly at a show of roses any gardener would claim with pride. The discovery that she *didn't* long for Reggie was a shock. It had taken well over a year, but she no longer wanted him or needed him or felt like weeping at his loss. All that time? Or *was* it the passage of time?

Was it, heaven forbid, the advent of Pierce? Joanna strolled on, trying hard to read what was happening to her heart. Had her mourning state become nothing but habit? How awful. And Pierce . . . Had he walked in and renewed his claim? Just as he'd done during her one and only season before she'd learned from Cressy his wretched plans for her future?

Joanna stopped once more. This time her eyes rested, again without seeing, on a fine statue her grandfather had brought back from Italy. Those plans which had turned her love to disgust had never existed. Pierce hadn't expected her to play the docile wife, the doormat. Come to think of it, it had been a silly notion even then if she hadn't been too naive to see it. Pierce must have known her well enough to know she'd be a rug under no man's feet! Ooooh . . .

Tempting visions of tearing out handfuls of Cressy Clayton's brassy blond hair filled her mind. Further visions of boiling the other woman in oil, of putting pins into her pampered flesh, of—

"Ah, there you are." The voice of Joanna's enemy forced its way into her mind. "Is my brother here?" asked Cressy.

Joanna blinked away the red distorting her vision,

waiting for it to fade. She put still more effort into producing a smile as false as Cressida's. "Lord Halford? I believe you'll find him in the library. I'll answer the question you won't ask: the duke is there, as well."

Cressy's eyes narrowed. Had the little Ransome, now Wooten, lost all her naiveté while off with her soldier? Cressy stared into Joanna's limpid gaze and decided it wasn't possible. She couldn't know Cressy's current plans for remarriage—how near to the edge of social ruin she teetered, how badly she needed rescuing . . .

"Aunt Jo . . ."

"Elizabeth, you're limping!"

"Oh, 'tis nothing." The girl surreptitiously rubbed her hip, which she believed must be black and blue from the jouncing ride back from White Stones. She eyed her aunt with a scowl. "You look a vision in that blue, Aunt Jo."

Elizabeth had some difficulty accepting just how much a vision her aunt had become. Last night, too. That rose gown had been lovely and her aunt more so. It was a vision to which the duke must not be exposed.

"I thought you'd be back in your blacks," suggested Elizabeth, her eyes wide. "As you've told me again and again—"

"I think, my dear, that what I've said needn't be told to the winds."

"You malign me, Joanna." Cressy's bored tones reminded Joanna of her existence. "I'm many things, but a gossip I am not." Cressy had the satisfaction of seeing a blush on her hostess's cheek and the assurance that Joanna had forgotten her while bent on reprimanding Elizabeth. "Ah. You didn't mean me."

"I merely meant to suggest my niece not bore on forever about trivial matters. You'd better run and change, Elizabeth. Luncheon will be served before you know it."

"Then I, too, had better change out of my dirt. Is my brother staying for lunch?"

"I haven't the least notion. I assume Henry will ask him."

"And Pierce, too, of course."

Joanna found Cressy's easy use of Pierce's name a stab straight into her disobedient heart. "Pierce, too," she returned lightly. "He needs no invitation, of course, having run tame here at the Court since before he was breeched." She smiled at Cressy's obvious chagrin, nodded politely, and, telling the older woman she'd see her at lunch, walked on, all thought of her unwelcome guest fading immediately as her mind returned to its current obsession.

She was again staring blankly, this time with an unhappy expression, at the long view framed by two rows of gigantic cedars as she dwelled on her belief Pierce was merely trifling with her affections. She *must* remain on guard against him. She *must* control the stupid attraction she felt, the *need* to feel his arms around her again, the heat of his body close to her and that unnervingly sensuous mouth finding hers . . .

Blast and damn. She must not allow base desire to overcome her good sense. Joanna glanced around, determined that she was alone and uttered, softly, a string of oaths that stuttered to a halt as the words and phrases brought to mind Old Hooky's "scum of the earth" front-line soldiers from whom she'd learned them.

A smile touched her mouth as a much quoted remark from one of the Duke of Wellington's letters crossed her mind. Something along the lines of "I do not know whether my soldiers frighten the enemy, but, by God, Sir, they frighten me."

Joanna tipped her head, thinking back to her days following the drum, to the rough men she'd observed in the Peninsula. She had to admit there was something in Wellington's remark. But she appreciated the strong language she'd overheard and carefully tucked away in her memory. There were times such unladylike expressions came in useful indeed. Why, just now it had taken only a handful to raise her spirits immensely!

Six

When the men joined the women in the dining room, only Henry, who already showed signs of over-indulgence, actually filled a plate. Pierce and Robert were, they claimed, satisfied with the large mugs of home-brewed ale the housekeeper brought them personally.

"Thank you, Mrs. Landy," said Pierce. "No one has your touch with the home brew. Are you sure you wouldn't like to come to White Stones? I'll double your salary."

"Away with you, Your Grace." The woman's cheeks turned rosy and she curtsied as she left the room.

"Here, here now. What's this? Pierce, are you trying to steal my housekeeper again?"

"Yes."

Henry's jaw dropped. "Well, I say, that's not very sporting of you."

Fortunately Henry was not the sort to become upset when his friends laughed at him because his expression just then was exquisitely humorous to all who saw it. Even his daughter stifled giggles behind her hand.

"Well, well," he said, when the chuckles and chortles died away, "I'm sure Pierce didn't mean a word of it."

Joanna interrupted before Pierce could tell his friend he most certainly did, and suggested Henry make a few visits that afternoon to tenants who would speak to him of things they would not mention to herself. "You'd better take your agent with you in case you discover a problem or two. That way Mr. Douglas can discuss it with you and a decision may be made right then and there."

Her brother looked harassed, agreed it was something he should do while home, but insisted there was plenty of time. Joanna did not persist. She had accomplished her goal of turning the conversation from Pierce's teasing.

Conversation dragged. Cressy appeared to be flirting with Pierce, but His Grace ignored her. Elizabeth kept her pretty little mouth shut but divided her attention between Pierce, at whom she scowled, and Robert, toward whom she sent several speculative looks which, when he noticed, left him with dots of color high on each cheek. Henry was very busy cleaning his plate and selecting second servings—too busy to play host and keep a conversation going as he should have done. And Joanna found the headache that she'd first noticed when fending off Pierce that morning bursting into full bloom. She decided she'd spend the afternoon in her room.

"Aunt Jo . . ." began Elizabeth when they left the small dining room together.

"I think you should put in an hour practicing," said Joanna in an absent tone.

Diverted from what she'd been going to say, Elizabeth entered a protest. "Oh, Aunt Jo . . ."

"If me sister says you're to practice," said Henry,

coming up behind them, "then be off with you to the spinet, Lizzy."

"Lizzy! Please, Papa, do *not* call me by that nursery name." Knowing she'd lost her opportunity to warn her aunt against the duke, Elizabeth stalked off toward the music room.

"Just a minute, Jo, a word with you," continued Henry as Joanna turned toward the stairs. "Come along now."

"Not now."

"Now, m'love."

Joanna reluctantly followed him into the library, and when he didn't go on but looked exceedingly perturbed, she found a chair and sat down. "What can possibly have you in the boughs, Henry?" she prompted when it seemed as if he'd never speak.

"It's that sweet puss of mine." Henry frowned. "How the devil did the minx grow up so fast? How old is the girl, Jo?"

"She was seventeen her last birthday."

"*Seventeen*. Pish. Tosh." He cast her a defiant look. "Can't be."

Jo smiled at his blustering. "I'm afraid she is."

"Nonsense . . . You sure?"

"Henry, I've written you more than once on the subject of Elizabeth. How can you pretend you don't know her age?"

Henry sighed. "Tell you what, Jo. This being a parent is a terrible thing. First one problem and then another. Just can't keep up with it all."

Joanna might have told her brother exactly what she thought of how he cared for his daughter. Because she was amused by his obvious bewilderment, she resisted. "The *first* thing is to decide if she's to have her come-out this fall or next spring."

"I *see* that." Henry mumbled some more. "See we have to do something about her. Is there never an end to it, Jo?"

"Once a parent, always a parent, Henry."

He looked horrified. "You can't mean that?"

Well, I suppose once she's married, her husband will take care of her and you'll have little to do. Until her children start coming and you become a grandpa."

"Grandpa? No. No, no, no. I'm too young to be a grandpa."

Very true, thought Joanna, looking at her brother, twelve years her senior. He'd been married very young to the woman chosen for him when the couple had been tots. It had, she thought, been a surprisingly good marriage despite her sister-in-law's weak constitution which had led to her early demise. But all that history was irrelevant. She brought her mind back to the subject at hand.

"Then you don't wish Elizabeth to have a season this year?" she asked. Henry mumbled some more and Joanna, her headache fading beneath the humor she found in the interview, relaxed into her chair. "Well, Henry?"

"You say it's time?"

"Quite time. She's driving me to bedlam."

"You don't think Pierce . . ."

"Get that notion out of your head. He'd murder Elizabeth within a week of marrying her."

"Very likely," agreed her brother, who then sighed deeply. "Well, well." He looked sadder than ever at the thought that his hedonistic life must be interrupted by the exigencies of bringing out his daughter. "You'll have to take her to London a few

111

weeks early for all the folderols you and she will wish to purchase, I suppose."

"I was thinking, brother dear, of returning with you to Brighton."

"What's that? Go to Brighton?" His eyes bugged like a frog. "You? No, no."

"You look perturbed by the notion."

"Can't have you in Brighton. No room," he added as if from a flash of enlightenment. "No room at all. Haven't enough space for you and Elizabeth and your maids and a groom and the extra horses and . . ."

"We weren't thinking of staying forever, Henry. But I find I'm quite tired of my blacks. I wish to consult the mantua-makers."

"What's wrong with that thing you have on?"

"It is nearly two years old."

Henry peered at her more closely. "Fiddle. Can't be. Not at all in the fashion of two years ago."

"My maid and Mrs. Landy spent hours last night remaking it."

"Did they now?" Joanna nodded. After a moment Henry asked, "Why'd they do that?"

She laughed. "Oh Henry, you are a delight sometimes."

"Well," he said, flustered, "I know I'm not sharp like Pierce or Robert, but I'm not stupid. And I'm right up to snuff when it comes to fashion, Jo. Know that dress isn't two years old because the sleeves and the neck are all wrong."

"Two years ago it didn't look like this. That is why they spent all night changing it."

Henry digested that. "Don't suppose they'd like to spend a few more nights sewing?"

"No, they wouldn't. It was kind of them to do this one."

A crafty look wasn't missed by Joanna and she wondered why Henry didn't want her going to Brighton. "Seem to remember an old lady in the village. Me wife used to—"

"*Old* is right. She can't see to thread a needle and her ideas on fashion are twenty years out-of-date. She won't do. I must go to Brighton."

Henry looked hunted. "Well. Well. I'll think on it, Jo. That's what I'll do." He headed for the door. "Yes, Jo, I'll think on it."

When the door closed behind him, Joanna laughed heartily. "Oh, Henry. You do that," she said as his footsteps disappeared down the hall. "You think on it." She chuckled. "I fear," she muttered as the giggles faded, "you'll find yourself so out of practice you'll get nowhere, however."

A deep baritone voice commiserated. "Poor Henry." A dark head popped up from the sofa on the other side of the room.

Joanna jumped. "Pierce!" She straightened her skirt and sat more primly wondering why he'd not revealed himself sooner. "I thought you'd gone."

"Robert went walking with Cressy. I didn't care to fend off her flirtatious ways so I stayed behind."

"And eavesdropped," said Joanna, an edge to her voice.

"And eavesdropped. Had a devil of a time not laughing out loud, too."

Joanna smiled, then forced the smile to fade into a stern look. "It was not polite, not telling us you were here."

"I'd dropped off and when I awoke you were discussing me. I felt too embarrassed to reveal myself!"

"Embarrassed? You? I don't believe it."

He bowed slightly but otherwise ignored her comment. "Did I hear Henry suggest I might be interested in that chit of his?"

"You did. My buffleheaded brother got the notion from that note you sent him."

Pierce looked thoughtful. "Can't remember a thing in the note which could give him that impression. Quite the reverse, I'd have thought."

"He told me you wrote something about his responsibilities."

"So?"

"So what responsibility does a doting father have for a daughter except to accept some poor deluded man's offer of marriage?" Joanna didn't attempt to hide her exasperation.

"I've no experience, of course, but quite a few I should think."

"Ah. But then, you *do* think. Henry doesn't." Their laughter mingled. "Why doesn't Henry want me in Brighton?"

Pierce frowned. "I haven't a notion, Jo. That bit about no room is nonsense. He took a rather ostentatious house this year. It's on the Steyne, which isn't exactly the street one likes for housing one's female relatives, of course. The front windows along there look directly out onto the paving, allowing any passing buck to ogle the occupants. But for his daughter and sister to visit for a week or two? Perfectly acceptable."

"Then why . . ."

"I'll see if I can find out for you."

"Please. I must visit the warehouses for material and find a decent dressmaker. Now I've decided to come out of my blacks, I find I can't stand the thought of them."

"What puzzles me is why you've waited this long." He held up a hand in a fencing posture. "Hold hard, Jo. Just because I can't understand doesn't mean I don't respect you for it."

"That doesn't make sense."

"That loyalty of yours, Jo. Once given, you live by it. That is a characteristic one has to admire even though it plays the devil with one's own plans."

"Pierce, if you are going to start that nonsense again . . ."

He strolled toward her. Bending from the waist, he laid his hands on the arms of her chair, bringing himself far too near to her. Joanna found it hard to breathe properly and knew her cheeks were warming to much too rosy a color for her peace of mind.

"Hello, love," he said softly and bending still nearer, his lips brushed hers with the softest of touches. He raised his head and looked into her startled eyes, that smile she could never resist appearing. "It's been so long, my love."

His mouth touched hers more firmly this time and Joanna's traitorous mind echoed the thought: so long. So very long . . .

Unexpectedly he lifted his head and her hand followed willy-nilly to be left touching the ambient air. She didn't understand why he was suddenly standing by the mantel, half-turned from her, his fingers caressing a Meissen statuette.

"This is a lovely piece, Jo. Is it new?"

Her confusion cleared when she heard what Pierce had heard: the shrill voice of her brother's guest as Cressy and Robert neared the library. Joanna struggled for poise.

115

"Not new. Mrs. Landy and I found it in a cupboard and thought it should be on view."

The door opened and Joanna glanced from Cressy's stormy face to Robert's tight-lipped expression. The relationship between brother and sister, it seemed, had not prospered during their walk.

"Pierce, tell my brother it is none of his business what sort of stable I keep."

"It is if you expect him to support it."

"How dare you? How dare you suggest I can't afford . . ."

"Cut line, Cressy. The whole *ton* is aware you've not a feather to fly with. They've expected you to find yourself in River Tick any time these last two years." A frightened look appeared in the blonde's eyes but turned to ice when she met Joanna's sympathetic gaze. "So, if Robert has advised you to sell off some of your cattle and carriages," Pierce said with a shrug, "then I'd advise that you listen to him."

Joanna frowned. Cressy had always been the merest whipster. Why would she be keeping an extensive stable?

"My new carriage is all the crack. One must keep up appearances."

"It is hardly keeping up appearances when you can't control your horses," suggested Pierce sharply, referring to a recent incident Cressy had hoped was decently buried and forgotten. He went on in a kinder tone, "Tell you what, Cressy. I'll buy that phaeton and the new team of grays from you for whatever you paid for them."

Cressy eyed him speculatively. "That's a kind offer, Pierce."

Joanna, looking from one to the other, wondered if Pierce had less honorable motives than kindness

116

for helping Cressy. Not that Cressy would need to be bribed into Pierce's arms but he might not know that. Men, she had learned, could be complete dunces where women were concerned. Cressy was beautiful. Her figure was magnificent and she was, despite her malicious ways, an intelligent woman. Suddenly, once again, Joanna felt as if her head were about to explode. She shut her eyes for a moment wishing she'd gone to her room immediately after lunch as she'd planned on doing.

Cressy sidled closer to Pierce, laying her hand on his arm. "Thank you, Pierce. I'll have them sent round to your stables first thing when I get back."

"And I'll send the money to your carriage maker and . . . where did you get that team, Cressy?"

Cressy bit her lip. "'Twas a private sale, Pierce. You just give me a draft . . ."

"No. Don't think I can do that, Cress."

"Pierce . . ."

"Don't try that wheedle on me." Pierce lifted Cressy's hand from his sleeve. "And don't go wrinkling the material of my coat, either. I made the offer to pay off some of your bills, not to let you get yourself deeper in debt."

"Of course I'd use it to pay my creditors!"

"Debts of honor, Cressy? Oh, no. I'll have nothing to do with those."

"Ohh . . ." Cressy stalked off, slamming the door behind her.

"Now why did you do that, Pierce?" Robert looked thoughtfully at his friend.

"To get you off the hook for a bit, I think. Besides, I like the look of that team and would prefer to get my hands on it before she ruins their mouths. You

117

must admit she's a cowhanded whip." Pierce grinned crookedly. "Just how deep has she plunged?"

"Don't ask. Deep enough I can keep her in line for a while."

"Ah. That was why she looked like a thundercloud when you came in. You'd been laying down the law, had you?"

Robert looked at Joanna and back to Pierce. "I don't think this is the time to discuss it."

"Why not? Oh. Joanna. Jo don't blab, Robert."

"I still prefer to wash my dirty linen in private. And there is none dirtier than that my dear sister can bring to light," said Robert with more than a tinge of exasperation.

"Testy, testy. Oh, all right. But if you need help, let me know."

"I can, if I choose, take care of Cressy's debts. But I'm not sure I choose. My sister needs a lesson."

"You wouldn't actually let her fall into debtor's prison, would you?" asked Joanna. As much as she disliked Cressy, she wouldn't wish a life in King's Bench Prison on anyone.

Robert laughed. "No. But I'd just as soon you didn't let my charming sister become aware I'm such an easy touch. I've got something to hold over her head and don't want it spoiled. Pierce, think it's time we were getting back?"

"I want to talk Jo into riding. She needs the exercise."

"I do, do I? Well, I've much too much to do to take off on a pleasure ride with you, Pierce."

"Mrs. Landy is competent to deal with any emergencies which arise in the next hour or two. Be a good girl and get into that atrocious habit. Robert and I will have another brew while we wait and then walk you to the stables. Twenty minutes, Jo."

"Pierce, this is *my* home and I'll thank you not to give me orders."

"But it is the only way to get you to do anything. Run along now."

A short but pregnant silence was broken by a strange sound, the low growl startling the two men.

"Jo, is that *you?*"

"It is. I'm near exploding. Robert, I think you'd best take yourself off so I can tell this man exactly what I think of him."

"But Jo, we *know* what you think of me. Which doesn't mean you wouldn't be better for some exercise. Please?"

Joanna determinedly controlled the sensation of pleasure rippling up her spine at his husky pleading. "That's an underhanded trick, Pierce."

"Jo?"

"Oh, all right." She allowed him to help her arise. The warmth of his palm against hers added to the sensations filling her, and she dropped his hand as soon as she was on her feet. "I'll be down as soon as I can be." *As soon as I get my mind in order*, she thought, *and remember just who and what you are, Pierce Reston, m'buck!*

As the home wood thinned out the three riders came abreast. Lord Halford lifted his crop and pointed. "That's the way we came this morning, isn't it, Pierce?"

He nodded. "Straight over the top of the hill and take the right hand ride. It'll bring you out nearest the stables."

119

"I'll see you later, then." Robert turned toward Joanna. "Thank you for a delightful morning."

Joanna, remembering his expression when he and his sister had entered the library, gave him a speaking look.

Robert laughed. "Don't expect me to comment on my sister, Lady Joanna. Excepting her, the day was delightful."

"Thank you. You are, you know, welcome anytime you wish to ride over. Henry would want you to feel free—"

"You spoiled it," said Robert on a teasing note. "Now if you were to say *you* would like . . ."

Pierce interrupted with a testy question. "You did say you were on your way, didn't you, Rob?"

The men exchanged a look, Pierce's eyes flashing and Robert's twinkling in response. "Come now, Pierce. You must expect any man worthy of the name to engage Lady Joanna in a little light flirtation. Someone so lovely must expect . . ." Grinning at Pierce's thunderous expression, Rob raised a hand. "All right. I'm off. Have a good ride, Lady Joanna."

"Joanna. Please. You needn't be so formal, Lord Halford."

"Ah. Then *you* must call me Robert. Yes, Pierce. This time I'm really off." He grinned engagingly.

Joanna laughed, then turned to look at Pierce as he maneuvered nearer. "Careful, Pierce. Lad has been known to kick."

"As one hears Wellington's Copenhagen did after the long day's battle at Waterloo? Was Lad there?" He nudged his mount's sides and the two horses set off at a walk.

"Yes. Reggie had three of his string up near the battle. One was killed under him, another badly

120

slashed when he got caught in the midst of a cavalry charge and, toward the end of the battle, when he took that shot, he was riding Lad. Reggie fell and Lad stood over him, lashing out at anyone who came near."

"That's impressive detail, Joanna. How did you learn it all?"

"Reggie was popular with his men and he had many friends amongst the officers. They came to tell me bits and pieces when they learned he was dead. Those that survived," she added bitterly. "Waterloo was hell."

"Yes. I've heard tales of the carnage. I'm sorry, Jo."

She glanced at him, not sure if she believed the sincerity of his tone. He saw her uncertainty and his serious expression faded to be replaced by a rather mocking smile.

"I can't regret you were widowed, Jo. That would be asking too much of me. I am sorry for anyone who had to endure that day. And for all those brave men who died."

For a moment they stared at each other. Then, finding it difficult to shake off the memories she'd revived talking about the battle, Joanna turned to stare between Lad's ears. "Where would you like to ride, Pierce? Since you insisted we go, I'll leave it to you to lead the way."

"How about a game of fox hunting, Jo?"

A quick glance his way proved he was grinning just as she'd suspected from his tone. She smiled in return, some of the sadness fading.

"How angry I was at my father that day he insisted I was too young for the hunt." Her smile broadened, memories chasing away her moment of melancholy. "You were very kind to that young hoyden, Pierce."

"You were better able to keep up than some who showed up at the hunt. Your father should have let you go. I suggested our game to relieve your disappointment, but I enjoyed it, too."

For a moment Jo was tempted. "I'm no longer half a boy, Pierce," she said wistfully. "'Twouldn't be proper."

"Who's to know?" he teased. "You'd enjoy the run, wouldn't you?"

"Of course I would. But I shouldn't. Besides," she said mendaciously, "I've forgotten the rules."

"Simple enough. We take turns following the 'fox.' We must go a minimum of twenty yards before shouting right or left. Then it is the other's turn. Remember?"

"I remember how my governess ranted when I finally came home all spattered with mud, my new hat lost, and my hair in tangles."

Her rueful tone was belied by the excitement in her eyes. Lud, she was tempted.

"I dare you," he said softly.

Joanna straightened. Hoof and horn! He knew how she'd react to that. How *dare* he dare her? But the chance to really run, to take the fences and ditches and ride until she was breathless? How Lad would enjoy it.

"Double dare you."

No one would know, she argued silently. And maybe she could get rid of some of the nervous energy making her so miserable. "We'll do it!"

"I'm first then. We'll start toward that gate and once over it I'll take my twenty yards. Agreed?"

"Ready, Pierce. Anytime you are."

Pierce, his eyes laughing into hers, put his hands to his mouth and yodeled a tallyho as he kicked his mount. Joanna, half a stride behind, laughed as the wind took the first of the pins from her hair.

They had been riding hard for over half an hour when Lad threw a shoe. "Pierce!" Joanna shouted as she pulled Lad up.

Hunched over his stallion's neck, the duke glanced over his shoulder, noted Joanna dismounting, and, reining in, turned and trotted back to her. "What's the matter?"

"Lad's lost a shoe."

Pierce, too, dismounted, glancing around as he did so. Where had they gotten to? Just to be sure, he lifted Lad's leg, checked the loss, and glanced at Joanna who was staring at him, chagrined and slightly worried.

"What's the matter, Jo?"

"I told myself when I agreed to this madness, no one would ever know."

"Need they?"

"How can they help it? We must be five miles from home. Walking Lad back will take forever."

"Where are we?"

It was Joanna's turn to look around. She frowned. There wasn't a house in sight. She hadn't wished to be seen riding like the veriest hoyden, sometimes following, sometimes leading Pierce's stallion. Now she realized they were a mile from the nearest possible help. She sighed, brushing her hair from her face as something more than a fitful breeze tossed it around. Her eyes flew to the sky and dismay filled her.

Following her gaze to the clouds boiling up and over them, Pierce grimaced. A storm had come up from behind them without either of them noticing.

123

Unless they had a quick change of luck, Jo would be soaked to the skin before they found shelter.

"Which way, Jo," he asked urgently. "You know the area better than I."

Jo's exasperation lightened his mood: "If you'd spent anytime at home, Pierce, you'd be aware where we are. And that's a mile, at least, from anywhere. Why did I allow you to talk me into this nonsense?"

"That far? We'd better move." His beloved hesitated, her temper rising. He chuckled. "Jo, you can berate me all you want, but not while standing here waiting for the heavens to open. Which way?"

"Lady Keaton's manor is that way." She pointed.

"Old Lady Keaton is the worst gossip in the home counties, Joanna."

"Who better to give me a good character once you've taken yourself off and left me there. *You* can have the honor of riding to my brother and asking him to send a carriage for me."

"I can, can I?" He laughed. "A fitting punishment for leading you into temptation, you think? You never could resist a dare, Jo."

She sighed. "I know. It isn't entirely your fault. I should not be so childish as to be unable to say no to something I know is wrong. Hurry, Pierce. The wind is rising much too quickly for comfort."

"I'd ride ahead and bring back help except I do not believe it wise to leave you here alone."

"No. I'd prefer you didn't." She'd been lucky to recognize Turner when she'd been accosted before, but she shivered as she remembered Martin's dirty hand closing over her mouth. No, she would not like to be left alone this far from anywhere for any length of time!

"Cold?" Pierce was unbuttoning his coat when

124

Joanna looked at him and shook her head. He left it open in case it became necessary to shed it quickly to protect her from rain. "We could leave Lad in that field and ride double to Lady Keaton's, Jo. Apollo would carry us both."

"I'd rather not arrive on Lady Keaton's doorstep in your arms, Pierce. Your reputation would put me in the suds in an instant."

"You think it won't in any case?"

"Lud! What a thought. You'd better disappear when we get close. I'll tell her I rode farther than I'd expected and lost the shoe and could she please give me shelter until my groom returns with a carriage. That should do it."

"But I've heard many rumors about your unbelievably loose behavior."

"My *what*?"

"Loose behavior," he reiterated with a straight face. "It is common knowledge you *never* take a groom with you as you should."

"Gossip." Disgust dripped from her tone. "Why can people not find better things to do than gossip?" She sighed. "I'll just have to tell her that today I took a groom. Please, Pierce? I do not want my reputation ruined."

He studied her drooping shoulders. She didn't expect him to agree and he was tempted. Because old Lady Keaton was the biggest tattlebox in creation, Joanna might find it necessary to marry him out of hand! But he could see she was distressed. Forcing her into his arms was not the way. He'd rejected that means when Henry would have abetted him after the kidnapping five years previously. He wouldn't resort to it now, however badly he wanted her. It was Pierce's turn to sigh.

125

"I'll ride off as soon as I see you into the house, Jo. And I'll stay far enough away I'll not be seen myself."

She glanced at him, stumbled over a stone, and found herself caught—and held.

"But if I'm to be so noble, my love, I'll have my reward in advance."

There was no stopping him. And, much against her firm intentions, Joanna found herself lacking the will to try. His lips touched hers. Touched them more firmly and then slanted knowingly, his tongue tracing her closed mouth, probing for entrance. Groaning inwardly, Joanna relaxed into his embrace. So long . . . it had been so long without the feel of a man's desire arousing hers. And this was Pierce, her first love and, she very much feared, her last.

Rain poured down over them, drenching Pierce's hat, dripping off the brim and down Joanna's neck. She jerked away as the cool water trickled down her spine. Pushing at his broad shoulders, she stared at him. "There are rewards, Pierce Reston, and then there are rewards. You, I think, have had reward enough."

"I don't think I could ever get enough of that, Jo."

His eyes held hers, the flame in them telling her just how much more he wanted. She felt her skin warming, felt shame she'd allowed the kiss, let alone allowed herself to, just for a bit, respond. Well, more than a bit. If the rain hadn't come . . . Lud, she might have made a complete fool of herself. Damn the man. Did he have to be so utterly attractive? So irresistible? She renewed her resolve to avoid him in the future. There would be no more tête-à-têtes. There would be no more rides, certainly no more games. And she *would not* allow him to lure her into

126

an affair. Whatever her heart was saying, her head told her that was the best thing to do.

"We'd better get on, Pierce."

"You're going to pretend you didn't enjoy that, aren't you, Jo?" he asked in a conversational tone, staring straight ahead as he stalked along beside her.

"No. Why should I?" she surprised him by replying. "I did enjoy it. But it will not happen again, Pierce. I daren't. You are not used to denying yourself. I'm no green girl, and I know where such behavior can lead. I couldn't take an affair with you, Pierce."

"I do not want an affair with you. I want to marry you. You know that."

"I know you say that. I don't believe you." She heard his teeth gritting together and tried another tack. "Do stop teasing me or you'll ruin our friendship."

"I am your friend and have been since long before you put your hair up. For a long time I've wanted more than that. Why do you disbelieve me?"

She chuckled, blew upwards to shift a sodden lock of hair which was tickling her nose. "Pierce, perhaps it is because I've known you for ages that I don't believe you. You must remember all those years I trailed after you and Henry and all the things you two discussed, forgetting my tender years and listening ears."

"Are you saying you *understood*?" Pierce, still aroused from their brief lovemaking, remembered far different things than the plans to get even with one person or another to which Joanna referred.

"Outrage?" She realized what he was thinking and chuckled. "Come now, Pierce. What I didn't understand I discussed with Henry later. Sometimes he'd remember I was a girl and he shouldn't tell me, but often I could trick him into explaining whatever it was I wanted to know."

"I'll black his daylights . . ."

"Why? For things *you* could have prevented my knowing simply by not discussing the subject when I was around?"

His wry laugh was full of self-disgust. "You are, as usual, quite correct, my love."

"Then you'll leave me alone in future, Pierce?"

"How," he stopped and turned her, his free hand on her arm, "did you come to such an asinine conclusion?"

"But—"

"Whether you believe it or not, Joanna, I love you. I have loved you for years. *Nothing* will stop my attempts to convince you of that fact or the obvious conclusion one reaches from that knowledge. We will be married, Jo, as soon as I can contrive to break through your stubborn resistance to what we both want. It'll be years later than we should have wed, but we *will be married.*"

They trudged on side by side in silence until Pierce allowed her to go on alone toward Lady Keaton's front door. Hidden behind a hedge, he watched it open and saw Joanna admitted into the dry warmth beyond. Jo was safe and out of the rain. Pierce looked from one horse to the other. "Well, Apollo. Was it worth a soaking?" His stallion nuzzled him and Pierce grinned. "Yes. Of course it was worth it, but it's always nice to have one's opinion confirmed." He mounted and, with Lad trailing behind, started on the miserable, wet ride back to Midbourgh Court.

Seven

"Lady Joanna!"

"Timmons, is it not?" Joanna, bedraggled and dripping, maintained as much poise as she could in the difficult situation. "I am very sorry to intrude this way, but as you see, I find myself in difficulty."

"Dear me. How *wet* you are." The tall, thin, and very bald butler wrung his hands.

Joanna pushed aside the persistent lock that dripped onto her chin. "I am, aren't I? Of all the ridiculous times for Lad to throw a shoe!"

"Dear me, dear me . . ." The old butler's dithering stopped and his expression lightened. "I know. I'll send Mrs. Timmons to you. Immediately. I'm certain we can find something . . ."

His voice disappeared behind the green baize-covered door at the back of the hall. Soon he reappeared followed by a birdlike little woman wrapped in a voluminous apron who clucked at the sight of Joanna.

"Oh, dearie me. Oh, dearie dearie me. Lady Joanna, you come along at once. At once, do you hear?"

If not "at once," Joanna took only a moment to

assure herself her unexpected arrival would be announced to Lady Keaton. "I'm sorry to be making such a bother of myself, Mrs. Timmons." She indicated the dripping habit and her muddy boots.

"Not to worry, m'lady." Her voice held only the faintest of regret for the ruin of her highly polished floors. "The maids have little enough to do. 'Twill be good for them to busy themselves." She gave sympathetic little clucks as they climbed. "In here now," she ordered with kind brusqueness when they'd topped a second, less impressive, flight of stairs and entered a small bedchamber where a fire was already laid. "I'll have a bath brought up at once." She lit the fire. "I'm certain I can find something for you to wear while we dry your habit . . ." Her voice trailed off as she eyed Joanna's tall figure. "Well, hmm, *something* . . ."

Joanna laughed, already undoing buttons and stripping off sopping material, dropping it on the tiles fronting the fireplace. "At this point, dear Mrs. Timmons, even a nice warm blanket would do. I'm not the least fussy, you know—not at all high in the instep. I suffered far worse than this in Spain."

"Oh, you poor dear . . ."

With a last sympathetic look, Mrs. Timmons bustled out and Joanna continued removing her sodden clothing, wrapping herself in an extra blanket she found at the end of the bed. Three-quarters of an hour later, seated before a warm fire in a small back parlor, she was sipping hot tea with Lady Keaton and apologizing for her intrusion.

Her back as stiff as a board, that lady's gnarled fingers gripped the arms of her chair, but her dark eyes glittered with avid interest. "I hadn't heard you

130

ever rode this direction. How did it come about that you were caught so far from home, Lady Joanna?"

"It was such a fine day when I started. And I was much in need of exercise. So was Lad, poor fellow. My favorite mount, you know. For once, thank the Almighty, I took a groom with me. I had a rather bad experience recently and was reminded it is not always safe to ride alone."

As Joanna had hoped, the old woman was immediately alert to what might be a very interesting tidbit of news indeed. "Oh?" she probed. "How is that, my dear?"

"I had been informed that two out-of-work soldiers were about, but since I intended staying on my brother's property, it didn't occur to me there could be any danger."

"You were set upon!" Wide eyes glazed over with pleasure at the visions flitting through the old woman's head.

"Not exactly. I don't doubt I *might* have been if I hadn't recognized one of them. It is so sad, don't you agree, that the men who fought so bravely to keep us safe from the Monster must now resort to such tricks in order to survive?"

"You say you recognized one of them?"

"My husband's batman. I'd wondered what had become of him. After the Lieutenant's death at Waterloo, I was so distraught I didn't think of Turner, and when I did, I couldn't find him. They'd been together since my Reggie first went to the Peninsula, you see, and Reggie would have wanted him looked after. If it weren't for Turner, I'm not certain I'd have survived my first months as an officer's wife. I was such an ignoramus," Joanna said with a laugh. "Turner taught me everything I needed to know and acted as houseman." As an afterthought, Joanna added, "When we had a house, that is. He looked after me when Reggie was about his duties."

"You are a lucky young woman," scolded the neighborhood gossip, but again her eyes betrayed her thoughts.

Joanna sighed. She'd gone too far. Now Lady Keaton was making up scandal from the fact Turner had been a trusted servant during those difficult years. "Poor Turner. He isn't much to look at, of course, but he's loyal to a fault. Reggie rescued him when he was wounded at the battle of Ciudad Rodrigo and, once the man recovered, had the poor fellow assigned to himself."

Disappointment at this news wasn't entirely hidden. *Now,* thought Joanna, *if the old besom never sees Turner, just maybe I'll be safe.* The former batman was no nonesuch, but his looks were tolerable and he was just barely young enough Lady Keaton would have a field day making up fitting tittle-tattle should she choose to do so.

"I should," said the old woman, "have someone ride to Midbourgh Court with the message you are safe."

"You are forgetting, Lady Keaton," said Joanna softly, "that today I had a groom with me. My brother is in residence at the moment. But even if he weren't, I don't doubt they'll send a carriage for me immediately when word is received. I shouldn't be a burden to you for long."

Joanna turned the conversation by asking about an acquaintance who had grown up some miles beyond the Keaton estate. Lady Keaton happily filled her in on years of news, dishing out stale gossip Joanna not

132

only found lacking in interest but felt was, most likely, equally lacking facts to back it up.

Two hours later, Joanna was still prodding her hostess with questions whenever the garrulous woman seemed about to run down. Jo was heartily glad when Mrs. Timmons appeared, announcing m'lady's habit was dry and as clean as she could get it.

"I will change back into it if you don't mind, Lady Keaton? It was very kind of your second housemaid to loan me her best dress, but, as you can see, it doesn't quite fit!" Joanna twirled, showing Lady Keaton far more ankle than any proper lady would reveal. "It is such a nuisance being so tall."

Joanna dawdled as long as she could in the bedroom she'd been given. When she could justify staying there no longer, she returned to the parlor, praying little more time would pass before rescue arrived. Unfortunately her hostess had had time to think while Joanna was dressing and her first question was one Joanna had been dreading.

"I hear the duke is at White Stones?"

"Yes."

"You've seen him, then?"

"Of course." Joanna pretended astonishment the lady would assume otherwise. "He and my brother are friends from childhood, you know. They always visit back and forth."

"I thought you'd marry him. It was, in fact, all but settled, according to the duchess. A very old and very dear friend of mine, you know."

Joanna, remembering the duchess, doubted that very much. "There was," said Joanna carefully, "some talk of an alliance, I believe. When we were both much younger. But nothing was formalized and

I was allowed a choice." Again she tried to turn the conversation. "Nothing like the times in which you grew up, Lady Keaton. I've heard that in your day it wasn't uncommon for a new bride to have spoken, previously, no more than a word or two with the man chosen by her family as her husband."

"Young girls are given much too much a say in the matter in these lax times," responded Lady Keaton tartly. "Why, look at yourself. You made such a mull of it. A mere lieutenant with little more than his pay and a fancy red coat, yet he won one of the biggest prizes on the marriage mart that year." Joanna held on to her temper with both hands. "And only because your brother didn't put his foot down as he should have done. Pierce Reston would have been a proper choice in all ways. In place of your father, it was your brother's duty to see that you did yours, Lady Joanna."

"Lieutenant Wooten and I were very much in love, Lady Keaton." Joanna's eyes glittered dangerously, but she managed a polite response. "Despite the difficulties, I enjoyed following the drum."

Lady Keaton eyed her. "Yes. As young and heedless as you were, I suspect you found it exciting. What a blessing that young man died at Waterloo."

Joanna clenched her teeth against such callousness. Hidden by her skirts her hands clenched as well.

"Think how you'd feel as you got older, Lady Joanna. How disagreeable to aging bones such rough living would be and how boring for you a time of peace when you'd be living on an officer's half pay and unable to take your rightful place in society."

Joanna gritted her teeth. With great self-control she avoided reminding her hostess of the tidy fortune she'd inherited from her mother—it occurred to her just in time the woman would then accuse Reggie of being a fortune hunter!

"No," repeated the old woman waspishly. "It is just as well that young man didn't survive."

Goaded beyond endurance, Joanna's temper gained the upper hand. Lady Keaton looked shocked as Joanna loomed over her, her eyes flashing and anger giving color to cheeks previously too pale.

"Lady Keaton, you go too far."

"Lady Joanna!"

"Such sentiments are unworthy of you. I loved my husband very much. I cannot bear to listen to such callous words. The weather is clearing. May I impose on your, er, kindness a little further and borrow a horse and a groom? I will ride until we come up with the carriage, which is surely on the way, and your groom may return here with my mount."

"Oh, do climb down off your high horse, young lady," blustered Her Ladyship. "I've said nothing but the truth. And if you have one iota of sense in you, you will heed my words. You have a second chance at the Duke of Stornway. Don't muff it again."

A knock at the door prevented Joanna from blistering her hostess with the words on the tip of her tongue. The carriage, she thanked heaven, had arrived in the nick of time. Joanna forced herself to thank Lady Keaton for her hospitality. She gave much warmer thanks, far less stiffly phrased, to Mrs. Timmons and asked her to pass on to the maids her appreciation for their work and, also, special thanks for the loan of the dress.

Timmons held an umbrella over her head against the drizzle as she stalked to the carriage. He closed the door behind her. Joanna had settled her skirts if not her temper when she noted who else occupied the wide seat.

"You!"

Pierce chuckled. "Who else?"

"I'm surprised my brother allowed it."

"He cannot forbid what he knows nothing about. It occurred to me White Stones was a trifle closer than the Court. I went there."

Joanna remembered there'd been no crest on the door and felt a modicum of relief. The carriage wouldn't, automatically, have been identified by Timmons as one of His Grace's. "Which means my brother and my household think I'm missing and are worrying about me. I hope Sam hasn't sent out search parties."

"Calm down. I sent a groom with a message."

"So they *all* know I'm with you. Thank you very much, Your Grace!"

Exasperated, Pierce scowled at her. "Good Lord, Joanna. You are not a young thing anymore. You are twenty-four and a widow. What possible damage could there be to you in this situation?"

"Given *your* reputation, a great deal!" Joanna sighed. "Pierce, don't pretend. You know it will be all over the county I've ridden miles in a closed carriage in your company. I'll be ruined forever."

"I can trust my coachman. He'll not talk. What about Sam and Dawson?"

"Of course I can trust them. But what of all the others who will whisper and—"

"And nothing, Jo. You'll be dropped at your front door. Dawson won't prattle about how you arrived. No one will recognize this old-fashioned turnout. It hasn't been out of the carriage house in decades!"

Having found a scapegoat for her temper, Joanna

couldn't stop. "Worse. They'll be speculating on how I got home!"

"They?" he growled.

Anger at her arguments—which Pierce knew to have foundation—grew to match that she was pouring over his head. When he'd set out to return for her, he'd had a moment's qualm, but repressed it in his desire to spend another hour with her.

"Well, if you're going to be hung, Jo, then let it be for a sheep rather than a lamb!"

One arm slipped about her waist and jerked her around until she was pressed against his chest. His free hand found her chin, firmed against her jaw and forced her head up.

"Oh, God. Jo . . . !"

His mouth claimed hers and her struggles against him ceased almost before they began. So long. So many years since Pierce had stolen gentle kisses from her willing lips. Kisses she had, at the time, wished were more like what she was experiencing now. The arm trapped between them worked itself loose, slid to his shoulder, upward until she could touch the hair at the nape of his neck.

"Jo . . ."

Dreamily she fingered his hair, her mind will-less, her body willing. She didn't notice when his marauding fingers breached the defenses of her habit. Not until they began an agile sortie against the buttons of her bodice was she roused to consciousness of their behavior. Suddenly aware of just where they were, who they were, Joanna struggled.

"Don't. Oh, Jo. Please don't . . ."

"Let me go, you libertine. How dare you . . ."

He straightened and held her stiffly. Slowly he set

137

her away from him and touched her cheek. "Tears? My Jo is *crying*?"

"I am not your Jo and I'm crying because I'm angry. I'm furious."

"I refuse to apologize. I've waited too long to hold you and kiss you. You made *me* angry. I had no intention of being anything but a gentleman until you goaded me with your missish behavior."

"I don't believe you know how to be a gentleman. You've had your way with women far too long. They've spoiled you, damn you."

"You were as much involved as I, Jo."

His quiet words penetrated the haze in her mind and Jo, slumped into her corner of the carriage, grasped the strap to hold herself steady. "Yes. Yes, I was. It only proves why a lady should never go unchaperoned. We must have protection not only against unprincipled rakehells such as yourself, but against our own base natures. I will not become your mistress, Pierce."

"I don't believe," he returned sternly, "I ever asked that of you. I *have* asked you to marry me."

"Why?" she wailed, her emotions a complete tangle.

"Why do you demand I repeat myself again and again? Because you are the only woman I've ever loved. The only woman I've ever wanted for my wife, the mother of my children."

"Why don't I believe you?"

"Perhaps because you feel guilty? Feel a need to punish yourself as well as me?"

"*Guilt*. Why should I feel guilty?"

"For believing tales you should have known were moonshine. For letting someone come between us as

138

you did. For encouraging another man whom you could never love as you loved me. For—"

"Stop. For God's sake, stop."

"Can you deny any of it?"

"That I believed the lies? That I let them come between us? Perhaps I did, Pierce, but if you remember, you'd given me no reason to believe you loved me until you knew you'd lost me. Only then did you pretend you felt anything for me but a mild affection because you found me amusing. I had every reason to believe those lies." Sensing his withdrawal, Joanna bit her lip.

When he spoke, Pierce's voice was tinged with a deep sadness. "Yes. I was an arrogant young fool in those days. I suppose I'll have to pay the price now. Just how long do you feel you must punish me—punish us both?—before you're satisfied? Before you do what we both know is right and agree to wed me?"

Ohh. Pierce would go too far one day and she'd turn on him like a tiger, biting and scratching and tearing at him. How could he always turn things so that she was at fault when he was so obviously in the wrong?

"Jo?"

"Don't speak to me." Her eyes flashed in the dusky light inside the coach. "You make me so furious I could scream."

"What have I done now?"

"On the one hand you say you were a fool and then you turn right around and say it was my fault. Nothing, *nothing*, was my fault, you insensitive, lying, sanctimonious, insulting—"

"More punishment?" he interrupted, his hand gentle against her mouth and his eyes smiling into hers despite the fierce way she glared.

He pulled back slowly, one finger running lightly across her lips, back the other way. Joanna fought against the sensation even such a gentle touch roused, fought the memory of how she'd felt when he'd kissed her—how much she wished she'd not come to her senses.

"I think, assuming you don't want me to lose control again, you'd better do up those buttons, Lady Jo."

His crooked smile, the one that always touched her deeply, appeared. Jo looked down and gave one low shriek of dismay. Her fingers fumbled and he brushed them away, doing the job himself.

"There. All prim and proper again." He tipped her head, forcing her to meet his eyes. "Truce?"

"I suppose so."

"Such generosity," he teased.

"Careful, Pierce," she warned, her fingers busily checking that he'd gotten all the buttons. "It'll be a very short truce if you keep on that way."

"Good. My tiger's claws have returned to kitten length. All right, Jo," he said with a laugh, "what do you propose as a safe subject on which we might converse?"

Joanna sighed. She'd had enough gossip today to last her a lifetime, but what else was safe? No, she couldn't listen to another shred of information about mutual acquaintances—even if true. What alternative was there? What had she been reading recently? Byron. "Has anything been heard of Byron since he left England?"

Pierce responded politely. Behind his deliberately solemn voice, Joanna heard a tiny echo of humor and in his eyes, carefully neutral whenever he glanced her way, she noted an ember of the same emotion. *Well,* she thought, as she listened to him expound on Shelley's *Proposal for Putting Reform to the Vote, it is funny, the two of us resorting to such trite and uninteresting but oh-so-proper conversation.*

The drizzle turned once more to a full-fledged downpour. The carriage lumbered on through the late afternoon, an afternoon darkening rapidly due to the heavy cloud cover. Inside the coach, two old friends pretended to be strangers and Joanna discovered she hated it.

Could she *never* be satisfied? It was what she wanted, wasn't it? That Pierce keep his distance, for him to refrain from tempting her beyond her capacity to resist? Oh yes, agreed that rebellious part of her mind. Certainly it's what you want. But, it went on in a whisper, you *do* wish he go on tempting you *up to that point!* Joanna pushed away the provocative yet unacceptable thought.

"Where have you been?" thundered Henry as Joanna entered the foyer.

It was so out of character, she blinked at him. "I was riding, as you know. Lad threw a shoe."

"That was hours ago. *Hours.*"

"Henry, whatever is the matter with you?"

His rage, something so rare most people thought him incapable of the emotion, evaporated as he assured himself his sister was all right. He threw her a sheepish look.

"Later. I'll tell you later," he muttered.

His eyes moved accusingly toward Cressy, who stood just inside the open doors to the salon eavesdropping without pretending otherwise.

Joanna, following his look, grimaced slightly. Ob-

141

viously the woman had been inserting naughty notions into her brother's easily manipulated thoughts. She met his eyes. Understanding passed between them and he nodded briefly. Both knew he'd have no need to explain.

"You'd best get yourself changed for dinner, Jo. We've held it back and held it back and I'm sure it must be totally ruined by now."

"Ah. Your very just anger is explained," she teased. "I'm sorry to have been the cause of ruining your dinner, Henry."

"Well, now," he blustered—then chuckled as he realized she was teasing him. "Enough, Jo. You run up and get into something decent. We'll wait a little longer."

As Belton was putting the last touches to her hair, Elizabeth tapped on the door and slipped into the room. "Aunt Jo? May I speak with you?"

"Of course. No, Belton, not the pearls. The coral set, I think, to give this gray a bit of color. And did you think to bring down the colored shawls from my trunk?" She turned from the dressing table and noticed how Elizabeth's knuckles were white where she clasped her hands together. "Why, whatever is the problem, Elizabeth?"

The girl glanced from Belton to Joanna. "I . . ."

When she didn't go on, but looked again at the maid, Joanna compressed her lips. She didn't wish to deal with her niece on top of everything else she'd been through today, but it looked as if she'd have to.

"Thank you, Belton," she said when handed a silk and worsted challis shawl. "That is all."

Elizabeth sighed when the door shut. "Oh, thank you, Aunt Jo, for sending her away."

"Now I have, do you think you could come to the

point? Your father is waiting for his dinner, you know."

"I saw you go this afternoon. With Lord Halford and His Grace . . ."

"Yes."

Elizabeth clutched her aunt's arm. "Lord Halford did stay with you, didn't he, dear Aunt Jo?"

"Why do you ask?"

"I've been so worried." Joanna, searching her niece's expressive eyes, believed her, but didn't understand. "So terribly worried."

Bewildered, Joanna's laugh trembled slightly. "But, Elizabeth, why? You know I'm an excellent horsewoman. I haven't been thrown since I was far younger than you are."

"I wasn't worried about your riding, Aunt Jo. It's *that man.*"

"Man? What man?"

"You know. The Despicable Duke. I fear . . . was afraid . . ."

"Yes?" probed Joanna reluctantly.

Elizabeth drew in a deep breath, let it out in a whoosh. "I was afraid he'd *kidnapped* you again," she said in a hushed tone.

Joanna laughed at her niece's theatrics. "Nothing half so exciting, my dear," she said. "It was anything but a romance out of one of those novels you love to read. Lad threw a shoe. Then the heavens opened and drowned us. I assure you, far from any excitement, we were miserable."

Joanna had never before deliberately lied to her niece. She had withheld information, such as the fact the girl might be brought out during the fall season, but until now she'd not lied. Pierce was always exciting. And she hadn't been particularly miserable. Al-

143

though wet, she hadn't been chilled. Although she'd ruined her boots—her favorite pair—and probably her habit—which was no loss—she wasn't concerned about them. Of course there'd been the misery of listening to Lady Keaton's interminable gossip, but that wasn't what Elizabeth had meant.

"I think we'd better join your father and his guest, Elizabeth, before he is reduced to eating his cravat."

Her teasing brought a giggle to Elizabeth's lips and a lightening of her mood. "I'm so glad you've returned safely, Aunt Jo. But please. Do watch out for the Despicable Duke. Promise me?"

Joanna sternly repressed a chuckle at the girl's nickname for Pierce. "I don't think you should call him that, Elizabeth. If I promise to watch out, you must promise to keep that phrase from your lips."

"I will. I'll remember not to call him that to anyone but you and Alicia. But you must promise, too."

"I will certainly not be taken in by the duke's blandishments, Elizabeth. I've known him, you must remember, since I was in leading strings. I am well-aware of his character. Are you satisfied?"

"I guess so," said Elizabeth haltingly.

There was something in her aunt's voice that still worried her. Despite the fact her aunt was seven years her elder, and despite the fact she'd been widowed, she often seemed to the precocious Elizabeth to retain a certain naive innocence.

"I suppose my father and Lady Cressida are waiting for us."

"I'm *certain* they are."

Joanna didn't allow her niece to suspect she hated the necessity of joining Henry and Cressy. On the other hand, sitting through a formal meal when tired and politely thwarting their guest's barbed questions

144

would be a fitting punishment for the indiscretion of riding alone with Pierce. She wondered just exactly what Cressy had said to rouse Henry's rare anger. They were starting the third course before Cressy began her inquisition, timing her first thrust just when Joanna had begun to hope she might avoid all explanations.

"You were gone a very long time, Joanna."

"Yes." Joanna continued eating as if that ended the discussion.

"Pierce must have been delighted."

"Delighted?" Joanna held her spoon steady, halfway to her mouth. She pretended surprise. "That Lad threw a shoe and he was required to ride miles in heavy rain for help? Nonsense."

"He left you alone while he went for help?" Cressy pretended outrage. "Why, anything might have happened."

"Yes. Anything. What didn't happen, Cressy, *dear*, is what you're implying." *Just as I thought,* fumed Joanna silently. "I spent two miserable hours listening to Lady Keaton go on and on about all our mutual acquaintance. I was surprised to discover that I have not one friend who has not provided the *ton* with titillating bits of scandal. Of course, I strongly suspect that where there was none, Lady Keaton is capable of cutting scandal out of whole cloth—"

"Lady Keaton?" interrupted Henry. "What the devil were you doing so far from home? Why, when the weather changed, did you not turn back?"

"Because the weather came up from behind and we didn't notice until it was too late."

"Didn't notice?" Cressy's voice was a purr hiding animosity. "How were you occupied that you didn't notice? I don't see how one could help but notice."

Yes, thought Joanna, *you really did fill poor Henry's head with salacious nonsense, did you not?* "Pierce," she said with composure, "knows how I like a good fast ride." Joanna continued reluctantly. She didn't want to explain anything at all but knew Cressy wouldn't cease her lewd suggestions until she knew it all. "He knows I rarely get it. We were moving fast and not looking back." She glanced at her brother and her eyes lit: "Henry, remember that stake fence and ditch along the Squire's long field? Lad took it right in stride. It was like flying."

"You took that jump? Pierce allowed you to take that jump?"

Henry's anger seemed to be rising again and Joanna interrupted before he could work himself up still more.

"Pooh! I led *him* at that point! Oh, Henry, it was so good to ride like that again."

Joanna hadn't revealed that episode to set Cressy's mind at rest, but her very obvious enthusiasm did more to appease the other woman's jealousy than anything else she might have done.

"Well, sister, I suppose if you enjoyed it . . ." Henry sighed and went on plaintively, "Why must I be burdened with a sister with such unladylike accomplishments? No other man must put up with such hoydenish behavior in his female relatives. Why, you might have come to grief at any point. What then, my dear?"

"Then I presume Pierce would have found a farmer and a gate and borne me home. Don't carp about it, Henry. I'm a very good rider. I won't come to grief over a hedge or a ditch."

"No, but," said their guest under her breath—but not softly enough, "you may over a rake!"

146

Elizabeth, seated across from Cressy, heard the comment. It emphasized her own fears for her aunt, and, for once, she found herself in charity with their guest.

Henry also heard. "Rake? Rake? No, no, Cressy. The farmers have long ago put away such implements." He accepted another helping of cherry sorbet from the hovering Dawson and turned the subject. "Well, well. Enough. Enough."

More than enough, thought his bedeviled sister.

"Elizabeth," he went on, "I hope you intend to entertain us with some music this evening? Hmm? Hmmm?"

At White Stones, Pierce was relieved to find Robert had not waited dinner. The duke ordered a tray to be served in the library as soon as he'd had changed. A short while later, clean and content, he joined Robert and found the earl lounging in his host's favorite chair before a cheery fire, his gaze fixed dreamily on the bright warmth.

"Made yourself right at home, have you, Robert?"

"Right at home. Couldn't be more comfortable in my own. What's more, I ordered up another bottle of that very fine burgundy your father laid down. Won't you," he asked with a mischievous smile, "have some?"

Pierce laughed at his friend's "hospitality." "I know just how good it is and will have a glass with my supper. I wish they'd hurry. I'm starved."

"It is a trifle late."

Pierce's eyes narrowed with amusement at Rob's subtle bid for an explanation. "We rode farther than we'd intended."

"Quite a bit farther." Lord Halford peered over the rim of the glass he held in both hands, his elbows comfortably settled on the arms of his chair. "Or did you find a convenient inn?"

"I may call you out for that, old friend. Joanna wouldn't."

If Rob hadn't been bored and feeling mischievous, he'd have heeded the warning in Pierce's voice and stopped teasing him. But he was, so instead of giving over, he added, "But you would."

Pierce closed his eyes, a pained expression crossing his face. He had to control himself, meet teasing with teasing. "Now Rob, how can you suggest that a proper gentleman such as myself would even think of finding a convenient inn and—"

"Because," interrupted Rob, "I've been with you when you have."

Pierce turned at Rob's tone. "But never, I think," he said, the warning stronger than before, "when with a lady."

"Define lady," promptly responded Rob, a devil pushing him to greater lengths.

Pierce studied Rob's heavy eyelids, his slack posture. "You're well on the way to becoming drunk," he accused.

"Nonsense. Not a bit of it. Or only the slightest over par. Not even half-sprung, Pierce. Well, maybe the least bit well to go," he wheedled.

"You're so castaway you'd better put your head—"

A knock preceded the opening door and Pierce closed his mouth with a snap. Robert stared dreamily into the fire while the butler moved a table for Pierce and set it. Once his meal, complete with cold meats and a bowl of soup, was laid out on a convenient table, he forgot to reprimand his friend—much too hungry to care.

"Thank you, Brownlee. That will be all for this evening."

"No, no, Brownie, old boy. Another bottle if you don't mind? *Then* that will be all."

Rob didn't say another word even when they were once more alone. The room was quiet except for small sounds: the fire popping, a tiny scrape when Pierce cut another bite from his slice of ham, the clock on the mantel tinging the half-hour. . . . Pierce relaxed, assuming Rob had ended whatever game he'd been playing.

"If you weren't at a convenient inn this afternoon, where were you?"

The sudden question breaking into what had been an almost somnolent silence made Pierce jump. A laugh erupted from him before he could find the anger Rob deserved. "That trick for surprising information out of someone is so old I wonder at your using it on me."

"It didn't work?"

Pierce grinned at his friend. "Why don't you simply ask what happened this afternoon?"

"What happened this afternoon?" asked Rob obediently.

"Lad threw a shoe in about as benighted an area as one could find in the home counties."

"You always did have the luck, Pierce," said his friend wistfully.

"If I'd any luck," admitted Pierce ruefully, "it wouldn't have poured rain not five minutes later."

"Only five minutes?"

Eight

"Five minutes is barely time for a single kiss," said Rob, sending an innocent look Pierce's way.

Pierce laughed but didn't respond to the inquiring tone. "We had to walk over a mile to Lady Keaton's where I left Joanna and rode home for a carriage. A very wet and lonely ride, Rob."

"And then?"

"Why, the carriage returned for her and took her home."

"And *you*," said Robert, "have spent the last several hours soaking your feet in a mustard bath to ward off chills! I don't believe it."

Again Pierce refrained from satisfying his friend's curiosity. "Rob, I acquit you of being out-of-sight drunk, so what's the matter?"

"Boredom, old boy. Nothing but boredom. Life is becoming a complete waste. Perhaps we should plan a trip." He stared into the fire, fondling his empty glass. "Egypt, maybe. Or the Balkans, following old Byron's footsteps. If that don't appeal, we could see the Levant. Sound good, Pierce?" he asked.

"No, it does not. I'll not be leaving England until

150

I can go with Joanna as my wife. And you won't be invited to join us on *that* journey!"

Rob scowled. "You, too, become a bore, Pierce. Never thought I'd think that, but you are as obsessed with her as you were five years ago."

"I never stopped being obsessed. However, when she married her redcoat there was nothing I could do."

"Been a widow for two years and you've done nothing."

"Not two years. Only a year and a half."

Rob let his sleepy-lidded gaze rest on his friend. "Not like you to procrastinate about a thing."

Slightly flustered by the look, Pierce continued. "I explained that last time we talked about this, didn't I? I expected," he went on, "to see her last spring during the season. I thought of coming down here when she didn't arrive in Town but my plan demanded she be surrounded by others where she wouldn't feel threatened." He paused. "In any case, I've waited. I wonder. Have I waited so long it has given her the wrong impression?"

"Wondered when you'd see that."

"Rob, what am I to do? She loves me. I'm sure she does. But she don't trust me. She won't believe me."

Pierce reached for the burgundy and a glass and poured, passing the bottle on to his friend. Rob took it, and once he'd poured for himself, set it beside the chair.

Pierce paced, returning to stop beside his friend. "I'm fast running out of patience now that I've seen her again, talked to her, kis—"

He glanced at his friend but Rob seemed totally preoccupied, his eyes fixed on the fire, a little dreamy, a little bit up in the world, perhaps.

"Well," Pierce finished, "I'm out of patience."

Rob waved one finger admonishingly. "Have to kidnap her again, I expect." Having said that he sent a surprisingly sober look toward Pierce to see how he took it.

"Try the same trick twice?" This time Pierce was staring into the fire, a frown creasing his brow. "I can't resort to that sort of thing a second time. She'd hate me all over again."

"Just an idea."

The duke studied his friend and concluded wrongly, "You are drunk as a lord."

"Am a lord."

"If you think that justifies dipping deep, think again." Pierce stared at Robert, a half-rueful, half-irritated expression on his face.

"Don't be cross, Pierce," said Robert, meeting his friend's gaze, his own warmly coaxing. "I'll come out of the sullens tomorrow. Just a little lonely and depressed tonight." As an afterthought he added, "And I'm not drunk."

Pierce forced his thoughts to veer from his uncooperative love to his bedeviled friend. "So how about a hand of cards? Or chess?"

"With my head working at half pace you think I'm stupid enough to engage in a game with you?" Robert shook his head carefully. "As I said, I haven't had *that* much to drink, my boy."

Pierce, giving up, said good night. On his way to the door, he once again missed the alert knowing look in Robert's expression.

"I will ask one of the footmen," said Pierce, "to look in on you later. He can help you to bed. I am retiring before I catch your illness."

"Not ill. Told you. Just bored."

"Isn't that a form of illness?" asked Pierce lightly. He got no answer. "Good night, Rob."

Joanna, feeling hunted, looked from her stubborn brother to her hopeful niece. Blister Lady Bradford anyway. "I am not officially out of mourning. Elizabeth is not yet out. It would not be proper." The unending argument was driving her crazy.

"Lady Bradford very kindly sent a special invitation, Joanna. Your birthday party must be considered the end of your mourning period." Henry mopped his brow. To him, also, the argument seemed interminable but he'd made up his mind, had sent their acceptance and he would not now be shamed by his sister. She would go to the ball if he had to dress her himself. Knowing how stubborn his sister could be he was a trifle worried it might actually come to that!

"Aunt Jo . . ."

Elizabeth's voice had a breathy note, a diffidence quite unusual in the girl. Joanna noted the restraint, wondered at it. "Yes, Elizabeth?"

"Alicia Staunton went to the Bradford Hunt Ball before her come-out. She said her mother thought she'd be more comfortable once they were in London if she'd had some experience of a formal ball, that here, where she knew so many people, she'd be more relaxed and that—"

Joanna interrupted her. "That is the first argument which holds the least bit of sense. But . . ."

She put a hand to her head, walked toward the window, and turned to face her puzzled brother and trembling niece. She looked from one to the other and sighed. Could she do it? Chaperon her niece properly? No. She couldn't. She wasn't ready. She'd had so little experience. She didn't know enough!

"Elizabeth, will you please leave us? There is something I must discuss with your father." Elizabeth hesitated. "Please?"

Wide-eyed, the girl stared at her aunt. For once she was being treated like an adult. It was a request, not an order. Biting her lip, wanting desperately to stay and hear what Joanna had to say, wanting to fight for the right to attend the Bradford Ball, still, she felt she had to give in. She nodded finally and walked reluctantly to the door. With her hand on the doorknob, she turned, staring at her father, her big eyes pleading. He nodded, made pushing motions with his hands. She left.

Before Joanna could speak, Henry took on a pompous stance. "I will have no more arguments. I want to hear no more excuses. It is settled," he said in a tone she knew was one part determination and six parts bull-headed stubbornness. "We *will* go to the ball. I have said so."

Joanna was beaten and knew it. "All right Henry. We'll go to the ball."

No longer wanting to explain her state of mind to Henry, she left the library, going straight to her room. There she donned the ruined habit she'd insisted Belton leave for her until something better could be contrived. Soon she was riding wildly across the long meadow, Lad's legs stretching into the easy loping stride that had carried his master to safety more than once when in the Peninsula. But today Joanna was not thinking of Reggie. Her thoughts were on the future. How had she gotten into such a ridiculous position?

Behind her she heard Pierce's tallyho. Instead of

slowing, she dug her heel into Lad's side, urging him to even greater effort. Slowly Apollo gained on Lad. Joanna turned her head when, out of the corner of her eye, she caught sight of the beautiful animal. She grinned at Pierce and he smiled back. Soon they were racing side by side.

Finally after crossing several fields, they slowed, walking on to let the hot horses cool. A trickling stream appeared and they stopped, dismounted, and let the animals drink. Joanna looked across Lad's neck at Pierce. It had been so good to race like that. Only one other man had understood her need to ride like the wind, and he more from heedlessness and the assumption that everyone wanted that sort of danger in their lives than any deeper motive. Reggie had had no true understanding but Pierce did.

"Thank you."

He nodded. "What were you running from this time, Jo?"

This was understanding indeed. How had he known? She bit her lip.

"Tell me?" he coaxed.

Again she hesitated. Then, needing someone to whom she could express her fears, she decided to try. "I don't even know where to begin."

"Has Henry upset you?" His hands tightened on Apollo's reins. "Or that woman?"

"Cressy?" Joanna laughed, feeling another increment of tension drain away. "No. Not Cressy. I suppose in a way, it is Henry. My idiotic brother accepted an invitation from Lady Bradford, a more inclusive one for the three of us."

"Quite proper of her. Although, with that plain daughter of hers, I'm surprised."

"Why?"

"She can't want Elizabeth there in competition with Lady Anne."

"Pierce, that's not nice." She tried to repress a smile. "Although, if the truth be known, I suspect the invitation was Lady Anne's idea and that Lady Bradford gave in to her generous daughter's demand on the assumption we'd turn it down." She sighed. "I hold no brief for Lady Bradford, but Lady Anne is another matter entirely. She is a wonderful young woman with an exquisite dry wit and more kindness than anyone else I know. If men weren't always so blind to true worth, she'd have been married long ago. But that is not to the point. We are, if you please, attending the ball. And I don't want to."

Pierce's gaze sharpened. "Why?" Was she still mourning that young cub of a husband of hers? Would she never lay that marriage to rest?

"I'm afraid."

A choke of laughter at the unexpected response was instantly stilled. *"Afraid?* You?" His disbelief was obvious.

"I said it was silly." Joanna allowed Lad's reins to drop, walking away. "I am no proper chaperon for Elizabeth, Pierce. I feel a complete fool. Why, when I've been begging for Henry's permission to bring Elizabeth out this fall," she whirled to face him, letting the truth out in a rush, "should I now feel so totally inadequate? Who am I to guide a high-spirited girl through the dangers of a season? I feel shattered by the thought of the responsibility. I don't see how I can do it."

"Of course you can do it."

A scornful look scorched him. "Little do you know about it." Her shoulders rose and fell with a deep breath and her worried look returned. "And that's the problem. I know far too little myself. I had barely half a season and that years ago."

"Don't be missish, Jo. You are an intelligent woman. What is the worst that can happen? That she be courted by fortune hunters on the lookout for a rich bride? You are qualified to determine which of Elizabeth's suitors are out to feather their nests. And if you are not certain, you will ask either Henry or myself. For the rest, you are a lady and you know how to behave. You will guide her quite capably."

"If only I could believe it."

"Believe it, Jo. If you need help, you'll have it. You know I will do anything I can for you."

Her gaze sharpened. "Will you? Why?"

"Because I don't want my future wife falling into the briars, of course." He grinned at her, but she didn't smile back. "Oh, Jo, how much longer am I going to have to wait?"

"Likely forever, Pierce." He shook his head. "Oh, I don't know. I wish . . ."

"What do you wish Jo?"

"I wish I weren't so confused. I wish I weren't so worried about Elizabeth. I wish . . ."

"Yes?"

Joanna realized she didn't wish for Reggie. It was the second time the thought had been acknowledged, but it was something of a shock nevertheless, and a vague feeling of guilt filled her. She told herself she was silly to feel that way and, with a little effort, washed it out of her system for the last time. She'd been a good wife to Reggie, but Reggie was dead. She was alive. And Pierce made her feel more alive than she'd ever felt before. If only she were the sort to indulge in affairs. Perhaps if she were, she could get over the hold he had on her. But she wasn't. She sighed.

"Joanna?"

"Pierce, please don't pressure me. I simply can't deal with you and Elizabeth, too."

"I don't believe I can leave you alone, love."

"You said you'd do anything."

He grinned. "Anything to help you. Leaving you alone wouldn't be a help."

"A help to whom?"

"Joanna, I will court you as you should be courted. But that is all I can promise."

She sighed, wishing she could tell him to go away and mean it. Because she couldn't, because she didn't really want him to leave her alone, she nodded. "Just so you behave."

"Behave?" He strolled nearer and she backed up. "Is this what you mean by behaving?" He reached for her.

"It is not."

"I'd better make absolutely certain I understand. Just so I'm sure what it is I'm not to do." His hands rubbed up and down her arms. She trembled. "This is misbehaving?" Again she nodded, biting her lip. "And this?" he asked softly as his head bent, his lips brushing hers. He looked at her before lifting her arms and placing them on his shoulders. Then he gathered her close. "Just a test, you know," he whispered and kissed her deeply.

Some minutes later Joanna found herself released. She fought to regain her poise. Blinking rapidly, she forced herself to face him and speak sternly. "Yes. That is exactly what I mean by misbehaving. Now you know and you won't do it again, correct?"

He grinned unrepentantly. "I won't promise."

Joanna stalked over to Lad and caught up his reins. Immediately Pierce was there to hand her into her saddle. She looked down at him, shaking her head. "You, Pierce Reston, have been spoiled rotten. You are impossible."

"And you are the most stubborn woman I've ever known."

A thoughtful look crossed Joanna's face. "You know, Pierce, I wonder if I'm not the only woman you've ever known."

He laughed ruefully. "Do you realize what you just said?"

Her lips tightened. "I meant what I said. The other women in your life have been there only superficially. You have not wanted to understand them, wanted to know their thoughts or their feelings."

Pierce flushed. He hadn't blushed in years. It occurred to him that to have Joanna thinking of the women who had shared his bed off and on over the years—although far less often than the gossips would have believed—was not a direction in which he wished her thoughts to go.

"You are right, Jo," he finally responded in a quiet, serious voice. "Be logical, Jo, if you can." Jo's eyebrow rose, a silent question. "The only woman I wish to know that way is the one I'll wed."

This time Joanna blushed. She swung Lad around and was gone before he could reach Apollo and rise into his saddle. Mounted, he decided not to follow. He set his stallion into an easy canter and headed for home thinking over the conversation that had passed between them. He felt he'd erred again and wondered if the path of true love ever ran smoothly for anyone. His path had been long and rocky and he could see no end of barriers yet ahead. But he'd persist. He laughed softly and Apollo twitched back his ears. "She loves me," he informed the ears that were sensitive to the tone of his voice if not the meaning. "I'll win her yet.

Belton finished a new and somewhat more elaborate hairdo for the ball, then held her breath. Joanna checked her image in the mirror. "Thank you, Belton. It's very nice. You've outdone yourself."

"Too bad you haven't had time to acquire more gowns," said her maid, regret in her tone.

"Yes, but I haven't so I won't repine."

Well, not much, Joanna added silently as the new rose gown was thrown over her head. Once it was fastened and she'd added a strand of well-matched pearls, she took one more look at herself and nodded.

"I'll do. Now I must see to Elizabeth."

Joanna searched her small jewel box and, finding what she wanted, left Belton straightening her room. She walked down the hall, irritated she wasn't at the forefront of fashion, but her new gown *would* do for a lady of advanced years who had dwindled into a chaperon, or so she lectured herself. Elizabeth's appearance at her first formal ball was far more important than the emergence of still another widow. It was necessary her charge make the best possible impression. If only Elizabeth hadn't taken things into her own hands. . . .

Joanna knocked at the closed door and entered when she heard Elizabeth's cross voice asking who was there. Her eyes flicked around the room, checking the disarray. Elizabeth, she thought, had tried on

160

each of her three newest gowns before deciding on the one Joanna had suggested as most suitable.

"That dress looks lovely, Elizabeth. Why are you frowning?"

"My *hair*," wailed the girl.

Joanna, biting her lip, refrained from laughing at the long curls half up and half down. She dismissed her niece's harassed maid and reached for the brush.

"Can you do anything with it, Aunt Jo?"

"I believe we can achieve something you'll like."

She swept the lush locks up and formed an unexceptionable Grecian knot. Glancing into the mirror, she watched Elizabeth's eyes widen, and smiled at the approving look.

"Now, where are those flowers I asked be delivered to you?"

Joanna found them eventually, amongst a pile of sheer scarves and a tangle of beads. Having retrieved them, she approached her niece who still sat before her mirror.

"It is quite proper to wear them in your hair, you know."

"I thought I was to carry them. And I didn't know what one does with them when dancing. Oh, Aunt Jo, I will be allowed to dance, won't I?" Joanna couldn't help liking this version of her usually willful niece. "And . . . and I *will* be asked, won't I?"

"Calm down, Elizabeth. Of course you will. All your friends will be there and I can't see the young men allowing you to be a wallflower when they know how graceful you are on the dance floor. Alicia's brother, Albert, for one, will ask you." She thought of the small informal country gatherings they'd attended and how Elizabeth had been the belle of the impromptu dances. "Simply remember you aren't,

161

under any circumstances, to waltz. Since you know that, you'll do very well I'm sure."

Elizabeth giggled. "Nor will I allow some young buck to guide me out into the garden or into an empty room. Nor will I laugh too loudly. Nor will I forget my partners are to return me to your side or to my father—"

"Or," interrupted Joanna, "contravene any other of the many rules your governess has pounded into your head. At least she seems to have succeeded in teaching you social niceties if she didn't manage much of anything else."

"Yes, but I knew I'd need them," her niece explained with unexpected candor and no sign of contrition. "I still don't see the use in studying the globes or about those old kings and things like that," she went on. "They are so dull."

Joanna fixed the flowers into Elizabeth's coiffure. "That will do, I think. Now, one more thing." She reached for the reticule she'd laid aside and pulled out a string of pearls. "My Aunt Henrietta gave me these at my come-out. Since I have the longer string Henry gave me before my wedding, I'd like you to have these. They are perfect for a young girl."

"Oh Aunt Jo!" Elizabeth's eyes gleamed as she put out one finger and touched the pale pink sheen of the pearls. "Ohhhh." She stood up and hugged her aunt before waltzing around the room, turning back to add, "Thank you very, very much."

"You're welcome, my dear."

Joanna, although she didn't say it, was rather touched by Elizabeth's enthusiasm. She should have known better, she thought a moment later as she listened to Elizabeth's guileless confession.

162

"I was afraid I'd be the only girl there wearing a string of beads. It was such a lowering thought."

Joanna stifled a laugh and suggested they go down to the drawing room. "Your father ordered dinner a little early since we've the carriage ride and don't wish to be the last to arrive."

"But not the *first*, I hope," Elizabeth objected, justly horrified by the notion.

"No, certainly not the first," Joanna pretended equal horror, but went on to tease, "unless everyone has decided to arrive an hour late, of course."

Elizabeth gasped. "Surely that couldn't happen . . ."

"I'm quite sure it won't."

Joanna's eyes widened as she stopped on the top step. Dawson had just opened the door to Pierce and Lord Halford. He was taking their capes, hats, and canes, and passing them on to the footman. "If you'll follow me, Your Grace, m'lord . . ."

Pierce ignored him. He walked, instead, to the foot of the stairs. Slowly Joanna floated down toward him. He raised a hand and she put hers into it, blushing slightly as he gently squeezed her fingers, his eyes telling her he found her beautiful. She'd forgotten, she thought, how handsome he was in formal evening dress. The dark coat fit perfectly and the old-fashioned knee breeches above tight white stockings—still common on formal occasions—allowed the strength and perfection of his limbs to show. The white vest faithfully followed the lines of his well-muscled chest and formed a frame below the perfection of his cravat.

"Lady Joanna, Lady Elizabeth." Lord Halford bowed.

Joanna forced herself to remember the proprieties

and forget the unwelcome thoughts that suddenly filled her mind. She simply mustn't lose her head over Pierce. Besides, her duty was to Elizabeth that evening and nothing must interfere with that.

Elizabeth hid her irritation at the unexpected guests. Her father made no secret that he enjoyed the company of the men. Of course he'd have invited them to dine and travel to the ball with them. She should have foreseen it, she thought as she led the way into the parlor where her father was enjoying a glass of wine. She smiled, gratified, when he poured a few sips into a glass for herself when he served the rest of the party.

"Where is my sister?" asked Robert.

"Late," said Henry with no sign of rancor. "You've known Cressy all her life, Halford. Have you ever known her on time for anything?"

Robert chuckled. "Come to think on it, no. Ready for your first ball, Lady Elizabeth?"

Robert had watched the chit since their arrival and concluded Pierce had a serious problem. His question startled the girl from her frowning preoccupation with the Dreadful Duke and her eyes widened.

"You have certainly made yourself lovely for it," he continued.

Elizabeth's eyes widened even more.

"Well, girl?" Henry nudged his daughter. "Can't you thank Lord Halford for a very pretty compliment?"

"Oh. Yes. To be sure. Thank you, m'lord." Her blush of confusion brought laughter to everyone's lips.

"Halford's quite correct, Elizabeth. You'll outshine everyone but Lady Jo," added Pierce teasingly.

The duke's qualified compliment reminded Elizabeth of his despicable intentions toward her aunt and her reply was more restrained, inadvertently more mature.

"That's the way, brat. Cool and just a little distant. You'll take London by storm." Pierce chucked Elizabeth under the chin, which made her fume. He followed Joanna, who seated herself near the fireplace. "The chit is determined to dislike me," he said in a low tone.

"I don't believe she's forgiven you for the things you said the day she was thrown."

"I think," he said, turning and noticing the glare Elizabeth sent his way, "there is more to it than that, but I don't understand why. Surely she can't be jealous of my love for you."

"Please. None of that tonight." With effort Joanna met his eyes, kept her own stern. "I beg you."

"I fully intend that no one mistake my feelings for you."

His serious expression convinced her he meant what he said, and Joanna felt that all too giddy sensation once again. It wouldn't do. Firmly she put aside all thoughts of a flirtation with Pierce and turned the stern look on him.

"Don't, *please* don't put me to the blush tonight. I'll have my hands full merely seeing Elizabeth does nothing foolish. I haven't time to deal with your machinations, too."

"First Elizabeth and now you are cross. I seem to have lost my ability to charm."

Joanna laughed at his pretended concern. "I'm sure you'll have no trouble charming any lady you wish this evening."

"You?" She shook her head, lowering her eyes to where she clasped her reticule tightly. Pierce went on

165

more brusquely, "Will you really be upset if I show my interest tonight?"

"Any night." Joanna's voice was half-choked.

"At this ball, but this one only, I promise to behave."

He looked around as the door opened and Cressy entered. Pierce had time for no more because immediately Dawson announced dinner and they moved to the dining room—where he teased Jo at every turn about every topic raised. She gave him a reproachful look.

He didn't behave in the carriage either. There was room for the six of them, barely, in Henry's well-sprung traveling coach. Pierce had maneuvered the seating so Joanna was crowded between himself and Elizabeth, their backs to the horses. Seated in the middle, there was nothing to hang on to and, when the coach swayed, Joanna found herself pressed against him again and again. She didn't like the way it increased her awareness of him, and, as they went around another curve, she glowered.

"What's the matter, Jo?" His low voice, covered by the conversation going on around them, wasn't so soft she didn't hear the humor in it.

"You know very well what the matter is."

"And you know how to take care of that problem, my dear," he whispered into her ear, his tongue flicking into it with the last word.

Joanna gasped. "You promised . . ."

"We haven't yet arrived. In the meantime I intend to enjoy every moment of this, er, unexpected intimacy."

"Ohhh . . ." Joanna gave thanks the moon was hidden by a haze of clouds and the coach dark enough to hide her blush.

166

Elizabeth, unable to hear the exchange but knowing something was going on, demanded Joanna's attention. "Tell me again what I'm to do. Please, Aunt Jo."

"If you aren't sure how to behave, you shouldn't be going," inserted Cressy, her voice irritable because Henry, whom she'd about decided might do as a husband, had just lifted her palm from his thigh and set her hand back in her lap under cover of her cloak.

"I do. I just wish to be sure I make no dreadful error. Please, Aunt Jo?"

Glad of distraction, Joanna repeated what had already been told her niece twice. "There will be a reception line. You will make your curtsy to Lord and Lady Bradford and their daughter—"

"Poor Lady Anne," interrupted Elizabeth, who had asked the question merely to interfere with the duke's attentions to her aunt "This will be her third season, won't it?" she asked, but not unkindly. She was never unkind to girls who couldn't compete with her beauty, and Anne, with not a jealous bone in her body, had long shown her admiration for the more beautiful younger girl. Her mother, however, had never been so generous and the thought made Elizabeth cringe inwardly. "Will Lady Bradford introduce me to people?"

"Not if she can avoid it." Cressy laughed harshly.

Her fear intensified and Elizabeth reached for her aunt's hand.

Lord Halford said, "If she forgets herself to the point of being rude, Lady Elizabeth, I assure you there are others who will be able to take her place. Young men clamoring for introductions are quite adept at finding someone who will present them to the lady of their choice."

Elizabeth relaxed at his words but stiffened at Cressy's next comment. "Oh yes. The fortune hunters will be after you in force. You must watch her closely, Joanna. After all, our naive little Elizabeth will be quite a catch."

"We'll all watch," stated Henry, closing the conversation by asking Pierce if he'd enjoyed the hunt that morning.

The men took over, reliving every jump and run until the final denouement when the fox had been cornered. Joanna fumed. How she would have loved it. Except the finish, of course. She pitied the fox. She wondered, not for the first time, why her brother must be so old-fashioned when their father had been so different.

"Why weren't you at the meet, Jo?" asked Pierce, reading her mind.

"You know my feelings," Henry answered for her, "about women and hunting."

"But what are Joanna's feelings?" persisted Pierce.

"I would, as you know, have enjoyed the ride."

Joanna spoke repressively. She was still angry at her brother's adamant refusal to allow her to go. His attitude was a grievance that went back many years, but she'd thought herself old enough now that he'd have felt relieved of the responsibility of making the choice for her.

"You'd have been too tired for the ball this evening," soothed Henry, voicing a fallacy he persisted in believing.

"You think me such a poor puss, Henry?"

Pierce laughed. He touched her hand and she turned to him. "When we are married," he whispered, "I'll expect you to ride with me, shoulder to shoulder. We will take each jump together."

It was almost enough to make Joanna willing to accept him right then and there.

"You will, won't you?" he persisted.

"If I were in a position to do so, I expect I would."

"What *are* you two whispering about?" inquired the petulant Cressy. Henry had, this time, pinched her fingers sharply before pushing her hand away from him. Just when she had given up on the Duke of Stornway and turned her attentions to Henry Ransome, the lazy earl was proving most difficult to seduce. What if he weren't so easily caught as she'd believed? This might take some plotting. Surely Henry would not be difficult to trap. *Rich,* easygoing, Henry . . .

Elizabeth had once again asked a question, and ignoring Cressy's cross demand to know what was being said between herself and Pierce, Joanna soothed her niece. She was very glad when they turned in behind another carriage and followed it up the long drive to Bradford Hall. Her patience, which she'd once believed one of the strongest of her character traits, was about at an end. Nevertheless, as the coach slowly followed others setting guests down at the door, she felt an unexpected lift of excitement.

A ball. How long had it been since she'd last attended a ball? The unexpected elation faded as memory returned. Brussels. The Duchess of Richmond's ball, which had been interrupted by impending battle. She recalled the hasty parting from Reggie, his excitement tempered by the knowledge that the coming battle would be the hardest fought of his career. Letting him go with a smile on her face had been nearly impossible. Joanna, too, had understood this first meeting between Wellington and Napoleon would be bitter to the very end.

169

"Forget it, Jo," said Pierce quietly, squeezing her hand as the others stepped out of the coach. "If he were half the man you think, he'd expect you to enjoy yourself, not beat yourself that you're alive and he is dead."

Her head rose and she glared at him. "Reggie would be the first to agree with you."

"Then heed his wishes. Put him behind you."

"I fully intend to. If you weren't so insensitive, you would understand I needed a moment's reflection, a moment to honor his memory."

"I do understand." Judging by the tone of his voice, Joanna believed him. "But you've had far too many moments, my girl. It is fully time you returned to the life to which you were bred."

Her momentary belief ended in irritation. "I know that, too." She discovered he still held her hand when he squeezed it again. He didn't let it go when she tugged. She was glad of an excuse to leave it in his possession but couldn't allow him to realize it. "I had already made that decision."

"If you know and have come to your senses," he asked in a lighter tone, "why are we arguing?"

Jo grimaced. "I don't know. Except we seem to do a lot of that." She finally managed to regain her hand. "Now remember your promise. Please?"

"I will. I never forget a promise. But I demand at least one waltz, my love. And I'll ask for two. There is nothing out of the way in your dancing twice with me."

"One."

"The supper dance," he bargained.

"I should—"

"We will. In order to have the favor of your company, we will join your abominable niece and whomever partners her."

"Well . . ."

Waltz with Pierce? What a joy that would be and not just because it was Pierce, although that was a factor: for some reason their steps had always matched perfectly although he wasn't the best waltzer she'd ever known.

"Well?"

"If you are willing to put up with Elizabeth, I suppose you may have the supper dance."

"Good." He stepped out of the carriage and, forestalling the footman, helped Joanna down. She put her fingers daintily on his arm and they joined the rest of their party in the front hall. Cressy, she noted, was looking sour and unhappy.

Cressy's temper was exasperated almost beyond control when she discovered Henry had his daughter in tow, that Pierce was partnering Joanna, and that she was left to make do with her brother as they started up the broad steps to the receiving line.

Facing straight ahead, her brother whispered sternly, "Remember those debts."

Cressy fumed. The world was not treating her well. She couldn't understand it.

The party went on to the ballroom and Elizabeth gasped, clutching her father's arm. "Ohhh."

"Here, here, puss. Careful there or you'll crease me coat!"

"Isn't it beautiful?"

Joanna, remembering ballrooms swathed in pink silk or turned into veritable fairyland gardens, looked around the room. The chandeliers sparkled, their light reflecting from the mirrors hung between each of the tall windows. More candles glowed from wall

171

sconces, adding to the brilliance. A dais, where four musicians played, was almost hidden behind potted palms, ferns, and large bouquets, but that was all the decorating Lady Bradford had done. Joanna, much to her surprise, found she liked it better than the often fussy and overdone decors of her memory.

As they moved around the side of the room, Elizabeth watched the dancers with a mixture of excitement and envy. As they strolled, nodding to acquaintances and stopping to exchange commonplace remarks with friends, the set ended. Joanna sensed Elizabeth's excitement, heard the girl's breath quicken as two young men, brothers of her friends, made their way toward the small party. Elizabeth touched Joanna's arm, her fingers trembling, and Joanna smiled at her.

Henry surprised them all, however, when he insisted he have the first dance with his daughter. For a moment Elizabeth looked daggers at him, but Joanna, pinching her lightly, reminded her where she was and she smiled. The girl's dance card filled nicely, and when Joanna checked it a bit later, she discovered Lord Halford had put his name down for the supper dance. Because it would almost certainly be a waltz, she looked from the card to the man. He smiled, shaking his head slightly, his expression soothing her fears that he would forget Elizabeth's age and break convention by actually dancing with the girl.

Preoccupied with Elizabeth, Joanna was surprised when she noticed she'd absentmindedly promised dance after dance. That would teach her to pay attention, she thought, stifling a laugh as she went with her first partner to join the set just beyond the one Henry and his daughter were in. She looked back

172

just as the music began and discovered Cressy, her face closed in and proud, staring blankly at nothing at all. A moment's pity stirred in Joanna's breast, but when she saw Cressy turn toward Pierce and almost drag him onto the floor the pity changed unaccountably to a deep and hurtful jealousy. It was well-known Pierce never danced the country dances. That he would do so with Cressy made it worse. And the fact he'd had no choice, unless he wished to make a scene, didn't alter Joanna's admittedly irrational feelings one whit.

Nine

Joanna relaxed as the evening progressed. Elizabeth was behaving beautifully. Henry and Cressy had disappeared into the cardroom. Lord Halford and Pierce, however, had taken up a position near where Joanna stationed herself. In the role of chaperon, Joanna danced only if Elizabeth already had a partner, and, because Elizabeth danced almost every set, Joanna danced many more than she'd expected to do.

Lady Bradford, sensitive to both the conservatism of the local guests and the sophisticated tastes of those more *ton*ish, had allowed only a few of the controversial waltzes. Joanna sat beside Elizabeth during the first, having refused two gentlemen who'd asked for it.

"Why did they make that stupid rule a green girl mustn't waltz?" asked Elizabeth, her foot tapping in time to the music. "It is by far the nicest kind of dancing, Aunt Jo."

"You must have overheard older ladies discussing the waltz."

Elizabeth giggled. "Oh yes." Her pert nose pointed upward, she mimicked one of the more straitlaced of the local squiredom. "So *fast*. Quite scandalous. An excuse for *embracing in public*." She sniffed haughtily—then spoiled it by giggling, her dimples showing briefly. "I've heard it all. But I don't know why they feel that way."

"You do understand, Elizabeth," said Joanna repressively. "Remember how embarrassed you were when you were taught to waltz?"

"But that was because I was sure I'd never learn the steps, Aunt Jo."

"Was it?" Joanna persisted. Elizabeth blushed and hung her head. "Just so. You know very well why you felt that way." Joanna tapped her niece lightly with her fan. "Now hush, Elizabeth. Lady Keaton is coming this way."

Joanna's nerves stretched taut as the strings of the violin a young musician on the dais played with abandon. She wished she'd warned Elizabeth to say nothing about her disastrous ride with Pierce and feared the chit would give her away if Lady Keaton referred to it. Pierce must have read her mind, she decided. His Grace and Lord Halford joined them, found a chair for Lady Keaton, offered to fetch lemonade, and, in general, behaved in such a way it was impossible for the old gossip to insert more than commonplace statements into the conversation.

The waltz ended, and relieved by the addition of several young men to the group surrounding them, Joanna allowed herself to relax again. She felt even better when Alicia's brother led Elizabeth onto the floor—quite ready to fend off any of the questions Lady Keaton was organizing at that moment, obviously deciding between the fascinating question of the duke's renewed interest in Joanna and the unknown young man who might also be a suitor.

"I believe this is our dance, Joanna," said Pierce mendaciously.

"I thought—"

"I'm sure I'm not mistaken. Hurry or we'll not have a place."

Joanna, unable to decline without making a scene, excused herself to Lady Keaton and walked onto the floor. "I'm sure you said the supper dance."

"I did. I also said I'd beg another from you as well."

"But you are known to never dance country dances. Tonight you'll be dancing two."

"Perhaps more. I could wring Cressy's neck."

"Ah. You mean you must make it look unexceptionable that you danced with her." Joanna nodded briskly. "I understand."

"That I was forced to dance with her." Joanna knew it was true but didn't allow her features to relax. "You appear to understand nothing, my love," he whispered so only she could hear. "If you did, I could ask Lord Bradford to announce our engagement."

"Pierce, you promised . . ."

Beginning to believe he was serious, but confused by her suspicions and troubled by her rebellious emotions, Joanna was thankful that the forms of country dance made it impossible to continue the conversation. Her emotions congealed into anger, however, as she realized the supper dance followed. Pierce had promised he'd not make her conspicuous, but he was doing just that: dancing two straight sets with him would have every tongue in the room wagging. . . . She glared at him and he pinched her fingers lightly.

"You'll only add fuel to the fire, Joanna, if you

persist." She knew it was true and bit her lip. He went on softly. "I apologize. I didn't realize we'd progressed so far into the evening and only thought to get you away from Lady Keaton."

Probably it was the truth, but given Pierce's reputation, the resulting talk would not give him the benefit of the doubt. She watched Elizabeth approach and a bitter feeling welled. It wasn't her niece whose behavior would have the gossips smothering smug smiles. It would be herself.

Well-aware of Joanna's simmering temper, Pierce spoke coaxingly, trying to undo his error. "Elizabeth must sit this one out. Why don't we join her and Robert and, as soon as possible, sneak out to the dining room?"

Wondering if she were simply contrary by nature, Joanna, when given the choice, immediately decided to dance. Pierce smothered a grin, and once they knew Elizabeth was happily settled with a few friends, Pierce led her back onto the floor. Lord Halford was left playing rueful chaperon to three young girls and two equally young men.

Her laugh brittle, Cressy rose from the table. "Well, gentlemen, I believe that hand quite ruined me for the evening." There were teasing remarks, a few of them slightly off color, but she ignored them. "Frederick, your luck appears to be as out as mine. Will you join me in returning to the ballroom?"

The tall man to whom she spoke leaned back in his chair, his heavy-lidded eyes narrowing, the expression in the black depths totally hidden behind ridiculously long and thick lashes. The white prematurely dusting the temples of his coal black hair added a cachet to a face and form already distinguished. "Asking me to dance, Cress?"

"I'd enjoy it. You waltz better than almost any gentleman I know," she returned, forcing a smile.

"*Almost* any?" Sir Frederick Carrington slapped his cards flat on the table. "You put me on my mettle. Gentlemen? You'll excuse me?"

"I'm surprised you're here, Frederick," said Cressy as they left the room.

"I've not been ostracized from polite society, Cress—which has become a distinct possibility for you, or so I hear?"

"I should," said Cressy, forcing a nonchalance she didn't feel, "have remembered you are not a gentleman. If you'll excuse me, I think I'll have a few words with my brother."

"No dance?"

Cressy smiled sweetly. "No dance. I thought I'd refuse it before you had the chance to refuse me!"

Sir Frederick chuckled. "The one thing which makes you tolerable, Cressy, is the fact you're reasonably intelligent."

"How strange. I hate to admit it, but we must be two of a kind. I find your wits the only thing about *you* to admire."

Frederick watched her join her brother, draw him a little away from the small group of young people with whom he'd been talking. He wondered if he knew any of Rob's friends and lazily looked them over—and drew in a sharp breath. What a beauty! Who, he wondered, was she? He worked his way closer and chuckled softly as he overheard a bit of the conversation between Cress and her brother.

"Lost again, have you?" he asked.

"Yes. But I didn't write any IOUs."

"Only because you knew I'd refuse to pay them." The argument grew quietly heated.

Sir Frederick approached Elizabeth and, gaining her attention, subtly maneuvered her away from the others. "The most beautiful young woman in the room," he growled playfully when certain he'd not be overheard.

Elizabeth felt her cheeks pinken. She didn't know this man and something about him both excited and frightened her. She glanced to where Lord Halford was gesturing in tightly restrained movements, his back to her. She wished he'd notice her difficulty and come to her rescue. But he was deep in argument and didn't turn around.

"Might one ask why such a lovely young woman languishes on the sidelines while much less attractive girls whirl joyfully around the floor?"

"I think you know the reason quite well, sir."

"I suspect I do. It's an unfair world, isn't it?"

Elizabeth, not immune to his charm, smiled, a dimple peeping in one cheek. Again Sir Frederick's breath caught at her loveliness. The newest beauty was an unflawed diamond.

"Tell me you wouldn't prefer to be out there waltzing with the others," he challenged.

"I would and I wouldn't, sir."

"A riddle! I can understand why you would. Now tell me why you would not."

Elizabeth, a faint frown not marring her looks at all, gestured to a passing couple. "There's the explanation."

Carrington glanced at them, groped for his quizzing glass, and eyed the pair. "Ah, but not all gentlemen are such boors, my child. Not all ignore the

179

obvious distress of their partners as Herman is doing. He lacks finesse."

"You know Squire Herman, sir?"

"One knows nearly everyone when one has been in the world as long as I. I do not, however, know the lady he holds so tightly." He tried to catch Elizabeth's eyes, but she continued to watch the dancing. Who was this delightful chit? No matter. He could discover her identity easily enough.

"Matilda Storling," Elizabeth responded when he'd almost forgotten the implied question he'd asked to keep her talking, "a particular friend of mine. She and my best friend's brother are in lo—Oh, no!"

"What's the matter, my dear."

"That awful man . . ."

Elizabeth, forgetting all she'd been taught, headed toward the French windows that led onto a balcony. Matilda had had a look of fright, almost terror, and Elizabeth was determined to put a spoke in Squire Herman's lecherous plans.

"Careful," purred the voice at her elbow. She glanced up at the gentleman with whom she'd been talking. "You don't wish to cause a scene, I'm sure."

"I must save Matty." Elizabeth tried to shake off his restraining hand. "That disgusting old man . . ."

"I understand. But it would be better—would it not?—if I were to go to the rescue?" *Thereby*, thought Carrington, *putting you into my debt, you little darling, you.*

"Would you?" Wide-eyed, obviously admiring, Elizabeth stared at him.

"For you? Yes, I will. Wait here, my dear."

Elizabeth peered out into the shadowy ill-lit darkness. If it hadn't been unseasonably warm, the doors would have been shut and Matilda never put into such a situation. Elizabeth's quick ears caught a stifled shriek, the sound of flesh hitting flesh, and the patter of feet. Matilda ran straight into Elizabeth's arms.

"Oh dear. Oh dear . . ."

"Stop it, you silly widgeon," hissed Elizabeth. "Do you want everyone to know what has happened?" She held on to her friend's arms, assessing the minor damage to the girl's gown and the tear-streaked face. "Do you want a scandal?"

"You don't understand . . ."

"No. You can explain while we fix you up. Come this way. Quickly now," ordered Elizabeth as Matilda dithered.

Her friend, keeping her face turned toward the wall, followed Elizabeth through a nearby door into the hall. There Elizabeth hesitated. The women's retiring room was undoubtedly full of too many eyes and ears. The bedrooms on the floor above, however, would be empty and might contain a pitcher of water and a comb they could borrow. She glanced both ways, saw the hall was temporarily free of prying eyes, and whisked Matilda up the nearby set of secondary stairs. Almost at once they were around a turn and out of sight.

Joanna's heart beat faster and faster as she whirled around the room in Pierce's arms. Could a man have that look in his eyes and not feel something for the woman toward whom such fervent emotion was directed? Her eyes never left his, and gradually, between the movement of the dance and the beating of her heart, she felt as if she'd lost all common sense and with it her will to resist him.

181

She barely noticed when the music ended. Still in a dream world, Joanna followed blindly as Pierce led her toward their party. Her thoughts on the dance, her eyes didn't comprehend anything around them until she heard Pierce's voice:

"What do you mean you don't know where she is?"

Pierce's hissed question and Robert's worried expression brought Joanna sharply back to reality. "What's the matter?"

"Elizabeth has gone off somewhere."

"Oh. *Oh, no.* How dare my idiot niece do such a thing?"

Joanna glanced around, searching the sea of faces. She met Cressy's malicious gaze for an instant before Robert's sister turned away and her suspicions were aroused.

"What has your sister been up to?" She, too, hissed and the melodrama plus rising hysteria roused a hastily suppressed giggle.

"Cressy? Nothing . . ." Robert's face firmed, his eyes darkening with anger. "Or perhaps she saw something when we were . . ." He stalked toward where his sister sat alone and bent over her.

"Pierce, what am I to do?" Joanna fretted. "Where can she be?"

"You check the lady's retiring room, Jo. I'll see what Robert discovers from Cressy."

"That woman. I'm *certain* she knows what has happened. But would even she allow something to befall a girl as young as Elizabeth?"

"If you're suggesting she might stand by and watch your niece ruin herself, you'll get no argument from me. Now go, Joanna."

Joanna returned immediately to the rapidly emptying ballroom. "Pierce?"

182

"Cressy says Sir Frederick Carrington was talking to her."

"*Sir Frederick?* Oh, my God!"

"Relax. I saw Frederick myself only moments ago. He was partnering the Willingham filly to supper and Elizabeth was nowhere in sight."

"We don't know what happened while we were dancing. He might—"

"No man could have managed it in the time, Jo," soothed Pierce. "Relax."

"We must find him, ask him . . ."

"And publish to the world your niece has disappeared?" He squeezed her hand. "Do hush, love. Here comes what looks to be an agitated hen and you don't wish her to know—"

"Mrs. Storling," interrupted Joanna, sotto voce. "She's the mother of one of Elizabeth's friends."

Wringing her hands, Mrs. Storling approached Joanna with nervous steps.

"What is the trouble, Mrs. Storling?"

"I can't find Matilda *anywhere*. She was dancing with Squire Herman and she didn't return to me when the set finished." Almost as an afterthought she added, "I can't find him either."

"You allowed Matilda to dance with Squire Herman!"

Mrs. Storling, forgetting her concern for a moment, straightened to her full four feet ten and a half inches. "Lady Joanna, you know our circumstances. Squire Herman has made his intentions known to me. Matilda is aware of what she owes her family and will—"

"But not if the Squire manages to ruin her in the meantime," cut in Joanna and was immediately appalled at herself for suggesting such a thing. "No,

183

no, Mrs. Storling. Don't faint. I'm sure I didn't mean it . . ." Joanna looked at Pierce for help, but he was obviously trying to contain chuckles. She glared at him and he bit his lip.

Carefully he composed himself before speaking. "Joanna, Matilda is a friend of Elizabeth's, is she not?"

"Yes."

"Then, might I suggest the two girls are together?"

Joanna stared at him. Unperturbed, he stared back. It was possible, she supposed. And Pierce's suggestion was more tolerable, certainly, than any other that had flitted through her mind.

"That's entirely possible," said Mrs. Storling, "but why has the Squire disappeared?" Joanna, ignoring her, stared over her shoulder and Mrs. Storling turned. "Matilda! Wherever have you been? And Elizabeth." Clucking and scolding, she moved to her daughter's side. "You naughty children have frightened us out of our wits." Pierce muttered a "speak for yourself," but Joanna shushed him. "You have been quite inconsiderate and thoughtless."

"Yes, but Matilda tore her dress and we had an awful time fixing it, didn't we, Matty?" The last was said in a bracing tone that immediately raised Joanna's suspicions but, happily, satisfied Mrs. Storling. She hustled her daughter away and Elizabeth, defiant, met her aunt's eyes.

Joanna, lips compressed, glared at her niece. "Now they are gone, what is the true story, Elizabeth?"

"It wasn't my fault. Oh, Aunt Jo, do you know what Matilda told me? It is awful. Simply awful. That terrible old man has asked permission to court her. She hates him. He has behaved in a dreadful manner and . . ." Elizabeth suddenly realized she had no idea who her knight in shining armor had been. "Well, there was this man talking to me and when I saw how frightened Matilda looked, I was upset and started after her. But he didn't think it was a good idea for me to go, so he went. Out on the balcony, you know." She spoke more quickly, trying to get it all out before the anger she could see in Joanna's eyes exploded into words. "Well, Matilda says he behaved wonderfully. He simply tore Squire Herman away from her and landed him a facer—"

A painful blush raced up her cheeks at having revealed knowledge of boxing cant and her gaze, mortified, touched her aunt's, the duke's, then traveled on to Lord Halford's.

"You mean the gentleman hit the squire and knocked him down?" Robert suggested smoothly.

"Yes." Her eyes thanked him. "That's the way it was. And Matilda ran back in and she was crying and her dress was torn but not too badly and I took her to a room where she could recover herself and—"

"That's enough, Elizabeth," Joanna interrupted.

Elizabeth seemed more upset by Matty's predicament than ready to develop a dangerous *tendre* for the wicked baronet who had come to her aid—for which Joanna was thankful. She couldn't, however, decide what to say for the best. Postponement of any discussion seemed prudent.

"In fact it is too much to sort out in the middle of a ball. We will discuss this tomorrow, but now we'd better go down and have supper before the whole world knows something has happened."

Pierce took Joanna's arm and Robert offered his to Elizabeth. They strolled down the wide stairs to the supper room. Pierce, irrepressible, whispered in

Joanna's ear. "So, the prodigal returns a heroine in fact."

She gave him a reprimanding stare.

The men managed to find a table for four and went to get plates for the ladies. When they were gone, Elizabeth clutched Joanna's wrist. "Aunt Jo, we must do something. Matilda must not marry that awful man."

"Elizabeth, dear," Joanna said with a frown, "there is nothing we *can* do. Her mother has accepted his suit and—"

"You told me I should think of others, and now when I am, you . . ."

"Hush. I know Matilda will need your support, my dear, but this is neither the time nor the place for a discussion of what you might do."

"I will do something," muttered Elizabeth.

"Yes. I hear you. But not right now! No more or I will find your father and insist we leave at once."

Silenced, Elizabeth pouted, scheming ways and means of saving her friend. Joanna, equally disturbed but for reasons having to do with Sir Frederick, was determined not to show it. In an attempt at normality, she instigated a conversation with the two men so banal that it had Pierce manfully containing chuckles.

The company thinned out as more and more couples returned to the ballroom. Finally coming out of the brown study into which she'd fallen, Elizabeth looked around her. She tugged at Robert's sleeve. He ended his part of a conversation with Pierce and turned to her.

"What is it, Lady Elizabeth?"

"That gentleman." She pointed surreptitiously. "The one talking to your sister. Who is he?"

186

"Sir Frederick Carrington." Robert took care to blank all emotion from his voice. "Why do you ask, little one?"

"He's the one who rescued Matilda."

"Sir Frederick?" Robert choked, coughed, set his wine glass down very carefully. He was aware Frederick had talked to Elizabeth while he'd argued with Cressy, but he'd assumed some other man had gone to the Storling chit's rescue. "Are you certain?"

"Of course I'm certain." Robert's eyes remained on his sister and the rake with whom she was speaking. Elizabeth looked from one to the other, then back to Robert. "Why do you look that way?"

"Hmm-Hmm?" He forced his gaze back to Elizabeth's. "Why? 'Tis just that it seems a bit hypocritical of Carrington, that's all."

"Hippy-cri . . ." Elizabeth frowned. "That word. What does it mean?"

Robert swallowed a grin. "That his behavior tonight contradicts his behavior in the past."

"I don't understand."

"Sir Frederick, my dear, is a dangerous and unprincipled man where ladies are concerned. His attitude is understandable perhaps, given his mother and what happened when—but never mind *that!* I called Sir Frederick's behavior hypocritical because young girls are more often in need of rescue from *his* machinations. If he went to your friend's rescue, it is because he had a reason to do so. I don't wish to frighten you, Lady Elizabeth, but I suspect *you* are that reason."

Elizabeth thought about that. "Do you dislike Sir Frederick?"

Robert hesitated. How did one explain that a person could be liked in some situations and not in oth-

187

ers? Carefully choosing his words, he said, "When one meets him at Whites or Jackson's or some other place men gather, I like him." How to go on? "When among men, he is as honorable as anyone. More than once in our checkered past I have depended on him and trusted him completely. What I do not like is his behavior toward young women."

"He is a rake?"

"He is worse than a rake."

Elizabeth frowned. "I don't understand how that can be."

Again Robert had to choke back laughter. "Lady Elizabeth, rakes, just like other varieties of the human animal, range from the more or less acceptable to the very, very bad. Some rakes have rules which limit their, er, rakish behavior to a certain class of, hmmm, women. Other rakes are less discriminating, in fact seem to gain joy out of, er . . ."

"Seducing?"

Robert frowned repressively at the girl while restraining himself from tugging at a cravat that seemed suddenly too tight. "That, young lady, is something you should know nothing about."

"Nonsense, Lord Halford." Elizabeth pretended greater understanding than she actually had as she continued. "If young girls were taught about such things, we'd know better how to avoid situations which might lead to disaster."

A measure of respect slipped into Robert's assessment of the beauty he'd assumed was merely another feather-headed minx. "I may agree," he said cautiously, "but it is not a fit subject for you to discuss. At least not with me. Your father . . ."

"Would become red in the face," she interrupted

tartly, "and harrumph and stutter and send me to my room most likely."

"Then your aunt . . ."

"Yes, Aunt Jo, is a great gu—"

Her eyes flew to his and this time he didn't try to repress his sense of the ridiculous. Politely he finished her cant phrase. "A great gun. Quite." Noting Joanna was preparing to leave the supper room, he went on quickly, "Lady Elizabeth, however charming you find the man, remember Sir Frederick is dangerous. Very dangerous."

"Thank you for telling me." She smiled slightly, turned to Joanna, and went docilely when her chaperon suggested they retire for a moment to the room set aside for that purpose.

"You seemed to be having a very serious discussion with Lord Halford."

"Yes." Elizabeth spoke thoughtfully. "He is a very interesting man, isn't he?"

It occurred to Elizabeth that Robert Merton would be perfect for her aunt and a speculative gleam came into her eyes along with a tiny flame of despair somewhere much deeper inside her—an emotion she didn't understand so she pushed it away. Yes, Robert Merton was a wonderful man, just the sort Aunt Joanna should marry.

She added, "Quite good-looking, too."

"You like him?"

Joanna hoped Elizabeth wouldn't set her heart on Robert Merton. Even the most assiduous of the husband-hunting mamas had, for years, considered him a hardened case and ignored him. She'd been told he'd never shown the least interest in any of the young girls thrust upon the *ton* year after year—he was polite, but with it, kept a distance, a certain chill in his relations with them.

Because Elizabeth didn't understand her feelings for the man, she equated them with those with which she'd had experience. "I wish he were my father," she muttered. "He'd be so much better than the one I've got," she added bitterly.

"Hush." Elizabeth blushed, and Joanna, her mind at ease, went on to tease, "If you aren't careful, I'll be demanding more lines on the subject on which you recently were required to write!"

"I don't think that's fair. All I said was—"

Realizing there was some justice in Elizabeth's wish, Joanna placed her fingers over her niece's mouth.

"That, my dear, is *enough*. Now sit down so I may fix your hair. It would not do if it were to come down during one of the more boisterous dances. There," she said, her hands at the back of Elizabeth's head. "Just as I thought. It has begun to loosen dangerously."

It wouldn't do for her niece's hair to fall down her back. Such a mishap would pique the old cats, always avid for scandal. They would interpret it as deliberate provocation, labeling Elizabeth "fast," and that was to be avoided at all costs. As she replaced the flowers, Joanna wondered how to introduce the subject of Sir Frederick when Elizabeth did it for her.

"I asked Lord Halford to identify the man who saved Matilda. He said it was Sir Frederick Carrington and that he was a dangerous rake. Why, then, did he go to Matilda's aid?"

"Perhaps to make himself look good in your eyes," suggested Joanna, thanking heaven for such an unexceptional opportunity to tactfully say what had to be said.

"That's what Lord Halford said." Elizabeth giggled, her eyes twinkling and the dimple making an appearance. "What you mean is that you think he wishes to pursue me?"

"You are a lovely young woman, Elizabeth. It is suspected he has done more than pursue young ladies such as you," said Joanna as repressively as she could. "He would do his best to ruin you."

Joanna didn't like the look in Elizabeth's eyes. It would be just like her silly chit of a niece to think she could give the dangerous rake a set-down—which was a thought foolish beyond permission.

Elizabeth sat silently until her aunt finished repairs and, deceptively meek, followed Joanna to the ballroom. But just outside the door, she laid a hand on her aunt's arm, halting their progress.

"Aunt Jo, explain something to me. If it is known Sir Frederick is such a bad man, why is he invited to *tonish* parties?"

"Because he has always managed to avoid a public scandal. Do not let that confuse you, Elizabeth. It does not mean he has not acted in the most improper of fashions."

"You mean people ignore his behavior. I understand." She nodded thoughtfully. "Do you know? I think life in society may be far more complicated than I believed."

"Yes, I've always thought it ridiculous that, just because a person has never been called to account for his behavior, the *ton* ignores it."

"Then there are other people, decent-seeming people, whose sinful behavior is ignored? Or is it only because Sir Frederick is so charming he gets away with it?"

"Think about it Elizabeth."

The girl frowned balefully at such serious and complicated thinking and inadvertently frightened away a very young man who turned on his heel and moved off at the look. "Squire Herman!"

"Definitely a case in point. Quiet now. We can't talk about this sort of thing here."

Elizabeth felt no desire to cease discussing such interesting problems but was already surrounded by a covey of young men, all begging for the next dance—although it was known her card was full. Elizabeth accepted the arm of the favored beau and, smiling a bit absently at the rest, stepped into a set forming for the next dance.

"Well, Joanna?"

Joanna's glance slid away from Elizabeth to meet Pierce's eyes. "I don't know. I just don't know. She seems to understand she must avoid Sir Frederick, but I know my niece. I don't trust her, Pierce."

"We'll keep an eye on her."

"I know you'll help, Pierce. And I'll warn Henry of my suspicions although I'm not certain just what good that will do."

"Speaking of Henry, Joanna, I think I know why he doesn't want you in Brighton." His diversion worked, he noted, pleased when Joanna turned impulsively toward him, losing the worried look he hated to see on her face.

"You do? Tell me."

But before he had a chance to elaborate, they were interrupted by Lady Bradford who simpered up at Pierce in a manner more suited to a young girl. "Your Grace, I believe you've met my daughter?"

Joanna had to keep tight reins on her sense of humor as she watched Pierce, maneuvered by an expert, forced to ask Lady Anne for the next dance. It was a waltz, and as Pierce and Lady Bradford's daughter took the floor, Joanna heard a deep sigh from her hostess.

"Such a suitable match that would be," said Lady Bradford wistfully.

"Has His Grace shown a partiality?"

Joanna was quite certain he had not. Small, fat-hooded eyes turned haughtily to stare at her. Joanna met the look innocently.

"Given your extremely inappropriate alliance, Lady Joanna, I assume you do not believe in arranged marriages. Most people of our station understand such things. My daughter will have a large dowry. It will include a portion of Lord Bradford's estate. That portion," said Lady Bradford significantly, "which abuts White Stones."

"Ah. Stornway is looking to increase his acreage? I didn't know. I'll have to let my brother in on the secret," she teased. "Perhaps he'd add some land to Elizabeth's portion." She tipped her head thoughtfully. "There is a meadow in which the duke has expressed an interest . . ."

Yes, recently Pierce had shown a strong interest in that meadow. Joanna repressed a smile at the thought of how often she'd met him there.

"A long meadow with a stream in it," she went on, "The farm beyond that would make it an unexceptionable addition to . . ."

Joanna bit her lip and stared at her hostess's stiff back. Lady Bradford marched off with her nose in the air, obviously deeply insulted. Matchmaking mamas were one of Joanna's pet peeves. She must be sure to tease Pierce about his soon-to-be-announced engagement by asking him when all the documents would be ready for signing.

Ten

Calculating nicely, Joanna managed to enter the breakfast room the morning after the ball and find it empty. Which was just what she wanted. She needed time to think through the several problems that had arisen the night before. Particularly Carrington. Henry must be informed. That would be, however distasteful, her first task this morning. She rang for Dawson and asked if her brother were about.

"His Lordship is with his agent, Lady Jo."

Of all times for Mr. Douglas to catch up with Henry, thought Joanna peevishly. She forced a modicum of patience. "Will you please inform me as soon as he's free?"

"Certainly, m'lady."

Joanna managed to hide her irritation from Dawson at the thought of postponement. It was a distasteful task, informing her brother a rake was very likely pursuing his daughter and she wished it over.

Dawson left the room, and Joanna, unable to prevent herself, found her thoughts on Pierce. She remembered their waltz. It was, she thought, too bad of Pierce that he could make her feel so much like a chit in her first season merely by waltzing with her. As if she were young again, free to hope and dream and plan a future with the love of her life.

Why did he affect her so? Was it only that she had denied herself even the most innocuous of male companionship for so long? Was she imagining the flutters in her very soul when he was near because she wanted so much to feel again those things Reggie had taught her to feel? Needed to feel them?

"Good morning, Aunt Jo."

Joanna, barely retaining hold of the cup of tea she'd let grow cold, gave herself a little shake. "Elizabeth? I didn't expect you up for another two hours. At least."

"Pooh. I feel wonderful." The dimpled smile faded. "I wonder if Matilda feels the same."

"Elizabeth, you know you mustn't interfere, don't you?" How harsh that sounded, thought Jo. "Contracts cannot be set aside, my dear."

The girl turned from the sideboard, and Joanna, unable to face more than her morning coffee, felt ill at sight of her niece's well-filled plate.

"If the contracts are signed, nothing may be done. I know *that.*" Elizabeth seated herself and thanked her aunt for a cup of tea. "Unless, of course," she added thoughtfully, "Matilda were to cry off."

"Matilda will obey her mother." Joanna swallowed her distaste at the necessity of forcing her young and idealistic niece to face hard facts. "It is not our business, Elizabeth." Joanna didn't like the mulish expression hardening Elizabeth's face. "Mrs. Storling is responsible for Matilda's future and it is up to her to determine what is best for your friend." Why did saying the proper thing seem so wrong at times?!

"I don't need to like it, do I?"

Joanna sighed. Everyone knew Squire Herman had buried two wives, one dying at the premature birth of his eldest son and the second after the birth of two babies that died in their first year, several miscarriages, and then the birth of his only daughter.

"No one of any sensibility could consider the match suitable, Elizabeth. The Squire's son would be a more likely husband for Matilda, come to that. However, we are not in a position to know Mrs. Storling's problems. She is widowed and, I know, not well-off. She may feel such a marriage is better than—"

"Wed to the Squire? Better to trim hats or . . . or go on the stage!"

"Matilda on the stage?" Joanna forced Elizabeth to meet her eyes. "Elizabeth, you must promise me you won't put notions of that sort into the poor girl's head!"

"I promise. I wouldn't, but Matilda is a mouse and could never carry through such a scheme anyway."

"I will assume you are joking. There is no more to be said. This is the end of this discussion."

"Yes, Aunt Jo." Elizabeth finished off her excellent breakfast and stood to go. "Oh, Aunt Jo?" Joanna looked up. "Do I have permission to drive over to Alicia's? We promised to meet today."

Joanna chuckled. "I'm sure you did, but isn't it a little early?"

"If Alicia is still abed, I shall get her up. Don't expect me back until tea, please."

Had she given permission? Joanna decided not to make an issue of it. "You will take Jem or your maid, won't you?"

Elizabeth's eyes widened. Her mouth rounded to an o of horror. She shuddered dramatically. Then,

196

in a hushed voice, she said, "Of course. Do you think me *fast*?"

"I think you abominable," said her much-put-upon aunt, chuckling for the first time that day. "Don't be late for tea."

Joanna gave up all pretense of breakfasting and, after checking that Henry was still occupied, went to her daily consultation with Mrs. Landy. She was leaving the housekeeper's rooms when Dawson stopped her. "Yes, Dawson? Is my brother free now?"

He grimaced. "Mr. Douglas has gone, Lady Jo, but Lady Cressida is with His Lordship. She caught him in the hall just a moment ago and drew him into the library. I will tell you when she leaves him."

Cressida spent all of fifteen minutes with her host. It had taken no longer than that to discover that, although Lord Midbourgh might not be the sharpest wit in the *ton*, he just might be the wariest bachelor. She decided to return to Brighton immediately and begin a new campaign for a ring on her finger amongst men who did not know her so well. There was, obviously, no reason to waste more time in the country.

Dawson again found Joanna—this time to tell her Lady Cressida wished to speak to her. Joanna was much surprised to find her brother's houseguest dressed for traveling. The older woman was standing in the front hall, tapping her foot impatiently.

"Cressy? Dawson said you were looking for me."

"Oh. There you are. I suppose I should thank you for a pleasant visit, but since it wasn't, I won't."

Joanna blinked. "You're leaving? Now?"

"I'm leaving. I came for the ball and it's over."

197

"Only for the ball." Joanna kept a straight face with difficulty.

Cressy laughed, one of those rare instances of honesty overcoming her. "You know very well why I came. But," the frown returned, more deeply engraved than ever, "when I saw the two of you waltzing together, well . . ." She shrugged. "I must be off now."

Joanna nodded, feeling an unwanted touch of pity for the woman. "Dawson, find Lord Midbourgh. He should be here."

"Never mind, Dawson," countermanded Cressy. Remembering their interview, her voice filled with venom as she continued. "Henry knows I'm going. I'm sure I'll see you in London this fall."

Ah yes, thought Cressy. London and Carrington's very obvious plans for Elizabeth. She felt much cheered at the thought that the Ransomes, whom she'd always detested, would get their comeuppance one way or another. She added a lilting goodbye to her exit.

Cressy traipsed out the front door, down the steps, and into the carriage. Her maid followed, juggling a jewel case, a bandbox, and other paraphernalia. As she climbed in behind her mistress, she dropped a book. "Clumsy oaf. I wonder why I don't turn you off." Once the book was retrieved and the maid seated, the carriage door shut on a diatribe which sounded more habit than truly vicious.

Joanna, confused their guest had left so abruptly, was pleased to see the last of her and waved. Ten minutes later she'd run Henry to ground.

"Carrington? And Elizabeth? I won't have it."

"The problem is how to *prevent* it," repeated Joanna with what patience she could muster. "I've a suspicion Cressy may have had a hand in introducing them—however," she added thoughtfully, "in justice to Cressy, their paths would have crossed at some point. Carrington has a knack for discovering all the greatest beauties—or so I've heard."

"You've warned Elizabeth?"

"I have." Joanna couldn't help a troubled "But . . ."

"No buts. Surely my daughter understands her danger?"

"I'm not sure she does. Henry, you know Elizabeth . . ." Her brother looked flustered and Joanna grimaced. "Or perhaps you don't, but I fear she's plotting a set-down for the man."

"What? A chit like Elizabeth? Carrington? Pish. Tush." Henry thought for a moment. "Nonsense," he added for good measure. "She can't think such a thing?"

"Elizabeth is quite capable of thinking it."

Henry harrumphed. He made the disagreeable noise again and stood up. "Then the only thing to do is put off her come-out. There. It is settled." He smiled benignly and nodded several times.

"It is not settled." Henry looked hunted. "She must be brought out this fall."

Henry blinked. He paced from one end of the room to the other, looking occasionally at his sister. Finally his pale gaze focusing on her, he asked, "Thinking of going back into harness yourself, Joanna?"

"Me? What have I to do with this?"

"Blushing, sister? Well, it would please me no end."

"What would please you?"

"You and Pierce, of course. So, if that's in the wind, of course you must be in London this fall. In fact, if that's the way of it, I have no objections to you returning with me to Brighton."

"And if that isn't the way of it?"

There was a sweet, almost syrupy note to his sister's voice, one Henry hadn't heard in a long time. "It ain't?" he asked cautiously.

"It most definitely *ain't*. But I go to Brighton nevertheless."

Henry paced, glancing at Joanna now and again. "Can't take you," he decided.

"Of course you can."

"Won't, then," said Henry stubbornly.

"Then once you've left, I'll follow. That's simple enough."

"Don't want you in Brighton, Joanna. Not if you haven't set sights on Pierce."

"This is the most ridiculous conversation I've ever had. Why are you so against my coming to Brighton?"

"Don't want you there."

She could get no more out of him. Joanna gave up and went to try on an ancient habit Belton had found in the attic and restructured to fit her mistress. It needed a touch more work at the shoulders, and although Joanna wanted nothing more than a long run on Lad's willing back, she gave into Belton's pleading that she not allow herself to be seen in the ruined habit.

An hour later Joanna took one last look in the mirror and sighed. The remade habit was forest green. The color gave her complexion a sickly cast that was not at all becoming. Worse, the worsted material was too warm for the season which was far more temperate than usual for the time of year. Joanna almost wished for the old brown habit she'd come to hate.

"Jo!" called one voice as another yelled, "Lady Joanna! Hold up." Joanna pulled Lad up and around, watching as Pierce and Lord Halford raced toward her. "Good afternoon," said the latter while Pierce scowled and said, "That habit is worse than the other."

Joanna ignored Pierce's comment and smiled at his friend. "It's a beautiful day, isn't it?"

"It certainly is." Rob smiled as he edged Pierce's Apollo away from Lad. "I'm surprised to see you out, though. Aren't you tired after last night?"

"I've been up for hours. Did you enjoy the ball?"

"More than I expected. Most entertaining."

There was a wry note in his voice, and Joanna looked him in the eye but could read nothing from his expression. Pierce had come up on her other side and now caught up her reins. "Your Grace?" she asked with all the reserve and hauteur she could manage. She looked from him to her reins.

"Don't ignore me. I won't have it." His voice, though soft, held a determined note.

"You won't?"

She turned back to Robert, noticed his expression as he glanced across Lad's withers, and realized he was flirting with her in order to tease his friend. She sighed. Men. They never grew up. Joanna faced straight ahead.

"Boredom is no excuse."

Pierce's strange comment made Joanna blink, and

she wondered what he meant but refused to look at him.

"No," sighed Robert, "I don't suppose it is. Good day to you, Lady Jo." Before she realized his intention, he tipped his hat and rode off.

"That's better." Satisfaction saturated Pierce's tone.

"You think so? I don't agree." Joanna gritted her teeth. "*Will* you let go my reins?"

"In a moment. Jo, look at me."

"I'm angry with you."

He chuckled. "Yes. I seem to have that effect on you. I really would like to see your face."

The coaxing note in his voice very nearly made her give in to him, but it was an unexpected thought which changed her mood for the better. "Pierce, last night you began to tell me why you thought Henry didn't wish me in Brighton."

"So I did."

She turned. "Well?"

"Ah. Your face. Such a lovely face."

Joanna's teeth snapped together and she drew a deep breath through them. When he let go her reins, she kicked Lad and took off across the meadow, letting the wind blow away her temper, and leaping the stream, she pulled Lad up and around on the other side. She grinned at Pierce who had caught up with her, their horses jumping side by side.

"That was wonderful." She fanned her face with her hand. "Oh, it is so hot."

"It is warmer than one might expect but not hot. It's that heavy habit. Where did you get the atrocious thing?"

Joanna grimaced and undid the hooks at the high collar. He was right: the material was much too warm for the pleasant autumn day. "My old one couldn't be saved. Thank heaven!" She flicked a smile at him and was rewarded with an understanding look. "This was in the attic and will have to serve until I can get a new one made up."

"Ah. Brighton."

"Well, no. Not for a habit. I'll only go to Roberts for that so it'll have to wait until I get to London. No one else can make a proper habit. But I must have gowns made and other things. So," she glared at her tormentor and demanded, "why does Henry wish to keep me away from Brighton?"

"Redcoats."

Joanna frowned. "I'm not in the market for a coat. And it wouldn't be red even if I were."

"Come, Joanna, don't be bacon-brained. You once succumbed to the lure of a redcoat. Henry fears you will again." He paused, studying her features carefully. "One of Prinny's favorite regiments is based near Brighton."

Joanna perked up. "Oh! *That* sort of redcoat. Which regiment?" Cautiously Pierce told her. "Wonderful. I know half a dozen officers. Now I certainly *will* go, Henry or no."

Pierce dismounted and came to her side. He gripped her waist and lifted her down slowly, his eyes catching and holding hers. Joanna felt her breath catch, wondered if he would kiss her and what she'd do if he did . . . and was disappointed when he set her a little away from him. But he didn't release her, and his eyes, suddenly very solemn indeed, still held hers.

"Pierce, let me go."

"No. Is Henry correct? Will you look for a husband amongst the officers?"

"I've told you my future. It does not include a

203

husband, officer or not." Her temper, volatile ever since Pierce's reentry into her life, took off like one of Whinnyates's rockets. She very nearly stamped her foot in childish rage. "Does Henry intend that I should never again have contact with old and very good friends?"

"Bother Henry." His face reddened at her speculative look, and he shifted his weight from one foot to the other. "Settle down, Joanna. I can't help it if I'm jealous of every man who looks at you. Give me the right to protect you and you can see any friends you wish."

"Will you please stop that nonsense, Pierce? You know you don't wish to be married."

"I do. To you. Someday I'll manage to convince you of my sincerity. For now?" He smiled sadly, the smile growing at her wary look. "For now perhaps we should ride or," his hands moved suggestively against her waist, "I'll be tempted far beyond what a man should have to bear."

Joanna had never heard him so serious. It was her turn to search his features and what she saw made her blush. Could her new interpretation be correct? Had she misjudged him? But if she had, then that meant—a shiver ran down her spine. "Yes. Let's ride."

As she settled her skirts, she searched her mind for a topic to lighten the mood. There was something about Pierce today she didn't quite understand, something that made her as skittish as a colt. Marriage? Dare she believe it? Pierce had the same reputation as Robert. He was the bane of the matchmaking mamas hunting husbands for their daughters. Wasn't he? On the other hand, perhaps he'd decided it was time to settle down and set up his nursery. In that case, he might truly be courting her. Not that she'd marry him for that reason, but at least she could trust he wasn't looking for revenge. Marriage. Hmmm. Joanna's eyes twinkled as she turned Lad downstream.

"Pierce, I heard a rumor last night."

"Only one?"

"Only one which would interest you, I'm sure. I'm to give you congratulations, I believe."

"You are? For what?"

"Aren't the documents being drawn up? Haven't you written the notice for the papers? I have it on the best of authority, you'll be unable to resist . . ." She trailed off, her eyes twinkling.

"Joanna, what *are* you talking about?"

"An arranged marriage, of course. Lady Anne's dowry."

His sharp crack of laughter made her grin. She couldn't know he was remembering his dance with Lady Anne the night before and the young lady's dry comment: "Do relax, Your Grace. I have no ambitions to become a duchess." Her wry words had reminded Pierce of Joanna's comments concerning Anne and he'd taken care to draw her out. Now his grin widened.

"Joanna," he said, "whatever Lady Bradford is plotting for her daughter, I have it on the best of authority Lady Anne hasn't the least ambition to marry me."

Joanna's smile faded. "Oh?"

"Yes. She told me so."

Joanna felt as if someone had hit her in the stomach. My God. It was true. He'd offered for Anne and been turned down! For a moment she couldn't breathe. Her attention wandering, she let Lad pick his way along the bank of the stream that was widening slightly as they neared the river. Now Pierce was offering for her. Perhaps it was true he was only interested in adding to his acres. If she'd agreed, would he even now be bargaining with Henry for the meadow and tenant farm she'd joked about the evening before? Had he truly become so mercenary?

"Pierce . . ."

Pierce was standing in his stirrups, his hand shading his eyes. "Jo! Isn't there a mill just around that curve in the river?"

She tried to see what had his attention. "Yes. Of course. But . . ."

"Is it working?"

"What a question." The low rumble of the distant mill had been a background noise for some time. "It is the harvest season, Pierce. . . . Where are you going?"

Then she saw what he'd seen. Fear clutched at her at the sight of the child's bonnet, an arm raised, splashing. Setting her heels, she flipped her overlong reins onto Lad's flank. The surprised gelding took off after Apollo but was soon pulled up in a flurry of dust as they caught up.

"Pierce!" she cried.

He was pulling off his boots. His coat already lay in the dirt. His eyes never left the bobbing head and flailing arms which were approaching them much too quickly on a current swelled by the recent rain.

"Ride, Joanna. See if you can get the mill wheel stopped. Hurry, my love!"

He jumped into the river, striking out for the child; she wheeled Lad and raced for the mill, grim determination keeping her eyes forward rather than turning to search the waters for any glimpse of Pierce. The miller's wife was feeding her chickens and

Joanna pulled into the clucking flock, sending feathers flying in all directions. "Quick! No time to explain. Stop the wheel. Instantly."

The chubby cheeks paled, eyes flying upstream. "Someone in the water, m'lady?"

"Yes. A child. Hurry!"

Skirts flapping, the miller's wife raced for the open half-door to the mill, and Joanna, thankful the woman had her wits about her, headed back upstream, her eyes anxiously scanning the water.

"Joanna!"

Frantically she focused on the sound of his voice. *There*. Pierce held the struggling child's head above water with one hand, his other grasping the slick branches of an overhanging willow. Joanna slid off Lad's back only feet away. "Pierce. Oh, God, Pierce!"

"Don't fail me now. Grab the child. Can you reach her?"

Praying fervently, Joanna stretched for a limb, tested her grip, and leaned out into the water. "A bit farther, Pierce. I can't . . ."

"Try."

There was something stern and unyielding in his tone, in the eyes she looked into. Pierce was counting on her. Joanna tried a new grip, reached farther.

"I have her. Pierce, I have her!" He let the girl go just as his other hand slipped from the slippery leaves. "Pierce!" Joanna's heart constricted.

The child, coughing and spitting clutched at her but Joanna gently pushed her farther from the river even as she whistled for Lad. Grasping Lad's reins, she raced downstream, calling to Pierce who was, despite his attempts to gain shore, being pulled remorselessly toward the still-turning wheel.

Positioning herself yards downstream from him, she stood as close to the low bank as she could, waiting.

"Pierce, the reins!"

She tossed the loop toward his hands, watched as he caught them, winding them around his wrist, and saw his body twisted by the current until his feet pointed downstream. Joanna turned to Lad who was twitching, nervous at the pull on his head. She stepped between her horse and the water, one booted foot slipping in the marshy edge as she pushed at the bridle, her hands on either side of Lad's head.

"Back, you fool. Back. Slowly, Lad. That's a boy. Back."

She didn't stop until she heard Pierce laughing and turned to see him lying full-length on the bank, one arm stretched up in the air, the rein still wound tightly around it. Water ran down his neck, disappearing under the nearly transparent material of his shirt.

"Oh, Pierce." They stared at each other, and Joanna, knowing he was safe, succumbed to panic at the thought that she might have lost him to the mill wheel. "Oh, Pierce, Pierce . . ." She helped him free himself from the rein as running figures came up the path, the miller's wife panting.

"Oh, my gracious, it's the duke himself!"

"Where's the child, Joanna?"

Joanna blushed. In her fear for Pierce she'd forgotten the girl. Now she ran toward the willow. The little girl was wound into a tight knot, sobs shaking her, the slight body shivering from the cold wet clothes dripping into a puddle around her. "You poor baby. You poor, poor baby. Who are you, child?" Disregarding the girl's soaking clothes, Joanna knelt and scooped her close. Rocking her against her breast, Joanna soothed and gently scolded, and the child gradually calmed.

"Land's sake, why, that's the Sanders child. Whatever was the poor baby doing so far from home as to get into the river?"

"You know the girl?"

" 'Tis Abigail, milady. Abigail Sanders."

"But it must be two miles to their farm."

"Aye." The miller's wife took the toddler into her own plump arms. "Oh, milady, you've ruined your habit. And, His Grace, why, *his* clothes. Oh dear . . ."

His teeth chattering, Pierce spoke for them both. "Forget the clothes. It's the child that's important. Confound it, woman, you can't think either of us is worried about clothes."

Joanna noticed how tightly he clenched his jaw and the involuntary tremors occasionally running down his back whenever the wet linen of his shirt was pressed against his skin by a gusting breeze.

"Clothes, no, but your health, Your Grace, is something else." Joanna spoke firmly, despite her own chattering teeth, before turning to the woman cuddling the child. "Would your husband have a shirt and trousers the duke could borrow? He left his jacket and boots farther down the bank."

"Dearie me. Where is my head? Of course. Come. Both of you. John? Find His Grace's jacket and boots, now. And you, Your Grace, you'll be warmer in the sun if you're out of that shirt. Come now. Take it off."

Pierce's eyes went to Joanna, a faint flush reddening his neck. "If Lady Jo will turn her back . . ."

"Nonsense." Joanna's fingers were already undoing tiny buttons. "Don't be a stick, Pierce. Yours

209

won't be the first bare chest I've seen. Oh, these stubborn buttons!"

"Not the first, Joanna, but it isn't right." She heard his teeth chatter. "I'm not your husband." He chuckled. "Yet," he whispered for her ears alone.

"I'm not referring to my husband. There." She pulled the sopping material away from his flesh. "Pierce, for heaven's sake, cooperate. Ah. Here comes the miller with your coat. If modesty requires it, get this off and get yourself into that."

As he did so Pierce glared at Joanna. "You've seen other chests than your husband's?!"

"Hundreds. Do hurry, Pierce. You and the child need warmth."

"I'll want that explained, Joanna."

"Later. Please. I feel almost as if it had been I in the water. Oh, Pierce, I might have lost . . ."

"Lost me?" His eyes warmed, then his expression faded to one of sober concern, remembering. "Love, I very much feared when I looked upon you as you took the child from me, it might be the last time *I'd* see *you*. What if you, too, had fallen into the river? I couldn't have borne it. I hated it that my last view of you was with fear in your eyes."

"Not fear for me, Pierce. Fear for the child. Fear for you." A vision filled her mind of Pierce being pulled under the wheel of the mill, his crushed body flung out into the pond wash beyond, bloody and disfigured, and with a wail of pain, she reached for him.

"Jo!"

She shuddered in his arms and he held her close. "Jo, Jo," he crooned. "It's over. All is well."

When he realized she was sobbing, he looked helplessly at the miller who waited patiently, the reins of a horse in each hand.

"Aye. Just like a woman." Flour whitened the burly man's hair, fluffed out his eyebrows, coated his clothes. "The trouble is past so they fall to bits. She'll recover, Your Grace," he added in a laconic burr.

Later, home-brewed ale in Pierce and perhaps a touch too much homemade blackberry wine in Joanna, the hysteria was pushed to the back of her mind. The child was with her mother and the whole story told over and over again. Finally the two of them were allowed to leave. Joanna let Lad carry her toward home, Pierce riding beside her and keeping an eye on her sagging figure.

"How do you like being a heroine, love?"

"Heroine? 'Tis you who are the hero, Pierce. I'd not have seen the poor child. 'Twas you who spotted her and raced to the rescue."

"I couldn't have done it without you." He smiled. "Shall we share the honors?"

"I'd rather forget the whole thing."

The haunted look he'd begun to dread was back in her eyes when she turned toward him. Pierce wondered how to make it go away.

Joanna's voice was tight with strain when she said, "I swear I was never more frightened in my life."

"You behaved beautifully, Joanna. I know no other woman who wouldn't have fallen into hysterics or fainted away and been totally useless." He reached for her hand and she allowed it to lay in his as the horses paced side by side. "I suppose your experience in the Peninsula gave you such courage. There must have been many occasions more frightening than what you went through today."

"Never. I swear it."

"I can't believe that." He glanced at her, noted her white cheeks. "Your husband was in constant danger."

"But he was bred to it. He lived for it, loved it. It was his life's blood, danger."

A deep hurt filled Pierce. "And it isn't mine. I see."

"He knew death could come at any time. You . . ."

"I live a soft life and don't expect it? That makes me something less of a man, perhaps?"

"Don't be silly. That isn't what I meant at all. You are willfully misunderstanding me! You have a different sort of duty. Yours is to see to your tenants, keep your land in good heart . . ."

Joanna turned angry eyes his way and it occurred to Pierce that rousing her temper was just the thing to drive away the horror.

"You must have felt I'm a coward. Not to be compared to Wooten. After all, my love, you married him."

"That's ridiculous, Pierce." Pierce pretended to be unconvinced. "I married him because I loved him."

He pounced on that. "You married him because someone lied about me. You married him because you wished to escape the destiny you believed I'd planned for you. You married him—"

Joanna jerked her hand from his. "Nonsense."

"Don't try to convince me you loved him as you loved me."

Joanna's temper blossomed. She didn't want to admit there was any truth in what Pierce insisted was the correct version of their history. But deep inside she knew that if Cressy hadn't lied to her she'd have done no more than flirt lightly with Reggie as she had with all her many suitors. Only because she was

212

disappointed in Pierce, only because she'd believed he'd never feel for her what she felt for him had she allowed herself to become infatuated with Reggie.

"Joanna?"

"I've had quite enough of this subject, Your Grace. We've been over it far too many times as it is."

"Then we'll discuss another. All those bare chests you claim to have seen." Joanna glared at him. "Well, Jo?"

Once again his hand closed over her reins and once again she found herself angry at his temerity, the audacity that made him feel free to control her.

"We'll sit here until you explain if it takes all night."

She gritted her teeth, debating whether to do just that. She knew she could pit her stubbornness against Pierce's and win—or at least reach stalemate. But then she remembered his ordeal and swallowed her pride. "In the Peninsula and again in Brussels," she admitted. "I worked with the wounded."

"In the hospitals?" Pierce had never seen wounded men in agony but he had a vivid imagination. "Joanna, that's no work for a lady!"

"Someone had to do it. And what else was I to do? Sit nearby plying my needle and ignoring those poor men when there was much I could do?"

"You and your needle?" Pierce smiled. He was well-aware Joanna had never been one for embroidery or any of the other handiwork common to women. In fact, remembering her first—her only— sampler, he wanted to laugh. But the thought of her amongst the wounded and dying men brought off a battlefield horrified him.

If she'd been standing, Joanna would, for the second time that day, have stamped her foot in childish

213

temper. "I could give them water, feed them. I could write letters for them. I could even, when necessary, change bandages, and once, during an emergency, I helped the surgeon . . ." The horror of that experience blended with the day's terror and she turned tear-bright eyes on Pierce. "Do you have the least idea what tortures you'd have suffered, what that wheel would have done to you?"

So that was it. Most women had no basis on which to judge, but if Joanna had worked with the wounded in field hospitals, she had vivid memories of the ways a human body could be mutilated. He could see, almost feel, what she was suffering. He dropped down between the horses, pulling her off Lad and into his arms. When he cradled her head into his shoulder, her hands clutched at him, her body pressed into his, and the tears trembling in her eyes flooded over and down her dear face. Pierce picked her up and carried her a few feet into a sun-filled corner where two hedges met. He laid her down, coming down on the grass beside her and, his cradling arms surrounding her, rocked her. His voiced soothed with soft wordless murmurs.

The tears slowed and her sobs became soft gasps. One finger under her chin, Pierce tipped up her face until he could look into her ravaged features. For him. She'd cried for *him*. A wave of tenderness engulfed him, and he touched her damp cheek, lightly touched spiked lashes, gently pushed her face into his neck. The reality of death touched him, the very real possibility that he might have lost her before ever having had her sent tremors through his body. When her lips opened against his throat, every muscle in Pierce's body tensed. Greedily he brought his mouth down on hers, his hands moving less tenderly, less randomly than when he'd soothed her.

Moments? Minutes? Pierce rolled away from Joanna and covered his face.

"Pierce?"

"No. Not this way. Not when we're both upset by the day's events. I won't make love to you when you will only regret it later. I won't have you blaming me . . ."

His muffled words trailed off and Joanna looked blindly around the meadow, golden now in the slanted beams of the late afternoon sun. She saw the horses standing rump to nose, the swish of tails protecting noses sensitive to buzzing biting insects. Into the peaceful scene floated trilling notes, the melodious song of a high-flying lark. She blinked, looked down her length and slowly, painfully, hooked up her habit, not bothering with the tiny buttons of the bodice beneath. Pierce had touched her. Touched her and made her feel alive and real and unbelievably good. And then he'd stopped.

Regret it? Would she have regretted it if he'd made love to her? As he'd wanted to do. She'd been close enough there was no doubting he'd wanted to. Her neck felt stiff as she turned to look at the man stretched on the long meadow grass beside her. He was alive. He hadn't passed under the mill wheel. He wasn't lying mangled, perhaps dead . . . He was *alive*.

Joanna drew in a deep breath and plucked a long blade of grass, passing it between nervous fingers. "Thank you."

"Thank me tomorrow when I'll feel less like a fool for not pressing my advantage."

"No. Thank you for not going on. I'd never have forgiven myself. You knew that, Pierce. But I couldn't have stopped you. I didn't want to stop you. It's been so long . . ."

Joanna remembered the gentle kisses he'd stolen in days long past. She'd dreamed about those long lost days of her innocence. Then she had only guessed at the glory that might have been between them. Now she knew how wonderful it would be to lie with Pierce. Oh, why couldn't she trust him to love her as she loved him?

"So very long . . ." she mumbled.

Pierce felt every muscle tense. Misunderstanding, thinking she was remembering her life with her husband, he wondered: was that all it was? That she'd been so long without a man she'd responded to him only because of need? No. He wouldn't believe that. She wouldn't have responded to just any man. He couldn't believe that and retain his sanity.

"We'd better go, Jo."

"Yes." She struggled to her feet, glad he made no move to help her. "Yes. We'd better go."

Eleven

Occasionally as Belton brushed the heavy habit, she turned a speculative eye toward her mistress. It wasn't difficult to imagine how a woman got grass seeds and dust on the back of her clothes and in her hair. On the other hand it was unlike her mistress to play such games. Nor did she have the look of a woman deeply satisfied, and Belton was woman enough herself to believe the duke wasn't the sort to leave a woman any other way. She sighed.

"I'll wear the rose again tonight, Belton."

"Aye, Your Ladyship." Belton waited, but the formal use of the title didn't bring the usual lecture down on her head. Joanna remained as withdrawn and looked just as sad. The maid offered more provocation. "'Tis just the thing for a quiet family evening."

Still no response. Joanna never turned from the window through which she'd been staring for the last half-hour. Finally, "You can pack a portmanteau. Ask Lady Elizabeth's maid to do the same."

"We're going to Brighton?"

"Yes. Tomorrow."

For a moment Belton forgot her concern and listed

things which were most urgently needed, Joanna's wardrobe having had no attention for over a year. Her mistress's lack of interest soon brought her back to her senses.

After another silence Belton suggested, "About time, if I might be so bold, *Your Ladyship.*"

"Don't, Belton." Joanna's voice was dull and lifeless. "You know I dislike it."

This lack of animation worried the maid and Belton tried another gambit. "Lady Jo, whatever is the matter? Why are you moving like you're half asleep?" No answer. "Why do you look very much as you did when you returned from Belgium?"

Startled by the comparison, Joanna gasped, revealing the truth without thought. "There was very nearly a fatal accident today." Wan already, she paled still more. "I haven't quite recovered."

After arriving home she decided the gentle loving Pierce had demanded of her in the meadow had been nothing more than an attempt to turn her mind from the horror. Lud. If only he hadn't stopped. If only he'd demanded more. She'd needed, oh how she'd needed, still needed, to know he was alive and well, that they were both alive . . .

"An accident?"

"What? Oh. A child was in the river above the mill. His Grace went in after her. He might . . . *they* might have been pulled under the wheel. He might . . . *They* might both be dead. I can't stand it, Belton."

"You love him."

"*No.*"

But she did. Too weary to lie to herself, she remembered admitting it when she'd feared for his life,

218

realizing then that she'd never stopped loving him. And in the meadow . . .

"A woman doesn't keep the horror by her for so long if she hasn't very deep feelings for the man, m'lady."

Belton's gentle tone only made it worse. Joanna stared blindly through the window, fighting the tears that wanted to run, stream down her face. What was she to do? If only she could believe him, believe he loved her as she loved him. Believe he wanted more than a wife, a mother for his heirs . . .

"Exactly when do we leave for Brighton, Lady Jo?"

"Lord Midbourgh goes tomorrow after breakfast. We'll go with him if he allows it, follow if he remains stubborn."

Again there was no emotion, no expectation in her mistress's voice. Belton hung the habit and reached for the dusky rose dress. She checked it and decided it needed a light pressing to freshen it. "I'll have a bath sent up, m'lady. You'll feel better after a soak and a rest," said the maid as she folded the gown over her arm.

Just as Belton was exiting the room, Joanna made an effort at normality. "Has Lady Elizabeth returned from the Stauntons?"

"Yes. And like a cat in the cream she was, too." That would give Lady Jo something new to think about, thought Belton.

"Up to mischief, you think?"

"I do."

Joanna sighed. She couldn't deal with her niece just then. She pulled her oldest but warmest wrapper more tightly around her shivering body and didn't hear the door close quietly behind her maid. Gradually Joanna talked herself around to a decision. Or more exactly, she decided she needed time away from Pierce to reach a decision and her impulsive words to her maid about going to Brighton exactly expressed her need of the moment.

Later that evening Joanna entered the small salon where the family met when there was no company for dinner and found her brother there before her, a glass of wine in his hand. "I'd like a large sherry, Henry, if you don't object—or even if you do, for that matter. Then I wish to talk to you."

She walked to the couch pulled up near the fireplace, was glad someone had started a small blaze against the evening's chill. Autumn was finally making itself known after long days of unexpected sun, she thought, remembering the pleasant, uncomplicated summer days and wishing she could return to them. A sudden change that evening meant frost tonight for the first time.

"Something on your mind, Jo?"

"Yes. Pierce tells me the reason you don't want me in Brighton is that I'll meet many of my old friends from the regiment. Very selfish of you, Henry."

Henry's cheeks took on a mottled look. "Don't want you in Brighton."

"Why? Do you fear I'll run off with a half-pay officer?" She noted his lower lip protrude. "At my age?"

"You did once," said Henry, stubborn to the end.

"*Not* a half-pay officer, Henry."

There was no use discussing that point further. Reggie might have had a small income from money left him by his godfather, but he hadn't, by any reckoning, been wealthy.

"If you were home more often," she went on sternly, attempting to hold his wandering gaze, "perhaps you'd have learned I've grown up. I am no longer a skitter-brained hoyden, and I will not make an unconsidered decision to wed the first uniform I see."

He didn't respond except that his mouth formed a pout.

"I need a new wardrobe."

The mulish look characteristic of both her brother and his daughter firmed his soft features still more.

"Henry," she sighed, "if you will not take us with you, I swear I will follow after. You can't stop me. I have my own monies and I am of age. But I would prefer to have your escort and to live in your house under your protection rather than in a hotel."

He looked baffled, and Joanna's shoulders rose and fell as she drew in a deep breath. Her will had always been stronger than Henry's, but she hated pitting herself against him. He was her brother and, despite the difference in their ages, she loved him. When they were miles apart, she managed respect for him as well! In any case, she very much disliked upsetting him, but his fears were ridiculous and she *would* go to Brighton.

He took a turn around the room, his eyes flicking toward her again and again. Finally he said, "All right, Jo. But I'll be watching. I will not have you running off to any more wars, is that understood?"

She smiled. "I've no desire to see more battles, Henry. I lived through quite enough horror."

"See that you remember it." He turned at Elizabeth's entrance, obviously relieved they'd been interrupted. "Well, puss, seems you're off to Brighton tomorrow."

Jo saw the unconscious shake of the head her niece

gave the news, the lack of enthusiasm. Now what was the chit up to?

"You will enjoy Brighton, Elizabeth," she ventured.

Joanna could imagine the whirlwind in her niece's mind and quite forgot her own problems while wondering what the minx was plotting.

"Tomorrow, you say?" The girl's words were tentative, cautious.

"Yes," answered Joanna, "I've asked Belton to tell your Betty to pack for you."

"Surely we could wait a day or two?"

"Don't you wish to go to Brighton?"

"Oh yes. Just not right now." Elizabeth moved to her father's side. "Couldn't you put off your return for a few days?"

"Now, now, puss, don't crush me coat sleeve." Elizabeth jerked her hand away from his arm and reached to smooth the creases she'd made. "It's all decided, me girl. As your aunt says, you'll enjoy Brighton. The promenade. Seeing Prinny's Marine Pavilion. Perhaps your aunt will allow you to go to one of the subscription balls, and I've a box at the theater, you know. You'll like that."

For a moment, Joanna thought Elizabeth would forget whatever was on her mind. Her eyes glowed just as they ought and an excited smile hovered on her face. Then both faded and she shook her head. "I think I'll ask Alicia if her mother will allow me to stay with them."

"Elizabeth . . ."

"Dinner is served."

Dawson's voice intruded and Joanna sighed. She'd have to talk to Elizabeth but it could wait until after dinner. A problem, however, arose. After dinner, her niece disappeared. Not until bedtime, when the girl showed up in her bedroom, was Joanna able to corner her charge.

"All right, Elizabeth. What is this all about?"

"All about? I don't understand?"

"Why do you wish to stay in the country when you've been so insistent on going to town?"

"I insisted I have my come-out this fall. I've never suggested we go to Brighton."

"That innocent look does you no good, Elizabeth. You must tell me what you're plotting, for plotting something, you are."

"I don't know what you mean. But I can stay with Alicia, Aunt Jo. A message came just half an hour ago." Elizabeth handed over a note.

"Elizabeth . . ."

"If I promise to do nothing which would shame you, will you allow me to stay with Alicia?"

Joanna frowned. If only her head didn't ache so badly it made thinking nearly impossible. What could the girl possibly be up to? "Elizabeth . . ."

She shook her head. "No. I don't wish to tell you. But truly, you would approve. Please?"

Joanna searched her mind. "Matilda . . . ?"

"Oh, that. No contracts have been signed." Elizabeth waved a hand, her voice dismissive. "Squire Herman has merely talked with her mother. He hasn't even spoken to Matty. Nothing is decided."

Joanna stared. Could it be true? "You are not lying to me?"

"I do not lie. At least," she blushed, "not about important things."

"No. I don't believe you do." Joanna frowned.

"So you'll let me stay with Alicia?"

"You truly wish to remain in the country? Knowing all the delights which await you in Brighton?"

223

For a moment, longing was apparent in Elizabeth's eyes, but she shook off the mood. "I truly wish to remain in the country."

"And you will do nothing you shouldn't?"

Elizabeth's eyes wavered a moment then met her aunt's. "*I* will do nothing I shouldn't."

Had there been a very slight emphasis on the pronoun? Joanna wasn't sure. If Elizabeth wasn't worrying about Matilda and if she wasn't plotting anything out of the way, then perhaps . . .

"Please?" Elizabeth moved to Joanna's side. "Oh, Aunt Jo, you don't know how important it is . . ."

"Important?"

"Matilda is frightened, Aunt Jo. She needs Alicia and me."

That might be true. Perhaps the girls only wished to support their friend. She'd encouraged Elizabeth to think of others before her own desires and this indicated the chit had listened. Joanna sighed. "All right, Elizabeth. But you are on your honor you'll not make a scandal."

"*I* will do nothing."

Had there, again, been the slightest emphasis on the pronoun? Joanna, struggling with too many problems of her own, decided she was imagining things. Besides, the headache was very nearly unbearable.

"Tell your maid what you'll need. I should be gone no more than a week. By then the fittings will have reached the point they can finish without me."

Before going on to Brighton, Henry detoured by the Staunton estate and dropped off Elizabeth, her maid, and portmanteau. The short day's journey left Joanna more tired than she'd have expected. But

224

when she'd spent the hours in the coach thinking about Pierce, wondering what Elizabeth and Alicia were up to—and that they were up to something had been obvious from the moment she'd seen them together—and, occasionally, in an attempt to escape further thoughts of Pierce, planning the wardrobe she'd order, she felt it was no wonder she was tired.

Three days later, following hours of fittings, Joanna, Belton, and the footman Henry insisted she required, were making their way home from the mantua-makers when a curricle and a team of magnificent grays pulled up by them. "Lady Jo! Well met."

Joanna looked up into Pierce's eyes. It was their first encounter since his close escape from death, and Joanna, certain she'd disciplined herself for such a meeting, discovered there was no such thing as discipline when it came to her stubborn foolish heart. He looked so good, she thought. "Good afternoon, Your Grace."

"Send your maid home, Jo, and I'll take you for a drive. It'll blow away the cobwebs I see in your eyes."

Not cobwebs, she thought. Dreams.

Pierce searched his memory. "Belton, isn't it?" Her maid nodded. "Tell Lord Midbourgh, if he asks, I'll have Lady Joanna home for tea."

Still dreaming, Joanna put her hand in the one held out to her and climbed up to the seat. Pierce squeezed her fingers before releasing them, and Joanna, forced wide awake by the intimacy, folded her hands in her lap, safely away from temptation.

They were out of Brighton and up on the cliffs before Pierce spoke again. "It wasn't kind of you to leave without sending me a message."

"There is no reason why I should send you messages, Your Grace."

"Back to that, are we?"

"I don't know what you mean." Joanna, hating the half-choked sound of her voice, cleared her throat.

"Where is the woman I kissed in the meadow? Where the loving embrace?"

"Forget that. Pierce, please don't be cruel."

"Cruel? Is it cruel to remember the wonder of it? Of you?"

Did his tone have to be so soft, so tender? "It was cruel. The whole of it. You took advantage that day. The ri—" she gulped and finished the word "—ver, my fear, that dratted blackberry wine, your . . . gentleness. Why Pierce? Why did you do it?"

"Was I," he asked, deliberately avoiding her true question, "to let that child go to her death?"

Joanna turned her face away. "I think we should return to town."

"Not just yet." They drove on in grim silence, turning away from the ocean until Pierce found a lone wind-tortured tree which provided a bit of shade. He pulled off the road, tied the reins to the whip, and turned to her, not touching her with anything other than his eyes. "Jo, I can't, *won't*, forget that hour with you. Touching you as I did fulfilled a dream I've had for many years." He touched her cheek gently. "Well, part of the dream."

"I will not become your mistress, Pierce."

"Have I asked it of you?" Joanna remained silent. "I have not. What I have asked and will continue to ask is that you marry me."

Joanna bit her lip. How could she put him off now she knew her own heart? Oh, if only she knew *his*. "I do not trust you." Trust you, she thought, to love me as I love you.

Pierce was not a mind reader. "I thought we'd settled that nonsense. I've told you some enemy told you lies."

"And I believed you."

Pierce twisted in the seat, reached for her shoulders, and turned her. "Joanna, look at me." Pride forced her to do so. "If it isn't that, then why don't you trust me?"

Now what could she say? She recalled her fears when he'd first come back into her life. "Your very nature . . ." She looked down at the hands twisting painfully in her lap.

"Riddles? I've never like conundrums, Jo."

If only she could believe he loved her. But he didn't. If he did, then once she was widowed, he'd not have stayed away from her a moment longer than custom demanded—if that long—wouldn't have asked Lady Anne first . . .

"I can't explain. Please take me back."

"I love you."

Why did he lie? Why pretend he loved her? If only he did, she'd gladly give in, marry him . . .

Pierce sighed. Joanna was deeply upset. He could read it in her posture, in the taut skin over her cheekbones, the dark look in her eyes and strain around them. "All right. For now. Somehow, some way, I'll convince you I mean what I say and we will wed, Jo, because I know you are not averse to my suit." He gathered up the reins and turned them, heading back for Brighton.

If only he hadn't offered for Lady Anne. If only she dared believe him. Sometimes she wondered if she couldn't, didn't, simply because she wanted so badly to do so. Did that make sense? Joanna wasn't sure. Again they were silent and Joanna was glad. Between the continuing strain of her impossibly tan-

227

gled emotions and the weariness brought on by hours of standing for the modiste, she simply couldn't cope with Pierce if he were to press her more.

The wheels hit the paving stones and rumbled along the Marine Parade, bringing her out of her brown study. She looked around, saw an officer she recognized and nodded, smiled, when he waved at her.

"An old friend, Jo?"

"Yes. We knew him in Spain."

"Henry has the right of it?" There was a resigned note in his voice. "You are looking for another officer to marry?"

Joanna sighed. "Pierce, will you get into your head I have no plans to marry anyone?"

"Good. I'll carry on with *my* plans."

He turned off the Marine Parade into the Steyne and Joanna straightened at the scene farther up the street.

"Looks as if you have company, Jo. Expecting anyone?"

"Oh my God." For good measure she added a few of the less colorful of the oaths she'd learned in the Peninsula.

"Softly, Jo. You don't want the old tabbies hearing you!"

"Did you see? That's Elizabeth."

"I know."

"Can you hurry, Pierce?"

"Certainly. We'll run down that bakery lad and leap over the cabriolet, then follow that by sliding under the mail coach in order to avoid the knife grinder; we'll sideswipe that farmer's cart and push it out of our way and . . ."

Joanna chuckled in spite of herself.

"That's better," he said, smiling down at her. "It's the first laugh I've heard from you today."

She shook her fist at him but sobered almost immediately. "Why would Elizabeth be here? How did she get here? I knew she was up to something. What has she done?"

"You are terribly suspicious, Jo. Perhaps she simply missed you. Or perhaps, lured by the delights of Brighton, she decided to join you."

"Abominable man. You know it isn't so. Oh, why won't that carriage *move.*"

When they approached the house, Pierce's waiting groom stepped away from the wall and came to the grays' heads. Pierce helped Joanna down and told the man to take his team on to the stables, that he'd walk home.

"Pierce, it isn't necessary that you come in."

"Forbidding me the premises, Jo?"

"Don't be absurd. In the first place they are Henry's and I'd have no right, and in the second . . ."

"In the second you don't wish to. Come along. Let's see what the brat has done now."

Elizabeth was standing in the hall, her bonnet hanging untidily down her back by ribbons tied loosely around her neck. She had her hands knuckled into her hips and her nose in the air. "My father will—Oh, Aunt Jo, thank goodness you've come. This man is being most disagreeable. He will not believe I am who I say I am."

The butler's nose, which had been raised to a more haughty angle than Elizabeth's, came down to a more reasonable altitude. Was it possible, he wondered, that this young person was really not a young person at all? But she had no maid, no luggage, and was so

229

free with her smiles, so . . . so unlike a *lady*. His cheeks reddened as he met Pierce's mocking gaze.

"No one informed me His Lordship's daughter would arrive today."

Elizabeth, not restrained by the advanced years plaguing her aunt, stamped her foot. "No one informed you, you looby, because no one *knew* I'd arrive today."

"That will do," said Joanna, finding her tongue. "Come up to the salon while the housekeeper prepares a room for you." Joanna turned to the butler. "Chitters, bring tea as soon as you can. I'm feeling a bit chilled." She turned back to her niece when the butler's stately tread bore him toward the back of the hall. "You are behaving badly, Elizabeth."

Pierce fought a laugh at the disgust and impatience he read in Elizabeth's face. "Hello, brat. Show your manners like the good girl you aren't. Your aunt is upset enough without you adding to her burden. She's tired after hours standing still while pins were poked into her, so behave. If you can." At his teasing, Elizabeth pouted—but she did as she was bid.

The doors closed behind them and Joanna turned on her niece. "Now, Elizabeth, you may explain why you are here. I can't believe Lady Staunton allowed you to come all this way unescorted."

"Oh, I was escorted. Their solicitor. You know, Mr. and Mrs. Williams?" Joanna nodded. "They were coming to Brighton and brought me. But there wasn't room for my box or my maid. She's coming with the carrier."

"It was nice of the Williamses to bring you," said Joanna, not restraining a tendency toward sarcasm. "I hope you remembered to thank them. But what I wish to know, miss, is *why* they brought you."

230

Elizabeth sighed, but Joanna sensed the excitement underlying a slight case of nerves. The girl looked at Pierce but found no help there. She raised rueful eyes to her aunt. "I suppose I must give you Lady Staunton's letter?"

"I suspect you'd better."

Joanna held out her hand and Elizabeth, sighing more deeply, dug into her reticule, handing over the crumpled sheets. Joanna took them to the table by the window and spread them out, wondering after the first glance, if she'd be able to make out a word. It had been written obviously in great haste and even greater agitation. She couldn't decipher every word, but gradually Joanna understood.

"Well, Elizabeth? Lady Staunton recommends locking you up and giving you naught but bread and water until you confess."

"Confess what?" asked Pierce.

Both irritated and a trifle amused, Joanna explained, "Nothing of any importance, Pierce. Simply her part in Matilda Storling's elopement with the Staunton's second son."

"Albert and Matilda have not eloped. We told them and told them but no one would listen."

"It says they have disappeared. Lady Staunton writes that her husband is still searching for the pair."

"They did *not* elope. Albert and Matilda have known for years they would marry someday but Albert cannot wed until he finishes at Oxford and takes up the living his godfather is holding for him. They both know that. But if Mrs. Storling forces Matty to marry that awful man then . . ."

Jo interrupted what threatened to be a long and

irrelevant lecture. "If they have not eloped, then where are they?"

"I will not tell you until tomorrow when Matilda will be safe."

Joanna looked hard at her niece who looked back with the stubborn expression she'd inherited from her father. Jo sighed. "All right, Elizabeth. I see I must take Lady Staunton's advice."

Still there was no reaction from Elizabeth—except a slight tightening of her lips. Jo moved to the bellpull and yanked it. The butler, who must have been hovering right outside the door, stepped in. Jo turned her glare on him and the man had the grace to flush slightly.

"Ask the housekeeper if Lady Elizabeth's room is ready for her, Chitters."

"And no more listening at doors," said Pierce with a chuckle—his voice an undertone but very likely loud enough the man heard him.

The butler returned and informed them that not only had Lady Elizabeth's room been prepared but that her maid had arrived. The girl followed him out. She wished to wash and change her travel-wrinkled gown. Elizabeth considered she'd been punished quite enough for her part in the affair. After all, she'd had to listen to Mr. Williams prose on and on about wills and deeds and other boring things all the way to Brighton. But if Aunt Jo was going to be gothic about the whole, she wouldn't repine. It was, after all, in a good cause and for only one night.

Joanna wondered where their tea had gotten to but Pierce asked, "Are you sure you do not wish something stronger, Jo?"

"No—"

She closed her mouth on what she would have

232

added when the door opened and the butler ushered in two footmen carrying trays. He seemed to have ordered a surfeit. Joanna closed her eyes, opened them, and raised them to the ceiling. Pierce stifled laughter only until the door closed.

"I think," he said between chuckles, "it isn't only Elizabeth's behavior Chitters deplores, but also your own. Do you suppose he supplied such an overabundance of food on the theory that feeding one of my appetites, you'll be safe from another, you abandoned creature, you?"

"Abandoned? Oh. Because I receive you here alone, I suppose." She shrugged. "The man can think as he pleases. I must admit to feeling a bit as Elizabeth does about him. I cannot like him."

"Have you informed Henry of that?"

"Hmmm? Henry? Told him I don't like his butler? Why would I do a thing like that?"

Pierce chuckled again. "If you ever dislike a butler of mine, be sure you tell me."

Joanna looked mystified. "Pierce, why are we talking about butlers?"

"I am expressing my desire to please you." Joanna drew in an exasperated breath. "But I see you are not interested. Are you worrying about the brat's escapades?"

"Pierce, she will have ruined herself as well as that poor Storling child. And it won't have been Matilda's fault." Joanna put her hand to her forehead. "Obviously Elizabeth . . . Oh dear. I don't know what to do."

"It appears there is nothing you *can* do until tomorrow when your abominable niece has promised to confess."

Jo nodded but was obviously not satisfied.

"Jo, do you think Elizabeth's friend and co-conspirator is equally stubborn?"

Jo looked at him, her eyes widening. "Alicia! No, she is not. She draws most of her spirit from Elizabeth—which is why everyone will know the plot, whatever it is, is my niece's."

The thought that Lady Alicia would not hold out against her mother's determination soothed Jo's conscience and she busied herself with the tea tray, automatically preparing Pierce's cup just as he liked. Finding it comforting that she remembered, Pierce searched his mind for a way of distracting hers from her chit of a niece. He chose the obvious.

"How goes your shopping?"

For a moment Joanna stared at him, then sighed and followed his lead. "Slowly. I detest fittings. I believe I ache in every muscle from standing still for so long. If only there were some alternative! The result will be pleasing, I think, but the process! Such a bore."

"Tell me about *all* you've ordered."

Joanna gave him a repressive look and he chuckled, knowing full well some of her order would be of a delicate nature. She did fill in the next twenty minutes discussing styles and materials but broke off halfway through a description of a blue sarcenet gown with darker blue appliqué.

"This is nonsense. You can't be the least interested."

"If it were any other woman, I suspect I'd be bored to tears. Nothing you do bores me, m'love."

A little later Pierce rose to go. "You must tell me what the brat has been up to. I swear," he said, adopting a lisp and just a hint of foppish posture, "I'll not sleep tonight for the excitement."

Joanna laughed at his antics but ended on an exasperated sigh. "*I* won't sleep for the worry. When she becomes stubborn, there is really nothing anyone can do although I'll have one more try this evening."

Joanna walked into Elizabeth's room just as her maid was setting out an illicit cold collation. The maid sent a fearful glance toward her young mistress who sighed hugely. Joanna motioned for the maid to leave and the girl did—with alacrity.

"I became hungry."

"It was expected you'd be hungry."

"Well, don't blame Betty. She only obeyed orders."

"She disobeyed mine."

Elizabeth picked up the tray and took it to the door. Joanna opened it for her. The maid was dithering, waiting in the hall, and Elizabeth told her to return all to the kitchen—grabbing a roll and a slice of ham for herself before it was carried off. Defiantly she looked at her aunt.

Joanna, knowing she shouldn't, ignored it, "Are you ready to tell me what you've done?"

"Tomorrow. I told you I'll tell you tomorrow."

"You do realize you've helped ruin Matilda?"

"Oh no. You don't understand at all. It will be quite all right. You'll see."

"I can see you believe that but if she left in the middle of the night with only Albert Staunton as escort . . ." Jo caught a gleam of amusement in Elizabeth's eyes. "Ah. Not alone with Albert." Elizabeth looked sullen and refused to speak. "I wonder who has gone with them. You did say it was not an elopement?"

"It is not an elopement."

"And she has not been alone with Albert?"

"She has not been alone with Albert but how you guessed I don't know."

Joanna decided she wouldn't explain to her niece just how expressive a girl's eyes could be. After all, in the war between chaperon and chaperonee, one needed every advantage!

"All right. We'll leave it until tomorrow since I don't believe in thumbscrews and the rack. Then, once I know exactly what you've done, I will try to discover a way to save you from ruin as well as Miss Storling. Oh?" she asked politely when her niece turned a startled face her way. "Didn't you realize you'd be ruining yourself as well as Matty? Ah well, it'll give you something to think about tonight."

Jo left before Elizabeth could open her mouth and hold her with a question. Once one had spoken an obvious exit line, it was best to leave immediately.

The next day the duke and Lord Halford arrived at an unsuitably early hour for a morning visit. They were announced and entered the salon to find an exuberant Elizabeth dancing around the room and a very prim and disapproving Joanna seated at a delicate desk writing a letter.

At the entrance of the two men, Elizabeth paused and, belatedly, assumed the manners of a young lady. She noted how the Dreadful Duke went immediately to her aunt's side. In the pressure of saving Matilda, she'd totally forgotten the man was out to ruin her aunt. Well, now Matilda was settled, she'd have time to put a spoke in the Despicable Duke's wheel! But how?

Lord Halford approached her and Elizabeth turned, a smile lighting her face, her dimple flittering into and out of existence. She didn't understand why, but she was very happy to see Lord Halford. She curtsied, and he took her hand, and—improperly, given her age and unmarried state—bent to kiss her fingers. She felt a blush. Rising from the curtsy she raised her eyes and met his, found amusement there and something else, a warmth she didn't understand.

"This is a surprise, Lady Elizabeth. I'd heard you were settled with your friend." Elizabeth stifled a giggle and flicked a look at Joanna. "Ah. A mystery," suggested Lord Halford.

"Well, Lady Jo?" Pierce's eyes twinkled.

"Since Elizabeth assures me Lady Alicia will have confessed, I suppose there is no hurry with my letter. It's your tale," she told her niece, "and you may tell it."

Joanna turned farther away from the desk, the pen still in her hand and looked at Elizabeth, exasperation mixed with something very like admiration in her expression.

"Well, brat?" Pierce took a chair near Joanna and Lord Halford settled himself on a chair beside the girl. "We've slept scarcely a wink in anticipation, so get on with it with no roundaboutation," suggested Pierce so drolly that, despite her antipathy toward him, Elizabeth giggled, hiding her mouth behind her hand.

"It is perfectly simple," she said. "Lord Albert took Miss Storling to her grandmother."

"And don't, dear sirs, say, as I did, that she has none." Exasperation was definitely the dominant emotion in Joanna's voice.

"I should think she'd have two," Robert teased.

Joanna shook her head. "No. Mrs. Storling has never spoken of her husband's mother so I'd assumed her dead. And I knew *her* mother died just before my come-out. Elizabeth had some difficulty persuading me as to the existence of the other."

"Mrs. Storling doesn't approve of Matilda's other grandmother." Again Elizabeth giggled. "Matilda says it is because Grandmother Storling refuses to set the dibs in tune."

"Elizabeth!"

The girl blushed, rueful eyes moving from Pierce to Robert. "I *meant* to say Grandmother Storling won't give Matilda's mother a healthy allowance, which Matilda says she easily could do." She ducked her head, obviously embarrassed by her wayward tongue.

An arrested look in Pierce's eyes stopped Robert's next teasing comment. Robert recognized that look and wondered what his friend had remembered. He watched Pierce closely when his friend asked thoughtfully, "Tell me more about the old lady, Elizabeth. Where does this grandmother live?"

"In Devon, which is the cream of the jest. Everyone searched to the north, believing they'd run off to Gretna. As if Matilda would! Or Albert for that matter. They took Matilda's old governess along for chaperon, so you see all is right and tight."

"So they headed south and west. Is it certain her grandmother will want Miss Storling to live with her?"

"Oh yes. She's wanted all of them to come live with her ever since Mr. Storling died. She won't send them money, hoping they'll come, you see. But Mrs. Storling won't. She doesn't approve of her mother-in-law."

"Yet she expects the old lady to give her an allowance?"

"According to Matilda, her grandmother could set them up in style and never miss it." Pierce gave her an encouraging look and Elizabeth went on repressively, "Mrs. Storling says the old lady smells of trade."

Pierce's thoughtful look changed to one of expectation. "Trade."

"Yes. Matty says her great-grandfather left her grandmother a fortune. Something to do with locks, I believe."

"Light dawns." His satisfaction at solving the puzzle was clear in Pierce's words. "Robert, did your grandmother never tell you tales about the Caplan heiress who, in their youth, took the *ton* by storm? The one they called the Gilded Lily?"

"Caplan? Caplan? *Caplan!* My God. The Caplan fortune? Do we have a downtrodden friend we'd like to see wealthy, Pierce? Someone we should send to rusticate in Devon? Does Matilda have sisters? Surely if La Storling is related to that fortune she might look as high as she likes for husbands for her daughters."

"If I'm right, Mrs. Storling is a fool." Pierce turned to Joanna. "That is a letter to Lady Staunton, is it not?"

"Yes." Setting down the now-dry pen, she frowned, perplexed. "Pierce, I'm not sure I follow you. Are you suggesting Matilda's grandmother is wealthy beyond belief?"

"The Caplan fortune is definitely beyond belief. Golden Ball's may be larger, but not, I imagine, by much. I suggest you hint to Lady Staunton that before she discourages a marriage there, she'd better discover the facts. It could be a very good thing for the boy."

239

"Albert loves Matilda!" Elizabeth rose to her feet, scowling at Pierce.

"Ah, but does *Lady Staunton* love Matilda? Don't the lovebirds need all the help they can get?"

For a moment Elizabeth glowered, but his questions weren't easily brushed aside. Her features lightened into a smile. "Yes. Lady Staunton *was* threatening to disinherit Albert for his part in this—as if she could!—and Lord Staunton was exceedingly angry because he had to miss a day's hunting."

"He wasn't angry his son had run off with a neighbor's chit?"

"Oh, no. Just said Albert had always been a fool but he wasn't stupid so there must be an explanation." Elizabeth cocked her head to one side. "Does that mean he'll listen to Albert when he gets home?"

"I suspect so. Joanna, do add the likelihood of a healthy inheritance in the offing to that note you are writing Lady Staunton. Miss Storling will not be ostracized if it turns out she's an heiress."

"If you'll excuse me, I'll finish and send it off. Martin is saddled up and waiting for it."

Joanna turned back to the writing table and tried to concentrate on soothing the irate Lady Staunton. If Pierce was correct, then the children had, somewhat unbelievably, acted for the best. The thought of Matilda marrying Squire Herman made her stomach turn when she'd first learned of the proposed union. Now, assuming Matilda was an heiress, the thought of him getting his greedy paws on the girl's money was more distressing than ever.

Finishing, she rose and called in Chitters. Handing over the sealed letter, she gave instructions and turned back to the three seated near the empty fireplace where Pierce smiled at Elizabeth's chatter while

Lord Halford sat quietly watching the pair. A pang arose in her breast. Pierce, she thought, looked far too well-amused. It took as long as the walk to join the trio for her to recognize the feeling swelling into her throat. Heaven forbid! She was jealous of her niece!

"Aunt Jo, it is a wonderful plan."

"What is, Elizabeth?"

"That since it is getting on for time to go to London anyway, we do so immediately. If my father were to open his town house a bit early, it will give us that much longer to choose a wardrobe for my come-out. You, too, need to order those special items one can only acquire in London. I think it a wonderful idea."

It occurred to Joanna that gossip would be rampant through the countryside around Midbourgh Court. Their friends would be aware of the young couple's escapade; anyone knowing who was involved couldn't fail to lay the plot at Elizabeth's feet! Joanna didn't look forward to facing Mrs. Storling's more or less justifiable rage to say nothing of Lady Staunton's fury. Giving the matter careful consideration, Joanna believed it might be in everyone's best interest to go straight to London.

The fact Pierce had suggested it to Elizabeth rather than to herself upset her no end. Why was he being so friendly to the girl? Had she been right all along? Was his desire for revenge so extreme that he'd brought her to the edge of capitulation only to humiliate her by declaring for her niece instead?

There was a lack of animation in her when Joanna eventually agreed to the scheme that had Pierce watching her closely. That Elizabeth watched him watching her neither realized because Joanna kept her gaze firmly on the hands in her lap.

Lord Halford watched all three, his boredom a thing of the past. Concern mingled with curiosity, however, as he wondered at the animosity in the girl's face. Was she angry at Pierce's attentions to her aunt? Robert wondered if his nascent interest in that direction was to be blighted. The minx was so natural and unspoiled. Well, unspoiled in one way. All beauties were petted and indulged and it was to be expected they'd be a bit spoiled in another sense.

A cynical thought crossed Robert's mind and he shrugged slightly, telling himself not to be a fool. Elizabeth, like all the rest, would change once she'd been introduced to the delights of the season. Almost certainly, in a very few months, he wouldn't like her at all. Once she gained the sophistication of a little town bronze she would become a dead bore, and that being the case, he really shouldn't be concerned by his suspicion Elizabeth had, indeed, set her sights on Pierce.

Twelve

Joanna had forgotten how noisy and dirty London was. Or perhaps she'd been too young and excited to notice back when Henry took her and her aunt to Town for her short season. It seemed she had a constant headache and was forever in the mopes. Today was certainly a case in point, she thought. Joanna hung back as Pierce arranged seating for his guests in his town carriage. She knew all of the party except for Sir Rupert, a dour man with a missing leg and badly scarred face. The duke put Lady Anne facing forward in the far corner and Sir Rupert across from her. Then he helped Elizabeth in and motioned Robert across from her.

"Jo?" He chuckled. "No, don't glower at me that way. We're all friends here and have no need to stand on ceremony. Come along now. You're holding up the rest of us."

"I don't believe I'll go. With Lady Anne along, you have no need of me."

Pierce glowered. "Jo, I have every need of you. As you know." He held out his hand imperatively and she put hers into it. Once she was seated beside Elizabeth, he had another word with his coachman and climbed in facing her.

"Everyone comfortable? Good."

"How long will it take to reach Richmond?" asked Elizabeth.

Once he'd satisfied her on that point, Pierce leaned forward slightly and, speaking across the others, asked Lady Anne if she'd located the book for which she'd been searching when he'd seen her the day before at Hatchard's.

"The tome on herbal remedies? Yes, but I don't think I'll like it half so well as the one I have."

"You delve into folklore and herbal medicine, Lady Anne?" asked Sir Rupert, his scowl lightening.

"Yes . . ."

Joanna shut her ears to the ensuing discussion, except to note that Pierce asked a question every time it seemed about to flag. Elizabeth, beside her, fidgeted and Joanna pinched her. The girl might be bored, but it was very bad manners to show it.

As she herself was doing, thought Joanna a bit ruefully. But when had Pierce discovered such a deep interest in herbs? She didn't believe it. It was out of character. But he was deliberately drawing out Lady Anne and making her laugh—Laugh? Even Sir Rupert chuckled. What had she missed? Joanna decided it was time she began attending.

There was a pause in the conversation then, and Joanna, thinking of Reggie, asked Sir Rupert if he'd been wounded at Waterloo.

"No." The man seemed to draw into himself with the one rude word.

Pierce kicked her shin and both he and Robert jumped into the breach. Robert spoke quickly to Elizabeth, asking where she'd acquired her bonnet, and Pierce, talking across that conversation, asked Anne if she grew her own herbs.

Again the conversation bored Joanna, but this time she pretended interest. She felt a great deal of relief when they arrived at Hampton Court where her spirits drooped as she watched Elizabeth coax both Robert and Pierce into the maze. Lady Anne chose a bench some distance away in the shade where she continued her animated conversation with Sir Rupert, who, when alone with her, seemed to thaw. Joanna, feeling very much alone and unneeded, chose a path at random and strolled down it.

She felt a great deal of surprise when Pierce joined her some minutes later. He mopped his brow and resettled his hat. "I thought I'd not escape that easily," he said, "but when Elizabeth chose one path, I took another and, once she was out of sight, retraced my steps."

"You left Elizabeth alone with Lord Halford?" Joanna was not so outraged as she sounded or as she felt she ought to be. It was, she'd discovered, a heavy burden chaperoning a chit like her niece.

"You dared," Pierce mimicked her tone, "to leave Lady Anne unchaperoned with Sir Rupert?!"

They stared at each other and Joanna couldn't repress a giggle.

"That's better. You know the guard in the middle of the maze is sufficient chaperon and Lady Anne and Sir Rupert are far too respectable to need one."

"What you mean is no one would think to accuse Lady Anne of dallying with Sir Rupert. Pierce, what happened to him? I realize I put my foot in it when I asked if he'd been at Waterloo, but what else was I to think? A lost leg, those scars on his face? Was I truly out of line?"

"No. But he's sensitive. He feels he made a fool of himself and has been punished far too severely—and believes himself a monster in the eyes of others. It happened years ago, a curricle race that went wrong, but he's never been the same. It is a ridiculous attitude, and Robert and I occasionally try to bring him to his senses. We practically had to kidnap him to get him to come along today."

"But why did you?"

Pierce opened his mouth—then closed it. He frowned slightly. "Joanna, if you are so dense as to be unable to explain that for yourself, I don't believe I'll tell you. Shall we return to the others?"

Joanna felt like an idiot. She also felt small and unhappy. Pierce's disapproval of her had been clear and she resented it. If she weren't so unhappy and if her head didn't ache so abominably, perhaps she wouldn't be acting like such an old cat. But watching Pierce make up to Lady Anne right under her nose was more than she could bear.

Pierce, decided Joanna, was behaving like the veriest coxcomb. Not satisfied with making a conquest of Elizabeth toward whom he'd shown lazy attention ever since they'd come to London, it appeared he had to have every female in sight in love with him. But Lady Anne? The woman had no extraordinary beauty and had already turned him down. She did, however, have an excellent dowry. Pierce couldn't have become so mercenary he was playing the heiresses, one against the other, until he could determine which would do him the most good. Could he? Or was he planning still another revenge, this time against Lady Anne for rejecting him?

Suddenly Joanna remembered her brother's gossip about Pierce going the pace just after her marriage to Reggie. Could he be under the hatches and no one have guessed? That would explain his interest in a large dowry. Joanna put the unpalatable idea to the back of her mind and did her best to join in the entertainments of the rest of the afternoon.

But back in her room in Henry's house on Grosvenor Square, Joanna frowned, pacing back and forth, the thoughts going round and round, her headache growing more severe with every new theory to cross her mind. The one thought never to intrude was to wonder why, if he were in need of money because of that long-ago spree, he'd waited years before doing anything about it.

Robert Merton, Lord Halford, paced with equal determination. Unlike Joanna, whose room was spacious and allowed such occupation, he was confined to the limited area of the rooms he kept in Little Ryder Street just off St. James. No matter which way he turned it seemed he was always bumping into some item of furniture. If not a table in his way, then a chair or a stool. For once, Robert wished for his town house.

He told no one why he habitually let out his perfectly situated mansion, the existence of which meant he needn't live in such obscurity. Of course his friends needed no telling. They knew his ambitions didn't run toward *ton*ish entertaining. His chief reason, however, was a desire to keep Cressy from running tame in his home—which she'd do, given half a chance.

Robert paced and wondered just what his old friend was up to. Unlike Joanna, he acquitted Pierce of flirting with Lady Anne. He'd noted the shy interest Sir Rupert expressed in Lady Anne's conversation and how, as the day drew on and the two found more and more in common, Pierce had thrown out comments or questions only when needed to keep the other two talking.

If Pierce was matchmaking between Lady Anne and Sir Rupert, Robert was all for it. Their old friend had practically withdrawn from the world since his accident. He was much too touchy about the loss of his leg and his scarred face, and indeed the face had looked rather awful before the red faded. Now the scars were more raffish than off-putting, although no one could bring Rupert to believe it. If Lady Anne's gentle interest was an indication, a match there might be possible.

Elizabeth was another matter altogether. Robert, much against his will, was falling deeper and deeper into an infatuation with the abominable girl whose liveliness was enhanced by occasional flashes of wit and intelligence. A smug smile crossed his face as he remembered how he'd managed to lose Pierce in the maze, spending a delightful half-hour following Elizabeth while the chit attempted to find her way to the middle. She had, predictably, refused all help from the guard seated in his high chair, ready to give aid to those who became too confused. As predicted, Elizabeth had enjoyed the maze. Even so, Rob couldn't quite acquit his old friend of monopolizing her attention at other times.

Or was that the other way around? Was Elizabeth monopolizing Pierce? Thinking back, it seemed that whenever Pierce showed signs of turning to Joanna, Elizabeth was right there, teasing and cajoling, lightly flirting or asking questions. Pierce had shown no sign of irritation, however, which he would surely if he'd wished a tête-à-tête with Lady Jo.

Robert flopped into the rather tatty but exceptionally comfortable chair near his small fireplace but jumped up immediately. He removed a quirt, a dirty glass, and a glove he'd thought lost, looked wonderingly at the glove and then, deciding it wasn't important, dumped them all on the floor before returning his tall form to the chair.

This evening they'd all been invited to the first ball of the season, and before it was over, if he watched carefully, perhaps he'd have a better idea of what was going on. Assuming, he thought ruefully, he and Pierce didn't have to forcibly dress Rupert and didn't, as a result, arrive far later than was polite, considering there weren't six or seven parties to attend each evening as there would be later in the season.

Joanna, surrounded by officers, smiled and laughed and agreed to dance after dance, each time with the proviso that she would not take to the floor if her niece were in need of chaperoning. But even as she laughed at a sally made by a major in one of the light brigades, her eyes were searching for Pierce, wondering why he'd not yet appeared. He'd asked for the supper dance several days earlier and she was saving it for him, but if he didn't arrive soon she would find herself without a partner.

Elizabeth, her face flushed after a particularly boisterous country dance, came off the floor with something less than the expected enthusiasm.

"What is it, child? Have you ripped your gown or did someone step on your toes?"

"Young men are so silly. Would you believe my last

partner says he's a poet of all things and promises to write an ode to my eyebrows? And the one before that compared my dancing to a daffodil blowing in the breeze? You might be a daffodil, Aunt, with your blond hair, but me, with my dark locks? More nearly a chimney sweep's brush than a daffodil!''

Joanna laughed at the scorn in the young voice but noticed that her niece, too, seemed to search the crowded room for one person in particular.

"There are the Bradfords, Aunt Jo. Let's join them for a moment.''

Was Lady Anne the person for whom Elizabeth had searched? Joanna thought not. "They are across the ballroom, Elizabeth. Besides, haven't you promised this next dance?''

"Good heaven's no!'' Elizabeth gave her aunt an exasperated look. "It is a waltz. Do you wish me to lose my reputation?''

"I seem to have lost track. Oh, Lieutenant Netherton, did I promise you this dance? I'm so sorry. I did warn you, didn't I . . .''

"You go along, Aunt Jo. Lady Staunton won't mind if I join her, will you, ma'am?'' Elizabeth raised limpid eyes to the formidable matron who'd just strolled up beside them. "You'll tell me all about how Albert found Matilda's grandmother, won't you?''

Lady Staunton tried to look severe, but, meeting the mischievous eyes of her daughter's friend, found she couldn't. "All right, child. You sit here and I'll tell you all about their adventures. Run along, Joanna. I'll see to your ewe-lamb.''

Joanna gave the lieutenant her hand and moved toward the dancers swirling around the floor. Lieutenant Netherton was an excellent waltzer, and almost in spite of herself, Joanna enjoyed the dance.

The officer answered questions about the recent doings of many of her old friends in his regiment but seemed much more interested in hearing about Elizabeth. Laughing, Joanna promised him an introduction and laughed still more when he pretended to wipe sweat off his brow and said he'd brushed through that better than he'd expected. When they left the floor, it was to find that Pierce, Robert, and Rupert were talking to Lady Staunton and Lady Bradford. Anne and Elizabeth were nowhere to be seen.

Joanna looked at Lady Staunton who informed her a very rude gentleman had stepped on Elizabeth's gown and ripped the ruffle loose and that she and Anne had gone to find a maid to mend it. "I'd better go after them," Joanna said but her next partner came up and delayed her long enough that the girls returned.

Elizabeth's color was high and Joanna noted a slightly disapproving look on Anne's face. *Now* what, she wondered, but before she could ask, Robert led her niece into a set forming nearby and her own partner insisted they, too, find a place before it was too late. Pierce, she thought, glimpsing his face before he turned to talk to Anne and Rupert, looked very angry about something, but she had no time to worry about him now.

That changed soon enough; the supper waltz arrived and with it the necessity of facing Pierce's black mood.

"Well, Joanna?"

"The evening has gone very well, I think."

"It was a lie, was it?" He swung her in a wild circle and her feet very nearly left the floor. "All your protests that you aren't husband hunting were twaddle."

Joanna frowned. "Pierce, what are you talking about?"

"You've laughed more tonight than you have in weeks. I've been watching you. Laughing and flirting with every uniform in sight. Damn your eyes . . ."

"I have done no such thing. And if all you can do is insult me, I'd like to return to Elizabeth."

Realizing Joanna's temper was rising, Pierce backtracked to the first thing to come to mind. "Speaking of Elizabeth, she ran into Sir Frederick when off fixing her frills."

Joanna felt the blood draining from her face, her eyes lifting finally to meet his. "Pierce . . ."

"Lady Anne has a good head on her shoulders. She allowed no more than polite greetings, but as predicted, the chit must be watched. Relax, love, no harm will come to your charge." His hold tightened momentarily as they circled again and then again. "I didn't tell you to worry you, Joanna, only to warn you."

"Thank you." Joanna fixed her eyes on his cravat, allowed her feet to float to his guidance.

"I'd like to see your face, Joanna. Your hair is very beautiful, but it's your eyes I dream about." She flushed, looked up with an angry gleam but, confused by the soft expression she saw, set her gaze again on the elaborate folds of the starched muslin at his throat. He continued in a dry pedantic tone. "I've come to the conclusion playing chaperon is not good for your character."

Joanna blinked. What on earth did he mean by that?

"Hmm," he said thoughtfully. "It seems to have dulled all your enthusiasm for life, love." Just a touch of anger could be heard in his next words: "Except, of course, when with your *old friends*."

"I *am* tired, Pierce. Bear-leading Elizabeth is more a strain then I expected, choosing just the right styles and finding just the right accessories. And when we aren't shopping, which has never been a favorite pastime of mine, we seem to be running hither and yon and, up till tonight, the season hadn't yet begun. I will be so glad when it is over. And so very glad when Elizabeth's future is settled. Then," she lifted her chin, "I can think of my own."

"I, too, will be glad when you can think of your future, Jo. As you know."

The throbbing in her temples which had disappeared while talking to various officers of her acquaintance, returned with a vengeance.

"What is it Jo? Are you ill?"

How had he guessed? And why, occasionally, could he sound as if her welfare was his concern? His only concern? When that kindness appeared in his voice, she wanted desperately to lay her head on his shoulder—and her heart at his feet. Oh, if only she could believe that he loved her.

"Come, Joanna, let us find the others and go down for supper. You'll feel better for getting off your feet for a time." She frowned at him. "What now? How have I insulted you this time?"

"Am I so ancient a few dances wear me down?"

"No, but constant attendance on the brat would exhaust the strongest among us."

The twinkle in his eyes brought a lightening to her mood and she smiled in spite of herself.

"Better," he said with a thoughtful nod.

When she chuckled, he smiled.

"Much better."

He whirled them around once more and stopped right where Elizabeth was chattering to two young men, Lord Halford's hand set possessively on the back of the delicately wrought chair in which she sat.

"Tell these fine gentlemen they'll have to run along, brat. We're off to the dining room before it becomes too crowded."

Elizabeth, much to Joanna's surprise, obeyed docilely.

Across the ballroom, Lady Cressida Clayton bit her lip as the second matron that evening gave her the cut direct. She looked around a bit wildly and her eyes lit on Sir Frederick who stood, arms folded, against one wall. She noticed how his eyes followed the Ransome women as they left the ballroom on the arms of Pierce Reston and her brother. Cressy, forgetting her problems when confronted by Sir Frederick's obvious lack of success, wended her way to the baronet's side.

"Well, Frederick?"

"I've noticed just how well it is with you," he said, his lip curling.

Cressy flinched at his sarcasm, but matched it with some of her own. "And, of course, with you. You've danced so often with the newest beauty, haven't you?"

"I plot my own course, Cress. Don't interfere."

"Such an odd course. So successful . . ."

"Don't play games with the master, my dear. You'll lose."

He offered his arm and Cressy, pleased by the attention, took it. Even Sir Frederick, with his tarnished reputation, was better than no escort down to supper. He seated her at a table for two and walked off toward the groaning buffet, returning with just the delicacies she most enjoyed.

"Sometimes I wish you were the sort one married, Frederick. You remember just exactly what most pleases one."

"That is because knowing what pleases another gives one an advantage over them."

Cressy lowered the forkful of creamed crab to her plate. She looked from it to him. "Advantage?"

"It puts the recipient into a good mood. You'd best remember that."

"You are laughing at me."

"Just giving you a word of advice, Cressy."

They ate in silence for a few moments, Cressy's eyes on her food and Frederick's flicking occasionally toward the corner where Elizabeth's laugh floated on the air. God, the chit was a beauty, he thought. Lively and unaffected. And well-chaperoned. 'Twould be a challenge, winning the chit's favor.

Joanna was ambivalent about the evening she'd just passed. True, she'd enjoyed joking and reminiscing with old friends, but there'd been sad memories, too: so many had died at Waterloo and every man she talked to had called to mind another she'd never see again. Then there had been Elizabeth's brief but unsettling meeting with Sir Frederick. Anne had assured her it had involved no more than a few polite words, but Joanna knew her niece. The chit would quite happily ruin herself in an attempt to give the rake a set-down.

Pierce was still another problem. He'd had the supper dance and then, when he'd found her card full, had stolen two more later in the evening. He'd cut out one man too young to have any idea how to handle the situation and very nearly caused a scene with another who had, half seriously, threatened a duel over the abduction of his partner. Three dances in one evening! Joanna could only pray no eagle-eyed dowager was counting. Pierce would cause a scandal yet. Lord, she was tired. If only she could close down the squirreling thoughts going round and round in her mind and *go to sleep*. One last yawn and she did just that.

"It is *too* warm enough." Elizabeth insisted one morning ten days later. "I won't wear a pelisse."

Joanna stared at her niece until the girl lowered her gaze. "I understand very well, Elizabeth, that you wish to show off that dashing new ensemble, but if you come down with a chill, you will be confined to your room and unable to show off that or any of the others now crowding your wardrobe."

Elizabeth sent a startled glance across the breakfast table, then giggled. "You, Aunt Jo, are a complete hand."

"Allow me to drop a word in your ear, my dear," drawled Jo. "Don't go around spouting cant phrases. It sets up the backs of the old tabbies and isn't much appreciated by the patronesses either. You *do* wish to be approved for the waltz, don't you?"

Elizabeth bit her lip. "You know, I'm not certain I do."

"What?!"

"Remember the night Matilda was in trouble? The Bradford ball?"

"Yes," said Joanna drawing the word out slowly.

"She got into that situation because she was waltz-ing. When a gentleman controls one's steps, he can lead one anywhere. And one mustn't make a scene. So, you see, I'm not so certain I do wish to waltz."

Joanna stared at her. "Sometimes, Elizabeth, you amaze me. Now, if you've finished playing with that poached egg, send for your pelisse and let us be off to the park."

"I thought the proper practice was to sit in the salon and wait for callers the day after a ball, and we attended *two* last night."

"Elizabeth!"

"Oh all right. But you know I hate to walk."

Joanna knew that full well, but she badly needed the exercise and fresh air. As she waited for Elizabeth, it occurred to her that a cottage in the country might appeal to her more than a place in Town. She could ride in the country as one could not in the park where convention held one to a strict trot at best. Still considering that point, she automatically checked that her niece was properly turned out and that their maids were in attendance before nodding to Turner who was attending the door, obviously proud of his new uniform and his duties as under butler.

Joanna reminded herself to have a talk with Turner. In his new role the former batman looked disapproving every time she smiled at him or stopped to ask how things were going with him. He needn't think she was less his friend now than he'd been to her in the Peninsula. In fact, she thought with a rueful chuckle, how dare the man get so uppity!

Half an hour later, encountering them near the Serpentine, Lady Anne invited Joanna and Elizabeth into the Bradford's carriage—much to Anne's mother's chagrin. Lady Bradford shortly changed her mind. While the young bucks flirted with Elizabeth and the Corinthians traded quips with her aunt, there were a couple of the more sober gentlemen, drawn to the carriage by the presence of the Ransome women, who actually seemed charmed by Anne's dry wit. One of those men had considerable expectations and might not be such a bad match. Lady Bradford was becoming very worried by her stubborn daughter's continued single state.

When the Duke of Stornway and then Lord Halford rode up, she was more than pleased by the exchange of looks between her daughter and His Grace. Not that she understood it. In fact the slight shake of his head was quite confusing. But it did mean the two had an understanding of some sort and that was quite enough to push aside all thought of "considerable expectations" and set Lady Bradford dreaming—again—of her daughter, the duchess.

Later, when set down by the park gate nearest Grosvenor Square, Elizabeth seemed pleased enough to head for home. "Did you see Lady Cressida?"

"No, I didn't. Was she in the park?" Joanna felt faintly surprised. Cressy was not one to come to the park even at the most fashionable time of day when all the *ton* went to see and be seen. Certainly not at this early hour when the fading beauty was known to keep to her room—and out of the sun.

"She was riding in a carriage with a very odd-looking man."

Joanna swung her head quickly one way and then the other. "Lud, child! Watch your tongue."

"Pooh. No one is about but a few maids and the tradesmen. Who do you suppose he was?"

"I haven't a notion." Joanna drew in a deep breath. "It is not your business, Elizabeth," she said repressively.

"I just wondered." They walked in silence for a ways. "I've heard she must marry soon if she isn't to find herself beyond the pale."

Joanna shushed her, but Elizabeth was in search of information and ignored her aunt's request she be still.

"Aunt Jo, just how does a woman put herself beyond the pale?" She jerked at Joanna's sleeve.

Like Lady Bradford, Joanna had noticed the secret exchange of information between Lady Anne and Pierce. Now she shook her head clearing it of renewed dreams of a quiet cottage in the country where she wouldn't be constantly battered emotionally as she was here in Town. She discovered she'd lost track of the conversation: "Beyond what pale, Elizabeth? What are you talking about?"

"Lady Cressida, of course. Do come down out of the clouds, Aunt Jo." But just then they came within sight of their front door, and Elizabeth lost interest in the subject. "Hurry. We have company." She quickened her steps.

Joanna sighed. Avoiding the sort of company to which Elizabeth referred was precisely why she'd gone to the park. She'd hoped to avoid another morning playing propriety in the salon while Elizabeth made eyes at every rogue who called. Not that either of the gentlemen watching their approach qualified as a rogue. In fact one of them had eyes only for Joanna. A dull throbbing set up housekeeping in her temples as they led the way to the salon and Joanna prepared herself for a boring half-hour.

Lord Halford appeared before the first two callers took their leave and soon still others arrived. Joanna wondered how she was to survive the weeks they'd be situated in London. Worse, what if Elizabeth left unbetrothed! They'd have to return and do it all over again in the spring. What an awful thought.

Joanna was very conscious that Pierce was not amongst the crowd of young sprigs decorating her brother's salon. The fact any number of the other gentlemen found her company interesting did nothing to assuage her headache.

"Oh, please, Aunt Jo. Say we may go."

"What?" Joanna looked around the salon and discovered all their guests but Lord Halford had left. "Go where?"

"You aren't attending. Ro—" Her eyes darted toward Robert and she blushed. *"Lord Halford* has invited us to the theater and supper afterwards. Do say we may go. I've never been to a play, Aunt Jo. I'd like nothing else half so well." Big eyes begged for permission. "Please say yes. Please?"

Joanna blinked at Elizabeth's enthusiasm. Several days earlier when, at her instigation, her brother suggested taking the two of them to see a Shakespeare production, Elizabeth had vowed the evening would be dull beyond bearing. "Lord Halford?"

"May I add my plea to that of your niece? I've suggested the Theatre Royal in Drury Lane, Lady Jo. They've mounted a new comedy which seems to be doing quite well."

"Oh. A comedy. I see." Joanna's eyes twinkled. A comedy was a far different proposition indeed than one of the Bard's tragedies. "When do you propose we go, m'lord?"

"I thought on Friday. So far as I'm aware there is nothing more important than a musicale scheduled for that evening."

"I believe I've kept that evening free of engagements. Well, Elizabeth, if you would really like to go . . ."

"Oh, I *would*."

"Then we shall."

"Excellent." Robert lifted Joanna's fingers and kissed the air somewhere above them. She noted he held Elizabeth's small hand a trifle longer and that her niece blushed beautifully before he released her. "I will, I hope, have the pleasure of seeing you, er—" he glanced at Joanna—"*both* of you, long before Friday. Good day."

Was Lord Halford flirting with Elizabeth? How strange. Surely her abominable niece didn't believe she could lure the elusive Robert to the altar, did she? But then, wasn't the earl acting quite out of character in paying attention to a mere chit of a girl just out of the schoolroom? And what about Pierce? If he were truly enamored of Elizabeth, instead of toying with her as Joanna feared, would Robert yield the field to his best friend? Joanna longed for the long busy, *boring* days at Midbourgh Court. It was far more likely, she thought then, that Robert was merely being kind to a friend's daughter. She must remember to warn Elizabeth not to take him seriously.

That evening, at a soiree, she once again found herself wondering at Pierce's abominable behavior. Lady Bradford made a point of telling her the Duke of Stornway had called at the Bradford town house that afternoon and stayed very nearly an hour!

It would have eased Joanna's mind no end if she'd known Sir Rupert had arrived with the duke and stayed even longer, but since Lady Bradford had no interest in the baronet, with his battered body and lesser title, the lady made no mention of the fact her daughter had spent most of the afternoon with him discussing the benefits gained by the proper use of Boraginaceae—whatever that was—and other such oddities. Lady Anne had suffered through a long lecture from her ambitious mother as soon as the salon was cleared of company. Lady Bradford wasn't quite sure her daughter had been attending, however, and that was something else she had no intention discussing with Joanna, who had a tiresomely lovely niece. Lady Bradford had it quite firmly settled in her mind her daughter would be Duchess of Stornway before Christmas.

Pierce grew more and more worried about Joanna as the days passed. She seemed to have lost all sparkle, all energy. On Thursday he tricked her into a ride in his phaeton and got her away from Town, reaching the Chelsea road before she came out of her protective cocoon enough to notice.

"I think—"

"So far as I've been able to determine, you don't think at all," he interrupted.

"You said . . ." She glanced at him. "I'm sure you said the park."

"You never believe what I say." Exasperation was evident in his tone. "Why did you this time?"

"Pierce—" she sat up straight and glared at him— "you aren't kidnapping me again, are you?"

"It may come to that, but I'm still hoping you'll come to your senses and it won't be necessary."

His teasing, so different from the first taunting remarks, relaxed her and Joanna slid back into the well-padded comfort of his carriage, pulling the soft woolen rug more tightly around her shoulders. "Well, in that case, I suppose you'll eventually tell me where we are headed."

"Good girl."

"What have I done to deserve your approbation now?"

"Decided to trust me."

"Have I? I don't believe I have."

Pierce cast a wry look her way. "In that case, perhaps I should turn this drive into a kidnapping."

"Don't be a great silly."

They drove in silence for nearly half a mile before Pierce cleared his throat, drawing Joanna out of her preoccupation. "What has you in the mopes, love?"

She ignored the endearment, having discovered that objecting only led to his taking further liberties. "Elizabeth. Of course. What else?"

"Don't sound so despairing. Tell me what's bothering you."

"It is none of your business. Besides, why should I worry you with my concerns?"

"Because I wish to be concerned? Because I wish to lighten your burdens?"

She chuckled. "How out of character for you, Pierce. Should I spread the rumor you're going soft?"

"Don't make jokes, my love. You've become skin and bone. Your brother has a responsibility for the chit. If you won't talk to me, talk to him."

"Such excellent advice, Your Grace! Of course, I'll have to get his attention first. Perhaps if I were to knock him over the head with the fire irons? Or lock him up and promise to feed him only if he takes the time to listen to me first? Or perhaps—"

"All right. It was a rotten notion. But I'm worried about you, Jo."

"Worried?" Joanna thought about it and decided it couldn't be true. Pierce never worried. He never had anything about which he need worry. So he

263

wasn't worrying now. She sighed at the logic of that conclusion. It was just the sort of thinking which caused one headache after another.

"You don't believe me. This lack of faith in me will drive me to desperate measures, Jo."

"Pierce?"

"Yes?"

"Please, just for an hour or two, can we forget all about my bothersome niece and the season and everything else? Just pretend I'm seven and a nuisance?"

"We can forget your niece and forget the season, Jo. But there is no way I can pretend you are only seven. I haven't been able to pretend that since you were seventeen. And it only gets worse."

"What gets worse?"

"My need for you. Wanting you in my arms—my bed."

Joanna compressed her lips tightly. "Must you have every female you know at your feet?"

Pierce frowned. "Now what?"

It all boiled up and Joanna reached for the reins, tugging until he pulled the horses over and stopped by the side of the road. "It's true, Pierce. I've watched you. Elizabeth. Anne. Every woman you talk to. You need their constant attention, their . . . regard. I will not add to your consequence by becoming just another conquest."

"You have lost what little wits you ever had, love."

"No, I have not. You seem to think it a game. Elizabeth, for instance. Your friend Halford shows more interest in her than he has ever shown a green girl, but you have to cut him out! It's despicable, Pierce."

Very slowly Pierce tied the reins. Slowly he turned until he faced her. Tension trembled through him and Joanna edged back until she was trapped in the

264

corner and could get no farther. He reached for her and she shook her head. Then, fingers biting into her shoulders, he shook her.

"How dare you?" Her bonnet tumbled down her back. "How dare you say I'd do such a thing to a friend?"

"If it isn't true, explain away your behavior. If you can."

"I have done absolutely nothing I need explain."

"You have. You visit Bradford House daily. Everyone is waiting for the announcement of your forthcoming nuptials. You—"

"My visits to Lady Anne are a cover for Sir Rupert. Lady Bradford must not interfere in that courtship."

Joanna blinked. Could it be true? "Well, then Elizabeth."

"Haven't you figured out that abominable brat's tricks?"

"I don't know what you're talking about. She's infatuated with you."

"She is not infatuated. She dislikes me intensely."

"Then why . . ."

"Because she thinks that if she dominates my attention, I will not turn to *you*. She's protecting you."

"Elizabeth?! Ridiculous."

"Elizabeth, for reasons I don't understand, seems to have changed from the self-centered spoiled brat I first met."

"Elizabeth is *protecting* me? *From you?*"

Could their one conversation have had that much effect on the girl? Joanna, thinking back, decided it might have. Elizabeth had intelligence. If she was made to use it, she very well might change out of all recognition. And there was no doubting she'd given the girl a great deal to think about.

"Well . . ."

Pierce waited. When Joanna didn't go on, his grip loosened, changed, one hand moving down her back and pressing her toward him as the other tipped her face. "Joanna?"

A horn blasted behind them, and as a coach-and-four passed at a gallop, Pierce's team panicked, hauled back, lurched forward, rose on their hind legs, and suddenly required all his skill to quiet and control them. The moment was lost. Joanna found she was filled with regret.

It seemed she could not be pleased. It appeared, she thought, as Pierce turned the carriage with a dexterity she could not help but admire, that nothing satisfied her. Neither Pierce in a teasing mood nor when serious. Not when he cajoled her nor when he berated her. And although she knew it was the height of folly, she could *not* be glad their moment was interrupted: Pierce had been about to kiss her. Again. And she was dreadfully aware she had wanted him to do so.

Oh, for that blessed cottage and still more blessed peace! A silent and bitter laugh wafted through her mind; that, too, was a less-than-pleasing thought. Joanna was quite certain that escaping to the peace of her very own cottage in the country would be about as boring as anything could be. She shook her head. It was true. There was simply no pleasing her at all these days.

Thirteen

Elizabeth stamped her foot and stared down her maid. The girl, not much older than Elizabeth herself, looked at the floor, twisting her fingers into her apron. For weeks the abigail had gone along quite docilely with all her mistress's stratagems for escaping strict chaperonage. Suddenly she was irritatingly stubborn about the jaunts to shops and parks which Elizabeth enjoyed so much.

"You will stop lecturing me, my girl, and do as you're told."

"That's what I *be* doin'," said Betty with only the slightest whine to her voice. "Me orders be not to let you out alone. It was all right as long as no one knew, but when we got caught that day, I got me orders. I daren't let you go out walking no more. Not alone."

"I haven't asked you to let me out of your sight." Elizabeth pushed her parasol and reticule into the abigail's hands. "I have merely suggested you not bother my aunt with the fact of a mere stroll to Hookham's Lending Library."

"Library?" asked Betty doubtfully. "You said nothin' about a library."

"Library. Surely you do not think I may get into mischief at a library? Aunt Jo needs to rest. She is looking haggard. There is no reason she bestir herself for this."

"You mean to say you be going to a *library*?" Suspicion etched Betty's voice. "Sounds smoky to me, m'lady." Elizabeth's usually helpful maid frowned at her mistress.

"That is because you are an ignorant girl from the country, unknowing of Town ways." Elizabeth's pert nose rose a notch or two. "I have it on the best of authority that Hookham's Lending Library is a sociable place where one may meet one's friends and show off one's newest dress. And I very much want to show off this ensemble," she finished coaxingly. As her maid's eyes softened, she went on: "And I do *not* wish to add to Aunt Jo's burdens by suggesting she, too, make the effort. You know she isn't interested in such things."

This the maid couldn't contradict. Lady Jo always dressed up to the mark when going into society, but she didn't hold her wardrobe in such high regard that it took up nine-tenths of her time, thoughts, and energy as was true of so many ladies.

Elizabeth let the girl's mind work its way through the points she'd made. "Well?"

"I can see no harm in it." Betty spoke slowly, trying to find the flaw she was convinced existed.

"Nor can anyone else, Betty. Do hurry."

The weeks of the season had passed blissfully up until she and Betty were caught returning from an unauthorized shopping jaunt. Since then such excursions had been curtailed, but this was important.

Elizabeth had not lied to her maid. She was always pleased she needn't lie to get her own way. It was quite simple, however, to tell less than the whole truth. The evening before she'd overheard Lady Anne quietly mentioning to Sir Rupert she intended returning her books this morning. The comment had been accompanied by a significant look. Elizabeth, although preoccupied with her aunt's affairs, had not overlooked what appeared to be an assignation between the baronet and Lady Anne and she was curious.

For Lady Anne to be making assignations was out of character. Besides, why would a woman of her position and fortune look twice at so battered a piece of goods as Sir Rupert? Elizabeth knew for a fact Lady Anne had turned down three perfectly acceptable matches. Not that she had boasted of them, of course, but her mother had. Now it seemed to Elizabeth Lady Anne was flirting with half a man. Elizabeth, curious, wished to see the two of them where they would not be under Lady Bradford's basilisk eye.

Not quite so knowing as she pretended, Elizabeth misjudged slightly. In her concern to leave the house before her aunt could set her a chore or require she go for a fitting or suggest she practice—at that thought Elizabeth made a mental note that she really must spend some time with her piano—in any case, she'd misjudged. There was no one of note in the quiet library. Only a few elderly gentlemen reading newspapers and one equally elderly, exceedingly dowdy, and thankfully unknown lady with her long nose in a fat tome.

Elizabeth sighed. She'd arrived too early. She headed for the shelves where a helpful and instantly infatuated heavily freckled clerk said she'd find the newest novels. Absently she looked at one, then another, but nothing held her interest. Every so often she glanced around to see if Lady Anne had arrived, and sighed slightly when she discovered her quarry was still not in sight. Finally, seeing a title which intrigued her, she lifted on her toes and stretched for it.

"Allow me, Lady Elizabeth."

The soft but familiar voice tickled her neck, and with an uncontrollable but almost silent squeak, Elizabeth tried to turn and drop back down onto her heels at the same time. Hands, warm strong hands, circled her waist, steadied her.

"Sir Frederick. How you startled me."

Elizabeth felt a moment's qualm as the hands moved against her waist, but they dropped and the baronet stepped back, lifting his hat and bowing slightly. Again he was the friendly man who so often happened to appear where she happened to be. Elizabeth relaxed.

Frederick Carrington had played the game far too often to allow his quarry to fear him. "I apologize if I startled you," he said softly. "I saw you straining to reach for a volume and only thought to help."

"Well, so you may." Demurely Elizabeth pointed out the novel at which she wished to look. "I must say, Sir Frederick, this is the last place I'd have expected to find *you*."

Well-formed brows rose in query as he handed her the first of the three volumes. "Am I to feel insulted by your comment, my girl?" He noted her stiffening at that form of address and quirked one brow into a more sardonic but humorous twist.

"No insult was intended," said Elizabeth with cool restraint. "It just seems odd to find you here." Pretending sophistication, she added, "Your reputation, you know."

"Ah, you have been told I'm a rake and it is your opinion rakes have no interest in libraries?"

Elizabeth laughed, glad to be back on the bantering ground he'd taught her to enjoy. "Isn't it silly how one gets an idea in one's head and then thinks that is all there is to a person?"

"Quite silly. I find myself guilty of the same sort of thinking. To find *you* here seems a bit out of character."

Again he was rewarded by her delightful laugh. "But you are not wrong, Sir Frederick. I am here only because a friend is to be here this morning."

A chill swept across Frederick's shoulders. Was the chit intriguing with another man? When his tiger, set to watch her, had run to him with the word his current interest had walked to Hookham's, he'd found it surprising. It had been over a week since the girl had gone out with only her maid and he'd begun to wonder if she'd been forbidden the freedom. Having walked out, it had seemed to him a strange place to find her. But to meet a friend? Well, surely his experience would overcome any rival.

He spoke softly, insinuatingly. "Perhaps I, too, have come because I knew a friend would be here."

"Do I know your friend?"

"I believe you do."

"It's someone I know well?" she asked. He smiled knowingly. "Well?"

"Perhaps as well as anyone knows her."

Elizabeth giggled. "You're flirting with me. I wish you wouldn't."

Mentally Frederick made a quick adjustment. The little Ransome was not stupid. Nor did she make the usual pretense of not understanding him. "Do you not enjoy a light flirtation?"

"Now you are being quite nonsensical. *Everyone* enjoys a mild flirtation. However—"she tipped her head—"I do not believe I'd enjoy one with you."

"Why not?" The moment the startled question left his mouth, the baronet wished he'd bitten his tongue instead.

"You are angry with me. Please don't scowl."

"You mistake." He forced a smile. He wasn't angry with Elizabeth but with himself for blurting out his question like any green boy. "I'm interested. I know I'd enjoy a flirtation with you. Why would you not enjoy it, too?"

"Sir Frederick," said Elizabeth sternly but with mischief in her laughing eyes, "you know very well why not. To flirt with you would ruin my reputation and there is nothing more important to a lady than her reputation. There. Lady Anne has arrived. I must speak to her. Good day, Sir Frederick."

He laughed and chucked her under the chin. "Good day to you, minx. I promise I will not ruin your reputation."

"Ah, but that is not enough, sir. You must also promise not to ruin *me!*"

Touché, he thought but didn't say. She smiled at him, nodded, and crossed the room to where Anne had settled at one of the tables with a large book full of finely drawn pictures of plants.

Sir Frederick watched her go, a curious smile playing around his lips and a thoughtful look in his eyes. The Ransome chit was something new in his experience, and jaded as he was, new experiences were few and far between. He took his leave quietly. Lady Anne was not a woman he could cajole and it was better that she be unaware he'd had conversation with the beauty. He wondered if Elizabeth would tell her.

* * *

Joanna raised her fists and shook them. "I tell you," she repeated, "I do not know where Elizabeth has gone. I am about out of my mind with worry."

"When did she leave?"

"No one knows. Pierce, where can that abominable chit be this time?"

"Do not ruin that delightful coiffure, love. Tearing your hair will not help. Do you know if she is alone?"

"Her maid has disappeared as well."

"Then she isn't alone." Pierce lifted his head, turning it slightly, at the sound of Elizabeth's laugh coming from the hall. "Besides, it appears the brat has returned and in good health."

The door was opened by Chitters, Henry's supercilious butler, allowing a breathless Elizabeth followed by two guests to enter. "Do see who I ran into, Aunt Jo. Lady Anne and Sir Rupert have graciously agreed to have lunch with us." Elizabeth bit her lip over a smile, her eyes dancing. "You'll be pleased to know I remembered to inform the housekeeper." The joking reference to the fiasco surrounding her aunt's birthday didn't have the happy result Elizabeth anticipated.

Jo gnashed her teeth—twice—before pinning on a social smile and moving toward her unexpected guests. "How delightful."

Before it became obvious his love was having difficulty turning from the role of worried chaperon to that of hostess, Pierce stepped into the breach. When Henry joined them moments later, the situation was saved and he managed to isolate Jo and her charge in one of the window bays. He kept an eye on the exchange, noting Jo's frustration and Elizabeth's mulish look.

Blast the brat. How dare she upset the love of his life. Poor harried dear. If only he had the right to step in and take charge. Something must be done. He'd sacrifice anything to give Joanna peace. Peace, he thought sardonically, would come when the chit was married and some poor deluded man's responsibility. Pierce wondered whom he could push into declaring for the provoking chit. From nowhere Halford's name entered his mind. Rob? Robert *had* shown interest. Pierce was desperate. So desperate he found himself quite willing to sacrifice his oldest friend for Jo's peace of mind.

Pierce pondered the idea. It was true Rob had shown more than casual interest in Jo's troublesome charge. He'd even admitted to an infatuation, pointing out that his feelings would change as quickly as Elizabeth turned into a proper society miss hunting down a proper husband. But that had been weeks ago and, so far, Elizabeth had not changed. She was still the pert minx that had ensnared his friend—and Rob was revealing, now and again, a certain possessiveness toward the girl.

Pierce stared thoughtfully around the room. Lady Anne and Sir Rupert made no pretense of interest in anyone but each other; that, thought Pierce, was going very well. Their three-way plotting was close to maturation. Soon, he knew, Lady Anne would discuss the situation with her father, to whom Pierce had long ago introduced Rupert. Rupert would pay a formal call on the old gentleman and gain permission to address Lord Bradford's daughter. The announcement would be in the paper before Lady Bradford had time to interfere. And Jo? Her sotto voce wrangle with her unrepentant niece was over. Pierce made his way to his love's side.

"Had she an excuse?"

"It appears to be *my* fault, would you believe? I am so haggard she felt it cruel to ask me to accompany her to the library this morning. *Library?* Doing it way too brown, Pierce."

"She did run into Lady Anne and Sir Rupert. It seems a likely locale for that."

"What I can't discover is who else she 'ran' into."

"You fear an assignation?"

"What other explanation is there?"

Pierce studied Elizabeth as she bent her dark head over the latest issue of *La Belle Assembleé*. "I don't know, Jo. Should I try to discover who was there?"

"I can't see her telling you if she won't admit it to me."

"I won't attempt to get an answer from the brat. A few inquiries here and there." He waved a hand expressively. "Let me try, Jo."

"Why should you? She's my responsibility."

"Because in one respect she's correct." Stern eyes bored down into her wary ones. "You are becoming fagged to death and I can't allow it. I must, where I can, ease your burdens, love."

They were interrupted as Lord Halford was announced. Pierce, who had turned to stare at Elizabeth, was surprised to note her unmasked joy at Rob's entry—joy which immediately disappeared behind the polite facade every young lady was trained to wear. *Would* that be a match worth making? Pierce turned his eyes toward Rob. The earl made pretense of conversation with Henry, but too often his eyes strayed to where Elizabeth sat, her shoulder turned quite obviously against him. Hmmmm.

"That, at least, is something about which I needn't concern myself." Joanna, too, stared from Elizabeth to Rob.

"That? What?"

"I have warned Elizabeth Robert has no interest in marriage. She understands there is no hope for a match in that direction. He is simply being kind to the young daughter of his friend."

Pierce rubbed his chin thoughtfully. "Would you disapprove a match between them?"

"Theoretically? I don't suppose one could from a mercenary or social point of view. He's perhaps a little old for her—or rather she's too young for him. He'd soon find himself bored by her fits and starts, and assuming her affections were caught, she'd be badly hurt when he turned from her in disgust."

"I think you wrong my friend, Jo. Were he to marry her, she'd have no cause to complain."

"You aren't suggesting . . . ? No, of course not." Joanna laughed. "For a moment there, I thought you were seriously proposing . . . but of course that is nonsense."

Pierce bit the inside of his mouth, his lips pursed. Was Jo objecting so strongly because *she* had an interest in Rob? He turned to her, his eyes burning over her face, meeting her gaze and holding it. Joanna blushed. Pierce smiled, touched her cheek lightly, and bowed. "Perhaps you are right, love. Time will tell."

He crossed the room and joined Lady Anne and Sir Rupert. Moments later the butler announced that a nuncheon was waiting in the small dining room, and the party trooped out into the hall.

The absurd feeling she hadn't a notion what was going on around her followed Joanna into lunch.

276

When it was over and their guests left, she still felt that way. Elizabeth accompanied her up to her room and wandered around it, picking up a scarf here, a porcelain figure there, and gradually wound down until she agreed to rest on the chaise longue while Joanna lay on her bed.

"Aunt, why is Lady Anne making a dead-set for Sir Rupert?"

"What makes you think she is? They appear to have interests in common and Anne always has had a kind heart. Don't you think she is merely offering friendship to a lonely man?"

Elizabeth thought about that for a moment. "No. That won't fadge. I caught them making sheep's eyes at each other. And Anne touches him whenever she can without drawing attention to herself. I think it may be a match—which is ridiculous. I know of three much more eligible suitors she's sent to the right-about. So why would she throw herself away on a man like Sir Rupert?"

Joanna frowned. What had her niece seen that she had missed? Obviously something. Pierce, too, had commented on the courtship. Joanna berated herself for turning into just such a blind self-centered idiot as she most deplored. She thought about what to say to Elizabeth, afraid something she said might lead her niece into interfering between Sir Rupert and Anne.

Carefully Joanna suggested, "Anne is an extraordinary woman, Elizabeth. She has a good mind and strong interests, which are things uncommon amongst females of our set. Perhaps, having found a man who appreciates her mind and would allow her to use it as she wishes, she values him more highly than a coronet or fortune. Not that Sir Rupert is precisely *poor.* He is well able to provide his wife the elegancies of life."

"You mean she has looked for more than a socially acceptable arrangement."

Is that what she had said? Jo wasn't sure.

"I admire that." Elizabeth's sincerity couldn't be denied. "How wise of Anne to look beyond the surface things to those that are really important, things which will last for years and years and make the marriage a good one."

"I believe you are growing up, Elizabeth."

The mischievous look Joanna dreaded returned to her niece's features. "Mayhap I have. But what I think I've done is decide I won't worry about making a match this season. When I first yearned to come to London, I wished to be married just as quickly as I could. To show up Alicia, you know, who told me how hard it is to bring a suitor up to scratch. Most anyone would have done. Now I wish to wait until I may have more than a wedding band on my finger. I wish for a man who will love me."

Joanna blanched slightly. "Elizabeth . . ."

"Oh, don't concern yourself, Aunt Jo. I know how rare such matches are. But *you* chose to marry for love despite social and family pressure. I am young enough I needn't rush into marriage with the first man to ask. I have a chance of finding love."

"So you do," replied Joanna on a wistful note.

She wondered if she should explain to her niece just how foolishly she herself had rushed into marriage. Not that she hadn't loved Reggie. She had. But not with the depth of feeling to which Elizabeth referred. No. A certain duke, blast the man, had held her heart that way and she'd let pride and a sly woman drive her from him.

Did she have a chance to correct that mistake? Could she truly believe Pierce meant all those wonderful things he said to her? She glanced at Elizabeth and found, to her surprise, her niece had dozed off. The sweet innocence of the girl had Joanna smiling. With all her heart, she wished her niece would find the man she loved and discover the man loved her back. Her surprisingly pragmatic niece seemed to understand just how unlikely that would be but was willing to wait patiently to see what might occur.

Well, best of luck to her. Joanna found herself so impatient she could no longer lay still on her bed. Rising, she paced quietly on the side of the room opposite her sleeping niece. Did she really wish to wed Pierce? Yes, decided Joanna, she did. Strange as the notion seemed to her, given the disaffection in which she'd held him for so long, she *did* wish to marry him. Bless the man. Pierce had pushed and prodded and pricked at her until she'd been forced to admit, to herself, her true feelings. So, she thought, it is time to stop acting the looby and *do* something. But what?

Joanna paced and thought. She thought and paced. And was completely unaware when her niece opened one eye and watched her. Elizabeth was wondering what had her aunt in such a quandary but knew she'd get no answer if she simply asked. Elizabeth lay still and did some thinking of her own.

Later in the afternoon, as arranged, Lord Halford arrived to take Elizabeth up in his carriage for a drive along Rotten Row. She waited patiently until he maneuvered his lively pair through the obstacles of the street and into the park.

"Might we first drive along a less popular path, Lord Halford?"

"Do you truly wish to? A young lady wearing such a delightful costume must surely wish to show it off."

Elizabeth glanced down her length. She sighed softly. She did, of course, desire to let the *ton* see her smart new pelisse in palest green and the becoming Gypsy-style bonnet with matching ribbons. Unselfishly she put the thought aside. "I wish to talk to you, Lord Halford, and I have no wish to be overheard or interrupted at every other word."

Rob glanced at her profile, noted the serious set to her mouth, and turned off the Row into a less frequented part of the park. "Should I pull up? You appear to be thinking very deeply about something, Lady Elizabeth."

"Just drive slowly, Lord Halford."

For several moments she remained silent. Rob smiled, wondering just what sort of coil the chit found herself in—obviously one which she was reluctant to discuss with her aunt. He didn't believe for a minute it would be anything too serious, but when she still didn't speak, he said, "If there is ought with which I can help . . ."

"'Tis rather delicate, sir."

Robert blanched. "Then perhaps 'twould be best if your aunt—"

"Oh, no. You see, it is *she* I worry about."

Relaxing, Robert slowed the team to a walk. "I am a safe confidant, child. I promise to keep your problem secret."

Elizabeth drew in a deep breath and plunged in, speaking sternly: "I am very much afraid my buffleheaded aunt is about to be taken in by that rake of a friend of yours. Something must be done. I want you to do *whatever is necessary* to head him off."

"Him? Rake? You aren't speaking of Sir Frederick are you?"

Elizabeth threw a scornful look his way. "Of course not. That particular rake looks to make *me* his next conquest. No. I speak of your friend the duke."

"Stornway? You mistake, Lady Elizabeth. Pierce wishes to marry your aunt." Rob spoke absently, his mind on Elizabeth's caustic statement about Frederick.

"The Duke of Stornway is a rake."

"He has that reputation, child. But there is more gossip than truth in it." Elizabeth frowned. "Pierce is a prominent figure with his title and wealth. He has never, since your aunt married, shown the least smidgen of serious interest in any marriageable woman. Therefore, any female he speaks to, any female he walks with, or takes up for a ride is immediately suspected of being his mistress. If," Rob went on with a smile, "he had had in keeping or under his wing half the women he is reputed to have had, he'd be worn to a frazzle with the dissipation of it all."

It suddenly occurred to Rob he should not be speaking of such things to Elizabeth and he blushed. Unfortunately she noticed it.

"You are not a good liar, Lord Halford," she teased and his blush deepened. "However, I commend your loyalty to your friend."

"Believe me," responded the flustered man, "I have not lied. I am merely chagrined to have spoken of such things to an innocent. It is not done." He drove on a few more yards and, deciding he must make the minx understand, pulled over, tying the reins and twisting sideways in his seat. "Lady Elizabeth, you truly have a wrong impression of my friend.

He has a kind heart and generous nature. I would go to him before any other if I were in a quandary and needed help."

"But you are a man. It is different, between men, I believe."

'Hmm. Yes, I see what you mean." Robert spoke more sternly when he went on: "He loves your aunt, Elizabeth."

She dodged a quick glance his way beneath her lashes. Although he'd forgotten to use her title, she could see no flirtatious intent in his expression. She sighed. For just an instant she'd hoped . . . but that was for the future. When she was sure her aunt was safe, then she might think of the secret problem plaguing her dreams and, when she was off her guard, at other odd moments.

"How can you know that? That he loves her? Do you know how he tried to stop her marriage to my uncle?"

Rob chuckled. "He said you overheard that bit. Naughty minx."

This time Elizabeth blushed rosily, ducking her head. "Hmm. Yes. I think I was very much a child then."

"So many weeks ago."

"Much," said Elizabeth, "may happen in only a few weeks."

Rob studied her face, discerning a mild sadness which surprised him. "Can you tell me?" he asked softly. "May I help in some way?"

Startled, she again gave that sidelong glance, pushed away her vague depression that this man she admired above all others might never feel a similar admiration for her. She sighed. "My only concern is my fear for Aunt Jo."

"May I give you some advice, child?"

Would he never give over calling her a child? "I will listen."

He chuckled again softly. "Yes. You will listen and go your own way if you don't like that which I have to say. Well, minx, my advice won't be acceptable to you, I'm sure. It is only that I am older and have had much more experience than you that makes me say it anyway."

When he paused, she lifted her eyes to his and waited.

"Ah, Elizabeth, I remember so well how it was to be young and so certain one could make a difference, could cause things to happen as one wished." She frowned. "Now . . ." He paused, went on more firmly, "Now I know that more often than not, interfering between two people may only worsen their problems rather than help them."

"I only wish Aunt Jo to be happy."

"I wish for both of them to be happy. I believe they will be happy together.' "

"He is a rake."

"He is a man."

"He will make her unhappy with his philandering ways."

"He will have no need to, er, philander, when they are wed."

"Marriage? You are *sure* he has marriage in mind?"

"I'm sure."

Elizabeth sighed deeply. "If only I could believe it."

"Believe it, child. I assure you it is true."

"Then why . . ."

"Why what?"

"Then why, if all you say is true, did he wait one

day longer than her required year of mourning before approaching her again? He wouldn't have approached her even when he did if she hadn't been set upon by Turner and Martin."

"He admits that was an error. But he'd made a plan. He intended waiting until Joanna returned to society at which point he'd lay siege to her in proper manner. He was confounded by her extended period of mourning. But, having made the plan, one he felt had some chance of success, he waited. I believe your aunt, also, has some doubts about the legitimacy of his feelings, given that mistake."

Elizabeth turned this information over in her mind and decided it might be true. And if it were true, the Despicable Duke might very well be a Desperate Duke instead. "Can't we do anything to help?"

"Perhaps keep our eyes open. If we see anything interfering between them, we might remove that barrier."

Elizabeth flushed. *"My* interference, for instance."

"That is," he teased, "the sort of thing I have in mind, yes."

She compressed her lips against a gurgle of laughter. "It is getting late, Lord Halford. If the *ton* is to be given the exquisite joy of inspecting this newest creation by Lisetta, perhaps we should turn back to the Row?"

"Minx."

"Perhaps, but a rather decent minx, I hope."

Rob laughed. "Don't change too much. I'll miss the minx if she disappears."

Elizabeth settled her parasol at the correct angle, forced back a most unladylike grin, and presented a demure face for their friends and acquaintances as Rob made slow passage along the Row.

Rob, however, was aware his love was preoccupied. He had learned to interpret her well: whenever she responded with purely social responses to those she met, it invariably meant her mind was elsewhere and her words mere parroting of the proper thing to say. The chit had been well-trained by someone, he thought. He hoped her old governess wasn't an elderly woman. It seemed to him that someday he might want to hire the woman to train the daughters Elizabeth would give him.

In the distance he saw Sir Frederick on a high-stepping black and was reminded of her saucy remark. Deciding he'd get to the bottom of it at once and ignoring the approach of three mounted swains wishing speech with his passenger, he turned off the Row into another lane which would lead toward a gate not too far from the one by which he'd normally exit the park.

"Lord Halford?"

"It is my turn to wish to talk with you, Lady Elizabeth."

Her heart sped up, almost stopped, and then pattered in an irregular pattern. "Yes, Lord Halford?"

"You made a comment earlier and I wish to know the rights of it. Why do you think Sir Frederick has picked you as the next of his, er . . ."

"His next pigeon for plucking?"

Startled by her flippant tone Rob turned to look at her. She was pouting. Now why was she reacting that way? "He has," asked Rob, "suggested you gamble with him?"

It was Elizabeth's turn to look startled. "Why no. Why do you ask?"

Rob chuckled. "If you must use cant, Elizabeth, do it correctly. A pigeon for plucking is a greenhead ripe for gambling but without the head for it so he may be *plucked,* if you see what I mean."

"Ah. Thank you. I will remember." Once again Rob had forgotten her title. Could it mean . . . ?

"Which does not answer my question."

Elizabeth sighed. She *must* remember this man had only befriended her because he was fond of her aunt and a friend of her father. The foolish hope he'd been about to propose was just that: foolish. "What is it you wish to know?"

"Why you believe Sir Frederick has marked you as his next conquest."

"You do not think I am beautiful enough to attract him?"

"Minx. Please be serious, Elizabeth. It is a very serious subject."

She sighed again. "I believe it because he has made every effort to approach me. He flirts with me. He uses his eyes . . . *so.*"

She illustrated her point by running a hot gaze down her escort's well-muscled form. Rob first flushed and then laughed.

"It is most disconcerting, of course," said Elizabeth, her voice cool and unconcerned.

"I see that it is."

He felt the red rising in his cheeks again, remembered his grass time when he'd eyed women with just that stripping look. Good heavens! Was that how the women felt? How *very* disconcerting. And how effective. Rob wished he could pull up and carry his love to a bed of sweet-smelling grass right then and there. With great self-control he forced his mind and body to behave.

"Will you answer my question?" he asked.

"You mean I have not?"

Rob drew in a deep breath. "Perhaps you have. But are you aware how dangerous he is if what you believe is true?"

Elizabeth thought of all the meetings she'd begun to suspect were neither so accidental nor so innocent as she'd once believed. Her mind flitted to the most recent encounter.

"He has promised he will not ruin my reputation."

"The devil he did! What, my demure miss, was your response to that impertinence?"

"Why, that he must also promise not to ruin *me*."

"Did he respond to that, too?"

"He did not. But that was not entirely his fault; I left him at that point. He hadn't time."

"Elizabeth . . ." Rob trailed off, not quite certain just what he wished to say.

"Yes, *Robert?*"

He glanced at her, noted the half-teasing light in her wide eyes and laughed. Pretending a prim inquiry, he asked, "May I have permission to use your delightful name, Lady Elizabeth?"

"When we are not in society, I see no reason why not. We have become friends, have we not—Robert?"

"I very much hope we have. And now it is quite time I deliver you back to your aunt or you will not have time to dress for dinner."

Friends, thought Elizabeth. Well, it was a start. From what she'd observed in her brief life, the only marriages that seemed to prosper included friendship. They needed *more*, of course, but it was, she reiterated bracingly, a beginning.

Fourteen

"Jo," said Henry, capturing his sister's attention as she was about to enter the green salon. "I'd like a word with you."

He led her into the library—if a couple of low bookcases filled with an odd collection of novels and sermons, *Debrett's Peerage,* and several back issues of *Blackwoods* could be said to form a library. It was Lord Midbourgh's favorite room in his city residence, providing comfort and none of the formality found in the salons, for instance. It had been designated the library, partly for lack of a better name and partly because Henry believed every house should have one—however little interest *he* had in literature or study. Once the door closed behind them, he paced the floor.

Joanna settled herself in an overstuffed chair near the empty hearth and waited. Twice he looked at her and twice he looked away. Joanna folded her hands. Pretending to be attentive, she mentally went over plans for the musicale she was thinking of giving later in the season. In fact, she became so absorbed, wondering if she could coax La Taglioni into performing, she jumped when he came to stand in front of her.

"You wished to speak with me, Henry?" she asked when he still said nothing.

"It's that daughter of mine. Jo, can you tell me if her feelings are fixed? Has she shown particular preference for any of the young men cluttering up my house day in and day out?"

"Is there any reason she should? She's very young, Henry."

Her brother clasped his hands behind him and rocked up on his toes and back to the floor. Rather pompously he announced, "I've had a very advantageous offer for her."

"I'm not surprised. Can you tell me who? Have you told her?"

Coming down off his dignity, he became confidential. "Well, it is very strange, Jo. He has asked me not to tell the chit yet. Merely that he wanted my permission to attempt to fix his interest. I cannot understand it."

A deep debilitating chill filled Joanna. Pierce had finally shown his hand just as she'd begun to believe him serious about herself. He *had,* as she'd feared, been playing with her while all the time angling for a richly dowered match which would add to his acres. Damn the man. Outrage grew, seething inside her. *She would not allow it.* Elizabeth would not suit Pierce. He'd end up murdering the girl and going to the gallows before their first anniversary.

She *could* not allow it. Somehow she must turn the tables on him. She'd marry him herself if necessary. And when they'd married, she'd make him such a good wife he'd forget all about his desire for more acres. He had wanted her once, and, devil take it, he'd have her. But how could she bring it about? She'd have to think up the perfect scheme.

Henry had continued talking and Joanna tuned back into his words: "He is perfectly suitable," said her brother. "Perhaps a trifle old for the chit, but she is such a minx an older man would know how to deal with her fits and starts. I gave him permission, of course."

"I do not understand why you wished to speak to me. Are you merely informing me or is there something you expect of me?"

"I wish you to give him every opportunity to be with Elizabeth." Embarrassment at Joanna's shocked expression had him puffing. "Not alone, exactly . . ." said her brother hurriedly, twisting one of the buttons on his waistcoat. "But you know the thing. Keep others from interfering if he's talking with her. You might even let him have more than two dances if he asks. That sort of thing?"

"Did he suggest you ask for my help?"

"I suggested it. He thought you might prove an excellent conspirator."

"He did, did he?" Joanna fairly boiled with indignation. How dare he!

"Well, it's true, isn't it? As her chaperon you could help, could you not?" Henry looked bewildered.

Jo forced a sweet note into her voice. "Of course I could."

If I would. But I won't. Pierce would find her less a fool than he thought, *She* would make a fool of him. But what, the thought crossed her mind, if he truly loved her niece? The notion faded to naught. Despite recent suspicions to the contrary, Pierce loved no one but himself. He never had and he never would. So she would save her niece from that rake

290

and she would marry him herself. And then he'd see! Just what he'd see, she didn't bother to contemplate. It's enough that she was finally angry enough to forward her own interests.

"There are things I must do," she told her brother. He goggled at her and she asked him why he was looking such a fish.

"Why are you so angry, Jo?"

"Angry?" She gritted her teeth. "You mistake. I'm not at all angry." *Oh no. Not at all.* "Merely determined."

Uneasily Henry watched his sister leave the room. She *was* angry. But why? Lord Halford would be an excellent match for Elizabeth. Joanna had shown no signs of an interest there so it couldn't be jealousy. Well, it was beyond him what went through his sister's convoluted mind.

Perhaps he should discuss it with Pierce. The duke was a knowing un and seemed to understand Joanna as no one else did. Besides, although not so knowing himself, Henry was sure Pierce would renew his offer for Joanna and he wanted to help that courtship along any way he could. Discussing this situation might give Pierce a push in the right direction.

Pierce should have married her in the first place and would have if one of his team hadn't gone lame, requiring that he stop at that inn where Joanna's lieutenant discovered them. Henry hadn't thought the young officer would catch up with them—given Pierce's well-known expertise with the reins—and had refused to join in the chase. The lieutenant had had a few words to say about that, too. Henry shuddered at the memory. Well, Wooten had been Jo's betrothed. Perhaps it hadn't been quite the honorable thing to wish Pierce would succeed in carrying her off.

Henry sighed. It was all too complicated for his poor head and, besides, it was long over. Now was now. And this time Pierce would win his stubborn sister and all would be well. At least Henry sincerely hoped Pierce would win her—and she'd no longer get into his own hair as she tended to do. And that being the case, he concluded, it would be quite the thing to discuss the situation with Pierce.

He stopped short. Botheration. He couldn't talk to Pierce. He'd given Halford his word he'd talk to no one but Jo. Henry dug in his pocket for his snuff, sneezed mightily, and decided that, one, there was nothing he could do and that, two, Jo would go her own road in any case. Henry remembered he had an appointment at his club and, later, an assignation— unfortunately innocent—with a little widow. Putting his conversation with Jo out of his mind, he took himself off, expecting to enjoy himself immensely.

That evening when Jo and Elizabeth attended a levee at the home of the Russian ambassador and his wife, she watched Pierce whenever she knew his attention to be elsewhere. Much to her surprise, he seemed to pay less attention to Elizabeth rather than more. She decided there was simply no understanding the man but didn't object when he attached himself to her side, refusing to be edged away even when Sally Jersey made it abundantly clear she wished a tête-à-tête with Joanna. Sally told him he was a bad boy and it was about time someone brought him to order. Joanna blushed at the meaningful look the Jersey sent her way.

Much to Joanna's relief Frederick Carrington was not in evidence and, for once, she felt she could relax her guard. Twice recently she'd discovered Elizabeth talking to the man, the teasing glint in her eye and the amusement in his voice enough to frighten the wits out of any responsible chaperon.

Rob's sister was much in evidence, however. Jo wondered if the current *on dit* that Cressy Clayton was about to remarry—once again a man many years her senior—had any foundation. In support of it was the fact that she was on the arm of a tall gray-haired Scot, the laird of something or other. Jo had been introduced some days earlier but had been preoccupied with trying to overhear her niece and Sir Frederick and had missed the name. For Lord Halford's sake, Joanna very much hoped the rumor was true. If Cressida were to remarry, Robert would no longer feel responsible for her, and that would be a very good thing for him.

"You are quiet tonight, Jo. Something on your mind?"

Joanna looked up at Pierce and frowned. "Since you agreed Henry should talk to me, I should think you'd *know* what is on my mind."

Pierce searched his memory. "I did?" he asked cautiously.

"Oh, there's no talking to you." Joanna turned on her heel and strolled toward where Lady Anne and Sir Rupert were in conversation with several other serious-minded people. Joanna found herself bored with a discussion of the nesting habits of the common titmouse. The others scarcely noticed when she excused herself and walked away.

Anne was no longer hiding the fact she was a bluestocking and Joanna wondered how her ambitious mother felt about that. She looked around to see if Lady Bradford was observing her daughter's behavior, and, not finding her, she forgot she was angry with Pierce, who'd been following her. She asked, "Pierce, has Lady Anne's mother given up on her?"

"Lady Bradford is, I understand, in bed with a chill acquired when chaperoning a group of young people on a picnic on the Thames."

"Poor lady. It is not a topic for amusement, Pierce."

He sobered. "No, of course it isn't. And if she were really ill, I wouldn't find it at all amusing. But you must admit it is convenient. Lady Anne saw her chance for a bit of freedom. She convinced her mother she should not take the smallest chance the chill might develop into something worse and talked her father into escorting her this evening."

"I haven't seen Lord Bradford either."

"Of course you haven't. He likes Sir Rupert. They get on very well when discussing their acres and modern methods of tillage. When Rupert offered to see Lady Anne home, her father agreed with alacrity. He handed his daughter over to Rupert's care and immediately went off to his club. There was an added motivation, of course: he's uncomfortable at this sort of do and was thankful for an excuse to leave."

"Pierce," said Joanna, her eyes wide, "did Lady Anne plan all that?"

"Plan?" he asked. "Joanna, how dare you suggest a plot?" But the twinkle in his eyes belied his denial.

Joanna laughed. "I'd say it was brilliant of her."

"Yes," he said, studying his nails. "I thought so myself."

Joanna chuckled, "I begin to see the fine hand of an expert involved. I might have known Anne could never be so devious."

"Lady Anne, my love, has discovered a gift for subterfuge and has been making great strides toward becoming as devious as you please. She has, however, one lack I supply." Joanna's brow rose in inquiry. "Experience, my love."

Joanna's delighted trill of laughter turned heads. If she'd realized how obvious to others was Pierce's fond look, she'd have been gratified—but quite equally mortified. Gratified he made his liking for her clear, mortified they were making a spectacle of themselves. One simply did not draw attention to one's feelings. It was not done. She did not notice, however, and Pierce, who did, didn't enlighten her. Therefore, quite in charity with him for a change, she accepted his escort to the dining room and help in choosing delicacies for her supper.

Elizabeth and Robert soon joined them, and Sir Rupert and Lady Anne arrived almost on their heels. Their table was the center of much interest. More than one gossip left the levee to spread rumors, quite true of course, of three alliances in the making.

A few days later, right after his sister's hurried wedding had gone off without a hitch, Halford entered Jackson's Boxing Academy to find Sir Frederick there. He watched his sometimes friend batter one of Jackson's more promising young fighters. The earl's eyebrows rose at the force behind Sir Frederick's rather beautiful left. The baron was in a temper. Robert could think of no reason for it, and as he watched, Frederick finished pummeling his opponent. Overheard comments brought it home to him others had noticed as well.

Frederick left the ring, the scowl marring his brow no less black than when he'd entered it some thirty minutes earlier. "Going into training to challenge the champion, Frederick?" The taunt came from a rather plump but enthusiastic follower of the fancy. A lisping voice teased Sir Frederick about his terrible ferocity. Frederick very nearly landed the fop a blow that would have marred the man's prettiness for at least a week.

Lord Halford sighed and decided he'd better interfere. For reasons Rob couldn't guess, his cool saturnine friend, who usually ignored such irritating tulips and their nasty comments, was behaving in an odd fashion, indeed.

"Frederick? Join me for a stroll?"

Frederick shrugged into his coat and took the gloves and cane handed him by one of Jackson's servitors. Another handed him his hat. The scowl had lightened only slightly. "I'm not fit company for man or beast, Rob."

"Then we'll ignore each other, my friend. Just walk."

Walk they did, in a silence that stretched until Lord Halford led Sir Frederick into Green Park where buxom milkmaids coddled placid milk cows, keeping demure watch over the grazing herd. Here and there a nanny guarded toddlers at play; elsewhere maids, on their half-day, flirted with young men Frederick described as a bunch of cits.

"Why are we here?" he asked.

"You said you weren't fit for company." Robert shrugged. "'Tis the first place I thought of where you could be as private as in your own rooms."

"Which is where I should be."

"Come out of the boughs."

Frederick swiped his cane at a nodding daisy and missed.

Robert blinked, stopped short, and stared. The tension in the baronet's face and shoulders made him decide not to probe. But as they strolled across a broad green to where a path entered a small grove of trees, he searched his mind for clues to explain Frederick's behavior. Hidden from all eyes, Frederick suddenly attacked a tree trunk with the unlucky cane until that strong piece of highly polished ash broke with a loud crack. He threw it away and dropped to lie on the ground.

Robert lowered himself to the grass near the man who had once saved his life. "Frederick, what is the problem?" He got no response so he ventured, "By the way, I'll have a draft to you tomorrow paying off my sister's IOUs." She had handed them to Robert with the last of her bills, right after her wedding that morning.

"Tear 'em up. I never meant to collect. I couldn't forbear goading her into a game last night."

"No. I'll pay—"

"Don't. I'll only send it back to you." Frederick bit his lip, looked at Robert with dancing lights in his eyes. "Oh, the devil, man, I told you. I'd no intention of collecting when I set out to run up that score. And I *did* run it up, Robert, if you catch my meaning."

It was the closest Sir Frederick would come to saying he'd cheated. Robert didn't know whether to believe him or whether the man was suborning his honor in order to prevent payment of the debt. With Frederick one never knew. The man could, on rare occasions, be positively quixotic. He couldn't admire Carrington's principles where women were concerned, but that he was a good man at one's back in a fight and loyal to the Crown made up for a lot.

"Have it your own way."

"I will." Frederick gave a crack of sardonic laughter. "Not that I couldn't use the blunt."

Robert sobered. Was that it? "In trouble, Frederick? Can I pull you out of River Tick? A loan, of course," he added, thinking of the man's pride.

"I'm no more in dun territory than usual. In fact, at the moment I'm quite flush. But that won't last. It never does." Frederick rose slowly to his feet and held out his hand, helping Robert to his. "I just wish I might someday be enough beforehand with the world to set in motion some repairs needed to make the old place livable again. Who knows, with enough blunt I might even make some of the repairs my tenants are always urging on me." His expressive eyebrows quirked in self-derision.

Robert studied Frederick thoughtfully. "You could always do what my sister has done: repair your fortune through a suitable marriage."

The baronet grimaced. "I believe you've forgotten to whom you speak, Robert. Me? A respectable marriage?! Besides, I have discovered at this late stage in my life that I am, unlikely as it seems, a romantic." He laughed at Robert's astonishment. "I see you have difficulty believing that. Good. I'm not losing my mind when I think it odd of me. Thank you for lightening my mood, old friend. I've someone to meet now. At least, I believe I'll be meeting her, so I'll leave you while you and I are still speaking to each other." Frederick walked off.

Her? Elizabeth? Blast. Somehow he'd forgotten he'd meant to talk to Frederick about Elizabeth. Now, suspecting the man had had the gall to refer to his rakish pursuit of the minx, Robert very nearly went after him to begin a bout of fisticuffs himself. Then, once again drawn by the strange humor of the man, he chuckled, shook his head, and strolled on in another direction.

* * *

"I do not," Joanna said, "see what you find so humorous, Pierce. It can't have been easy to go into another marriage with an old man! I pity Cressida."

"I don't pity her at all. I hope he beats her. She deserves all she gets—if for nothing else, then that she drove a wedge between us, Jo." His eyes flashed.

"Ah." Joanna cast him a demure look from under her lashes. "You discovered the source of my misinformation, did you?"

Pierce's face hardened, his eyes cooling. "Yes, I did. It wasn't difficult. She admitted it when I taxed her with her lies. That is, she did when I made it perfectly clear I'd have nothing to do with her if there were no women left on earth but herself."

He looked so grim Joanna bit her lip. Did Pierce have something to do with Cressida suddenly finding herself on the verge of ostracism? "Pierce, you didn't . . ."

"Help along that wedding this morning? I did. At least I didn't object to answering questions the bridegroom put to me some time ago." Joanna relaxed. Pierce had not started any vengeful rumors as she'd feared. "He'd gotten an inkling of her character before they were introduced but it didn't put him off."

"I cannot like her but she can't be very happy."

"Perhaps not. But she brings her problems down on her own head. Don't waste any tears on her, Jo. He's taking her to an island off the coast of Scotland. She'll not bother us again. Are you attending the Blairmores' masquerade?"

"Forgetting Cressida is one thing, Pierce, but did you have to remind me of that idiotic masquerade?

Hairy Harry's pantaloons! Drat my brother's guilty conscience anyway."

Pierce maintained a solemn expression with difficulty. "Does that make sense, Jo?"

"Henry was forced to agree to take Elizabeth to visit our Great Aunt Tabitha. None of us can stand the woman, but none of us is able to say her nay. Although why that should be, since no one has expectations of an inheritance there, I don't quite understand. Merely force of character, I suspect." Joanna drew in a deep breath. "Whatever the reason, he feels he must accede to the old lady's desire to see Elizabeth. Elizabeth, needless to say, does not wish to go. Thanks to his guilty feelings about taking her away from London—and the fact Elizabeth can wind him around her little finger—we *are*, much against my better judgment, making a brief appearance at the ball. It was a combination of bribery on his part and blackmail on hers."

Pierce sorted her angry tirade into its parts, reached a conclusion, and shook his head. "Elizabeth is to be allowed to go? Not wise, love."

"Tell that to Henry. He pooh-poohed my concern. Said we'd all watch her. But how can one at a masquerade? Introductions are not required. There will be such a crush she may easily lose herself if she wishes—Pierce, it's enough to turn my hair white."

"Very pretty it'll be, too. But I'd prefer it to wait for the proper time, my dear, when you are a grandmother dandling your grandchildren on your gouty knee."

Joanna chuckled at the picture, but, ignoring the implications of his comment, returned to worrying. "What can be done?"

"Joanna, for no one but you would I put myself

300

out for such a rag-mannered chit. However, since it *is* you, I'll see what I can do to keep her unexceptionably involved with men one can trust to keep the line."

He paused, and Joanna knew he was running over the names of the men with whom he was closely acquainted.

"Do, however, see that you stay only an hour or two. I don't *know* all that many men who will toe the mark at a masquerade!" His eyebrows rose, inviting her to laugh.

Tears of relief beaded Joanna's lashes and she smiled through a rather watery chuckle. She thanked him with sincerity, holding out her hand in an automatic gesture. Pierce, being Pierce, immediately took advantage of her gift, kissing her palm, then her wrist, before gently pulling her trembling body closer. The next kiss took her lips.

Later, holding her in his arms, he tried to get her to look at him. She wouldn't, but the blush on her cheeks warmed his soul. "Drat it, Jo, will you get that chit off your hands so you can think of yourself?" His rueful look added to his further intense comment: "And of *me?* I'm like to die from frustration, my dear heart." He set her away reluctantly and began to take his leave. At the last moment he turned back toward her, a mischievous light in his eyes. "By the way, Jo, be sure to look at the announcements column in your paper tomorrow."

For one heart-stopping moment she thought he meant himself and Elizabeth and the kiss which had rocked her, in light of that, shocked her. Then she realized she'd have known if her niece had accepted an offer. She searched her mind, her eyes widening. "Lady Anne and Sir Rupert?"

"Always thought you a knowing un, Jo."

"That is good news indeed!" Joanna's smile faded. "Pierce, I can't help feeling a little sorry for Lady Bradford. Can you imagine what she is feeling now?"

"She'll survive. It is no one's fault but her own she's been spreading rumors about her daughter's glorious future."

Joanna sent him a warning look. "Be careful she doesn't sue you for breach of promise, Pierce!"

"I will." He chuckled and, bowing slightly, left.

It was only after he was gone Joanna realized he'd not made mention of marriage along with the unsubtle hint he wanted her in his bed. Unless that comment about grandchildren could be construed as an odd sort of proposal? In fact, he'd made no mention of marriage since—since when? It had been *weeks* since he'd last proposed.

Which was, she told herself, to be expected once he'd received Henry's permission to court Elizabeth. Knowing he'd talked to Henry, how could she have let him make mad passionate love to her as he'd just done? It was becoming obvious he wanted his cake and to eat it as well. She sighed before going to her room to check on the costume she'd wear the next evening. Something must be done and done soon. Pierce Reston could not be allowed to go on kissing her that way when he was about to ask Elizabeth for her hand in marriage. In fact, something must be done *before* he got that far. She wasn't about to allow a marriage between those two!

Belton looked up from her sewing and noticed her mistress seemed overly *triste*. Half an hour later, when more of the nap had been worn from the bedroom's pretty Axminster carpet, Belton was pleased to note a change for the better. The old twinkle denoting devilment was back in Lady Jo's eye. When her mistress grabbed an old shawl and headed, not for the front stairs, but for the servants' flight at the back, Belton shook her head. What was Lady Jo up to now? She'd have decided her much-loved mistress had lost her mind if she'd followed Joanna to the nether regions of the house where she collected Turner and the two went off to the stables to find Martin.

Taking the two men aside, Lady Joanna spoke rapidly. Not far into her monologue Turner took a rapid look around the stable. "This is no place for *this* discussion, Your Ladyship! Martin, harness a pair to the landau and we'll find ourselves some privacy." Soon the three conspirators were parked in Green Park where the two men sat on the driver's seat facing forward while behind them Joanna set forth her plan.

Once the shock wore off, they were agreeable despite the dangers involved in her plan. "Getting the information you need won't be difficult," said Turner slowly. "I've met His Grace's valet at the Old Man—a pub we all go to. He's a bit hoity-toity but always willing to take a free round." He mulled over the plot before asking, "How much time have we got?"

"My brother and Lady Elizabeth leave on Monday. They'll be a night on the road, a night at our aunt's, and another night on the road returning to London. I want to be back in London before them."

"Not much time, Your Ladyship."

"No, it isn't. Can we do it?"

Martin spoke for the first time. "We'll do it, Lady Jo. Somehow. Don't you worry none."

"I'll give orders when we return home that the two of you are released from normal duties for the duration."

Turner looked toward the sun and opined it might be best if they made for home quite soon.

"You understand what's in the wind?" Joanna felt a sudden qualm now it was settled. "If there are—objections—we may all end our days in less comfortable circumstances."

The two men looked at each other. Turner winked and Martin grinned. "Mrs. Wooten," said Turner, forgetting his newly learned lessons in the proper mode when speaking to his betters, "you don't know much about men, do you? What man would admit he'd been tricked so, by a mere female? He won't have us up before a beak. Ye needn't worry none you'll end your days in Newgate. Be too embarrassing to the poor man."

Joanna, thinking Pierce wasn't exactly a common ordinary garden variety of man, agreed—but with reservations. He would be *fair*. He'd not blame her servants for what he'd know was her plot. Ah well. It was settled now and Turner was quite right. They must return home. She'd barely have time to get ready for the very boring soiree to which they were invited that evening. She knew it would be boring because she and Elizabeth had been informed that Pierce and Lord Halford had other plans. Neither told their friends the "other plans" involved nothing more exciting than an evening alone together away from the social whirl in Robert's rooms.

"Tell me what I can do more than what I've done already."

Pierce looked over the rim of his glass to where Rob paced between the pieces of furniture crowding his rooms. Neither of them was exactly sober. Of course, neither of them was exactly drunk either, and Pierce was debating the pros and cons of remedying that situation. Unfortunately the decanter was across the room and it would take effort to go refill his glass.

"Pierce, you are not attending." Rob stood with fists pressed into his waist, glowering down at his friend. "Give me a hint. Just the tiniest clue. Some bit of advice, dammit."

"What are you going on about?"

Rob raised eyes to heaven. "What more can I do to attract my minx?" He sighed. "I know I'm a fool to have fallen for a babe barely out of the schoolroom—and at my age, too—but I have, so I need your help."

"Don't know how I can help you when I can't seem to help myself. My latest ploy was to see if I couldn't make Joanna jealous. Got the idea from something she said one day. So tried it. But it doesn't seem to have worked."

"I told you a long time ago you'd have to kidnap her again. Do you think Lady Elizabeth would find that romantic? Should I try it?"

"You very well know you cannot. The girl is far too young."

"She's no younger than Lady Joanna was when you carried her off the first time."

"But I had some excuse. For one thing I was much younger and for another there was no other way to get her. She'd engaged herself to that soldier of hers."

"Fiddle."

"You're sulking."

Rob sighed. He flopped into his chair and jumped right back out again—this time discovering where he'd dropped his best pair of boots. "No wonder I couldn't find them. Why do you suppose they're here in my sitting room instead of in the dressing room?"

"Why don't you discharge that excuse for a valet? He's supposed to take care of such things for you."

"I suppose it'll come to that, but Wiggins was with me during the war. Maybe I can make him a groom or something." He sat again and leaned back. "I know I can't run off with Elizabeth, of course, but I'm at my wit's end."

Pierce raised his glass to eye level and stared at the color of the last of his wine. "I thought you'd decided not to speak to her of marriage until the end of the season."

"When I'm rational, I still reach that decision. She should have the opportunity to look around her. Then we go to a party and I count the number of young men crowding up to her and I don't long remain exactly rational."

"I haven't noticed her show anyone any extraordinary attention, Robert."

Robert digested that in silence. He sighed, then asked, "What of your affairs?"

"I don't know. Maybe I should run off with her. If she disappeared, Henry would have to find someone else to chaperon Elizabeth. Which is something I'd very much like to see happen."

"Someone else bear-leading my minx? Why?"

"Because she's driving my poor Joanna to bedlam. The poor dear is exhausted, worrying about the chit."

"Don't insult my Elizabeth."

"Make her your Elizabeth and take care of her yourself and I'll shake your hand for you." Pierce sighed. "Calm down. You know she's a handful."

306

The friends were silent for a while, Robert not arguing his Elizabeth was not in the common way. Finally Pierce sighed again. And still again.

"What is it, friend? Anything I can do for you?"

"Yes," said Pierce, coming to a decision. "You can make my excuses to anyone who asks for me. I'll be back, assuming all goes well, in time to meet you at the Blairmores' masquerade. If I'm a trifle late getting to the ball, you'll have to be responsible for keeping track of which of our friends is supposed to be dancing with Elizabeth."

"Where are you going?"

"You mean you don't know?" Robert shook his head. "But it was your idea." Robert's eyes opened wide. "That's right. I've decided to toddle down to Canterbury and see the Archbishop, who, bless the man, is there instead of residing more conveniently in his palace west of London. Once I've seen him, I'll toddle home again. Shouldn't take more than eight to ten hours in all, should it?"

"Assuming all goes well, that should be about right."

"Then, since I'll have to leave at daybreak, I'd better take myself off home and get some sleep. I hope I don't have any use for a special license, Rob, but I think I'll get one . . . just in case."

Fifteen

"I don't see how you recognized us so easily, Your Grace." Elizabeth flirted from behind her Spanish fan, her eyes sparkling behind her mask.

The duke chuckled. "Have you never heard of a bribe, Lady E?"

"You didn't!"

"I'll certainly never admit it if I did."

Halford caught the girl's attention and bowed. Blushing, Elizabeth nodded when he requested a dance.

"Jo?" asked Pierce. "Will you waltz?"

Joanna watched Lord Halford lead her niece onto the floor and placed her fingers on Pierce's velvet sleeve. "Did you bribe someone Pierce?" He shook his head. "But then, how did you know to come as a Spanish Don?"

"Because I'm not stupid. The Widow Wooten would choose no other costume."

"I don't think that's a compliment. Besides, I chose it because of the necessary wigs. I think Elizabeth will be well-disguised by the wig. No one would think she'd cover up her own black locks with still more masses of black curls. By the time she is found out, we'll be ready to leave. At least, that is the plan."

"Please don't frown, Jo. White hair is one thing, but wrinkles, my love, are something else again. We'll watch her carefully."

Over an hour passed and Joanna began to breath more easily. Elizabeth, praise be, was behaving beautifully. Only one of her court of younger suitors had discovered her and he, for reasons of his own, was not handing out that information. He had, it was true, asked for a second dance and—because Henry, in his buffle-headed way, had interfered—been allowed it. Joanna had decided to sit the set out and was regretting it: Lady Bradford found her.

The lady's tirade was nearly impossible to follow as it gave equal value to her undutiful daughter's refusal to break the unsuitable engagement to Sir Rupert, her husband's stupidity in not discussing the matter with herself first, and the ingratitude of the servant class—her dresser in particular. The impertinent woman had objected to finding most of milady's scent bottles flying at her head when no more suitable outlet for Lady Bradford's temper could be found, and had given notice. The world, insisted Lady Bradford, was treating her very badly indeed. And why the duke, who had shown Anne such distinguishing attentions for weeks now, had not come up to scratch she could not understand. It was so clear he'd been courting her daughter.

Joanna, unable to get away from the woman's bitter animadversions, suddenly realized one dance had ended and another begun, and she could see no sign of her niece. With little courtesy and more haste, she escaped her neighbor's clutches and searched the crowd for one of the men who had made himself responsible for the minx.

Elizabeth had noted the Harlequin soon after entering the ballroom that evening. Dressed plainly in a silvery white and silvery black parti-color, he'd stood out among the kaleidoscope of brightly colored costumes, dominos, and sparkling jewels whirling around the room. She'd known almost immediately it was Sir Frederick, and she'd hoped he might approach her—a definite possibility at a masquerade! She'd never danced with the baronet and had long wished to do so. The rake rarely took the floor, but when he did, it was with a grace few men matched.

At the moment she especially wished he were her partner rather than the green young man who made still another mistake in the dance figure. When the set ended, her partner grasped her elbow in a tight hold and started off in quite the wrong direction. Elizabeth hung back.

"Mr. Lawson, where do you think you're going?"

"You recognized me?" The suitor stopped and looked at her. "Oh, Elizabeth, *Lady* Elizabeth," he corrected hurriedly when she stiffened and glared at him, "please honor me with a short walk in the garden. I've so much I wish to say to you."

"Return me to my party at once."

"Problems, little one?" The new voice was easily recognized and Elizabeth turned toward Sir Frederick, her Spanish skirts swirling. "Shall I call the dastardly villain out for you?" he teased.

Mr. Lawson sputtered but Elizabeth threw her young suitor another glare and laid her fingers on Sir Frederick's arm. They walked away leaving her partner mouthing a mixture of abject apologies to Elizabeth and threats to the Harlequin.

"You must forgive him, you know," said Sir Frederick softly.

"For trying to ruin my reputation?"

A waltz rhythm flowed around them and Sir Frederick looked from Elizabeth to the ballroom floor and back. "Shall we?"

Elizabeth, calculating the scold she'd receive against this one chance to dance with the best dancer she'd ever seen, nodded. And she'd been right, she thought, as he swung into a skillful turn. Enjoying the music, the smooth rhythm, the heady feel of a man's strong arm at her back, Elizabeth was out in the large anteroom before she realized he'd smoothly moved them through the doors. She lost a step, but the baronet, unlike the callow youth, knew to a nicety how to soothe a shy young miss.

It helped, of course, that Elizabeth was not shy. But was she, she wondered, a bit gullible? She shouldn't, she knew, allow herself to relax just because Sir Frederick continued dancing. But she did. There were two other couples in the room and, although she didn't really want to make a scene, she would if she found it necessary.

"Enjoying yourself, little one?"

"It's wonderful."

"I'd like to make your whole life wonderful."

"Careful, Sir Frederick," Elizabeth said with a laugh, "that might be construed as a proposal."

"So it might."

When he said no more, Elizabeth lifted her head a little to stare at him. "Frederick?"

"I suppose all men have a Waterloo in their lives."

"I don't think I understand."

"Don't you, my sweet?"

She shook her head but wouldn't meet his eyes.

Frederick smiled, a rather wry twist to his well-formed lips, but he didn't say any more. The music ended and his expression changed to one of sadness.

"I did promise not to ruin your reputation, didn't I? Come along."

Much to Elizabeth's surprise, he led her back into the ballroom where she recognized Sir Rupert. Making the best of his disability, he was disguised as a peg-legged pirate. And the lady on his arm had manufactured her own delightful lady pirate costume.

"You can go now, Frederick. I see someone to whom I wish to speak."

She nodded toward the pair, thanked Sir Frederick for the dance, and, pushing his odd behavior to the back of her mind, joined the group that included Rupert and Anne. Joanna found her there taking an animated, almost hectic, part in the conversation.

"Elizabeth," she hissed in the girl's ear.

Elizabeth jumped and turned. "Oh. You frightened me."

"What do you think you did me?" Joanna, with difficulty, forced a social smile when Anne turned their way. "The very best wishes, Lady Anne. Have you set a date for the wedding?"

"Almost immediately. Neither Rupert nor I have any love for society." Lady Anne grimaced. "We are here this evening because we will not allow my mother to set off a round of rumors which later, when she thinks about it, she'll regret."

"She isn't happy. I, hmmm, talked to her half an hour ago."

"You mean you listened to her ranting. Mother will

recover. I have never fallen in with her plans for me, and eventually she will turn her eyes to settling my brother appropriately." The happy young woman's chuckle tickled their ears. "Poor Mother. She'll find him no more cooperative than I've been, I fear."

Elizabeth searched the area for the Harlequin but didn't see him. "Aunt Jo, I think I've promised this dance."

"I think you've danced quite enough. We're leaving."

"Oh no, please. Not yet. It isn't time for the unmasking."

"I think it better if you do not unmask. Elizabeth, how *could* you—" Joanna bit her lip, glancing at Anne.

"If you are worried about Elizabeth's short disappearance, Joanna, please don't. They danced. I had my eye on them the whole time through that doorway." Anne frowned. "Elizabeth, the Harlequin was Sir Frederick, was it not?"

Belligerently Elizabeth nodded. "We danced. We did nothing wrong."

Joanna, too, frowned at her niece. "Sir Frederick forced you out of the ballroom and did nothing but dance with you?"

"I've told you and told you, Aunt, Sir Frederick has promised he will not ruin my reputation. He *danced* with me. That is all." A puckish grin followed her low-voiced tirade. "A very good dance it was, too. I've wanted to dance with him forever. I think he's the best waltzer there is."

"That's all very well, but now we'll leave. He will unmask, and if you are recognized, all the old tabbies will know you danced with him. Come along, Elizabeth."

The girl did, hoping that would be the end of it. Later, when Joanna arrived in her bedroom just as her maid was leaving, Elizabeth sighed. She might have known, she thought, and deliberately yawned.

"Elizabeth, we must talk."

"If it's about Sir Frederick, please don't."

"You simply do not understand how dangerous the man is."

"I suspect I have a better understanding of him than you do, Aunt Jo. I agree he set out to seduce me. His plans have changed." The last came out with a sadness Elizabeth didn't realize she'd allowed to show.

"Changed?" Jo's heart pounded. Had her niece wanted the rake to seduce her? No, of course not. She was going mad. "Elizabeth, you haven't formed a *tendre* for the man, have you?"

"For Frederick? Aunt Jo, are you quite well?"

"That is no answer."

"I have not fallen in love with Sir Frederick. Satisfied?"

Jo wasn't at all satisfied. "Then why does it upset you that you believe he no longer sees you as a quarry?"

Elizabeth smiled and her eyes twinkled. "Did I say that?"

"You implied it."

"Aunt Jo, it is late, we are tired, and I think we should stop talking about Frederick. You will never understand and I can't explain. It wouldn't be at all proper," she ended primly.

Joanna stared at her. Not proper? A new and still worse fear entered her mind. Had Carrington had the unmitigated gall to ask the minx to *marry* him? Almost immediately she thrust the thought away,

314

wondering if she would lose her mind before she got Elizabeth suitably engaged. Such a thought was impossible. The baronet didn't marry the girls he pursued. No. It couldn't be that, surely—but if not, at what was her irritating niece hinting?

"Good night, Aunt Jo." Elizabeth pulled the sheets around her shoulders and turned away from her chaperon. "Snuff my candle before you leave, will you, please, dearest of my aunts?"

The following morning Pierce watched his harassed love pace the green salon and wished the minx to the devil for upsetting her chaperon. "Joanna, come sit. Walking a path in the carpet will do no one the least bit of good." She glanced his way and succumbed to a coaxing look and proffered hand.

Joanna joined him where he stood near the blazing fire which had been lit against the damp, and after staring at it a moment, she seated herself in a nearby chair.

Pierce seated himself on the corner of the couch nearest her and pretended to wipe sweat from his brow. "There. That's better. You were wearing me out, my dear, just watching you."

"Pierce, please don't tease. Tell me I'm wrong."

"Perhaps if I knew what you are wrong about, I could make a decision on the point."

"You are still teasing. Pierce, it is impossible. I cannot believe it."

"Exactly what can you not believe?"

"I've told you!" Joanna glared at him.

"I dislike contradicting you, my love, but you have told me nothing. You've referred to Elizabeth's sly comment. You've referred to a 'him' I assume to be

Sir Frederick. You've mentioned—more than once, let me add—that you can't believe it, but you have yet to explain what 'it' might be."

Joanna stared at him. Had she been so bubble-brained? Perhaps she had. She would obviously be committed to Bedlam before she managed to get her niece off her hands. "Elizabeth made a comment which led me to wonder if Sir Frederick had had the supreme presumption to make her an offer. A *proper* offer."

Pierce blinked. "We are," he said carefully, "talking about Frederick?"

"I have said so, haven't I?"

"Then, if he made an offer, which he might have done, of course, it was not *marriage* he had in mind whatever that chit may think. Think, Joanna. We are talking about the infamous Sir Frederick Carrington!"

"She refuses to admit he made any sort of offer at all. She will only reiterate until I am ready to scream that he has promised not to ruin her reputation."

Pierce stared into the fire, thinking over what he knew of the baronet. The man had never been rumored to cheat. There was that odd friendship between Frederick and Robert he'd never been able to fathom. He was known as a boxer Gentleman Jackson would have been proud to train for the fancy and had never, to Pierce's knowledge, dealt an opponent a low blow.

These were things he would know since such items of masculine interest had a way of traveling through the male element of the *ton*. What else did he know? Not very much, he decided, except for the gossip surrounding his petticoat affairs—where he had a nasty reputation indeed.

"Pierce? Have you nothing to say?"

"I've been thinking. She is certain he *promised*?"

"She has repeated his exact words. He promised, Pierce."

"Then," he said slowly, "I believe you should stop worrying. For all his faults, Sir Frederick is an honorable man."

Thinking of all the gossip, Joanna's face wore a disbelieving look. "Honorable? Sir Frederick?"

Pierce laughed. "I know what you're thinking, Jo, but in the way of the world, he is. Believe me. If he promised not to ruin her, he won't. Which is, when one thinks about it, very strange indeed."

"Which brings us right back to whether he did or did not make an offer." Pierce's eyebrow quirked. "An *honorable* offer."

"Has he been to see Henry?"

"I haven't been informed if he has."

Pierce again stared into the fire. "It is a problem, love. Have you asked the chit her feelings toward Sir Frederick?"

Knowing how Robert felt about the girl, he waited a trifle anxiously for the response. Joanna, noting how worried he looked, stared into the fire.

"Jo?"

"She says she's not in love with him. What she insists is that he's her friend."

Pierce shouted with laughter. "And I thought her so up to the knocker!"

"It is *not* funny."

Pierce sobered. "No. Not at all humorous. Elizabeth may be a fool, love, but there is nothing you can do in the next hour or so. Come ride with me

317

and blow away the cobwebs?" He held out his hand, a coaxing note in his voice.

Joanna hesitated but, not exactly reluctantly, allowed him to help her to her feet. After all, if he were riding with her, he couldn't be forwarding his plans for Elizabeth. Plans she would soon, she thought with a smile, set for naught—assuming her own came to fruition.

She went to change into her new and very attractive habit while Pierce went to order up her mount. Before joining him, Joanna took one last look in her mirror. Yes, she thought. She'd been right. The deep blue, very nearly black in some lights, was flattering. The heavy fall of lace at her throat, over her wrists, and flirting occasionally from beneath the long skirts added just the delicate touch needed to set off the stark lines of the cut. It was, she thought smugly, the most attractively designed habit she'd seen for years.

The ride down Rotten Row, at the most social time of day, did not help the cobwebs much, but it was enjoyable. Joanna and Pierce had several short bantering conversations with old friends, saw and were seen—the prime purpose of presenting oneself in the park at that hour—and Joanna returned to her room more determined than ever to save Pierce from his intentions toward Elizabeth. He would thank her in time. And, apropos of those thoughts, a rather grubby and ill-spelt note awaited her, a maid having set the twist against her favorite scent bottle on her dressing table.

Joanna's hands trembled as she smoothed out the crinkles in the paper. For a moment the words blurred as she wondered if she actually had the nerve to carry through her plan. Then she thought of her lively niece, what was best for the lass, what was best

318

for Pierce, and for that matter, what was best for herself! Her determination restored, she raised the note, struggling to decipher the message.

"M lidy," she read and smiled at the tactful avoidance of a name. "Al set for Monday eve, 8 o the clok. Bloak walks to dinner and cards."

Joanna wondered how Turner had discovered that necessary bit of information. Probably through the servants' network.

"Coch wil wait ye at corner."

Joanna bit her lip. One more day and a bit. Henry and Elizabeth would leave late the next morning for their great-aunt's. She'd have to fill in the time until evening. Then once they had Pierce safe, she'd have forty-eight hours or so to accomplish her goal. Well, it should be enough.

While Joanna worried about Pierce, Elizabeth had her own concerns. Go she must, because she could not gainsay her father, but go without some means of entertaining herself she would not. So early the next morning, before the rest of the household stirred, Elizabeth again set off with only her maid to Hookham's Lending Library. On her last visit, purely by accident, she had taken out a novel with the odd title *Pride and Prejudice* by A Lady. It had, much to her surprise, delighted her; the story, about everyday people, had a subtle humor she chuckled over whenever she thought about it. Unlike the gothics she'd chosen in the past, the novel dealt with real life. If she must waste time visiting the old tartar, she would take along another book by the same authoress—if such could be found.

She strolled into the library with no thoughts in her head but to change her books. Therefore she didn't know whether to be glad or sorry when Sir

Frederick joined her amongst the shelves. "Good day," she said cautiously.

"I don't find it a good day at all, minx. Why didn't you tell me the *ton* would be deprived of your delightful countenance for a while?"

"How did you know?"

Carrington grinned knowingly. "How *does* one know these things? Word floats along on the wind to be whispered here and there and then elsewhere."

He spoiled the emotive style and grand gestures by laughing softly when she made a pert little moue of distaste. Elizabeth sighed.

"Please don't tease," she said. "Would you reach that novel for me?"

He took down the required set, looking at the back. "Ah, you've discovered the delightful Miss Austen, have you?"

"Is that her name? She is wonderful, isn't she? I've never enjoyed a story more."

Sir Frederick offered her the volumes and she clutched them to her chest. "Will you be off today, then?"

Elizabeth sighed again. "Yes." She couldn't help the mulish look, a curious mixture of depression and acceptance. "Not that I'll enjoy an instant of it. If only the old harridan didn't live so far from London. I could accept driving out for a day, but to be gone for three is outside of enough. Do you know I had to refuse invitations to a water party and a Venetian breakfast and a soiree and *three* rides in the park . . ." When Frederick chuckled, she glared at him. "Well, it is really too bad of the old lady, you know. Why she couldn't have requested our attendance on her before the season began or waited till after it was over or . . ." Elizabeth sighed. "But at least I'll have Miss Austen for company!"

"Just where does the old lady live?" Elizabeth told him and Sir Frederick nodded. "You'll be putting up at The George and Lion then. It is a very nice post house with an excellent table. Your father will approve their cellar, I believe."

"Yes. He says he wishes he knew where the innkeeper buys his brandy." Elizabeth, preoccupied with the wrong done her by her old relative, didn't observe Frederick's quickly repressed satisfaction that he'd guessed correctly. "I've been warned by Aunt Jo that once dinner is finished, it would be best if I went immediately to my room as my father will undoubtedly wish to sample the innkeeper's stock in peace."

This additional and gratuitous bit of information was a bonus and completed Frederick's plans to a nicety. He was well-pleased with their meeting and Elizabeth need never know his well-trained tiger had again run to tell him where she could be found.

"I must return to the house," Elizabeth continued. "No one knows I've gone out, and if they discover it, there will be another row. I am so tired of rows, Frederick. I do not care for them."

"Ah, but then you've never had a row with your husband and enjoyed the great pleasure of making up." Elizabeth, turning a sideways look at him, blushed rosily before turning away. "You will someday discover that it *is* a pleasure," he finished softly.

Elizabeth left him after a few more words, her mind roiling with questions. Sir Frederick had again insinuated he had marriage in mind. Frederick? It seemed so strange. Elizabeth had had stern warnings from all sides the man was not to be trusted. Were his hints merely a new ploy by a determined rake to get his way, or had he developed a *tendre* for her?

And if he had, wasn't that actually worse than the other? Because Elizabeth, much against her will and against other and equally stern advice, had tumbled head over heels in love with quite another party. She followed her maid into the house via a side door and whisked herself up to her room. There she changed costumes while her maid completed the last of her packing. Elizabeth presented a demure figure when she skipped down the front stairs to join her aunt and father in the small dining room.

Joanna studied her niece's traveling costume and raised her eyebrows as high as they would go. Elizabeth, to the degree she was allowed to get away with it, tended toward the extremes of style. Today she presented a picture of innocence that would have confounded all her friends and enemies. Not that she *had* any enemies, of course.

"Doing it up a little too brown, aren't you, my love?" Joanna suggested, tongue in cheek.

Elizabeth giggled. "But I wouldn't wish to shock the old lady, Aunt Jo." Her eyes widened in pretended concern. "At her age a shock might prove dangerous."

"Hmm."

"Oh well, if you must have it," went on her irrepressible niece, "I chose this dress because I don't half like it and I won't mind if it is ruined during the journey."

"Now that I can believe wholeheartedly."

Elizabeth chuckled. "I thought you might."

Soon after the early repast, Elizabeth followed her father into the traveling coach and waved goodbye. Joanna discovered her relief at the girl's departure outweighed every other emotion. Well, the girl couldn't get into much trouble while traveling with her father. At least she wouldn't if she followed Joanna's advice and pulled no hoydenish trick along the way. Joanna decided it wasn't worth worrying about the unlikely possibility and returned to her room where stealthily she filled a portmanteau with the things she'd need for her own disreputable escapade, then ringing for Turner to sneak it away to the carriage he'd hired for that evening.

Elsewhere, at about the same time, Lord Halford looked up when a curricle stopped beside him as he made his way toward his club. "Hello, Frederick," he said, eyeing the portmanteau strapped on in back and the two well-matched bays harnessed to the speedy vehicle. "Leaving Town?" he asked, the hint of a suspicion crossing his mind.

"Only for a few days. I'm rather surprised you aren't as well." Frederick quirked an expressive eyebrow.

Robert forced a laugh. "Yes. It will be dreadfully flat for a while." He frowned. "How did you know—" Or did he? Robert closed his mouth, determined not to let any cats from the proverbial bag.

"How did I know? But Robert," Frederick looked hurt, "I *always* know. It is my reputation to know." He chuckled. "It helps that I met her this morning at Hookham's. She didn't appear the least excited about the journey, poor child."

Robert sighed. "You are off to your estate?"

"I've put off a visit home far too long." Frederick studied the one man he actually liked and trusted. "Robert, may I ask your intentions toward the minx or would you find that question extremely impertinent?"

"I've spoken to her father. If she weren't so young, I'd have spoken to her as well, but I believe she deserves an opportunity to look about herself at the younger men before making a choice, so I'll wait until the end of the season before chancing my luck." Robert held the other man's gaze and was astonished at the rueful look returned. Frederick?! "Frederick, don't tell me—"

"I won't since you say not. Well, may the best man win."

"Yes," said Robert slowly. "Frederick . . ."

"No, do not strain our friendship, Robert. I know well I'm not the better man. But for her, I believe I could become so."

A worried look came into Robert's eyes. "I say . . . !"

A barked laugh cut him off. "Ridiculous, isn't it? Napoleon must have felt much the same way when he determined Wellington had him beaten."

"But Frederick . . ."

"I mean the chit no harm, Robert."

"No. If you truly love her, I know you will not harm her."

"Then peace. We'll find who wins her once she is won."

Robert bowed, but he could feel no peace at all. Frederick would not hurt Elizabeth. Not when he'd said he wouldn't. Rob knew that because he knew his man. That did not mean, however, that he'd play fairly in the process.

Robert, forgetting he was to meet a friend for lunch at their club, wandered back toward his rooms where he removed a creased cravat, a dirty tankard, and an old racing form from his favorite chair. He sat and sank into a brown study. Lounging in his

324

favorite posture with his feet up, his elbows on the chair arms, and his fingers interwoven, he went over every word he and Frederick had exchanged. Particularly Frederick's. It occurred to him, after thorough cogitation, that the baronet had not *actually* agreed with the suggestion he was off to his own estates.

Three-quarters of an hour later, Robert, too, had ordered a portmanteau packed, ordered around his team and curricle, and was to be seen leaving Town in the direction taken by Henry and Elizabeth earlier that day. If he were wrong, he would only be thought a fool; if he were *not* wrong, then he and Henry could prevent any damage being done—and if his groom had not spent the morning in his favorite tavern, he'd have checked the horses more closely and Robert's leader would not have thrown a shoe some ten miles from his goal. For the loss of a nail, his arrival at The George and Lion was delayed by half an hour too much.

Sixteen

"I wou' no try it, m'lord."

"Why not?" Pierce spoke with forced insouciance. The man was right. With that long-nosed barker pointed directly at his chest and no help in sight along the deserted street, he was in a spot of trouble this time.

"Because, m'lord, my friend is right behind you. Be pleased to hold out your hands."

Metal jabbed into his back and Pierce swore softly. Without speaking, he held out his hands. "Now what?"

"Together, m'lord."

"Hold my hands together?"

"M'lord," said his assailant politely, "we'll get along much faster if'n you cooperate. Be pleased to press the wrists together."

There was something smoky about this. Pierce peered into the dark, trying to get a better look at the man. That voice . . . There was something familiar about that voice. He made a wild stab at the truth. "Does Lady Jo know what you're up to?"

The man's head shifted slightly and Pierce saw the

gleam as his eyes turned toward the corner. "Come along now, m'lord."

Rapid calculations, a sense of humor, and a surge of hope combined. "Do you know, I think I will."

"Very good, m'lord."

His hands were tied with something soft and silky. Silk? Either kidnappers were being much more gentle these days or he was right! *Could* Jo be behind this nonsense? On the other hand, the silk was tight enough to be uncomfortable . . .

"The eyes next, m'lord."

"Now what?" asked Pierce when another soft cloth was wound tightly around his head.

"There's a coach just around the corner. Five steps straight ahead. That's right, sir. Now a turn left. A bit more. Another half-dozen steps, m'lord, and please to halt, sir." Pierce stopped, heard the coach door opening. "Put out your hands, m'lord. A little to the right. That's right, sir," the voice encouraged when Pierce found the doorframe. "The steps be about fifteen inches ahead and just a little to the left. Very good, Your Grace. If you'll please to be seated?"

Pierce sat, put one foot up on the cushions of the seat across from him. He sniffed, recognized the fresh clean scent he associated with his love, and smiled. The door was shut.

"Good evening, Lady Joanna."

"Is it?" She saw him smile. "How did you know?"

"Only you, my love, wear that scent. I would know it in Hades."

"You think I'm bound for nether regions, Your Grace?"

"Only if you leave me *bound* this way." Silence greeted him. "Could we do something about these ropes, my love? Your friend from the army is stronger than he knows."

"Not just yet. In time."

"Damnation . . ."

"Tit for tat, Your Grace. I recall begging you to untie *me* upon an occasion never to be forgotten."

"That's because I knew you were fool enough to try to jump from a moving coach. Are you planning to compromise me?"

"Of course. But have no fear. As a gentlewoman, I know my duty. I will marry you in order to save your reputation."

"I seem to remember several occasions on which I asked you to marry me."

"Yes. But you seem to have stopped asking." Joanna thought she managed that plaintive note quite well. "I can't very well tell you yes when you refuse to ask, now can I?"

"If I were to ask now?"

"But you won't, will you, Pierce? Not now." Joanna sighed. "You're having far too much fun, are you not? I can tell from that quirk to your mouth."

"I've decided to see just how you've decided to compromise me."

"I thought that would be the way of it. Stubborn man."

"Are you going to enlighten me?"

"I think not."

The coach rumbled over a bridge and Pierce frowned. For some reason he'd assumed they'd be headed for the Great North Road and Gretna. "We aren't eloping?" he asked.

"My goodness, Pierce," said Jo in pretended shock. "My reputation! I'd never live it down if I were to elope with you."

Pierce chuckled. "Do you think you might remove these ropes? I wasn't joking when I said your man tied them rather tightly." He held up his hands, shifting slightly to show her. There was the faintest of golden glow beyond the bandage over his eyes and he felt sure she had lighted the carriage globes. She'd be able to see for herself that his bonds, silken or not, were cutting into the flesh rather badly.

She saw. "Oh, Pierce. I'm so sorry."

"So undo them, love."

"Why? So you can throttle me?"

"That's an idea. This would have been unnecessary if you'd given even the slightest hint you'd abandoned your notion of a small house in some poor part of Town."

"I changed my mind and decided on one in the country."

"I assume," he said, exasperation showing, "you have given up that idea as well. As I said, the veriest hint . . ."

"Well, how could I know that? You dance attendance on Lady Anne. You are far more patient with my abominable niece than you ever were with me. In fact, Your Grace, you ceased showing me any particular attention at all."

He hadn't, but he could allow her the small self-deception if she liked. "How did you feel? Jealous maybe?"

"Pierce Reston, am I to understand that's what you intended?"

"Yes, but I was about to give it up and try some other means of attracting your attention. You showed no signs of jealousy at all," he ended on an aggrieved note.

"That's all *you* know about it."

"Mumbling, m'love?"

"Nothing to which you need pay attention."

He chuckled. "I think I'd better remember that when you mumble that is just when I most need to pay attention." She didn't respond. "Jo, I love you."

"Then why did you ask Henry's permission to ask my abominable niece to marry you?" The familiar anger boiled up again. "That, Your Grace, would be an absolutely disastrous marriage. You'd strangle the chit in a month or less."

"Definitely less. Where did you get the cockle-brained notion I had the least intention of asking the brat for her hand?"

"From Henry, of course. I couldn't let you do it, Pierce."

"Even if you had to sacrifice yourself?"

"Exactly."

"Chucklehead." He said it lovingly, softly.

"Pierce, please don't lie to me." This time the plaintive note was real. "Henry was not teasing me. I know you approached him. And I know you've been watching her closely."

"Idiot." The tone of this insult was a trifle less loving. "We've all been watching her. She's been playing games with Sir Frederick. Do you think we'd let her bring herself to ruin that way?"

"You can't be serious. She wouldn't . . ."

"My wrists, Jo. On my honor I will not try to escape whatever plans you have for me. I also promise not to do you damage. In fact, you'd pretty well have to try to kill me to get me to leave you now!"

"Oh, all right. But please tell me why you think my idiotish niece would be so imprudent when she knows . . ."

"Personally I believe—Oh! I don't know if that is

much better!" Pierce rubbed at the painful prickles running into his hands. Joanna took over and he leaned back into the corner, liking the feel of her flesh against his even if it were no more than their hands touching. "Where was I? Oh. I think she's playing dangerous games because my equally idiotish friend has come the coward and refuses to put his luck to the touch."

Joanna sighed. "You are making no sense at all."

"Then I'll spell it out. Rob is head over heels in love with the minx. He, not I, approached your brother. Amongst a slew of others, I'm sure. But he's been waiting until he's certain of her. Besides, she's so young he felt she should have most of her season to look over the younger men before settling on an old crock like himself."

"Robert? But he is a confirmed bachelor. The despair of matchmaking mamas for years!"

"The most complete bachelor will fall when his heart is touched, Jo."

"Oh, it is all my fault!"

Shocked by her tone, Pierce ripped off the blind-fold and stared at her. He grasped her hands and pulled them from her face. "Come now, Jo. I don't believe that."

"Don't you remember? I told you I warned her and warned her he cannot be serious, that the attentions he pays her are merely out of friendship to Henry, to you. In fact, now I think on it, it is your fault for not giving me a hint at the time!"

"Muttonhead."

Again the insult was an endearment and Pierce pulled her close. For a few moments they were lost in each other's arms, but the coach, a wheel pulled into a rut, jolted them, and Pierce set her back into

331

her place. "No. I will not make love to you for the first time in a bounding coach." He pretended to scold: "Behave yourself, Lady Joanna."

"I always find that difficult when you're so near."

"So do I. Jo, where *are* we off to?"

"To Cousin Lucinda in Canterbury."

"Where?" Pierce's look of loathing turned to one of speculation. "Your cousin is married to the dean, isn't he?"

"Yes. Once I tell her I've traveled from London with a man in a closed carriage with the windows covered, she'll bully her husband into approaching the Archbishop. We'll be married within an hour."

"Excellent planning, Jo. Why?"

"Why? Why what?"

"Why may we not be married in Hanover Square at St. George's?"

"Because I don't trust you not to leave me waiting at the altar."

Pierce turned to face front, but not before Joanna saw a hurt look in his eyes. He twisted away from her and twitched aside the curtain, staring into the countryside where a few lights gleamed here and there. Irritated beyond bearing with Joanna's lack of trust, he raised the curtain and continued watching the countryside. The coach turned a corner and a few straggling houses appeared.

"Pierce?"

He didn't take his eyes off the window as he asked, "What sort of man do you think I am?"

"One who will go to any lengths for revenge."

"I see. You remember the silly mutt I was as a youth and assume I've not matured beyond that." He straightened, yanked at the cord which would stop the coach. "I very much fear, Jo, this is an argument we'll have to postpone. I think—"

The door opened and Pierce pushed aside the hefty ex-soldier, lowering himself to the ground. "Here now, m'lord. Mrs. Wooten, you let him loose."

"Yes. You tied his bonds too tightly. Pierce, just where are you going?"

"Jo, do you recognize that livery? The tiger there by that curricle with the broken wheel?"

She looked to where he pointed in the small inn's yard. Her voice seemed lost. "Pierce," she managed to squeak, "it isn't . . ."

"I think it is. Elopements seem jinxed by this inn—remember, love?"

"Is it . . . ? It *can't* be where we stopped." She studied the cobbled yard, the low thatched roof and tiny leaded windows. "Oh, Pierce! I do believe it is."

"Shall we check and see if what I fear is true?"

"We most certainly will. If that is Sir Frederick's—Pierce, don't call him out. I couldn't bear for something to happen to you!"

"I doubt it'll be necessary. Unhitch the coach—Turner, isn't it?"

"Yes, Your Grace." But Turner had his eyes on his mistress.

"Please, Turner. I very much fear my plans have been overset by that minx of a niece of mine." She sighed, put her fingers on the arm Pierce held out to her, and let him lead her into the inn.

A flustered innkeeper met them in the hall. "M'lord. M'lady. I am greatly honored by your patronage, but I fear I have only the one private parlor and it's occupied."

"That's all right. We know your guests. No—" Pierce caught the man's shoulder as their host turned, ready to show them in—"We'll announce ourselves. Right down this hall, if I remember?"

"Yes, m'lord."

Pierce passed the man a guinea and suggested he make himself scarce. His voice low, he asked, "Now what, Jo? Have you thought how we should handle this?"

"First I think we should ascertain that Elizabeth is actually here. I'd hate to burst in on a tryst of any other sort."

"Wise woman. We will, quite indefensibly if we are wrong, listen at the door!"

"An excellent notion. As I remember," she said with a chuckle at the memory despite her worry, "it isn't much of a door."

"It may have been replaced by something better. As you will also remember, some damage was done by your rescuer's entrance into our rather heated conversation."

"So there was. Dear impetuous Reggie."

"Jo . . ." began Pierce in a warning tone.

She interrupted. "Pierce, I cannot, and would not if I could, forget my years with Reggie. However, I have long since come to the conclusion you were right about us. I loved him, yes. But not as I loved and still love you. So never, *never* try to run the man down to me again. He is dead, Pierce."

They stared at each other in the dim, dingy hall, and suddenly Pierce touched her cheek with gentle fingers. "You are right. By my own analysis I know you must have loved him. I'm very glad you can admit it was not so deeply or completely as you love me."

Jo swallowed. That had gone rather better than she'd expected. "Shall we on to the rescue?"

334

"I'm almost ready to leave the brat to her own devices. Somehow I have the feeling the minx will manage to save herself—assuming, of course, it is she in that room with Frederick." He took Joanna's elbow and they tiptoed down the hall. Looking at each other, they set their ears to cracks in the rickety door that had been mended rather than replaced.

"Frederick," a voice said, "this is outside of enough."

"Not nearly enough. Elizabeth, for the first time in my life I have fallen in love. I intend marriage, little one. And no more philandering."

Joanna heard a deep sigh. "Marriage? Then why haven't you done the proper thing, gone to my father and received permission . . . ?"

A harsh laugh interrupted her. "Permission? Me?"

"Oh, Frederick." There was a soft chuckle and Joanna gritted her teeth. "You are a lesson to us all. What it is to have ruined one's reputation."

"I want you, love. You'll see my reform is complete."

"There is a small problem, Frederick." Elizabeth spoke so softly Jo and Pierce had to strain to hear her.

"I see none."

"My heart is given to another."

Silence battered at all four sets of ears.

"I see."

"So I think it would be best if you returned me to my father. Please, Frederick?"

"May I ask the name of the lucky man?"

"I don't know if I should tell you." Again silence stretched. Elizabeth sighed. "He hasn't asked for my hand and my aunt is certain he will not." A short silence followed and Joanna could imagine the characteristic shake of the head indicating she'd made a decision preceding Elizabeth's next words. "I can't tell you."

"Halford?" Another silence. "Come now, Elizabeth. Don't be coy."

"Well then, it is."

Again there was silence. When Frederick next spoke, the listeners could tell from his voice he'd moved some distance away from her. "I should have left him on that damn beach for the smugglers."

His tone was low and bitter. This time the sigh was a masculine one.

"I can think of no other man to whom I'd let you go." There was a resigned note in his voice as he continued, "I'll see if a carriage is available for hire since they predicted an hour or more to fix mine."

Footsteps crossing the room could be heard. Pierce picked Jo up and moved them back nearly to the end of the hall. They were strolling along, retracing their steps, when the door opened and the baronet emerged from the parlor. "Sir Frederick," said Pierce jovially, "I thought that was your carriage in the yard. Well met. You can be a witness."

Sir Frederick glanced back into the parlor and pulled the door closed with a snap. "Witness? For what, Stornway?"

"My wedding. Is Lady Joanna's niece in there by chance? The chit would never speak to us if she discovered she might have attended her aunt's wedding and been excluded."

"Pierce, you are forge—" Joanna whispered shrilly but was interrupted:

"Quiet, my love. Shall we enter the parlor?"

Frederick, his face white and his eyes wary, bowed,

opened the door, and allowed Joanna to enter ahead of them. When she had passed him, he spoke to Pierce. "It is not what you think."

"Nonsense. It is exactly what we think, but I suspect the minx outsmarted you."

"If she lied to me . . ."

"Not by lying. By being just as sweet and innocent and loyal as she is. The truth outsmarted you—although none of this need have happened if my fool of a friend hadn't waited for some sign from her before proposing. She, little innocent that she is, is certain he feels nothing more than affection for the daughter of a friend and has demonstrated far more self-control than I'd have believed possible. She's not revealed a hint of her feelings. It's a pretty coil."

Frederick laughed but he didn't sound amused. He gestured toward the door and the two men entered the parlor. The low-voiced conversation between niece and aunt broke off abruptly.

"Now," said Pierce, thoroughly enjoying himself. Actually he felt a little on the go although he'd had nothing to drink. He was, he knew, drunk on the thought that, at long last, he was to wed his love. All looked at him. "We must get organized."

"Pierce," hissed Joanna, "I tried to tell you. My cousin's husband is to get the license, remember?"

He smiled and, with the air of a conjurer, removed a flat case from a pocket inside his coat and pulled out a paper with a flourish. He looked at it. "Oops, not this one. That's the one I've carried for years." He passed it to Joanna and pulled another from the wallet. "This will do the trick." He held the new license and looked at Jo, who was perusing the one she held. She raised her eyes to look into his. "For five years that has gone everywhere with me, Jo. Sentimental of me, I suppose."

"Then you were prepared for marriage when you—" Jo broke off abruptly, her eyes moving to where Sir Frederick stood, his face pale.

"Kidnapped her?" Elizabeth finished her aunt's sentence, interest in her voice.

Pierce chuckled. Jo, he knew, had not said the words because of the baronet's presence. "Yes, minx. But you needn't spout it to the winds."

"Oh, Frederick would never tell. He's my friend."

Joanna turned to where the rake stood near the low fireplace, his face austere, the bones hard below the taut skin. He bowed to her. Her eyes widening, she began to believe the man had really taken a tumble over her abominable niece.

"And the ring." Pierce opened a small chamois bag he'd removed from the same hidden pocket. He tipped it into his hand, firelight flashing off the rare yellow diamond. Extending it toward Joanna, he asked, "Will this do you, love?"

"I should think *so*."

It was Elizabeth answering him, awe in her young voice. Jo was too choked up to speak, her eyes saying all to her love. He held that gaze as he tested the size of the ring on her finger.

"Pierce," gasped Joanna, holding it up to the light, "It is beautiful."

"It'll do?" Jo nodded, her eyes misty. "Then the next thing is to rouse the vicar across the green."

Diffidently Joanna asked, "Will a stranger take part in such a ramshackle arrangement, Pierce?"

"I knew him when he was tutor to a friend of mine. He was given this living when the family ran out of sons for him to tutor. He's a nice old boy and will be happy to perform the ceremony."

The insistent voice of a new arrival could be heard in the hall, as well as the flustered shout of the innkeeper attempting to thwart entry to the parlor—but failing. The door burst open, again breaking the fragile lock.

"Oh dear. Pierce, do you think it is our responsibility to have that door replaced?"

"Oh, I don't know. This inn is so appropriately placed, a replacement might only make life more difficult for the next heroic rescue."

He grinned at her and then stepped between Rob and Frederick. From the black look on Rob's face, matters would soon be out of hand if he didn't take a hand himself.

"Wish me happy, Rob."

Rob's eyes traveled around the room. "I think—"

"Don't think," said Frederick languidly. "Instead, stop playing the fool and ask that chit to marry you. If you don't do it soon, I'll change my mind about leaving her alone."

"Why you—"

"Robert!"

Elizabeth's tense voice turned Rob in that direction. "Don't you dare touch my friend."

Rob's back stiffened. "I see."

"No, you do not see. You will *never* see." Elizabeth threw herself into Joanna's half-ready arms and began to weep.

"Robert, just see what you've done." Pierce's joy was irrepressible. "Now get over there and comfort the girl. I want Joanna in *my* arms."

"I don't believe I have the right, Pierce. After what she said . . ."

"Friend. Do you know the meaning of the word *friend?"* Elizabeth's muffled voice sounded irritated rather than sad.

"Frederick has never stood friend to a lovely young woman such as yourself, Lady Elizabeth."

"Oh, you're a fool. I sometimes wonder why I wish to marry you at all." Elizabeth realized what she'd said, turned anguished eyes up to Jo's, and buried her face against her aunt. She was gently removed from that position and turned into Rob's arms. "Robert?"

One finger under her chin, he tipped her face up so he could look into her eyes. "Will you marry me, love?"

Elizabeth, her dearest wish unexpectedly granted, recovered her poise instantly. A twinkle appeared in her eyes. "That wasn't the most romantic proposal I've received."

"You want me down on me knees, my hand on my heart?" Robert, too, had relaxed, was smiling.

"Well," she drawled, "it's traditional."

"But the floor is so dirty, little one, and my trousers so point-device."

"Hmm. A problem, that."

"And to place my hand on my heart I'd have to release you."

"An even greater problem."

"So, my love, I think you should simply forget romance and give me my answer."

Elizabeth drew in a deep breath and spouted prissily, "You do me great honor, Lord Halford."

Robert released her and, grasping her shoulders, gave her a shake. "Minx!"

"Oh well, if you'll have it with no bark on 't," she pouted, "then *yes."*

340

Robert whooped and scooped her back into his embrace. Joanna turned from their ardent display toward Pierce; the speculative, suggestive look in his eyes raised a blush in her cheeks and she turned to look at Sir Frederick, who leaned against the low mantel, his gaze trained on the smoky fire, a white line around his mouth and his jaw clenched.

There was a strained look around his eyes, too, which sharpened as he straightened, turning toward the door. Avoiding a glance toward the newly engaged couple entwined in each other's arms, he spoke softly to Pierce. "Were you serious about that wedding?"

"Quite serious."

"If I mistake not that voice, your future brother-in-law has arrived. I'd better leave before the chucklehead comes in and makes a hash of all we've accomplished. If you will trust me with that license, I'll rouse the vicar and meet you at the church in, shall we say, half an hour?"

Pierce stared for a long instant, then slowly extended the precious license. "Half an hour."

Frederick had been gone only a few moments when, once again, the door burst open. "Where is that blackguard?"

Pierce decided distraction was needed. "Henry, you are to congratulate me. Also Robert. Joanna and Elizabeth have finally said yes."

Henry looked around the room suspiciously. "Sir Frederick's curricle is in the yard being fixed."

"Oh?" Pierce winked at Joanna. "Someone else has arrived?"

"Sir Frederick, that villain. If he is not here, he is waiting somewhere to snaffle up me daughter."

"His curricle is being fixed?" Pierce's rollicking mood was getting out of hand. He couldn't repress

341

his sense of humor and went on, "Then how is he to, er, snaffle her? You think he has found one for hire? *Here?*"

"Brother, you are to felicitate me." Joanna pinched Pierce's arm in an attempt to bring him to order. "Are you listening?"

"Hmph. You finally came to your senses, did ye? About time." He stared at Rob and Elizabeth, who were oblivious to his entry. "But what about my minx of a daughter? I know I gave Robert permission to address her, but *that* is outside of enough." He pointed sternly.

"Quite enough." Pierce strolled across the room. "All right, you two. That'll do. I have need of you."

"Need?" Rob looked anything but clear-headed.

"Yes. You, my friend, must stand with me. Elizabeth is needed to attend Joanna." Pierce turned. "And you, Henry, *you* will give away the bride."

Elizabeth, standing now with her back to Rob but with his arms around her waist, clapped her hands. "'Tis an elopement."

"'Tis nothing of the sort," objected Pierce, his eyes on Joanna. "'Tis a kidnapping."

"Will someone explain what is going on here?" asked Henry plaintively.

"On the way to the church," said Pierce over his shoulder. More quietly, his features suddenly serious, he approached Jo. "Are you sure, my love? Will you not feel cheated of a wedding and reception and all that?"

"I had it all, Pierce. It is hectic and too much work and the bride too tired to . . ." She blushed deeply. "Well, er . . ."

"Enjoy her wedding night?"

"If you must have it, *yes.*"

"I most certainly must have a wedding night, and I will not have my bride too tired to enjoy it." His eyes twinkled with the joy he'd been feeling since Jo had said yes, but he made his voice stern with no nonsense about it: "You've no choice, my love. We'll be married here and now and that, my precious, is that."

"I say, now that's no way to speak to me sister!"

Both Jo and Pierce laughed and poor Henry looked more confused than ever. Pierce handed the hovering innkeeper another guinea and asked that everyone's carriages be ready in three-quarters of an hour. Then he led the way across the green, Joanna on his arm, her face glowing. At the church steps Pierce turned her, squeezed both her hands tightly, and looked into her eyes. "Follow in a moment, love?"

"Yes."

Joanna, her heart pounding, waited in silence. A shy, sleepy-looking maid approached from the vicar's small greenhouse and offered a bouquet. "The gentleman said you'd like flowers, milady."

"Thank you. It was very thoughtful of him."

Henry, willing if still not quite understanding all that was afoot, presented her his arm. She glanced at Elizabeth and the girl smiled and nodded. Joanna drew a deep steadying breath and started forward. From the choir stall above the door at the back of the church a beautiful baritone rose in song. Jo didn't glance back until she reached Pierce when they both turned and looked up to face the baronet. The rake's eyes were on Elizabeth, and just for a moment, Joanna's happiness was marred by pity for the man who had lost the one woman he might have cherished faithfully. His song ended, and Pierce and Joanna turned back to face the vicar.

The wedding was brief but quite moving. The small group returned to the green. Above them was a star-studded sky, a great golden moon just rising in the east. Joanna looked for Sir Frederick and found him in consultation with Rob. She approached. "Sir. Thank you. I had no idea you had such a beautiful voice."

"You're welcome." No one mentioned he'd sung the old love song to Elizabeth and not for the bride and groom. "I wish you every happiness," he added, his voice sincere.

"We'll hold a reception for our friends after a short honeymoon." Just a bit shyly, given her feelings about the man, she asked, "Will you come?"

"No. I fear I must forego that pleasure. Now that Bonaparte is out of the way, I've a fancy to explore the Continent much as an earlier generation did before the Monster made it impossible." Again his eyes trailed to Elizabeth who was approaching them. "Well, Elizabeth?"

"It is very well for me, Frederick." There was a small frown on her brow and the baronet touched it gently.

"It's well for me, too, child. Be happy."

She nodded. "And you?" She held out her hand.

Frederick reached for it, stared down at her, and grimaced. He pulled her into his arms and planted a quick but thorough kiss on her mouth, looked up and around, and grinned unrepentantly.

"Once a rake, always a rake," he quipped. "You owed me that much, Rob."

Frederick backed away, bowed once more, and walked quickly toward the inn across the way.

"What does he mean, you owed him?"

"What?" Rob was watching Frederick's swift exit. "Oh, he saved my life once. If he hadn't, I shouldn't be here to win fair maid."

"He mentioned smugglers whilst talking to Elizabeth in the inn, but I'd forgotten it," said Jo.

"Spies, Rob?"

"Yes, Pierce. One of the closest calls we had. Frederick not only rescued me in the nick of time, but managed to collect the memorandum we were after as well."

"Sir Frederick was also a counterspy?" asked Pierce idly, his hands occupied with Joanna's hair.

"What do you mean, *also?*" Elizabeth clutched at her betrothed. "You were in such danger in the war? You might have been killed? Oh, how could I have borne it?!"

"Heavens, Elizabeth, had I been killed you'd never have known me."

"Yes, I know. How could I have borne it?" she repeated, half laughing, half serious.

Henry yawned and said tolerantly, "Well, well, puss, that's a remark one would expect of the ladies." Everyone laughed and Henry looked affronted for a moment but yawned again. "Has anyone a thought as to how we are to proceed from here?"

Pierce took over, his patience completely gone. He wanted nothing but to be alone with his Joanna. "You, Henry, had best take Elizabeth back to your posting house and continue your journey in the morning. And you, Lady Elizabeth, will *not* make a fuss."

Elizabeth who'd been about to do just that, closed her mouth.

"Rob, I believe, will wish to return to London to

place an announcement in all the papers, is that not so?"

The earl nodded as Frederick's newly mended carriage turned out of the inn yard. Everyone watched it disappear almost immediately around a curve heading for Dover. Rob, after a glance at Pierce, managed to remove his future father-in-law and betrothed, hurrying them toward the inn.

Pierce and Joanna were left alone, standing in the middle of the green with the moon shining down upon them. "The only thing left to settle, my duchess, is where *we* are off to."

Joanna's eyes widened. It hadn't crossed her mind she would become a duchess with her marriage. "How I go up and down and up in the world."

"So you do. From my lady to a mere missus to Your Grace. 'Tis a rough life you have, my love." He kissed her much too briefly. "Where, dear one, am I to be allowed to have you all to myself?"

Joanna stared thoughtfully at the thatched roof, the tiny windows most hidden under the thick bundles of straw. The rooms would be small, the sheets very likely damp, and the service inadequate. "Do you think that poor innkeeper could be roused once more to unhitch the carriage and prepare a room for us?"

"'Tis a nasty little inn. Are you sure?"

"Pierce," said Joanna somewhat caustically, as she too was fast losing patience, "if you do not like it, then the nearest haystack or a deserted barn will do nicely. You are forgetting, my love, I am quite used to roughing it and not at all nice in my notions."

"I was forgetting, wasn't I?" He scooped her up into his arms and started across the road. "The inn it shall be."

346

The inn it was and the moon glowed bright, blushing, as it were, when it peeked into a small window of an upstairs bedroom. And well might it blush at the two who, finally at long last, found themselves alone.

Dear Reader,

I began *The Widow and The Rake* thinking Sir Frederick was a villain but, although I'm certain he's no saint, I've come to the conclusion he's not as black as he's been painted. But there's only one way to discover how a character fares in the future: one must write his book. So I am. I can't tell you much yet, but I know Sir Frederick returns to England in the company of a French aristocrat, the aristocrat's minx of a granddaughter (a young lady who reminds Frederick of Elizabeth) and the minx's companion, Miss Harriet Cole.

Eight years ago, during her come-out season, Miss Cole danced once with Sir Frederick, against whom she'd been warned. As a result Harriet came to the conclusion that the concept "rake" was a bug-a-bear designed to frighten young maidens—but despite that conclusion, Harriet doesn't trust Frederick an inch: her young lady is too much in the style Sir Frederick was known to "honor" with his attentions—leading far too often to a young lady's potential dishonor!

Sir Frederick has trouble convincing Miss Cole a rake may be reformed. He succeeds, of course. Eventually. He prevails by convincing her a rake may truly love—but not before everyone in sight must be saved from the machinations of a true villain.

If you'd like to read Sir Frederick's book, *A Reformed Rake,* it will be available in March 1994. I hope you'll enjoy Frederick's story and I'd like to hear what you think of him. Letters will reach me at the address given below.

Jeanne Savery
P.O. Box 1771
Rochester, MI 48308

A Memorable Collection of Regency Romances

BY ANTHEA MALCOLM AND VALERIE KING

THE COUNTERFEIT HEART   (3425, $3.95/$4.95)
by Anthea Malcolm
Nicola Crawford was hardly surprised when her cousin's betrothed
disappeared on some mysterious quest. Anyone engaged to such an
unromantic, but handsome man was bound to run off sooner or later.
Nicola could never entrust her heart to such a conventional, but so
deucedly handsome man. . . .

THE COURTING OF PHILIPPA   (2714, $3.95/$4.95)
by Anthea Malcolm
Miss Philippa was a very successful author of romantic novels. Thus
she was chagrined to be snubbed by the handsome writer Henry
Ashton whose own books she admired. And when she learned he considered love stories completely beneath his notice, she vowed to teach
him a thing or two about the subject of love. . . .

THE WIDOW'S GAMBIT   (2357, $3.50/$4.50)
by Anthea Malcolm
The eldest of the orphaned Neville sisters needed a chaperone for a
London season. So the ever-resourceful Livia added several years to
her age, invented a deceased husband, and became the respectable
Widow Royce. She was certain she'd never regret abandoning her girl-
hood until she met dashing Nicholas Warwick. . . .

A DARING WAGER   (2558, $3.95/$4.95)
by Valerie King
Ellie Dearborne's penchant for gaming had finally led her to ruin. It
seemed like such a lark, wagering her devious cousin George that she
would obtain the snuffboxes of three of society's most dashing peers
in one month's time. She could easily succeed, too, were it not for
that exasperating Lord Ravenworth. . . .

THE WILLFUL WIDOW   (3323, $3.95/$4.95)
by Valerie King
The lovely young widow, Mrs. Henrietta Harte, was not all inclined to
pursue the sort of romantic folly the persistent King Brandish had in
mind. She had to concentrate on marrying off her penniless sisters
and managing her spendthrift mama. Surely Mr. Brandish could fit in
with her plans somehow . . .

*Available wherever paperbacks are sold, or order direct from the
Publisher. Send cover price plus 50¢ per copy for mailing and
handling to Zebra Books, Dept. 4382, 475 Park Avenue South,
New York, N.Y. 10016. Residents of New York and Tennessee
must include sales tax. DO NOT SEND CASH. For a free Zebra/
Pinnacle catalog please write to the above address.*